Mi  Lyrics

What if everything you heard was wrong?

A Novel

By Mike Ellsworth

ISBN-13: 978-0-9884682-3-8

P2

Table of Contents

Foreword

Gentle Reader: The first chapter of this book sucks. It's intended to. Please read on.

Thanks.

The Management

Fleas naughty dog / There's fleas on your dad

José Feliciano—*Feliz Navidad*

The wind, unsettled and quarrelsome among dusty Bethlehem streets, blows down broken cobblestones as two hooded figures make their way. As they hurry, the taller whispers urgently to the other, who carries a small bundle. They turn down an alley, avoiding steaming piles of dung, toward the stable hewn into the rock behind an inn.

The pair step into the stable and the taller removes a cylinder from its pocket. It bends over the small bundle and sprays something from the cylinder. "There. Now he's protected from the brain virus the Enforcers have infected this planet with. At least his intellect won't be sapped, and he'll have a better chance of surviving."

The taller stands guard at the entrance, casting furtive glances toward the alley mouth as the other rushes deeper inside the stable, reappearing moments later without the burden. The two move quickly to cross to the other side, and hurry away, pressing close to the buildings like shadows.

In the opposite direction, a glow appears in the sky. The rough beasts in the stable shift and mutter restlessly. Suddenly, a burning armored figure of light screams down the street, faster than the fastest horse. It pauses briefly by the alley, inches above the street, then tears off after the figures, leaving a hole in the wind.

Moments later, the figures cower against the side of a carpenter's shop in the brightness. With a gesture, the entity disrobes them, revealing dark skin that quickly changes to match the sandstone of the building. A gleaming rope snakes from the glinting gauntlet and encircles the two. With a flick, the alien enforcer binds them to his back and rockets off into the sky, becoming a bright fading star above the sleeping village.

In the stable, in a manger, the bundle squirms. A curious cow nudges the covers with her nose.

Meanwhile, on the road outside of town, a poor cabinetmaker and his wife encourage their exhausted mules toward Bethlehem. They have come for the census but have made no plans for the night. Reaching the outskirts of the village, they stop at inn after inn with no luck. Trudging the deserted streets clutching their robes against the cold and leading their mules, they arrive at the inn by the alley and rouse the owner. Desperate, Joseph tells the man his wife is pregnant, ready to bear child. The wary innkeeper glances at Mary but cannot make out her form in the folds of her cloak.

"Alright," he says, "You can sleep out back in the stable. But don't disturb my animals!"

"Bless you, sir!" croaks Joseph. "God will surely reward such kindness."

"Bah! Begone by first light," the innkeeper growls and slams the door.

The couple walks down the alley and enters the stable. The animal stench overwhelms them at first, being more accustomed to the dust of the carpenter's bench. Joseph fumbles for a lantern and lights it with his flint. Mary crumples onto the hay and glares at her husband.

"I told you we should have left yesterday," she scolds.

"Enough, woman! Cease your infernal cackling. You know I had to finish the wagon for that Roman. He'd have my head otherwise."

"Well, I just don't know how I can sleep in such a filthy place as this! You could have sent word to your brother to expect us, at least."

"You're a riot, Mary . . . you're a regular riot," says Joseph, lowering his body to the straw. "One of these days, Mary, one of these days . . ."

Mary stands up and places her fists on her waist in defiance. "One of these days, what, Joseph? You'll be able to afford a room at an inn?"

"One of these days, pow! Right to the moon!"

Mary folds her arms in front of her, snorts and turns away from Joseph toward the animals. "What's that cow licking?" she asks, pointing into the shadows. Just out of the circle of light, the cow bends over something lying on the hay in the manger. Joseph gets the lantern and goes over.

"Why . . . it . . . it's a sort of a baby!" He bends down to examine the infant. "But it has monstrous horns on its head!" Joseph leaps back almost tipping the lantern. "My God, it's a little demon!"

Mary pulls at the blanket, rolling the infant towards her. "Oh, he's adorable!" She reaches out for the baby, pulling him into her lap. "And these aren't horns, you old fool," she says, "They look more like bumps." The baby opens his eyes and stares at Mary's face. His skin darkens momentarily to the color of her clothes, then lightens to mimic her swarthy face.

"Look they're almost gone now. Poor thing, he probably fell on his head." Mary pulls the child close to her breast. "I wonder whose he is?"

"Probably the spawn of some accursed slut, who dumped him here when he got in the way of business," Joseph said cynically. "No proper mother would leave a child in a hell-hole such as this." Joseph sweeps his arm to indicate the rotting timbers and leaking roof of the stable.

"Well we can't leave him here, Joseph. What should we do?"

Joseph turns to tether the mules and drops a few handfuls of straw in front of them. "I don't know, nor do I care what happens to that devil-child!" He spits on the straw. "I'm sure he's abandoned because his whore of a mother was ashamed of consorting with the devil."

Joseph comes over to peer at the infant. "What happened to the thing's horns?"

"He never had horns," Mary says." I told you, they were more like bumps. And they're gone now, anyway. Look, Joseph, doesn't he look like me?" Mary holds the baby up for Joseph to see.

"He's a changeling demon! That's what he is! And I want no part of him! Turn him out into the alley before he brings us evil." Joseph angrily moves to the door and slides it open. "I mean it, woman! Remove him from my sight!"

"Oh, be quiet, you old man. And close the door, he'll catch cold! We'll keep him, that's what we'll do. You told that innkeeper I was pregnant. Well, here's the baby you've been unable to give me these long years."

Joseph slides the door shut with a slam. "I warn you woman! Don't talk to me that way, or I'll . . . I'll . . . ."

"You'll nothing, you old blowhard. Come over here and see if you can get one of these mangy cows to give us some milk."

Grumbling, Joseph hunts up a stool and a pail, and begins milking one of the cows. Mary swaddles the child in her head cloth, cooing and singing.

Twelve nights later, still imposing on their host's hospitality for the sake of the newborn, Joseph watches three dark figures come down the alley toward the stable. Because of their strange clothing and their retinue of camels and donkeys, Joseph greets them warily.

One of the three, a short, wiry man with large eyes and a huge black mustache, says, "Good evening, my good man. We've come to see the baby, the Messiar—Messiar, I didn't even kiss her!" The small man rolls his eyes, squats into a duck walk, and turns circles in the alley, fingering an invisible object that seemingly dangles from his mouth.

Joseph, wondering how this strange little man could know of the demon child, says, "What are you talking about?"

"Look, your excellency, we're maguses. You know, wise guys from the East. Famed in song and story. We predict the future, follow the odd star, you know, like that." Melchior frames his face with his hands and bats his eyelashes at Joseph.

"We're Magi," interjects Balthasar, a stooped old man with a perpetual smile on his face,

"Magi, schmagi. Look, chief, we know you've got a kid in there, and we just want to see Him for ourselves. Do you mind?"

"Well, yes, there is a baby, but," Joseph feels a strange feeling pass over him, "You see, my wife's a virgin."

"Ah, oh!" Melchior raises his eyebrows and affects a conspiratorial leer. "Pull the other one, friend. Look, can we seem 'im or have we come hundreds of miles, against terrible odds, and worse evenings, for nothing?"

Joseph scratches his head in confusion but relents and ushers the three strangers into the stable. Melchior creeps on exaggerated tiptoes over to the manger and leans over to see the baby.

"It's Him! It's the son of God!" he exclaims.

"Wha? Now wait just a minute! That's my son!" Joseph insists angrily.

"Your son, His son, let's not quarrel. But he's the real Messiar! Ride through every village and town! Wake every citizen uphill and down! Tell 'em the King comes from afar—with a Hey-Nonny-Nonny and a Ha-Cha-Char!" Melchior dances a strange little dance in a circle and grabs Joseph, spinning the old man around.

"King?" says Joseph, pushing away from the little man and worriedly starting to collect their meager possessions. "What king? Is Herod coming this way?" Joseph begins to untether one of the donkeys.

"No, no, no, Colonel. Not Herod." Melchior leaps up on a haystack and crows, "The King of the Jews! The Messiar!"

"Messiar?"

Balthasar says, "He means Messiah. You know, King of the Jews? Savior of mankind? As Daniel prophesied?"

"So where are you kids from?" Melchior asks the startled Joseph.

"Nazareth," Joseph replies in a daze.

"Ah, Nazareth. I spent a year in that town, one Sabbath," Balthasar says.

"Well, go ahead, old-timer. Take a gander at the Messiar," Melchior says.

Balthasar approaches the manger on unsteady legs and peers at the baby. He gasps, turns, and nods to Melchior. "This is wonderful, to see the Messiah. It's good to be here. But let's face it. At my age, it's good to be anywhere."

"C'mon, Caspar. You're next," says Melchior, sweeping his hand back and forth as if directing traffic.

Caspar takes his turn at the manger, and soberly nods to the other two.

"Well, sport, looks like you've got the real McCoy here, a gin-u-wine Messiar. So, say the secret woid and you'll win a fabulous prize," says Melchior.

"What?"

"Close enough, close enough. Fellas, let's go get our gifts." The three men return to the alley. Melchior and Balthasar take packages from one of the carts and head back toward the stable.

Caspar hangs back as the other two men approach Joseph, who is standing at the doorway. Melchior turns around and says, "Come on, Caspar! It's time to give our gifts."

"Ah, just a minute," Caspar says. "Oh, Rochester!" he calls to one of the porters. "Yassir, Mr. Ben—Caspar!" says Rochester.

"Now, Rochester, how much gold did we bring along?"

"Pretty much all of it, boss," Rochester replies.

"ALL of it!" Caspar turns white. "Surely not my entire fortune!"

"Well, yassir, Mr. Caspar. You said you wanted to give the best gift to the newborn Messiah."

"Well, sure," says Caspar. "But surely we could give a quarter of this and still have a better gift than Melchior or Balthasar. They just picked up some lousy incense and oil at an oasis on the way here!"

"So, what do you want me to do, boss?"

"Look, let's just pull a few coins out of that sack there, and one or two of those gold candlesticks and call it even."

Melchior and Balthasar walk back and grab Caspar's elbows from behind, pinning him between them. "Come on, you old skinflint! Time to give the gifts!" says Melchior. "We need to get back on the road before that idiot Herod figures out where we are."

"Well!" sniffs Caspar. "I didn't come here to be insulted!"

"That's what you think," replies Melchior.

"Well . . ." Caspar stammers. "Just a minute, just a doggone minute." He tries to stuff a bag of gold under some baggage at the rear of the cart.

"What are you trying to pull, Caspar?" Melchior says with narrowed eyes.

"Well, I was just thinking, you see, we'll need plenty of gold to get home if we're going the long way, you see, to throw Herod off the scent," Caspar pleads. "So, I was thinking, a few coins, a candlestick or two, and we'll get out of here."

"Look, you cheapskate, are you going to give your entire gift now, or are you going to burn for all eternity?" Balthasar says.

The two stare menacingly at Caspar for a long minute. "Well?" says Melchior.

"I'm thinking it over!" cries Caspar.

"Come on, you old miser, let's go!" snarls Melchior.

Caspar glares at Melchior, who rises to his full height and glares back. "Old? Me, old? I'll have you know that on my last birthday I was 39."

"You must mean the last birthday you celebrated, back when you had hair," Balthasar says. "I always say, you can't help getting older, but you don't have to get old. Why, look at me. When I was a boy the Dead Sea was only sick. I'm at the age now where just putting a candlestick in its holder is a thrill. Why, at my age, I don't even buy ripe dates!"

"Come on you joker, let's gather up these bags of gold and give them to the Messiah," says Melchior. While Melchior maintains a firm hold on Caspar's arms, Balthasar and Rochester pile the bags onto a small cart and wheel it into the stable.

"Now cut that out!" screams Caspar.

"Hey," says Melchior, holding up a stringed instrument. "Maybe we should throw in the old man's fiddle, too?"

The three men brush past a goggling Joseph and enter the stable with their gifts.

O Come All Ye Fawfoo

John F. Wade, c.1743—*O Come All Ye Faithful*

Charles Beaumont DeFries, aspiring novelist, ex-college-teacher, moderately successful technical writer, and newspaper columnist, pulls the last sheet of the chapter out of the printer, squints at it briefly through the bottoms of his bifocals, then crumples the whole manuscript and tosses it angrily into the trash can.

Christ, he says, what a bunch of crap! Man, that was a strange turn it took: brain virus to three wise guys. Shit! I'll never get this goddamned book started.

Tempted to delete the whole misbegotten file from his hard drive, Charles instead stands up and walks over to the campy naugahyde bar by the window of his fourth-floor walk-up to pour himself a whiskey. He grabs the bottle of Jack Daniels, still fuming at his inability to write a suitable opening to his book on the life of Jesus. He spills some whiskey into an ancient Flintstones jelly jar and looks out the narrow window at the apartment building next door. If he cranes his neck just so, he can see a tiny blue scrap of Little River reflecting the brilliance of the Miami day.

Crap, I wish I could afford to move to the Beach, Charles muses. But that ain't gonna happen unless I can get one of these damn books published.

Although Charles makes a meager living writing software manuals and a column in the *Miami World*, all it buys him in high-priced Miami is a one-bedroom apartment in a two-rungs-up-from-fleabag residential hotel in Little Haiti, not far from the Interstate. It's a run-down area of the city, literally on the wrong side of the tracks, but only about 20 blocks from Biscayne Bay, and six miles due west of Miami Beach, the art deco heaven where Charles dreams of living. As skuzzy as the neighborhood is, it's as close to the water as Charles can afford to live.

Charles scratches his stubbly chin and takes a big swig of Jack. Over the last five years he's written two other unpublished books and managed to snag an agent, although not a very good or prestigious one. He'd hoped that his ex-wife's recent remarriage—to a longtime woman friend—and the accompanying cessation of alimony payments, would be enough to catapult him up to Miami Beach, but his column in the *World* doesn't pay much, his freelance work runs in cycles, and he's in the midst of a downturn.

As Charles stands squinting to see the half-imagined blue, there's a knock at the door. Who in hell is that, Charles thinks. With few friends in town, and even fewer clients, he rarely entertains visitors. Charles sets his glass down on the bar and walks across the thinning carpet to peer out the peephole. All he can see is a giant eyeball staring back at him, and he immediately knows to whom it belongs. Chuckling, he throws open the door. "To what do I owe the distinct honor or your presence, Reverend?"

Standing at the door, grinning broadly in a loud Hawaiian shirt and too-short shorts is the Right Reverend Lawrence Kenneth Martin, known as Chip to everyone.

"Well, you gonna invite me in?" Chip asks.

"By all means, Pastor," Charles says, sweeping his arm grandly over his cramped and cluttered apartment. "I've tidied up specially to receive you."

"Cut the crap, asshole!" Chip says jovially, smashing his huge fist playfully into Charles's shoulder. "Don't act like one of my star-struck congregants, afraid to so much as fart around the holy man!" With this he stands on one leg and lets one rip. Charles shakes his head and looks like he wants to spit. At 6'4", 300 pounds, with feet like hams—veritable slabs with blind toes, typically shod in flip flops—and decked out like a clueless New York tourist—pukka shell necklace around his neck and a slightly abused Panama hat on his head—only Chip's broad, raw-boned Midwestern face reveals his Nebraska origins. He brushes by his friend and flops heavily on Charles's ancient couch, causing one end to fall off the bricks that stand in for a missing leg.

"Shit," Chip says, bouncing up and quickly replacing the bricks. As he does this, he spies the crumpled pages of Charles's latest chapter peeking from the trash can.

"Oh, ho, ho! What's all this, then? Has my little Chuckster been busy on his widdle book?" Charles hates being called Chuck, and Chuckster even worse, and hesitates a second as he decides how to respond, before realizing that Chip is grabbing the pages from the trash can.

"Wait," he yelps, and tries to tear the wad of paper from Chip's hands.

"Not so fast, buddy boy," Chip says, shivering Charles with a stiff arm as he returns to the couch. "Let's see what you've got here."

"Now, look, Chip! I obviously am not satisfied with that draft, so please respect that and don't read it." Charles makes a feeble grab for the manuscript, but Chip holds him off easily with a massive forearm while running his eyes over the first page.

"Too late, Chuck, I've already read page one." Chip is a prodigious speed reader, often devouring three or four books a week despite his overloaded schedule as the pastor of the Haitian United Methodist church across the street.

Knowing that Chip won't be denied, Charles sighs and goes to the bar to retrieve his drink. "You want something?" he asks sulkily.

"Yeah, pour me a couple fingers of whatever you're having, no ice," Chip says distractedly as he plows through the chapter. Charles hunts around the messy apartment for another clean glass and comes up with a Yogi Bear jelly jar. He pours Chip's drink, freshens his own, and walks back to the couch. "Here," he says grumpily. Chip reaches out his hand to grab the drink without taking his eyes off the page.

Charles sits in a straight-backed chair across from the couch and fumes. He knows it's futile to try to stop Chip now, and he's slowly becoming embarrassed that his friend is reading his substandard work. A red flush is beginning to spread outward from the vicinity of his Adam's apple.

As Chip continues to read, it becomes obvious he is getting upset: His face, a ruddy barometer of his mood, is slowly turning red, and his already beady eyes narrow. Finally, he tosses the pages down to the floor and glares at Charles.

"You've got to be fucking kidding me. Groucho, Benny and Burns as the three wise men doing Borscht Belt schtick?! Joseph as Ralph Kramden and

Mary as Alice? It takes a lot to shock me, Chucko, as you know, but that really frosts my mini-wheats!" Chip stands up and starts to pace.

"I mean this piece of trash you wrote is wrong in so many ways! Alien Jesus, Honeymooner Holy Family, '50s comedians offering gifts, oy!" Chip strides over to Charles's chair and towers over him.

Charles is nonplussed and a bit intimidated by his looming buddy. He agrees with Chip that the chapter is a hunk of steaming shit, but he hadn't expected to hit this nerve in the normally extremely tolerant preacher.

"Chip, I don't get it. What's got you hot and bothered? And will you back off and give me some room?" Charles pokes feebly at Chip's substantial stomach. "I agree this chapter sucks. I threw it out, didn't I? And you insisted on reading it, so don't blame me!" Charles slips sideways out of his chair and backs off a few feet. Chip starts pacing back and forth across the small living room.

"Who should I blame, genius? You wrote it. This thing reads like a cheap joke," Chip says. "I was almost buying the alien Jesus, even the stupid brain virus vaccine from the stars—I mean, at least they're semi-interesting, if unoriginal, ideas—but, Christ, three Jewish comedians cracking jokes? Man, it's insulting! I feel like I've been sucker-punched."

"Take it easy, Chip!" He's gotten his friend pretty pissed off. The flush has reached Charles's cheeks.

"Look," Chip says, "I knew you were trying to start a new novel, we've talked about that, but I had no idea it was about Jesus. I don't know why a skeptic like you wants to write about Christ, anyway, and, knowing you, I guess I should have expected your flip attitude, but I got sucked in and then . . . and then . . ." Chip gropes the air for the words. "You stomped all over me!" Chip lands on the couch heavily, raising a cloud from the elderly fabric and rocking it momentarily up off the bricks.

"Don't take it so seriously, Chip. I threw it out, right? C'mon, man. I knew it sucked. And besides, it's really hard for me to buy this three wise men business. I mean, give me a break. They're guided by a star? Really? Have you ever tried to stand under a star? And they came from far away, so this really, really bright star had to guide them for days, and no one else notices? So, I thought I'd use three of my favorite Jews to liven things up a bit. Didn't work, but where's the harm?"

"I don't know," Chip says, picking at a rip in the sofa arm. "It just really got my goat. I mean, besides being blasphemous, which generally I'm not that upset with, it just felt like a slap in my face."

"Hold on, Chip," Charles says, a light dawning. "This wasn't targeted at you."

"No, just my faith."

"Well, as Tonetti says, 'Faith is a foolish thing,'" Charles says.

"No, you asshole, Tonetti says, 'Fate is a foolish thing to take chances with.' And so are you!" Chip's face almost betrays a small smirk. The two men share an obsession with Fred and Ginger's *The Gay Divorcee*.

"I know, I know. I was just riffing. But look, you can't possibly believe that every word in the Bible is the absolute truth, can you? Even the stuff about the subjugation of women, the keeping of slaves, keeping Kosher, for Christ's sake, and how about masturbation?" Charles knew that Chip, a lifelong enthusiastic masturbator, would rise to this bait.

"Well, Master Bates, as you probably know, since we've discussed it before, many United Methodists believe the Bible must be interpreted within its"—here Chip offers air quotes—"cultural and societal context. So, no, I don't believe every word is literally true, but it is the word of the Lord. That much I do know for sure." Chip seems a bit mollified by the discussion.

Charles says, "But how do you know what you should take as the absolute truth, and what is still true, but not actual, more a codifying or mythifying of actual events—revelation that is no less true for the fact that it did not happen? Like journalists lying to tell the truth, or like some manifestation of Jung's collective unconscious."

"Well, psychobabble-boy, that's where faith comes in. You gotta believe." Chip takes off his Panama and sails it across the room, trying for a ringer on Charles's tacky mechanical parrot on a perch. The hat spats against the motorized creature, which emits a slow-motion squawk.

Charles rolls his eyes and says, "But which to believe? That's what I'm asking. Believe that the world is only 6,000 years old? That we should keep Kosher? Never pleasure ourselves? Or love our brother as ourselves? How do you pick when the whole damn Bible is so contradictory and, frankly, confusing?"

Chip, calmer now, puts on his counselor's voice. "Like I just said, dude, that's what faith is for. You know the truth of the Bible in your heart, you feel God's love, and you know the right way."

"Yeah, well, I just can't believe in this magi fable, the stable, the manger, or the rest of the whole megillah surrounding the birth of Christ—the shepherds quaking, the angels and the star, the fucking frankincense and myrrh. I mean what possible use are these gifts to a poor little newborn?"

"Well, hold your horses there, Slick!" Chip says. "These three guys are honoring Jesus as the Messiah. Three types of gifts represent His three roles: He is the King of the Jews, as represented by gold; He is the Son of God, represented by frankincense; and yet He is a man, subject to suffering and death, represented by myrrh."

"Well, see, that's just what I'm talking about!" Charles fairly shouts, gesturing with his glass and sloshing some whiskey on the floor. He absent-mindedly covers the wet spot with his foot. "Where do these wise guys get all these ideas? How do they know Jesus is king of the Jews, son of God, and destined to suffer and die for all sins? Even if you accept that bunch of hooey, it's just too much for these guys to be sitting around the palace, or wherever, see a star, know its meaning, and then say to themselves," Charles hitches up his shoulders and affects a Scorcese gangster accent, "'Hey check it out, youse guys, dat dere star means de Messiah is born. So whaddaya think? You mooks got any idea what kind of highly symbolic gifts can we bring to the newborn king? Gold? Yeah, that's good, Nebuchadnezzar the Nose! What else we got? Incense? Hey great idea, Southside Shadrach. Now what else? We need one more thing. Perfume? Hey, whaddaya think this is, a friggin' chick wedding shower? Awright, awright, awright! Quitcher bellyaching. You win, Fat Meschach.'"

Chip smiles in spite of himself at Charles's awful Joisey accent, and says, "Fuggeddaboudit!

With a wry smile, Charles gets back to his point. "But seriously, I'm sorry, I'm just too well-educated to take such things at face value."

"Yeah, baby. You got two MAs and a Ph.D., Dr. MaMa Phud!"

Charles, annoyed, continues. "This is just like the Garden of Eden fable or the other creation myths. I mean, Mark doesn't even mention the birth of Jesus! Mankind cannot believe that the great have had inauspicious beginnings and so we concoct all these fake-o trappings of significance: angels and kings or magi or whatever the hell they were, and all that shit."

"Well I don't have a problem with the whole deal. It's God's word, after all. No room at the inn, born in a stable, angels and shepherds. It's all good," Chip says.

"So, what about the three kings, or rather, three astrologers, then? I mean, they figured out that the messiah had been born using a fantastical pseudoscience, astrology. Doesn't it all seem a bit farfetched?"

"Well, not necessarily. Matthew says that when they showed up in Jerusalem, Herod set the magi on their search for Jesus, asking that they find the baby so he could worship Him, too. Sure, they say they saw a star, but that was just God's sign, and not necessarily a reference to astrology, which, by the way, is one of the few occult sciences not condemned in the Bible. Anyway, the three men double-crossed Herod, and took another route home after worshipping Jesus. That sounds real to me; doesn't that seem like a real detail to you? It sounds authentic, and it all works for me."

"What, that a star led them to the stable?" Charles sits down on the other end of the sagging sofa.

"Why not? I believe in miracles. Matthew could have meant that the star appeared to rise above them, too. It didn't really need to move across the heavens. It coulda just risen, like the moon."

"OK, but why does Matthew say Herod and all of Jerusalem were frightened and disturbed by what the heathen magi said about the newborn King of the Jews? How come nobody else wanted to find him, besides that murdering asshole Herod?"

"That's the beauty of the passage, my bony boy. Pagan astrologers are digging on the newborn king, and devout Jews are ignoring or feeling threatened by the event. It's kind of a continuing theme in Matthew— Jews rejecting Jesus. But, hey, you know what? I'm over it. I'm cool with your draft. I think I get where you're coming from on the magi. Don't know as I would have selected the comedians you did. I'm more partial to a different Marx brother. Imagine Harpo doing that schtick—grabbing Joseph's hand and placing his leg in it! Honking his horn and waking baby Jesus. Heh."

Chip has clearly calmed down, and is smiling indulgently, which ticks Charles off. He leans back against the arm of the sofa and takes a big swig of whiskey. Then he rummages in the pockets of his sport coat but doesn't find the package of smokes he's looking for. Not only has his friend read, without asking, a manuscript he threw away, he has the temerity to get insulted by it. Then he ends the theological discussion just when Charles was making a few points.

"Well, Chip, you said you liked the brain virus business . . ." Charles gets up to get a new pack of cigarettes.

"Didn't say I liked it. Said I was almost buying it."

"OK, OK, whatever. What do you think of the idea?" Charles sits back down, opens the package, extracts a cigarette and lights it.

"Well, I'm not sure you've developed it properly. You just kind of throw it in at the beginning." Chip turns towards Charles and leans forward. "I don't really get the motivation of the aliens, here. What is their relationship with this brain virus? I mean, sure, it's kind of interesting, in a trite sort of way, to think that we're lots smarter than we act because of some external influence that makes us stupid. Reminds me of an old sci-fi story about the Earth finally, after eons, passing out of a cone of radiation or whatever that slowed down the neurons or something, and all of a sudden everyone became a genius. What the hell was the name of that one? You read it?"

Charles is now fuming. His friend hates his story, and now is accusing him of plagiarizing part of it. He opens his mouth to say something, but snaps it back shut.

"Where were you going with that?" Chip asks.

"Well, if I hadn't hated the whole chapter—like I told you, it took a damn left turn on me there—the idea was that the baby Jesus, being immune and all, is brilliant, in addition to being able to morph and present a pleasing image to all. He's able to pass this brilliance, or rather the immunity to the virus, down through the ages. So, all the major smart guys, Da Vinci, Galileo, Newton and so on, were of his line."

"Well I got to say, that bit I think is pretty good, although it smacks a bit of *The Da Vinci Code*."

"Oh, for Christ's sake, Chip! I've got drafts of a story based on this idea going back to the late '80s. Dan Brown can bite me!"

Chip grins at having gotten Charles's goat yet again. "Take it easy, buddy, I wasn't accusing you of anything. Although your choice of phrase there—bite me—has always puzzled me. I mean, when somebody says that, generally when expressing hostility, what is it they hope will happen? Surely it wouldn't be pleasant for Dan Brown to come over to your apartment and bite you, on the dick or anywhere?"

Charles sighs. "Well, it's not to be taken literally, obviously."

"True, true. But take a look at other hostile expressions. Say, fuck you, for example. Are you wishing that I would have someone make love to me? This is some kind of horrible thing to happen? I'm not so sure. Or do you mean you'd fuck me? Well, if a man says it to another—straight—man, perhaps that's a threat, but still equates lovemaking with aggression."

Charles says, "So what's your point?"

"Look, it's obvious that Western society at least, and probably mankind in general, is a bit, how shall we say, ambivalent about the physical act of love, right? But when did it become fashionable to use sexual terms to curse or put down another? I mean, I guess I can kind of see 'suck my dick' as an expression of dominance. You're commanding the other to service you sexually, but the rest of them, fuck you, eat me, bite my crank, and so on, just don't seem to make much sense."

"Well, I guess it's just the shocking use of mildly forbidden terms to associate with the person you're mad at, and nothing more," says Charles. "Of course, on the other hand, there is the tendency of some folks to refer to everyone as motherfuckers, you know like what that guy says in Blade, 'Some motherfuckers are always trying to ice skate uphill,' or pick just about any black comedian. Using about the worst epithet possible— implying that you fuck your mother—as a general term to refer to random other people without much of a value judgment just doesn't make any sense to me."

"True that, my brutha," Chip says, and reaches over to give Charles a clumsy white-guy high five.

Chip continues, "I remember seeing a concert, must've been back in the early '70s, by Lee Michaels. You remember him? Had a couple near hits, but I just really dug his organ playing. Anyway, he toured with just his keyboards and a fat drummer called Frosty, and I saw him at college, opening for somebody or other. Anyway, things were going fine until Frosty got out from behind the drums and did a Theremin solo. I shit you not. You remember the Theremin?"

Charles shakes his head no.

"It's this weird squat box with like an aerial sticking up. The Beach Boys used it to do that 'ooh-eee-oooh-ooooh' part in "Good Vibrations." Anyway, Frosty does like a 10-minute solo on this thing, and by minute two, he'd completely lost the audience, who started jeering at about minute eight. So, the second he's done, he sets the Theremin to scream this tremendously high-pitched tone, then turns his back to the audience and takes his right index finger and points to his asshole."

"Weird," says Charles.

"Yeah, it was an obviously hostile gesture, but what did it mean? Stick your dick in my ass? Fuck me in the rear? How exactly is this insulting? So anyway, about a year later, Jethro Tull was in town; this was during their *Passion Play* tour. And Martin Barre—one of the most underappreciated guitarists ever, by the way—does this stinging solo in the middle of this complicated bit of Tull music. I dunno what the deal was, but even though the crowd erupted in cheers when he was done, something pissed him off, I guess, and he turned his butt to the audience and made the same damn gesture Frosty had. I totally couldn't figure that out."

"Well," Charles says, "I guess that just supports my theory that the insulting part isn't the suggestion of a sexual act, but the use of forbidden words or gestures in connection with the person you're pissed at."

"Yeah, it's a conundrum alright," Chip agrees. He sits back, cocks his head and stares at the ceiling. "Anyway, getting back to the brain virus thing, think of how so many exceptional men and women seem to be so out of place in their times, having the ability to see things as they are, unclouded by the prejudices of those around them or the received perceptions of their times. What if it isn't some immunity to a brain virus? What if it's just the love of God that makes them great?

"Wait, wait, wait," Charles breaks in. "I think you're missing the point. I agree that there is inspiration, and by that, I mean inspiration in the original sense of being filled with some kind of spirit. But are these colossal geniuses freaks, mutations that just happened to wake up from the stupid dreams mankind is ordinarily dreaming? Or, they're just immune to the brain virus. Perhaps that's what genius really is."

Chip snorts. "Genius. God, I've known so many people who thought they were geniuses." He looks meaningfully over at Charles, arching an eyebrow. Charles grabs a pillow and fires it at Chip's head. "Shut the fuck up, you fuckin' motherfucker, and suck my dick! I point my asshole in your general direction!"

Chip roars with laughter. "I'm hungry. Let me take Mister, sorry, Doctor Genius to dinner."

As the two men get up to leave, Charles says, "You know Chip, I gotta say this manger story has always perplexed me. I remember when as a young child, if I couldn't sleep, my mother would hold me and softly sing Christmas songs. My favorite was one I called 'Come All Ye Fawfoo.' Even as a child, though, I wondered about the round virgin in 'Little Town of Bethlehem.'"

Chip throws his massive arm across Charles's bony shoulders and says, "Dude, she was pregnant, so of course she was round!" Despite himself, Charles laughs as they walk out into the hallway and down the stairs.

Chip says, "Hey, that reminds me of this joke I'm thinking of using in my next sermon." Charles rolls his eyes. His friend is constantly telling him terrible jokes, or jokes Charles doesn't really get.

"There once was a rich man who was near death. He's very upset because he worked so hard for his money and wanted to be able to take it with him to heaven. So, the rich man prays that he be able to take some of his wealth with him. An angel hears his plea and appears to him. 'Sorry Rich Man, but like they say, you can't take it with you.' The man begs the angel to speak to God to see if He might bend the rules. A week later, the angel reappears and informs the man that God has decided to allow him to take one suitcase with him.

"Overjoyed, the man finds his largest suitcase, fills it with pure gold bars, and places it beside his bed. Soon afterward the man dies and shows up at the Gates of Heaven to greet St. Peter. Peter sees the suitcase and says, 'Hold on, you can't bring that in here!' The man explains he has permission and asks him to verify his story with the Lord. Sure enough, Peter checks and comes back saying, 'You're right. You're allowed one carry-on, but I'm supposed to check its contents before letting it through.' Peter puts on rubber gloves, swabs down the outside of the suitcase with a piece of cheesecloth and opens the suitcase to inspect the worldly items that the man found too precious to leave behind. Seeing the gold Peter exclaims, 'God said you could bring anything at all with you and you brought pavement?!?'"

Both laugh, with Chip's booming laugh probably audible all the way to the beach.

Baby you're a rich fat, baby you're a rich fat, baby you're a rich fat Jew!

The Beatles—*Baby You're a Rich Man*

Stately, plump Jesús Christos came from the elevator, bearing a bowl of oranges upon which an iPad and a Wall Street Journal lay crossed. The billionaire scion of a Mexican pre-mixed concrete family crossed to the rampart on top of Christos Tower and surveyed his kingdom, laid out beneath him, through the haze of early smog. He cleared his throat and spat over the side; the sputum fell a few feet and then a gust caught it and threw it back in his face. Angered, he shifted the bowl into his left hand, wiped the spit off his face, and tried futilely to throw it back over the side of the hundred-story building.

Setting the bowl and its cargo down on a side table, Christos threw his bulk into the nearby lounge chair and scanned the newspaper's front page before lifting the iPad and settling it on the bulk of his stomach to get the real news. He checked his family's stock price and then checked Twitter for mentions of his dotcom company, Jewish.com. After answering a few text messages, Christos opened the manuscript he was working on, the story of his life. Most of the writing had come easily—the story of his successes online, his continuing conflict with his family and relocation to Bangladesh, his recent marriage to María Magdalena at 28. But he was struggling with writing about his early years, including his spiritual awakening at five, and a particular family trip to Jerusalem when he was 12.

Sighing, he began to write, again, his first chapter.

Chapter 1—My Young Awakening

From an early age, I felt alienated from my family. I remember at age five wondering who these people were. How had I come to be involved with a collection of semi-shady avaricious fools? These are not my real parents; my real father is coming back for me. My mother didn't help matters with her oft-repeated joke about finding me under a bush by the side of a country road. What a horrible picture this conjured in my young mind: lost among low hills of terraced farmland, baking under a hedgerow of agave.

I concocted a different fantasy: My real mom and dad live somewhere else and when they get enough money, they'll come get me. I'm just staying with María and José for a while until my real parents get on their feet. My real parents are fallen nobility, king and queen deposed by banditos. They placed me here for safety until the day I can regain my rightful place at the right hand of my father.

My alienation also stemmed from our family name. Like many Mexican Jews, my family did not have a typical Jewish name. My father couldn't be Josef; he was José. In fact, it was not until in my late teens, when I came upon my father's birth certificate, that I found out he was born with a different surname: Khaldei. I was further surprised and disgusted to learn that around the time I was born, the whole family, perhaps fed up with persecution, perhaps seeking a more acceptable identity to help extend the family business overseas, changed the family name to Christos. The name may have been chosen partly in sardonic honor of the religious crackpot Maria Devi Christos from our native Ukraine, a favorite obsession of one of my uncles, but probably primarily to fly under the anti-Semitic radar.

Consequently, my parents and the rest of the family were not outwardly, or even inwardly, religious and cared nothing for the Torah, which was my passion ever since I taught myself to read it at age five. My family only managed to drag themselves to temple a few times a year, mostly to hobnob with other important people on the various holy days. This secular disinterest in heritage and tradition helped make my growing obsession with the word of Yahweh seem even stranger to them. I was a precocious kid, and I yearned for a connection with God.

I learned Hebrew so I could know the word of God and I also taught myself Spanish so that I could learn more about the Jewish people in Mexico. Of course, Mexico in general, and Mexico City, where we lived, was not exactly a paradise for the Jews. I read the histories: the arrival of the Conversos with Cortés; the forced conversions to Paulicism brought on by the Spanish Inquisition and its Mexican counterpart that killed 29 Judaizers; the immigration of the Crypto-Jewish Carvajal family; the European Jewish influx of the late 19th century—especially the bankers who were invited by the government for their fiscal skills; Benito Juárez' Reform War, and on and on. I may have been precocious, but I was still a young child, and these terrible injustices affected me deeply, haunting my dreams, and causing me to hunger to learn as much as I could about my heritage to try to understand the treatment of my people.

My father made his fortune in concrete, a substance as hard and unyielding as his head. He took over the business from my grandfather and built it into a multi-billion-dollar international building materials company with a presence in 50 countries. In fact, cement is part of the reason I moved to Bangladesh, where the company has an outpost. It was an easy way to put an ocean between me and my family without seeming to escape their grasp.

From as early as I can remember, I detested being rich. Even while quite young, I felt demeaned by the attentions of the servants who performed all my grooming and toilet chores as if I were a cherished object to be polished rather than a person. Although I was this shiny valued thing, I felt I had no worth intrinsically. I was just a reflection of what my father owned. I began to feel that I was meant for better things, and that I needed to strive for some meaning to justify myself and break out of my father's shadow. Simply put, I felt destined for greatness, but in a way that transcended the materialist world of my family.

Around the time of my birth, my father was making the company's first international moves, acquiring European and South American companies. That's when he built his first palace, a ghastly faux Tudor affair, but actually quite tame compared to some of his hideous later mansions. I grew up on its cold marble floors. We had many servants, of course, and my parents treated them like dirt. I was aghast at the cruel treatment, especially by my mother, who would have the maid clean and re-clean a floor until she was satisfied, and the maid's fingers bled.

I hated all the cars, and boats, and airplanes my father bought, and all the clothes my mother wore once and then discarded, and all the diamonds and gold and other ridiculous excesses. The toilet in my bathroom was trimmed with gold.

There were various aspects of our wealth, however, that I did enjoy, sometimes to my shame. When my father determined that I would not be dissuaded from daily study of the Torah, he unloaded the dozens of bookshelves in his fake English library, tossed the books in the trash, and restocked with possibly the finest library of Jewish religious thought in the New World. I was like a kid in a candy store.

Another perk of wealth that I enjoyed was our frequent trips abroad. My favorite trip was one we took when I was 12, to Israel. We were only scheduled to be there for a day because my father had some business to do.

One thing that made this trip particularly memorable was the weird behavior of two old people we ran into while doing some sightseeing. One was a doddering old man whom we met at the Dome of the Rock. He said his name was Simeon, and he told us he was waiting for "the consolation of Israel." We had no idea what he meant by that. He raved on, saying that he had been promised by God that he would not die before he had seen the Lord's Messiah. As soon as he clapped his eyes on me, he embraced me and went on and on about how he could now die, because he had met the Messiah. He mumbled some other rubbish about rising and falling in Israel, and signs, and something about a sword as well.

I was pretty disturbed by this encounter, as were my parents who, once they recovered from their surprise, got their bodyguards to usher the poor fool away.

No sooner had Simeon been swept away than another old crank came up to me and started making a fuss as if I were something really special. She said she was the Widow Anna, and that she'd tell everyone about me. My folks were all shook up by that point and practically dragged me away from that holy place. I didn't want to leave because it was my fondest desire to seek out learned rabbis to discuss the Torah.

By that time, we traveled with quite the entourage. There were maids and valets, and perhaps a dozen bodyguards as well as three nursemaids for me, for around the clock attention. I had no use for any of them and, especially at age 12, was resentful of being treated as a child. My parents had a big diplomatic event of some kind that night, and I managed to run a little game on my nannies so I could slip away. Each thought the other would be in charge of me that night and the next day, when we were to take the family 757 on to Paris. This was the most tricked-out plane you would ever want to see, with multiple bathrooms, and several private compartments all resplendent in gold, diamond inlays, and other opulent decorations. I had often hidden myself for hours on the plane on longer trips, my nose in a religious book.

I was able to sneak off the plane and hailed a cab to take me to the Steinsaltz Center in Jerusalem where I was determined to find Rabbi Adin Steinsaltz and engage him in Talmudic discussions. When I got there, I found a great gathering of rabbinical scholars. When I asked to be allowed to join their discussions, they were at first amused, but when they realized I knew my stuff, they began to include me almost as an equal. Rabbi Steinsaltz himself was quite kind to me and expressed surprise as much for the questions I asked as for my answers to his. I can't remember a happier time in my childhood than the time I spent with these learned holy men. As I grew older, I harked back particularly to our discussions of the tribulations of Jeremiah and Job, and especially the prophecies of Isaiah. I often feel like a voice calling in the wilderness myself.

Because of my duplicity with my nannies, nobody noticed I wasn't on the airplane the next morning. My parents were quite used to not seeing me, sometimes for days, and assumed I was on board. When they got to Paris, they realized I'd been left behind, and immediately turned back to Jerusalem to search for me. After three days, they found me in the Steinsaltz Center, sitting among the teachers, listening to them and asking them questions.

When my parents saw me, they were astonished. My mother said to me, "Son, why have you treated us like this? Your father and I have been anxiously searching for you." Being a rebellious smartass, I replied, "Why were you searching for me? Didn't you know I had to be in my Father's house?" I had hoped this would particularly sting my father, whom I had regularly and loudly accused of not being my real father. My parents were flabbergasted and furious. They turned on their heels and let our bodyguards extract me from the company of rabbis and return me to the plane.

Around this time, I became obsessed with Paulicism and studied its version of the Bible intensely. How could this obviously crazy Roman Jew have concocted an entire religion out of whole cloth based on a few claims of miracles and mediated by a talisman so fraught with cruelty: the Roman crucifixion cross? And why did they revere the nails used to affix victims to the cross as holy relics? It doesn't make sense on so many levels. For example, kinesiologically speaking, the cross is a weakening symbol. Try it sometime. Lift a weight and then try it again while holding a cross. You'll be surprised.

The whole origin of this strange religion confused and fascinated me. The odd insistence that Paul was born of a virgin, baptized, and was a carpenter. It seemed to me that this was a mashup of the origin story for Krishna (second person of the Hindu Trinity, divinely conceived, son of a carpenter, baptized, called the Son of God), Buddha (entered his mother's womb from her side, in the form of a white elephant), the Akkadian birth of Marduk (created in the heart of Apsu) and the Persian god Mithra (born of a virgin on December 25th and known as "the Way," "the Truth," "the Light," "the Word," "the Son of God," and "the Good Shepherd"). Paulicism was plagiarism personified! The miracle birth meme was almost as old as civilization as an indication of holiness. Hell, I was a miracle birth myself. Mother was 46 and years into menopause when I was born, just like Isaac.

I felt the fact that Paulicism claimed a common heritage with Judaism was a particular insult to my religion. How could a religion with just Moses' 10 commandments truly be the successor to Judaism, with its mature, comprehensive laws for living and relating to God?

Even more insulting was my father's purchase of a firm that manufactured crosses and nail talismans. This was a type of business that was completely out of his bailiwick! In my self-centered young mind, this was a deliberate attack on my growing religiousness, and a way for him to assert the dominance of his materialistic worldview and lifestyle. I didn't speak to my father for weeks after I learned of the transaction. I doubt he noticed.

Judaism had become the central devotion of my life by my early teens. Two things obsessed my thoughts during this time: the worldwide persecution of the Jews, especially the Holocaust, and a growing conviction that the Jewish aversion to proselytizing would ensure that the hatred of my people would continue forever. It was in this period that I conceived Jewish.com as a way to spread the word about Judaism.

My religion had always been an exclusive club—the Chosen People. We begrudgingly accept conversions, but true Jews are those with a Jewish mother. I felt that as long as we held ourselves above others and made no effort to increase our ranks other than by in-breeding, we would continually suffer.

Jewish.com came into being in my bedroom. I had, like many of my peers, become fascinated with the power of the web as a communication tool. What better way to spread the word about Judaism than to harness this online power? I obviously had access to virtually unlimited funds, and so I bought a state-of-the-art web server and all the software necessary to begin to build a website. I took a number of online courses in web development and began to piece together the structure of the site.

My goal at first was to just create an online community for Jews all over the world, sort of like a Facebook for Yids, although I wasn't yet aware of Facebook, which hadn't spread far beyond a few colleges when I began Jewish.com. I thought if Jews from all cultures and walks of life could establish a kehila, a place to exchange thoughts, prayers, and viewpoints, then Judaism would not only be enriched, but could grow in stature and number.

From the start, I was conscious that there is no real tradition of proselytizing in Judaism and in fact, such an idea is anathema to the core beliefs of my religion. Traditionally we have believed that eventually all people will come to recognize the God of Israel as the One All-Powerful God of the Universe. It will either just dawn on people that Judaism is the one true religion, or the converted will otherwise fulfill the seven universal commandments God gave to Noah. In Deuteronomy there is also the belief that Jews adhering to God's commandments "will be proof of your wisdom and discernment to other peoples, who on hearing of all these laws will say, 'Surely, that great nation is a wise and discerning people.'"

Some Jews feel that to encourage conversions would doom many converts to fail, in part because to convert, one must accept all 613 commandments of the Torah. Discouraging conversion in this way weeds out those who aren't truly devout. Whatever the reason, the result is Judaism is one of the smaller worldwide religions: Paulicism and its offshoot, Islam, comprise well more than half the world's population—almost 5 billion. Judaism, claiming a mere 14 million adherents, doesn't even make the top 10; it's basically a rounding error religion.

At 13, in my first post on Jewish.com, I asked, irreverently, "How's that Chosen People thing going for you, Jews? Centuries of persecution and murder for our beliefs. Oppression and coercion and relegation to second-class status in society after society. It's just not working out." My young self's soul cried out for a better solution.

And so, I studied the Paulic evangelists, with their slick suits and eloquent speech, and their pandering to an audience that I—and they—regarded as morons. I also studied the sincere missionaries who, despite their sincerity, adopted often-horrific tactics to convert the heathens. I studied the Muslims, whose religion, although peaceful at its center, justifies holy war as a means to convert the unconverted. I concluded that unless the Jewish people adopted evangelism, not only would our numbers remain small, they would be small enough that another Holocaust could wipe us from the Earth.

Jewish.com is a major reason I chose to relocate to Dhaka. The history of our people in Bangladesh, a majority Muslim nation, is a sad one, but a typical one in Muslim Asia. After Shalom Cohen founded the Calcutta Jewish community in West Bengal, he started his trading company with Jewish employees in Dhaka. Cohen's son-in-law established a prayer hall in 1817 to serve the small Jewish community there. However, most Jews doing business in Dhaka did not live there, preferring to reside in Calcutta where there was a much larger Jewish population. Today, until recently, only a few Jews remain in Bangladesh, but most hide their Jewishness and are assimilated. Until I built the company headquarters here, there had been no synagogue in Bangladesh since the police seized the last one decades ago, although some Jews gathered privately to celebrate the feasts.

A country that lacks a significant Jewish population and which seceded from India based on its desire to become a Muslim state may seem like a poor relocation choice for a person seeking to spread the Jewish faith. My reasons for coming to Dhaka include my desire to separate myself from my materialistic, self-hating family, the convenient location of a family company office in Dhaka, and the extreme challenge of becoming a missionary in such an unpromising place. This challenge was brought home to me by the plight of Muslim Zionist and peace activist Salah Uddin Shoaib Choudhury, editor of *The Weekly Blitz* in Bangladesh. What a rare bird! A Zionist Muslim! Choudhury was accused of blasphemy, sedition, and treason for frequently writing pro-Israel articles and criticizing radical Islamists. He has had the temerity to say, in public, "I am a Zionist and a friend of Israel."

I simply had to meet this brave man who has been arrested and tortured with electric shocks, had his office firebombed, was kidnapped by the Rapid Action Battalion anti-terrorism unit of the Bangladesh Police, and was thrown in jail on fabricated charges of embezzlement. There is a Paulic parable about casting seed on rocky ground. Dhaka definitely was not fertile ground for a mission, but I've never been one to shrink from a challenge. I decided to march into the heart of the beast and change it with love.

To effect my relocation, I agreed to supervise the family company's construction of the tallest building in Bangladesh on the condition that the building include the country's first synagogue in many years. It was tough sledding to convince my father, but I actually think he would have done anything to get rid of me.

I now have built the tower, and the synagogue, and managed to get Choudhury released from jail. He now runs the synagogue outreach program, which numbers about a dozen souls. I maintain heavy security around the temple and the building, know whom to pay and with whom to ally, and am happy to report few incidents, and even a few conversions that add to the 3,500 Jews who lived in the country before I arrived. We are slowly convincing Bangladeshi Jews to stop claiming to be Jehovah's Witnesses and to reveal their true identity. Nonetheless, most Jews attend our services by entering through a special door in the underground parking garage of the building.

I am not confining my missionary activities to Bangladesh, of course. Through Jewish.com, I have organized missions throughout the Paulic and Muslim worlds. Interestingly, many of our missionaries were not born Jewish, and have converted as part of our efforts. My goal is that, in two years, by my 30th birthday, I will announce missions in every country on Earth.

Of course, I have faced opposition and death threats from all sides. The attacks from fellow Jews are especially virulent. My response to all attackers is that God loves them and will help them see the path to Judaism someday.

There are those who say that a person of privilege such as myself is not fit to minister to those less fortunate because I have never known privation. My response is that I have faced extreme privation of the soul growing up as a wealthy person. I have seen the disease of entitlement and arrogance that afflicts my family and others among the wealthy elite. I have seen scions of family friends turn to drugs or other risky behaviors because of lives barren of faith. I reject the trappings and privileges of wealth except in cases where my money can do good, and further my goal of converting to Judaism all those willing to be enlightened.

I know that some will fault me for fabricating a humble backstory, back when I started Jewish.com. To this, I plead youth. I was 13. And after all, for some time I had been creating a more acceptable family history—noble parents who would come back and rescue me from the filthy rich—and so it came easily to me. So, no, I wasn't the bastard son of a family of impoverished pretenders to the Ukrainian throne, although my family did emigrate from Ukraine to Mexico during the pogroms that accompanied the establishment of the Ukrainian People's Republic. And, no, I wasn't 28 when I created Jewish.com. Similarly, it's not true that I was a rabbinical student, and that's still not true. I've never met many of the prominent Jewish scholars I claimed to be associated with, although, as I mentioned earlier, I have met a few.

I concocted some of my story so that I could be taken more seriously, but mostly I was afraid that my message would be obscured by people's reaction to the wealthy messenger. Many believe the Paulic biblical verse, "It is easier for a camel to go through the eye of a needle, than for a rich man to enter the kingdom of God." In fact, even today, many have said, effectively, "How dare you try to advise us, when you've never suffered as we have!" Please rest assured I have suffered more than you can ever understand. Part of the reason I started my mission was because I felt unsuited to the life I was born into. I never felt I deserved the advantages I had; they embarrassed me. Our wealth made me feel overwhelmingly guilty. I felt like an imposter in my own life. And so, I created a new identity for myself so that I could avoid the implications of my heritage. On the internet, nobody knows you're a one-percenter.

I realize the irony involved.

María emerged from the elevator in a stunning one-piece swimsuit that accentuated her baby bump. "Join me for a dip, J?" This far above the Dhaka smog, the sun shines brightly, glinting off María's giant frog-eye glasses and making her look like a shapely alien.

"Not now, mi vida. I'm working on the book." Jesús regarded his bride briefly, flashed her a quick smile, and returned to his writing. Pouting slightly, María turned, dropped her wrap, and entered the gigantic pool. She swam over to the infinity edge and gazed out over the smog-fouled city.

"J, why don't you do something about this terrible pollution?"

Jesús looked up, glanced about, took a beat to process what she'd asked, and said, "I'm trying to heal spirits, not bodies. But I suppose I could close up Father's cement plants. That would be a good start at cleaning the air."

"I dare you!"

"Not even a gringo's double-dog dare would make me bring down the shitstorm that I'd be in if I ever crossed mi familia. Besides, I'm turning father's dirty money into clean Yechidah."

"Always the golden tongue," María sneered, sticking out her own tongue at her husband. "And are you talking about your own soul or your followers'?"

"For the millionth time, María, I do not have followers. I am a humble missionary attempting to spread God's word throughout the world."

"Well there's a few hundred thousand non-followers in the world who might disagree on that point." María returned to examining the smoggy city.

Jesús had indeed assembled a multitude of missionaries and converts. With Jewish.com as the center of his message, he had first reached out across Mexico City, then across Mexico, then North and South America, and now Asia. The website he created in his bedroom at 13 had evolved over the last 15 years into a virtual synagogue in the cloud, supported by an efficient hierarchy of missionary managers, volunteers and evangelists.

Along the way, the message of Jewish pardon—humility, resolve, and rituals of penitence—in which rabbis serve solely as facilitators, with God as the forgiver, had tended to take on some of the Paulic notion of the priests dispensing penance as de facto grantors of absolution. Jesús was concerned about this and similar shifts in dogma, but pragmatically reasoned that with a massive influx of Paulics and people of other faiths, dogma was less important than enlightenment.

After a moment's thought, Jesús replied to María, "I'm but a man. I do the best I can. If people start to regard me as some kind of prophet, there's little I can do about it. I can think; I can wait; I can fast."

"Yeah, amado, you could fast for a great while . . ."

Jesús tossed the newspaper in the general direction of his wife and returned to his writing.

Screw that lady

The Isley Brothers—*Who's That Lady?*

Charles presses print and hears the printer wake up and begin spitting pages. He stretches and shakes himself. I think I've finally got it, he thinks. After numerous false starts he's finally satisfied with his approach to the character of Jesus. Yah, he thinks, pulling a Marlboro from the nearby pack, this is just sacrilegious enough to make them think. Jesus, the son of a rich man! A man who made up stories about his origins because he knew no one would believe the soul of a rich man. It's just what Chip and I were talking about the other day.

Charles gets up and goes to the closet to get his coat. It was rarely cold enough in Miami to need it, but Charles felt naked without a sport coat. And besides, a coat was essential to mask the smell from his pits. Charles has bad B.O., and often changes shirts as many as six times a day, shucking them into a stinking pile in a corner of his closet. After years in Florida, his only concession to the muggy heat is to give up the tweed and wool in favor of linen jackets. Grabbing the sheaf of papers off the printer, Charles hurries out the door.

I must show this to Chip right away, he thinks. He takes the four flights of stairs two at a time down to the lobby. While crossing the street to the church, Charles runs his mind back over his chapter, stroking it as if it were a cherished pet.

As he walks into the church parking lot, he notices an unfamiliar car. Rats, Chip must have someone in with him. I'll probably have to wait.

Chip makes a little money on the side working for a pastoral counseling center. They primarily send him couples with marital difficulties, usually from other congregations. As Charles walks into the office, he can see that Chip's door is closed.

"Rita, is he busy?" Charles asks the church secretary, a voluptuous dark-haired Haitian with a taste for figure-enhancing yet somehow prim clothing. Charles has had many erotic dreams about her but has never gotten up the nerve to even ask her out for a drink.

"Yes, he's got a couple in there with him. But they should be out soon, their hour's almost up. How you doin' Charles?" Rita leans back in her chair and stretches, pulling the material of her blouse tightly across her bosom.

Charles tries not to stare. "Oh, fine. I finished a chapter that I'm pretty excited about and I can't wait to show it to Chip."

"Well, have a seat. Do you want any coffee or anything?"

"Thanks, Rita, no. I'm fine." Charles sits in one of the worn chairs in the waiting area and glances at the old pile of *Sports Illustrateds* on a nearby table. I wonder what his congregation thinks of Chip's choice of waiting room reading matter. Any other minister might stock uplifting religious magazines. But Chip has just about every old *Sports Illustrated* containing an article about Nebraska football.

He turns his attention to Rita, studying her perfect olive skin and examining the swell of her breasts beneath the demure blouse. The only thing that belied her otherwise proper appearance were full lips she always painted bright red. I'll bet she's a real hellion in the sack, he thinks. God, what thoughts to have in a church waiting room! Still, she's quite the hottie . . .

Chip sticks his head out of his office, and, seeing Charles, grins and says, "I see my 12 o'clock is here!" Charles, a bit embarrassed at the thought that he would need religious counseling, sticks out his tongue, but, failing to assemble a snappy comeback says instead, "Yeah, I need it bad," while glancing meaningfully at Rita.

"Rita, could you set the Taylors up for next week, same time? Chuck, I'll be with you in a minute," Chip says and closes the door. A few minutes later a middle-aged, rather frumpy couple walk out of his office, eyes straight ahead, and out the door.

Chip is speaking on his desk phone when Chip comes to the door, but beckons for Charles to come and sit. Charles slumps into one of the guest chairs and puts his feet up on the desk, inadvertently pushing over a stack of papers that cascade onto the floor. Chip mouths, "You idiot!" but waves Charles back into his seat as he rises to grab the papers.

"OK. Talk to you later. Be good," Chips says, and cradles the receiver with one hand while sweeping up a few of the papers with the other.

"What's with them?" Charles asks jerking his thumb in the general direction of the departed Taylors.

"He likes her clothes," Chip says.

"Well, so what?"

"Well, he likes them a bit too much . . . he wears them from time to time." They laugh. Neither is particularly aware of the breach of confidence Chip has committed.

"So, is the problem that they fight about who'll wear the new red pumps and push-up bra on Saturday night?" Charles asks.

"The problem," Chip says, "is that they are deeply committed Methodists, and Methodists don't do that sort of thing." Chip says this with a sad smile and a shake of his head, as if to say, "They don't get it."

Impatient with the small talk and excited about his new vision of Jesus, Charles thrusts the manuscript at Chip. Chip is a little surprised at his enthusiasm, but smiles, grabs the wad of print, tilts his chair back and wades in.

"Get us a coupla beers from the mini-fridge, willya?" Chip says. Charles crosses the room, grabs two cans of Bud from the fridge, pops them both and hands one to Chip. He's always amazed at how unlike a standard preacher his friend is. Beer in his office, in the middle of the day? Chip thinks nothing of it. He's more like your jolly, profane best bro than he is a preacher.

Charles sips his beer and tries distractedly to occupy himself while Chip reads. He gets up and wanders the room, examining the pictures on the wall, the book titles on the shelves, the toppled paper stack still spread out on the floor, the city street outside Chip's window. While cruising the bookshelf a second time, Charles idly wonders where Chip keeps the vintage porn he knows his friend buys with a passion verging on obsession. His wife Trixie wouldn't approve, so Charles is sure Chip is keeping it in the study. After much deliberation, Charles decides it's behind the picture of the Madonna on the wall behind the desk. He can imagine the safe that is set in the wall, with an old-fashioned dial set in burnished gray metal.

Chip's porn is relatively soft core: old issues of *Playboy*, *Penthouse*, a few *Hustlers*, the odd ancient *Stag*—nothing too depraved. Nonetheless, Chip is devoted to the magazines and has freely admitted to Charles that he has been a regular masturbator all his life. He calls it his deep relationship with Madame Hand.

Charles sits back down and again puts his feet up, feigning nonchalance. After a few moments, he fidgets in his seat then pulls his feet off the desk and stands up again. He's always uncomfortable when someone is reading his work, even his clients. In addition to his weekly column in the *Miami World*, opinion articles for national magazines and atheist blogs, and short stories in sci-fi mags, he takes several business writing jobs a year, yet it always drives him crazy when the client wants to read his work in his presence.

What do you do while they're examining your life, your thoughts committed to paper, he thinks. I should have brought a book. At least I could be pretending to read while I'm waiting. I wonder if Chip will get out some of the porn for me if I ask?

He wanders over toward the Madonna picture and stares out the window at the incredibly bright pavement. Girls in halter tops drift past the window in high-heeled sandals. The single-story pastel homes across the street bake beneath the palms. This neighborhood seems far from the art deco section of Miami Beach with its crass and compelling time warp ambiance, where Charles yearns to live. This area is in a different, less affluent time warp. Only six miles west of tony North Beach as the crow flies, the neighborhood might just as well be in a different country. The church itself, with its Haitian influence, is a spot of color amidst fading, peeling, sad houses with scruffy, sandy patches of front lawn.

How in hell did Chip get to be pastor of a freakin' Haitian church anyway? Charles is surprised he's never asked his friend this question. He knew Chip had served two stints with the Peace Corps in Haiti, but he was so not black, and so not Haitian. Yet his congregation loves him, and he's never had a problem with the racial divide. In fact, everybody loves Chip, without exception.

Wonder what that feels like, Charles thinks. I'm a bit of acquired taste myself. Charles has always had few friends and his introversion has often been mistaken for aloofness.

Chip is stirring. As he concentrates on Charles's chapter, he scratches his nose, and under his desk, he slips off his shoes. He idly reaches beneath the desk and pulls off his socks. Still reading the manuscript, Chip crosses ankle over knee and begins picking his feet. This is a trait that Charles finds particularly disgusting. Chip never thinks to ask if it's OK, but immediately becomes shoeless and odoriferous whenever he comes over Charles's place. Charles takes this somewhat as a compliment—Chip is so comfortable with him that he feels right at home. Still, these huge hams of feet—although they don't really stink, their aroma does tend to permeate the room.

Now Chip scratches behind his ear as if an insect has bit him.

Jesus, Charles thinks. When is he going to finish? It's only 4,500 words, for Christ's sake. Chip burps loudly—another endearing trait. Finally, he looks up.

"Interesting."

From his time living in Minnesota, Charles knows this is a Midwesterner's dodge—either a mask of annoyance, or contrary feelings, or an excuse for having no reaction or understanding at all. At least he didn't say "different," the Midwestern kiss of death.

"What do you mean interesting? My old roommate used to say interesting whenever he didn't understand something."

"No, I mean interesting. As in, really interesting, dickweed. What would Jesus have been like if he had been a one-percenter? Would the message have been the same coming from such a different vessel?"

"You mean, could God have inspired a rich man to say the same things a poor man would find easy to say?"

"Well, not exactly. The spirit takes different forms depending . . ."

"Depending on what? Isn't the truth the truth? Isn't there an absolute, as you are always telling me?" Charles moves from the window back to his seat but does not sit down. He always thinks better on his feet.

Chip regards him silently for a moment. "Yes, the truth is absolute, I believe, but the expression of the truth varies with the individual. For a rich man, the truth may mean: Give all your riches to the poor, or in this case, proselytize for the Lord. For a poor man, the truth may mean: Accumulate all the riches you can so you can help your family. You see what I mean?"

"I don't see what this has to do with the kingdom of heaven."

Chip scratches his stubbly chin. Despite his position as pastor, he can't be persuaded to shave more than every other day. "Well, I don't believe there's just one path. There are as many paths as there are people."

Charles won't take such relativism from Chip, who in Charles's eyes is a representative of dogma. "Didn't he say I am the way?"

"The interstate takes you to all destinations. There is no requirement for entry; just find an onramp. And there are many exits, not just one. But there is one final destination."

Charles is irate and leans over the desk towards Chip. "What the hell does that mean? Mumbo fucking jumbo. Religiosity for the sake of religiosity!" Charles feels he is somehow being attacked.

"No, I really mean it. The highway of life, the maze and the tangle of destinations. Who are we to say that a particular vehicle is not going to find the ultimate destination? It could be the Bangor, Maine of our dreams or it could be merely Pensacola." Chip snickers.

Charles, confused by the concept and irritated by Chip's attitude, says, "I don't get it. What does this have to do with what I have written?"

"Well, what is it you think you have written, Padawan?" Chip arches an eyebrow at Charles, drops one foot to the floor, elevates the other, and begins picking.

"Well what I think I am writing is an indictment of religion in general, and the whole idea that a simple carpenter, or a blood-thirsty Arab, or a Hebrew with a bad sense of direction and a God complex can be exalted and worshipped and codified into religions that have brought such misery to the planet. Any institution that brings about crap like the Crusades, all those nasty popes, Henry VIII, fatwas, war and famine, should be held accountable, that's what I think, and that's what I'm writing about. Frankly, I think religion should be banned or at least we should all be weaned from the idea that we must subscribe to a codified belief structure administered by a privileged few, whether it be worship of technology, sports, self, cars or other gods."

"Such big words, beloved!" mocks Chip. "So, you're against a spiritual life, an appreciation of something larger than yourself?"

"I believe in personal enlightenment, and although I hate the idea of self-serving bigots telling people what to think and how to be saved, I could support some kind of loose confederation of ideas, a communal or tribal feeling of closeness and common destination, with little dogma and, yes, an emphasis on spiritual life."

Chip is not smiling now, wondering if his friend truly sees him as a self-serving bigot. He's pissed by Charles's rant and its apparent ad hominem attack on him.

"Would you ban love because some people sin because of it?"

Charles smiles and says nothing; he likes to get Chip's goat.

Chip, now a bit red in the face, continues, "Think of all the monuments that came to be because of this terrible thing, religion—for the love of God. Think of all the good that religious institutions have done, all the refuge they have provided for the oppressed, all the comfort they've given the grieving. I grant you, in every human endeavor there are sinners, those who twist the goodness into evil, transmute gold into the base components of a man, but that fact does not invalidate the institution. Religion, which you defame, has exalted more than it has thrown down. Yes, I am ashamed of the Crusades, the error-filled popes, the Ayatollah, Al Qaeda, and fanatics of every kind. But I am not ashamed of the pious believers, who make all our lives richer by their devotion. Dammit, Chuck, it's not black and white, as you say. Why pick on one imperfect human endeavor, the feeble attempt of man to appreciate God, when all human endeavor is imperfect? Why not pick on, on . . . NASCAR, for Christ's sake, or Wall Street, or softball, or Mah-Jongg? It is not inherent in the worship of God to be deluded, yet some are still deluded."

Chip has been leaning far forward in his chair, hands gripping the arms with white knuckles. He collapses back, and the chair emits a loud squeak as it bears his bulk.

Charles smiles a bit to himself. He really got the old guy worked up this time. "I'm not surprised you mentioned monuments. Don't get me started on architectural excess in the name of the Lord."

Chip glares at Charles. "Look Chuck, the point is salvation. Not all followers will be saved. And, by the same token, not all followers will stray into these monstrous crimes and excesses you mention. That's just the way it is; it's a bell curve, the way it will be for any organized human endeavor."

Charles says, "It's just that religion purports to be different than these other activities you mention. Stock car racing doesn't claim to offer truth; that's your stock in trade, no pun intended." Chip rolls his eyes. "While you make a good point about the incredible, hopeless wrong-headedness of most human activities, I can't forgive religion, since it does claim to be above this, to be a path to truth and salvation. No, that's wrong. Religion claims not to be the way to the truth, but the truth absolute."

Both Chip and Charles are clearly weary of the conversation. "Let's get back to my chapter," Charles says. "I'm glad it's thought-provoking. What did you think about the missionary Jew stuff?"

Chip thinks for a minute. "Not bloody likely, is what I think. I can see a Jew being interested in proselytizing, and it sure could get him killed, but I don't see it succeeding to the point you mention in the chapter. Hundreds of thousands?"

"Yeah, I know. But that's what a messianic figure needs: a borderline heretical proposition. And I know a few people who have converted to Judaism, mostly as part of marriage, but one of them, she converted as part of her own spiritual journey. From Lutheranism, for God's sake."

"Mere anecdotes, Chucko." Chip smirks and picks up a partially smoked cigar from his desk ashtray and jams it into the corner of his mouth. "Is this guy in your chapter the Second Coming?"

"No. In this universe, it's the first coming. Paulicism is based on a false messiah, St. Paul, who creates the religion based on a bunch of memes that were floating around the Middle East back then. I figure Paulicism is pretty close to Catholicism, just no Jesus. Paul either fabricated some other messiah figure or chose himself. Since there's obviously crucifixion, I'm thinking Paul is still telling the story of another guy who got condemned, but it might have been him. I'm not sure which way to go with that. I'm expecting many of the same parables and scriptures get written. That way I can quote them as necessary."

"So, OK. That's interesting, the business of there not having been a true Messiah at the time of Christ, and I like your idea of Paul making up the religion out of whole cloth from ancient messianic myths. I'd like to see you expand on the creation of Paulicism. Just love the name, by the way."

"Yeah, I could do that, probably will. But where is this story going? That's what I can't figure. Does the rich modern Jesus still get crucified?"

Chip, who has been leaning back in his chair staring at the ceiling with fingers laced behind his head, rocks forward and contemplates the question. "Good question. As a rich man, He's more likely to be taken seriously enough to be made king, or president, or something similar. But I still think he would be enough of a threat to the Romans—or whoever is standing in for the Romans in your chapter, perhaps the Bangladeshis—

that he still would get crucified. Or maybe when the time came, he would feel he needed to masquerade as a beggar to get his message across."

"The great pretender. I like that."

Chip glowers at his friend. "That's not what I meant, you nut job. Not a pretender, he would assume the identity of a beggar in order to show that the mean shall be exalted."

"But isn't that a lie? He's not a beggar; he is already exalted. And he already tried that dodge when he created Jewish.com as a teenager with a false back story."

Chip scratches his chin, selects a particularly long hair and plucks it. "True, but I think the point is still the same. Material riches are not what counts in the world beyond. And certainly, just being poor is not enough to get you exalted in the kingdom of heaven."

"Well it sounds like a decent prerequisite. What about the rich man, the camel and the needle?"

"Not really relevant. It only is a rough measure of the crimes a rich man must commit to achieve or maintain his position. And this is only the average rich man we're talking about. Obviously, Jesús would not be the average rich man. Plus, you do have him, where is it," Chip riffs through the manuscript. "Maintaining 'heavy security around the temple and the building,' and he knows 'whom to pay and whom to ally with.' So, you got a pragmatic sinner on your hands."

Charles leans back in his chair thoughtfully, teetering on the edge of falling over. "I don't know. I don't know if this is really the way I want to portray Jesus."

"Well, dude, what is your point, anyway? You know this type of treatment would be considered extreme blasphemy by many of my colleagues. Remember what happened to Rushdie. You looking for a fatwa or excommunication or a just a good old-fashioned Southern lynching, boy?" Chip leers like a good southern cracker lawman, and the cigar drops from his mouth onto his desk.

"Methodism in madness, eh?" Charles laughs. "Yes, I remember Rushdie and his years of hiding. And probing underpinnings of faith is rarely rewarded, is it?" He sighs. "I guess I don't really know what I want to do here. All I know is that for as long as I can remember, I have wanted to write the story of Jesus. I never really felt comfortable with what the Bible says—all hearsay evidence and apostles' interpretation way after the fact—and I especially don't like the way religions have interpreted it. I think they have gotten it all wrong." Charles considers for a moment.

"Rather, I feel they have gotten Jesus all wrong. Or not all wrong, it's just that they've twisted what he said to fit preconceptions they have. He was a man, after all, but when do we see him sinning? I don't know . . . I guess I really don't know."

Chip, recovered from his exasperation with Charles's anti-religious rant, looks fondly at his friend. He retrieves the cigar from his desk and sticks it back into the corner of his mouth.

"You are exploring a different path for Jesus. You are enumerating one of the possible universes. Is it a requirement that Jesus be poor? I find this intriguing. Would a rich man's message have been significantly different than that of a poor man? I think that's an interesting idea. You've really got me thinking here." He leans back in his chair, again laces his fingers behind his head, stares at the ceiling, and starts to hum "If I Were a Rich Man" while chewing the stogie.

Charles is a bit mollified. At least Chip is thinking about what he has written. Perhaps all is not lost. Perhaps he can find a way to get this damn book written after all.

"Well," Charles says, "as you can see, this latest pathetic chapter grew out of our discussion the other night at dinner. Remember we were talking about what the manger means psychopolitically, and how although Buddha was a prince before being enlightened, Mohammed was an orphan; Confucius was from a noble family that had become quite poor. Remember? It was after many bottles of Cabernet, so I wouldn't be surprised if you didn't."

Chip nods and holds his head in mock hangover pain.

"You know, we talked on about the Jewish tradition of being downtrodden—Moses, Abraham, David over Goliath, that sort of thing. So, I got to thinking: What would have happened if Jesus had been born to a wealthy family? Would that have changed his message that the mean shall be exalted and the mighty brought down? Does the messiah need a rabble-rousing attitude—an understanding of the lives of the least of us? Is the messiah a revolutionary or, as in the Jewish tradition, merely a holy anointed king who will redress all the injuries visited upon the Jews?"

"It's true." Chip says. "The Jewish scripture regarding the messiah does stress the worldliness of his reign, building the third temple and reclaiming Jewish lands and such."

"Exactly. So, so his dad, José is a wealthy captain of industry who lives in a palace with servants. Despite his social position, though, Jesús feels he needs to justify his worth. An otherworldly—other kingdom—reason why he is special. Since José is a distant father, often away tending business, the son talks often of his real father returning for him. You know, I thought it would be a hoot for María to be a doting, carping Jewish mother. Might put that in."

"How stereotypical, beloved. I'd leave that out. You know, in both your chapters, there's almost nothing about faith. You're just describing events with no religious context."

Charles thinks a bit before replying. Obviously, his friend is big on the idea of faith, but Charles has a real problem believing in the unseen.

"I think faith is humanity's red herring. Unseen mumbo jumbo to enforce proper behavior, a convenient way to explain away some of the problems of life, like evil, and, ah, ah . . . hmmm. Rhetoric requires three points to an argument, let's see, OK. Point 3: a sop to the downtrodden."

Chip gapes at Charles like he's said the stupidest thing ever. "That was some weird-ass argument, even for you. It's not a red herring, mumbo jumbo or a sop. Faith has spurred mankind to do miraculous things: not just cathedrals—which I realize piss you off—and works of art, but lifting people out of poverty, enriching their lives with hope. All accomplished in the name of faith."

"Well, as Andrew Sagan said, 'Extraordinary claims require extraordinary evidence.' Where's your proof that these wondrous things were the product of unseen benevolent powers rather than an inherent goodness in the human being? How can you believe without proof?"

"Dude, the whole point of having faith is to believe in something unseen. God's influence is all around you."

"Yeah, right. In all the horrible things he lets happen."

"Free will, man."

"A convenient concept to explain away the problem of evil."

Chip points a finger at Charles. "Since we were cast out of Eden, we've had to find our way back to God—use our free will—to create the kind of reality that will gain us entry to paradise. The world is and always has been full of good and bad, for good needs bad, if only to enable us to make choices—free will. There's always been evil, sin, injustice, greed, lust, hate, but also goodness, love, beauty, and joy. How can you have free will if there are no choices? Like Pascal said, 'In faith there is enough light for those who want to believe and enough shadows to blind those who don't.'"

"So, it's like that, eh? OK, buddy. 1-2-3-4, I declare a quote war: 'Absolute faith corrupts as absolutely as absolute power.' Eric Hoffer. You go."

Chip says, "'Absolute atheism starts in an act of faith in reverse gear and is a full-blown religious commitment.' Jacques Maritain. And I'll give you a twofer: 'Faith is taking the first step even when you don't see the whole staircase. MLK.'"

"So, faith is like falling down stairs in the dark? Ha! 'Faith: not wanting to know what is true.' Friedrich Nietzsche."

"Oh no you di'n't! Quoting Nietzsche, that lowlife! 'Atheists are like fish who don't believe in the existence of water.' Anonymous."

"Anonymous, or you just made it up!" Chip opens his mouth to reply. Charles holds up a finger and says, "I know, I know. Just kidding. I've heard that one. You didn't like Nietzsche? How about a quote from another horrible human being who got at least one thing right: 'Faith is the worst curse of mankind, as the exact antithesis and enemy of thought.' Ayn Rand."

"You're really pissing me off now, 'cause I know you hate Rand. 'To sustain the belief that there is no God, atheism has to demonstrate infinite knowledge, which is tantamount to saying, "I have infinite knowledge that there is no being in existence with infinite knowledge."' Ravi Zacharias."

Once again, Charles is stunned not only at the breadth of Chip's learning, but at his encyclopedic memory. He might lose the quote war by running out of quotes. He replies, "'Religion is the masterpiece of the art of animal training, for it trains people as to how they shall think.' Arthur Schopenhauer."

"'If you believe in an unseen Christ, you will believe in the unseen Christlike potential of others.' Anthony Burgess."

"'Every man, who reasons, soon becomes an unbeliever.' Baron d'Holbach."

"'One person with a belief is equal to ninety-nine who have only interests.' John Stuart Mill."

"'Religion is like a blind man looking in a black room for a black cat that isn't there and finding it.' Oscar Wilde."

"'As for those who fear their Lord unseen, for them is Forgiveness and a great Reward.' The Quran.

"The Quran? Cripes. What's a good Methodist like you doing quoting the Quran? Ummm. Ummm. Hold on. I've got a list of juicy quotes on my phone."

"Well, if you want to cheat . . . I'm gonna stay with my own prodigious intellect, learning, and memory." Charles sticks his tongue out and blows a raspberry. Chip crosses his arms and starts humming the Final Jeopardy tune.

"OK. OK." Charles fiddles with his phone, scrolling madly. "Where is that damn file? Here it is. Ah. OK. Another great one from Eric Hoffer: 'Take man's most fantastic invention—God. Man invents God in the image of his longings, in the image of what he wants to be, then proceeds to imitate that image, vie with it, and strive to overcome it.' Eric Hoffer, my man!"

"'Faith is to believe what you do not see; the reward of this faith is to see what you believe.' Saint Augustine."

"'Faith is the denial of observation so that belief can be preserved.' Tim Minchin."

"'The man who flies an airplane . . . must believe in the unseen.'" Richard Bach.

"Was that from his crappy *Jonathan Livingston Seagull*?" Charles asks.

Chip shrugs his shoulders. "I dunno. I just read it somewhere."

Charles scrolls on his phone. "Ah! One of my faves. 'Christians keep saying that the God of the New Testament is completely different and more moral than the God of the Old Testament, not realizing what an insanely irrational argument that is. If you knew a man who was a serial murderer his entire life, committed genocide, demanded child offerings and crushed entire cities, would you suddenly start trusting him when he suggested crucifying his own son to make up for it?' Joshua Kelly."

"I have to admit, Kelly might have had a point. 'So we fix our eyes not on what is seen, but on what is unseen. For what is seen is temporary, but what is unseen is eternal.' 2 Corinthians 4:18."

Charles says, "And while we're on the subject of the Old Testament: 'The Old Testament is responsible for more atheism, agnosticism, disbelief—call it what you will—than any book ever written; it has emptied more churches than all the counterattractions of cinema, motor bicycle and golf course.' A. A. Milne. Winnie-the-Pooh got teeth!"

"'Faith is the confidence that what we hope for will actually happen; it gives us assurance about things we cannot see.' Hebrews 11:1."

"Great, Bible Boy! Let's see." Charles scrolls his list. "This next one's probably apocryphal, like the Bible itself, but it's a fave: 'Eskimo: "If I did not know about God and sin, would I go to hell?" Priest: "No, not if you did not know." Eskimo: "Then why did you tell me?"' Annie Dillard."

"'We are what we think. All that we are arises with our thoughts. With our thoughts, we make the world.' Buddha."

Charles give a big mock sigh, "Your story has become tiresome. You have disturbed me almost to the point of insanity . . . There. I am insane now."

"OK, Dieter, is now ze time on Sprockets vhen ve dance?"

Charles smirks. He's running out of quotes, though. "Here's my last one, a bookend to the Sagan quote: 'What can be asserted without evidence can also be dismissed without evidence.' Christopher Hitchens. Oh, wait! My all-time favorite: 'Prayer is like masturbation. It feels good to the person doing it and does nothing for the person they're thinking about.' Don Baker."

Chip erupts in laughter at this last. "That's a great quote! Who is this Don Baker guy?"

"He's a computer geek from Texas, big in the Free Thinker movement. He calls Christianity a meme, a mind virus."

"Kinda like that brain virus in your old first chapter, eh?"

"Yeah. He runs a site and organization called Christianity Meme. His idea is that the Christianity meme arose via natural selection and thus is a product of cultural evolution. As such, it is an amoral meme, and it is not bound by its own professed moral principles. And also, this virus is not subject to the normal error correction of living organisms, if you consider a virus living. Thus, errors can be introduced and perpetuated without check. Of course, you could argue that in Catholicism, the Pope is error correction, but we've seen where that has led."

The two men sit silently for a few minutes, drinking their beers.

Charles breaks the silence. "All this talk about unseen realms, heaven, hell, faith. It just seems so distant, and there seems no way our rational minds can touch these truths. So, I just don't know what the point is."

Suddenly there's a loud shout and a wolf whistle from the street outside. Charles, disturbed by the interruption, glares out the window. "I mean, what's the point of fleetingly glimpsing the beautiful women in their halter tops passing by your window?"

The two men move to the window and peer out. The shadows are a bit longer, but the street is still atomic bright.

Charles jabs his finger at the window. "We can't touch them; we can't directly experience them. There's little chance they'll ever have anything to do with our lives. Yet we still watch. We are still interested in their progression down the boulevard. Something about their experience connects with something inside us. In the case of this analogy, the connection is one of lust, but I am comparing lust to love. Lust to salvation, if you will. And I'm not at all sure I believe in salvation. I think the chances of me being saved are about as large as the chances of me bedding that woman there."

He points out the window at an incredibly lovely figure as she walks past them and continues down the street. She has an impossibly narrow waist and luxurious buttocks. Her figure is crowned with a fantastic bust line, neither too large nor too small, that swells up and down with the rhythm of her stride. As if she feels the gaze of the two men, she tosses her hair their way before disappearing around the corner out of sight.

"My friend, let's find out," Chip says, clapping Charles on the shoulder before firing his stogie in the general direction of his ashtray. The big man stabs his feet into his ever-present flip flops, grabs Charles's arm, and drags him out of the office, through the secretary's office and out the door to the hallway.

"Wait," splutters Charles, but Chip has him firmly in tow as they burst out upon the sunny street. The heat of the Miami day strikes them like a punch, staggering Charles briefly.

"Come on," says Chip as he takes off around the corner. Charles follows the lumbering big man reluctantly. They run for a block or so but fail to glimpse the beautiful young woman. Chip is breathing heavily when they stop.

"Damn...sonofabitch...shit!" he says, trying to catch his breath. "We missed her." Charles is similarly winded and already starting to sweat through his linen jacket. "What the hell was that all about?"

"That, my friend, was the leap of faith. You gotta believe before you're saved. You can't tell me that if you had met her you would not have been changed fundamentally in some way, maybe even saved. Or married. Who can say? Damn. I wish I knew."

"You see? That's just it. I don't think it would have meant, or changed, anything! She was just a shout in the street. Dammit, Chip. Why must you be so goddamn optimistic?"

A big smile spreads across Chip's face. "Same reason you got to play the faithless pessimist all the time, bucko! C'mon, let's go get a milkshake and some lunch. I'm broiling." Chip puts his arm across Charles's shoulders and turns them both around. "Say Charles, me boy, did you hear about the Buddhist who walked into a pizza parlor and said, 'Make me one with everything?'"

Cackling like a demon, Chip leads his groaning friend down the frying pavement in search of air conditioning and ice cream.

And I went to see the doctor of philosophy / With a poster of Rasputin and a beer down to his knee

Indigo Girls—*Closer to Fine*

Charles and Chip are sitting around Skip's office on a Saturday. Chip had some paperwork he needed to finish, so he invited Charles to drop over once he was finished and maybe play some basketball. The two are drinking Bud Lights, sitting at either end of Chip's office couch. They can hear a pickup basketball game on the church's court next to Chip's office. For while they just drink and listen to the young men slinging good humored insults at each other as they play.

"Reminds me of when we met," Charles says. "You remember?"

"Do you think I'm senile? Of course I do, it was only a year ago."

"I'd just moved into my apartment and was out walking, getting the lay of the land"

"And probably looking for a different kind of lay," Chip says, leering. "Know whatImean, know whatImean, nudge nudge, wink wink?

"I get your subtle innuendo," Charles says, rolling his eyes.

"In your endo, bucko!"

"Anyway, you were having a pickup game and needed another player. I ran back to my place, changed, and then we whomped the holy hell outta that other team."

"You were a monster on the boards, that much is true. But it was my outside shooting that made the difference."

"No, I think it was you grabbing the jersey of that hotshot, knocking the ball away to me and my subsequent layup that made the difference, you unethical piece of humus."

Chip puts on a wounded look and says, "Little ole me? Why I never!" Chip bats his eyes like a southern belle.

Charles ignores him. "Then we came in here after, got beers from the fridge and shot the shit for like four hours. I gotta say, though, initially I was shocked at your language. Why it almost gave me the vapors."

Chip leans over and lets out a massive, musical fart.

"That's what I'm talking about! I never met a holy man who swears like a sailor, let alone farts so unabashedly!"

"I remember it like it was 13 months ago . . ." Chip says, smiling. "Obviously, I think I should speak the vernacular, to remain closer to my flock. Doesn't bother you, does it?"

"Me? No. I like plain speak."

"Well, speaking of ethics . . ."

"Wait, what?" Charles says. "When were we speaking of ethics?"

Chip says. "You know, last week. We never finished that conversation."

"Hell, I thought we were finished the moment you said you didn't think there could be ethics without religion."

Chip says, "You blockhead, you know full well that I did not say that, nor do I think that. What I do think is that the subject is much broader than most people, especially conservative people, believe. For example, when I was in divinity school, I took an ethics class. We talked at length about the concept of an ethical life and how to lead it, as well as how to encourage others to do so. We all showed up for the final on a fine spring day. Birds tweeting outside the open windows. Breezes blowing dogwood petals. A perfect day. Out the window, we could see the building's janitor sweeping the petals off the sidewalk.

"My general tendency, by the way, in dealing with the people who serve us in our everyday lives, is to get to know them and to talk with them about their lives. There's many a waitress across the South who has poured out her life story to me because I took an interest."

"I'll just bet," Charles says. "Are there also any little Chips scattered about the South?" Chip just ignores him.

"So, anyway, on the day of the final, everyone's in their seats expecting the professor to distribute a thick sheaf of exam questions to each of us. But instead, he passed up and down the rows and placed a single sheet of blank paper in front of each student.

"My classmates exchanged puzzled looks. Was this to be an essay test? What were we to do with these sheets? The professor returned to the front of the room and said, 'OK. There's only one question on this final. If you get it right, you get an A. If not, you fail.' Well, we were all pretty shocked and worried by this. The professor continued, 'The question is: What is the name of the janitor?'

"My classmates gaped in horror. I, on the other hand, wrote down 'Monde Green,' stood up, delivered my paper to the professor and left with every eye in the room following me. I not only knew Monde's name, I knew he had three young kids and a wife who had a bum leg, and thus had a devil of a time looking after her kids. I knew he drove a beat-up Pontiac, and that he often stopped off at the bar on his way home on Friday nights. So, that's the foundation of ethics: Treat others as you would be treated—the Golden Rule. Most of your conservatives don't get this, no matter how piously they declare that all would be better if the country 'returned' to its Christian roots."

Charles burps and says, "I can actually get behind that. In fact, I'm in violent agreement with you on this point." Chip offers his beer bottle for a clink and drink. "So, did the professor flunk everybody else?"

"Nah. He just pulled out the mother of all ball-breaker final exams and told the class to think about how much easier their lives would be if they only would live ethics instead of just talking and reading about it. Most of them escaped the course with a gentleman's—and gentlewoman's because there were four women in the class—C."

"Hah! Serves 'em right. But when we talked about this before, you and I seemed to disagree. You seemed all dogmatic about following Christ's teachings and living a rigorous life bound to the Bible."

"Part of that was you and your preconceived notions about what I believe, and part of it was that I was baiting you a bit, just to see how you'd react."

"So how is that ethical?" Charles is mildly pissed, but mostly perplexed.

"It is ethical to play the devil's advocate to enlighten a student." Chip sticks his tongue out at Charles who leans over and tries to grab it.

"You rank bastard! Mr. I'm Holier Than Thou, Esquire!"

Chip just snickers and drinks his beer. "Oh," he says, "that reminds me of a favorite koan: A novice was trying to fix a broken computer by turning the power off and on. The Master, seeing what the student was doing, spoke sternly: 'You cannot fix a machine by just power-cycling it with no understanding of what is going wrong.' The Master turned the machine off and on. The machine worked.

"So ends today's lesson," Chip says. Charles groans and rolls his eyes. "Oh, brother! I like the koan, 'What is the sound of one hand clapping?' much better."

"That has an easy answer," Chip says, pulling off one flipflop and clapping his hand against the sole of his bare foot.

"Oh, that's good!" Charles says. "This novice is enlightened!"

Chip chuckles in delight and says, "Back to what we were talking about. You've made it clear you have no use for religion. What about philosophy?"

Charles replies, "Generally, a branch of religion, even when practiced by atheists. A different type of organized belief structure, but one just as prone to dogma and rigidity." Charles reaches down to the side of the couch, pulls his longneck beer up off the floor, and takes a swig. "I just can't accept these systems, these arbitrary systems, that enforce beliefs, demand obedience, and then fail utterly to inspire goodness, or even enforce goodness in their followers, or, for Chrissakes, at the very least prevent devastating evilness, like your basic Crusades or Inquisition and such."

Chip tilts back his beer, swallows ostentatiously and says, "Don't throw out the baby with the bath, Chucker! Just look at the alternative: A society with no moral underpinning can't hope to survive, much less be better off, as you seem to think. Humans need rules to live by."

Charles blows a mournful note across his bottle top. "What do morals have to do with religion? Or philosophy, for that matter. That's another thing that kills me. Where do religions get off claiming a monopoly on ethics and morality? Why can there be no moral choice besides theirs? It's just so hypocritical!" Charles slams his beer back down on the floor and grabs his head with both hands.

He continues, "It just makes me crazy! I mean, can a philandering preacher—like, say, that holier than thou Family Values asshole from Colorado years ago, the one with the male prosty on the side, what was his name . . . Haggard or something? Ted Haggard. How could a dickhead like him have anything to say to his flock about morals, or the blueprint for life? Idiot preachers who can't keep their dicks in their pants are so hypocritical, it makes me want to scream. Fucking Jimmy Swaggart, for crying out loud. Ach! I mean just look, look at this list I printed out from Wikipedia. It's not even close to a complete list of evangelist scum involved in scandals." Charles rummages in the folder he keeps his book notes in and thrusts a page at Chip. The page is filled, front and back, with evangelists' names.

Chip scans the documents. "Crap," he says. "I haven't heard of a lot of these. A. A. Allen? There's even the odd female, like Aimee Semple McPherson. Ooo, I like this guy's name, Apollo Quiboloy. But you've got some sincere evangelists in here, like Billy Graham."

"Yeah, they're not all crooks, but most of them use the same fire and brimstone and 'give me money for salvation' techniques. Some are self-righteous bandits, like Jim and Tammy Faye Bakker, Ted Haggard, Jimmy Swaggart. Others are perhaps more dangerous, because they were after political influence, like Jerry Falwell and Pat Robertson. But I think they're all despicable."

Chip finishes looking at the list, sniffs, and hands it back. "Dude, Ted Haggard's and Jimmy Swaggart's and a lot of these people's churches are non-denominational. They're not part of any organized religion. They're free ballin'. I agree there's some swine in the non-denominational evangelical 'churches.'" As usual, Chip supplies the air quotes.

"So, you're just glad they're not Methodists, huh? Give me a fucking break." Charles gets up and starts to pace. "It just proves my point about the dangers of religion. Any crackpot, even a mediocre science fiction writer or a loony guy from Ohio, can create a religion and be the authority, and start telling people how to live their lives, while they fatten their coffers."

"Well, if you want me to say just following a religion or being a member of a church can't prevent sin, I will. But that seems pretty obvious. Religions exist to inspire people to live better, more-moral lives and to avoid sin."

Charles sits back on the edge of the couch, leaning over with his elbows on his knees. His whole body is tense. "But where do they get off insisting that their way is the absolute truth? I'm definitely not an advocate of situational morality, but I'm also not comfortable with the idea of absolute right and wrong dictated by holier-than-thou-types. How can a pope, who decides to speak ex cathedra, be any more infallible than he is when speaking ex officio, or in normal discourse? And if you examine these pronouncements, it's clear they aren't any different from what the pope thinks in the normal course of events."

Chip spreads his hands and shrugs. "Don't ask me; I'm a Methodist. We got rid of the damn popes ages ago."

"Well bully for you! But to continue for just a little longer on the Catholic church, add to the ex-cathedra nonsense the fact that there are so many layers of truth in infallible teachings. There's ecumenical council infallibility, pope infallibility—as when a couple of them declared immaculate conception and the assumption of Mary as church dogma. There's explicit and implied infallibility. And don't get me started on the saints. Omigod, what a political cluster fuck beatification and canonization is, with the whole manufactured miracle stuff."

"Beloved, this is why there are Protestants. Exactly why. And why United Methodists view saints as sanctified members of the universal church to be celebrated for their lives and works, but not worshiped or treated as conduits to God."

"Well, that certainly seems like a more rational approach. But even Methodists believe in inspiration, as in the Latin *inspire*, and that the Bible was inspired by God. And that God helped men select which books would be in the Bible, right? Divine assistance and inspiration as determined by fallible men, that doesn't seem likely to me to produce truth. Just look at Leviticus!"

Charles takes a sip of his beer. "But don't get me wrong. I believe in inspiration. I do believe in some unseen magnificence that can break through and touch our lives. I don't think the fucking Pope has a monopoly on truth, nor do I believe any religion is even close to an authority on the subject. The Pope and all the religious figureheads are human beings, and will always be fallible, and subject to the restrictions and complications of their personalities."

Charles takes another long drink of his beer. Chip just sits calmly, sure that his friend will continue his rant.

"And, not to go off on a tangent, but the whole idea of the personality of God just seems to me to be so wrong. I have a really hard time ascribing a humanoid personality to whatever it is that is responsible for our existence and our inspiration."

Charles sets his beer down on the floor and crumples back onto the couch. "Think about it. A real, personal god, a male, of course, feeling human emotions like wrath and love. A jealous god of the Old Testament, prescribing crap like dietary laws and prohibiting masturbation and such, all that Leviticus stuff, letting your hair become unkempt or eating fat. A god who plays mind games with Abraham to see if the guy would really kill his own son. That god seems like a real eccentric crank to me. And, really, what would God want with a personality in the first place? It would just get in the way. A personality, to me, implies imperfection, flaws, variability, limitations. That's why machines have no soul. Nothing can go wrong." Chip sits back with a benevolent smile on his face as his friend gets more and more worked up.

Charles continues, "The idea of God with a human-like personality seems to me to be the ultimate blasphemy." Charles is rolling the beer bottle between his hands as if rubbing a lamp. "Think of all that makes you you. The foibles and flaws. The limitations and the separation from others, the distinctness of your loneliness . . . Take those away, and what have you got? A meat-based thinking machine with maybe a little bit of inspiration. Certainly not a whole human being, a whole personality. It makes no sense for God to have a personality. Tell me. What are God's foibles? What are his flaws?"

Chip has tired of Charles's tirade and says, "Well, he certainly doesn't lack a sense of humor. He made me funny-looking and you an ass."

Charles grabs a Nerf basketball from beside him on the couch and whips it at Chip's head. It bounces off and swishes through the nearby trash can basketball hoop. Chip crows, "You see? Kismet. He moves in mysterious ways! 'Hello? God here. Just sayin' hi.'"

Charles is not in the mood to laugh. "Oh, I don't believe it. I've heard unbelievable stretches to find meaning in the meaningless before, but that is ridiculous."

"Dude, lighten up! You're going to blow a gasket here."

But Charles is in not about to settle down. "You didn't answer my question. Doesn't the very idea that God has a personality seem preposterous to you? Wouldn't that necessarily involve placing limits on an all-seeing, all-knowing, omnipotent deity?"

Chip retrieves the basketball and rockets it back at Charles, who ducks, spilling the dregs of his beer on his shorts and down his leg. "Crap," says Charles. "Now look what you made me do!"

Chip laughs and says, "Like John Lee Hooker said, 'Serves you right to suffer. Serves you right to be alone.'" He sits back down on the couch like a load of bricks. "The Lord works in mysterious ways, and now He made it look like you peed yourself like a scared little weenie boy. That's your punishment for being uppity. How's that for personality?"

"Oh, give me a break! You're acting like a moron!" Realizing he may have gone too far, Charles looks apprehensively at Chip.

Chip, however, finds Charles's rants more amusing than insulting. He is, however, sick of this one, so he says, "Awright, boy. Ah mus' defend mah honor! Ah chellenge you to a duel. Jump shots at 20 feet. We'll jest let the Gud Lawd decide. Whatchew gonna dew?"

"Umm, I'm going to wipe the court with you."

"Waall, I reckon Ah'm jest gonna meck yew eet those werds, sport. After yew." They jostle one another as they leave the office on the way to the basketball court.

The pickup game has broken up and a dozen or so young men, mostly Haitians, are hanging out lying on the grassy mound adjacent to the court. Several others are leaning on cars in the nearby parking lot, shooting the shit with the drivers. They all start poking each other, pointing and laughing to see two old guys take the court.

"Give 'im hell, preacher!" one of them yells.

Chip beams at the young man and pounds his chest. He turns to Charles, who is dribbling the ball from hand to hand. "Oh, hey," Chip says to Charles, "before we get started, let me tell you my favorite Catholic joke."

"O, Lord, please prevent this horse's ass from telling me any more jokes. Amen." Charles tosses the ball to Chip who catches it with one hand and in a single motion puts up a set shot from 15 feet that swishes. The audience hoots and hollers.

"Hey, skinny dude! You in a world of hurt! Hope you don't got money on this," one yells as other young men start to gather around the court to watch the game.

Chip bows to the crowd, blows them a kiss, and says, "Now you all better be nice to my friend here, because I'm gonna wipe the court with him, and that's enough punishment for one day."

The crowd loves this and starts hollering, and laughing, and slapping five. One yells, "Yes, Reverend. We'll be good," which starts them again falling about with laughter.

"I'm counting on it—all week!" Chip replies, sweeping a pointing finger across the crowd, saying, "Alla yez!"

Chip then turns to Charles and continues, "No, you're gonna love this joke, although now that I think of it, it's pretty non-denominational."

"Please," Charles pleads. "No more!" He retrieves the ball and puts up a layup. The crowd yells in mock delight.

"Hey, you asked for it after that spew you made me listen to just now. You deserve this one, and it's a long one, so pay attention. A new priest at his first mass is so nervous during the homily he can hardly speak. After mass, he asks the monsignor how he had done. The monsignor replies, 'When I am worried about getting nervous on the pulpit, I put a glass of vodka next to the water glass. If I start to get nervous, I take a sip.'

"So, the next Sunday, the young priest takes the monsignor's advice. At the beginning of the sermon, he gets nervous and takes a drink. He proceeds to talk up a storm. Upon returning to his office, he finds the following note on his door.

1) Sip the vodka, don't gulp
2) There were 12 Disciples, not 10
3) Jesus was consecrated, not constipated
4) Jacob wagered his donkey, he did not bet his ass
5) We do not refer to Jesus Christ as the late J.C.
6) The Father, Son, and Holy Ghost are not referred to as Daddy, Junior, and Spook
7) When David was hit by a rock and knocked off his donkey, don't say he was stoned off his ass
8) When Jesus broke the bread at the Last Supper, he said, 'Take this and eat it, for it is my body.' He did not say, 'Eat me.'
9) Next Sunday there will be a taffy-pulling contest at St. Peter's, not a peter-pulling contest at St. Taffy's.

Charles lets out an extended groan. "Please, please, I beg of you, no more!"

Chip just shakes his head like Jimmy Durante and says, "I gotta million of 'em!"

After telling the joke, Chip notices a car pull up alongside the court. "Hold on a minute," he tells Charles. "I'll be right back."

Chip walks over to the car and speaks to the driver. The driver hands Chip a package and takes off. Chip walks past Charles, saying, "Be right back." He's gone for two or three minutes and returns without the package.

"What was that all about?" Charles says.

"Just some church business. I need to deliver a package. Now watch me deliver this." Chip is way outside the three-point line when he jumps and shoots. The ball rattles in and the crowd goes wild. "Thas the way, preach! You ready for the Heat!" Chip trots around the court with his arms outstretched like he had just won game seven of the finals.

There's a road and at this end love / Where the eagles fly when you're done

Stephen Stills—*Love the One You're With*

John Mittney, successful hedge fund manager, putative savior of the Olympics, and staunch Republican, put one booted foot up on the square prop hay bale and smiled at the small crowd. "Corporations are people my friend," he said with a twinkle in his slate blue eyes.

"No, they're not!" shouted several in the crowd.

"Of course, they are," Mittney said. "Everything corporations earn ultimately goes to people. Where do you think it goes?"

"To the Mormon Church," screamed one man.

John was taken aback by the outburst. In all the hundreds of political meetings he had attended in this campaign and the one four years ago, nobody had had the temerity to bring up his faith. While Mittney acknowledged that some Mormon beliefs were outside the general Christian mainstream, he was a Christian and had struggled to remove any whiff of scrutiny of his religion from his political life.

In his brief moment of shock and fear when the heckler brought up Mormonism, John flashed back to his childhood. He was a miracle child, since his mother, Elizabeth, was barren and past 45 when he was born. When he was young, his father, Zacharias, told him that his birth had been heralded by the angel Gabriel, who appeared to his father in the hospital waiting room. The angel said that John would be the forerunner of the Messiah.

It was many years before John understood what that meant. If the Messiah was returning to Earth, then these must be the End Times, he thought. What would be the effect of Jesus' return? Would the Messiah bring the Kingdom of God to Earth and peace and prosperity to humanity, ushering in the Millennium as his faith taught him? Or would there just be ruin, strife, and death? Looking around at the world outside his Mormon community, John was convinced that the Lord was planning on the latter. In Mormonism, the End Times were the key to the righteous being exalted, and to become God. The Earth would be cleansed with fire, Jesus would establish a true theocratic government that would last until the Millennium ended with the final battle with Satan.

Mormons were quite concerned with the End Times. Since only the righteous —meaning those who had accepted Jesus Christ and the Church of Latter-Day Saints—could enter the Kingdom of Heaven, the faithful attempted to qualify as many of their non-Mormon ancestors as possible by baptizing them by proxy.

As a young boy, John assisted in proxy baptisms of more than 100 of his forbearers, and later, as an adult, he assisted or attended thousands more with a fiery passion. His devotion to helping prepare his dead relatives for the Exaltation earned him the nickname John the Baptist, which John was ambivalent about. It was nice to be recognized, but the name had heavy connotations. Although he was quite devout, the fear and feeling of awesome responsibility instilled by his father's angelic visitation gnawed inside him. The magnitude of this responsibility and his indulgence in masturbation—a serious Mormon sin—made him question his worthiness to carry out the prophecy. When his 16-year-old friend Frank committed suicide, in large part because of his masturbation shame, John was terrified—of being discovered, of not being discovered, of being unworthy in all respects. He was living a lie in a community that abhorred falsehood.

Thus, although John was outwardly the model Mormon, he had a complicated relationship with his faith, and avoided mentioning it or identifying as a Mormon. When he embarked on his career in finance, he often declined offers to go out to the bar with his colleagues by saying he was an alcoholic rather than declaring his religion. The truth was much more shameful to him than this manufactured lie. As he rose through the corporate ranks, amassing a fortune and garnering respect for his business acumen, he was less secretive about his Mormonism.

Nonetheless, he continued to downplay the outward aspects of his religion.

So, when the Iowan heckler called him out, John was shaken to his core. Here he was, in his 60s, terrified that admitting who he was, in every sense of the word—a Mormon, a one-percenter, possibly a man whose destiny was to anoint the returned Messiah—would seal his doom. That things would only get worse if he went on to gain the nomination and then the presidency gave him night terrors.

It turned out that he needn't have worried about the heightened scrutiny that would await him as president. His flippant "corporations are people" statement and a pair of incidents in his private life combined with a secretly recorded private fundraiser speech to sink his candidacy. When he lost the presidential race, John was devastated, but a part of him was relieved. The cup had passed.

In the aftermath of the election, John wondering if his father's prophesy would ever be fulfilled. He had spent his life being apprehensive about what Gabriel told his father. Was it true? Or was his dad crazy? His father showed no other signs of being anything more than a successful businessman and politician. That was the legacy that John had taken as his mantle. There wasn't a crazy or mystical bone in his father's body. What should John make of his prophesy?

Thinking rationally, John realized he didn't have too many more decades on the planet. Had he missed his opportunity? Or was this burden the result of some momentary mental aberration suffered by his father? Were these really the End Times? Would Jesus come back and initiate the Apotheosis? John spent the first year after his election defeat wracked by these doubts and fears.

To find meaning in his life, John decided to rededicate his life to baptism, of the departed and, if possible, the living. As he studied the teachings of his church about baptism, he began to wonder why many modern Christian sects had abandoned the original baptism, which was accomplished by the biblical John the Baptist on the banks of the Jordan river. Convinced that convenience might have overcome tradition, he broke with the tradition of his faith—which involved immersion in a font in a church—and started planning to organize baptisms on the banks of the Virgin River near the town of St. George, Utah.

This site appealed to John for many reasons, partly the names of the river and the town, which was named after George A. Smith, a Mormon apostle, partly because Brigham Young had wintered there, but also because, to him, the place bore a striking resemblance to Bethabara, the site where John the Baptist had done his work. John had visited that site in the mid-80s while on a mission to lay the groundwork for what became Brigham Young University Jerusalem Center for Near Eastern Studies. He had helped broker the agreement that enabled the construction of the center by suggesting that the church pledge to not proselytize in Israel.

John decided to build a campus for Brigham Young in St. George, with an associated baptismal learning center. He would teach there and baptize converts and ancestors in the Virgin River. He had time; he had plenty of money, but, first things first: he built a palatial home on a hillside overlooking the town. Money moves mountains, and the $4 million 11,000 square foot (modest by John's standards) refuge was built in less than six months. The town fathers bent over backward to accommodate the relocation of Utah's most famous living son to their area.

Of course, John's plan to personally perform baptisms hinged on his being ordained. Although he had once considered the priesthood and had taken many relevant divinity classes at Brigham Young, he had not followed through to ordination. There was, however, one route open to him. Since he was a literal descendant of Aaron and a firstborn, he needed only to be called to service by the president of the church. John contacted some friends on the Brigham Young board of trustees and explained his plan to build an extension of the university in St. George, including his baptism education center. These men were opposed to ex cathedra baptisms, so John decided to talk to a member of the Quorum of the Twelve, the elders who helped run the church. His uncle had once been the president of the Quorum, so John knew he could use his influence to good effect.

John made an appointment with the Elder and showed up bright and early on a gorgeous Salt Lake City day. "Thank you, Elder, for making time in your day to see me," John said.

"How could I refuse to see such an illustrious and influential man?" said the Elder. "Please have a seat and tell me the reason for your visit, but first, before we begin, how are you doing? That was a devastating loss for all of us."

"Thank you, Elder. Yes, I was quite disappointed, and I confess it did bother me for quite a while. But then I realized that the Lord had other plans for me, and that's what I've come to talk to you about." John shifted forward in his chair to look the Elder in the eyes. "Let me be respectful of your time and get right to the point. I have a plan to increase the ranks of the faithful and to prepare even more of our ancestors for the exaltation."

The Elder fidgeted a bit in his chair while contemplating John's statement. Although John's family was honored and influential in the church, there were those Mormons who looked upon John as a bit too . . . worldly. He had pursued wealth and influence perhaps a little too keenly, although his faithfulness and tithing to the church were beyond question.

"Please continue," the Elder said after a moment. "What exactly do you have in mind?"

As John laid out his plan for the Brigham Young extension and the baptismal center, the Elder's eyes became slightly hooded. The Elder thought, now what could be driving him to propose this project? Why pick a remote outpost like St. George to build such a monumental structure? And baptism outside the confines of a church? It just isn't done. What would give him such an idea?

After John finished, the Elder said, "This is an ambitious project and I am worried about several aspects."

"Please, Elder, tell me your concerns."

"I suppose my biggest concern other than its scale is this idea of an outdoor baptismal structure. This is not done in our church as a regular thing, as you must know. Although it happens, it requires permission, and we generally discourage baptism outside a Stake's normal program."

"Yes, Elder, I do know this. But I also know that John the Baptist initiated the sacrament of Baptism in just such an outdoor setting. As we became more comfortable in indoor settings, our rituals moved indoors. Remember, Jesus preached on mountaintops and almost exclusively outdoors."

"You make a good point, but I'm afraid I cannot personally sanction this aspect of your plan. You'll need to take it up with the president."

"I thank you for your counsel. I hope that I can count on your support when I do so."

"We'll have to wait and see about that," the Elder said.

"There's one more thing I would like your help with, Elder. I personally would like to perform baptisms." The Elder's eyebrows rose in surprise. "Now, before you answer, let me stake my claim. I'm a literal descendant of Aaron. You may already be aware of that. And as you know, a literal descendant of Aaron may serve without counselors, if called by the President of the Church and ordained to that office. I am asking for your help in bringing this to pass."

"You know I cannot accomplish this. Only through that one man who is His mouthpiece on Earth will the Lord reveal instructions for His church, and that means the president must call you. As you must know, scripture says, 'a literal descendant of Aaron, also must be designated by this Presidency, and found worthy, and anointed, and ordained under the hands of this Presidency, otherwise they are not legally authorized to officiate in their priesthood.'"

"Yes, I do know that. I am hoping for your support. Ever since I was a young man, I felt called to the baptism. You may know that I personally was the surrogate for more than 1,000 baptisms of our ancestors and have thus saved them from the fire. I would agree to serve only in the role of baptizer, despite the fact that my lineage could qualify me to be the Presiding Bishop of the Church."

The Elder was flabbergasted by John's proposal. "It may not be as easy as you might think."

"I am prepared to offer myself to the scrutiny and process that the President will provide. Will you support me?"

The Elder realized that John would pursue this dream with the same doggedness he had pursued elective office. "I may indeed support you if you can find others. I know your influence, and I know your passion for our church. You have my blessing to proceed to convince others, and the President, to build your baptismal and convene the priesthood upon you."

"Thank you, Elder! You won't regret this," John said, standing suddenly and clasping the Elder's hand. "Once again, thank you for your time. You'll be hearing more from me."

I will be hearing more from others, too, the Elder thought as John left the room.

Despite initial resistance to baptism outside of a church, and to his being called to the priesthood, John's stature, both religious and secular, eventually persuaded the board, other influential Mormons, and the president of the church to ordain him and bless the project. He obtained an Aaronic priesthood and could therefore confer baptism on the living and the dead. By the time he moved into his new home, the construction of the center was well underway.

That left the last task: attracting converts and the faithful to his center. He stumped throughout the state and nationally, and soon the trickle of baptizees turned into a flood. As the crowds grew to fill first his makeshift riverside dock and later the grand stone baptismal that the river ran through, John finally became comfortable in his own skin.

John heard a rumor that one of the few surviving Nazi guards was living somewhere near St. George. What a coup it would be to baptize such a sinner and bring him to the light! And what a boost to his still-growing Baptism Center! John asked around and found the guard apparently lived in a closed movie theater on West Center Street in Kanab, about 45 minutes away. John got into his Maserati and motored east to Kanab. It's funny, he thought. So many western movies were shot in and around Kanab, and now the town can't even support a movie theater.

Arriving at his destination, John got out of the car and faced the blank marquee from across the street. Let's see, he thought. How do I get in? John walked up to the double doors and peered into the dark lobby. Inside he could see the empty snack bar adjacent to the velvet ropes and the ticket taker's stand, everything covered in a gray layer of dust. John tried the doors, but they were locked. He looked around and noted the winter grayness at the bottoms of the barn-board siding and the cracked concrete of the sidewalk. The town and the building had seen better days. He was walking over to the ticket window when suddenly a raspy voice from above stopped him in his tracks. "Who do you want?" John turned quickly, stepped back, craned his neck, and squinted in the sun to try to see the owner of the disembodied voice. The voice appeared to have emanated from a balcony next to the marquee. Finally, he was able to make out an old lady in a bathrobe leaning out of a second story window. He said, "I beg your pardon?"

"Who do you want? No one gets in the building unless I know who they want. I'm the conciurge. My husband used to be the conciurge. He's dead. Now I'm the conciurge."

"I'm looking for an old German gentleman . . ."

"Aren't we all!"

". . . and perhaps you'd be so kind as to tell me if he lives here?"

"Oh, the Kraut. Yeah, he lives in the back. Apartment 23," the old lady said and then wiped her nose on the sleeve of her robe. "But you won't find him there. He's up on the roof with his birds. He keeps birds. Dirty, disgusting, filthy, lice-ridden birds. You used to be able to sit out on the stoop like a person. Not anymore. No sir. Birds! You get my drift?"

"I ... uh ... get your drift. Thank you, Madam."

"I'm not a madam. I'm a conciurge!"

"So how do I get in?"

"Go around the back, and I'll let you in." John went around the back of the building and the door opened to reveal a truly ancient woman, hunched in a faded blue bathrobe. She ushered him in, and he followed her up the stairs, slowly. On the second-floor landing, she said, "Follow the stairs to the roof and you'll find him." Then she turned to dodder off toward her own apartment.

John climbed the stairs to the roof and found an old man feeding birds. But something seemed wrong. This man couldn't be much over 70, and even a guard who was a teen during the war would be pushing 90 by now.

"Excuse me, sir," John asked. "Would you mind if I ask you a few questions?"

The old man, startled since he hadn't noticed John's arrival on the roof, dropped the can of bird seed and swung around to face him. "Oh! You gave me such a fright!" His eyes narrowed. "What kind of questions?"

"Well, to be honest, I'd like to talk about what you did during the war."

"The Vietnam War?"

"Erm, no, World War II," John said, getting ever more puzzled.

"I was two when that war ended. Don't remember much about it."

"I'm sorry, sir, I must have you confused with somebody else. You see, I was told there was a man in town here who may have been a Nazi guard during World War II."

The old man bent over in laughter, which soon turned into a ragged cough, sending him digging in his pocket for a handkerchief. When he had recovered, he fixed a beady eye on John and said, "I think you are much mistaken, young man. There is a former Nazi guard in town, but it's a she, not a he. Perhaps you met her on the way in? The 'conciurge'?"

John reddened in embarrassment. "But . . . how?" he sputtered.

"Heh, the Nazis were equal opportunity offenders," the old man said. "The Aufseherinnen were female guards in Nazi concentration camps. There were a few thousand of 'em. Ruha was one of 'em. That schlub answered an ad in the newspaper looking for women to show their love for the

Reichland by joining the SS-Gefolge. Boy, do you got it wrong!" The old man giggled to himself, turned away, and resumed feeding the birds.

Apologizing, John took his leave of the bird man and made his way back downstairs to find the concierge's apartment. He knocked, and after a few moments, knocked again. Hearing nothing, he tried the handle. "Take another step and I'll drop ya." Ruha threw open the door holding an ancient Walther P38. "Oh, it's you. Well, whaddaya want?"

"Just a few moments of your time, madam."

"I'm the conciurge!"

"Right. OK. What's the preferred mode of address when referring to a concierge?"

"Aw, you can just call me Ruha. Sit down. Toss some of that junk outta that chair there and make yaself comfortable."

John looked around the dusty, cluttered apartment, which appeared to have been the theater's projection room. There were a few distressed pieces of furniture—a small round wooden table with two paperbacks propping one leg, a moth-eaten couch with one visible spring, a couple of low shelves filled with books, and an old TV/VCR combo. There were no visible running water or toilet facilities, just a large basin beside which sat a few plastic ice cream buckets. A battered cassette player played strange music that seemed vaguely Middle Eastern, as did the threadbare rug that covered part of the floor.

On the back wall were two small, square windows covered by sliding doors, probably the windows through which the projectors had shown the movies. On the floor opposite each of the windows were four brackets that once anchored the projectors in place.

John regarded the overstuffed easy chair that Ruha had indicated and saw that it held a dirty bird cage, some fast food wrappers, and a disheveled pile of loose papers. John shifted the junk to the floor and sat down. The cushion exhaled an aromatic cloud of dust as he settled into the seat.

"Ya want something to drink? I can run downstairs to the theater bathroom and get ya a drink of water. I'm all outta beer."

"No, that's quite all right, er, Ruha. I'm not thirsty and I don't drink beer."

"Well, Your Highness, I ain't got any wine," Ruha said. "Anyway, what brings ya here in your fancy-schmancy motorcar to visit the likes a me?"

John paused to consider how to broach the subject. He assessed Ruha, a tall, scrawny, hunched woman with a shock of white hair sticking out in all directions from her scalp. Despite her obvious age, she radiated a vitality, even a sensuousness. Her blue bathrobe featured a large embroidered L and two ragged pockets, one of them torn. There was something odd about the garment; it seemed to glow when the shadows fell upon it as Ruha walked about. On her feet were what once were probably bunny slippers, but which now looked like dirty string-mop-bottoms. Around her neck was a unique and beautiful silver necklace, which matched the bracelets on her wrists. The expensive-looking jewelry contrasted sharply with her apparent station in life. Her lined face featured high cheekbones upon which the flesh was taut, although somewhat yellowed. This provided an incongruous setting for bright blue eyes that were now peering at him warily.

"I want to assure you, before I ask my question, that I have only the best of intents in seeking this information."

Ruha clutched her Walther tightly.

"No need to worry. All I'd like to know is—well, I've heard that you might have been a concentration camp guard back in the second war." Ruha's eyes widened and darted from side to side. "Who told ya that?" she snapped.

John focused his attention on the pistol, which Ruha was waving in his direction. "Several people have mentioned that a Nazi guard lived here. It seems to be common knowledge. Please, Ruha, I mean you no harm. In fact, I've come here somewhat as a missionary from God." At this Ruha snorted and leveled the Walther at John.

"State ya business, directly and without no foolishness."

John held up his hands, palms out. "Ruha, if you are whom I seek, I would like to baptize you into the Church of Latter-Day Saints and ask you to help me in my work in St. George, where I have a baptism center."

This was clearly not what Ruha had expected. "What?" she said in a confused voice. "Baptism?"

"Ruha, you may have heard of me. I am John Mittney, you know? I ran for president? Anyway, I've decided to dedicate the rest of my life to baptism in the name of Jesus Christ."

"You are John, and ya baptize. Do ya pretend to be Yahya ibn Zakariyya come back to Earth?"

John blinked in confusion "Yaha who?"

"Yahya ibn Zakariyya, known to Christians as John the Baptist. Ya see I am Mandaean, not a Christian, and not a Jew. In fact, not being a Jew, and having blonde hair and blue eyes saved me during the cleansing."

John by now was completely confused. He had expected an Aryan, possibly a war criminal. He'd never heard of Mandaeism. And this old lady seemed off her rocker. "I'm sorry, I'm not familiar with your faith, or your story. Perhaps you could explain?"

Ruha sat back on the couch and placed the gun between the cushions. "Well, it's a long, sad story, and ya don't wanna hear it."

"No, please. I am fascinated to hear your story."

"OK. Well, first, ya need to know about my faith."

Ruha explained that Mandaeism arose around the first century after Jesus, but although its adherents revered Yahya ibn Zakariyya as a great prophet, they not only did not acknowledge Christ's divinity, Mandaeans regard him as mšiha kdaba, or "false messiah," who perverted the teachings entrusted to him by John. Not only that, Ruha explained, but Abraham and Moses were similarly false prophets. Mandaeans trace their ancestry back to Adam, directly from Noah through his sons Sam and Ram. Further, the holy spirit in the Talmud and Bible is an evil being to Mandaeans.

John, although listening quietly, was quite shocked by Ruha's explanation. Jesus a false prophet? The Holy Spirit evil? This was hard for a devout Mormon to listen to.

Mandaeans believe, Ruha said, in a supreme formless entity called the First Life that is beyond space and time, but who expresses itself in the creation of spiritual and material worlds and beings. Among the worlds created by this being is our own, created by Ptahil, the Fourth Life, who produced it in his own image. Our souls are exiled into our world, Ruha said, and yearn to return to their origin in the First Life. Mandaeans believe that the Zodiac, the planets, and the stars influence our fate and are also places of detention after death before, assisted by savior spirits, we can rejoin the First Life.

In Mandaeism, there is a light side and a dark side, the Light World and the Dark World. The darkness is ruled by Ptahil.

"So, we're souls in a prison, ya know? We believe in baptism, done by Mughtasila. Not just done once, but often, as often as necessary. Many call us Moghtaseleh, 'those who wash themselves a lot,'" Ruha paused to make sure John had taken this all in. Her whole demeanor and speech had changed during her recitation, and she seemed more focused and clearer. She almost seemed like a different person while talking about her religion, not the wizened, blunt crone that she had been at first.

"Please continue, Ruha," John said. "How did your religion affect your life in Nazi Germany?"

"Well, having blond hair and blue eyes saved my family from the Nazis, ya know? Most people think all people from the Middle East are brown and brown-eyed. As usual, most people are idiots, because many of us look like the Aryans, so we were spared the gas chambers. When I was 16, the damn Nazis pulled Jews, along with Gypsies, Jehovah's Witnesses, Communists, and socialists from their houses. My family was terrified that we would be found out, ya know? They decided I should join the Aufseherinnen, the female concentration camp guards."

"Yes," John said, "your colleague the Bird Man mentioned them."

"That old blabbermouth fool! It's a wonder the damned Nazi-hunters haven't found me yet. Ya better not be one of 'em!" Ruha glared at John.

"Don't worry, don't worry," John said, worried about the gun. "Your secret is safe with me."

"It better be. Anyway, my heart was breaking. I left my family and did the training. I learned how to punish prisoners and watch for sabotage and work slowdowns. I was assigned to Ravensbrück, a women's concentration camp." Ruha's eyes began to moisten as she recalled the devastation she saw in the camp. "But, honest, I never hurt nobody, ya know? I just helped keep order. I never had nothing to do with no gas chambers. Just kept order in the dormitories. Honest. I felt bad for those poor women. I cried myself to sleep every night but making no noise because if we showed even little bit of feeling for the women, we'd get discipline or worse—get killed like them."

John was saddened at Ruha's story and gave her an empathetic look. "I believe you, Ruha. I do. It must have been horrible." Ruha was now weeping, drying her eyes and nose on the sleeves of her bathrobe.

"So that's my sad story. What is it ya want with me?"

John thought for a moment. He had wanted to baptize and convert a guilty war criminal to show the world the power of forgiveness, and of his religion. Ruha did not appear to be a war criminal, nor did John believe she was lying about her past. It was funny how completely he trusted her story, despite having just met the woman. The Lord has led me to her, he thought. Perhaps He is displeased with my ambition and has shown me a different path.

"Ruha, it is as I said. I would like to bring you into the salvation of the Church of Latter-Day Saints by baptizing you, and also by asking you to work by my side to spread the gift of the Lord."

"You gotta be kiddin' me," Ruha sneered. "Why would I do that? Ya come here with your fine clothes and fancy car, and your flashy watch, and you say you want to help save me? And put me to work? I'm 90 years old. I ain't got much time left to save!"

"Ruha, I believe the Lord has led me to you. Please, at least come back to St. George with me. You can live at my house—along with my wife," John hastily added, as he saw the look Ruha gave him. "You can see how we live. You can watch the baptisms, and I won't make you do anything you don't want to. Please, let me help."

Ruha, still skeptical, said, "I dunno. Seems fishy to me. I need to sleep on it, maybe for a few days. Good day, sir!" Ruha rose, grabbed her pistol, and waved John out the door, which she slammed and bolted behind him.

As John made his way down the stairs and walked back to his car, he decided that, since he had no way of contacting Ruha to find out her decision, he would stay in town for as long as it took for her to decide. Once in the car, he phoned his wife to tell her about the conversation with Ruha and his decision to stay in Kanab.

John had always been fascinated by Kanab but had never been in the tiny town where hundreds of films since the '20s were filmed. Some of John's favorite movies used Kanab as a stand-in for the Old West, including *Brigham Young—Frontiersman*, and more recently, 1977's *Brigham*.

John settled in at the Canyons Boutique Hotel, which, although not up to his usual standards, seemed quite comfortable despite the in-your-face Western ambiance. He decided to give in to the vibe and have dinner at Little Hollywood Land's Cowboy Dinner Buffet.

John was quite used to being recognized in public, but for some reason he was surprised when he walked in and the host just about dropped the stack of menus he was carrying. A few spilled onto the floor and the host, now completely flustered, bent to pick them up. He only succeeded in dumping the whole pile all over the floor in front of the reception desk. "Let me help you," John said. "Oh, no, Mr. Mittney, please I'll get them." John insisted and the two soon had the plastic menus back in their cubby.

"Will you be dining with us tonight?" the red-faced host asked. He was a short, stout bald man wearing cowboy boots, jeans, a white Western shirt with a bolo tie, and a cowboy hat cocked way back on his head, exposing a shiny forehead and scalp.

"Certainly," John said. "I've heard good things." The host about fainted at John's little white lie.

"Wow. Wow. Wow. Uh, OK, I'll seat you immediately. Right this way please." They proceeded through the dining room, which featured long tables set end-to-end and covered with red and blue checkered plastic tablecloths. There were floor-to-ceiling windows looking out onto the parking lot along one wall and a buffet line at the end of the long narrow room. Every head in the place turned to stare at the celebrity, and many groped in their pockets for their phones to grab a picture.

Great, thought John. I'll be here all night taking selfies and signing napkins. Oh, well, I guess I'm stuck now. "Hello, folks! Sorry, I don't mean to interrupt your dinners. Please forgive me."

"I voted for ya, John," shouted a large gentleman sporting a 10-gallon hat. "Me, too!" shouted several others. Then the entire room burst into applause. John turned on his campaign smile and went up and down the tables, shaking hands and taking selfies until he had met everyone in the room.

"Now, please, folks. Please return to your meals and let's all pretend I'm not here." He flashed a big smile, turning up the lapel of his jacket and ducking behind it. The diners roared with laughter, as John took a seat facing the wall at the end of the room, next to the buffet table.

"What shall I get you, sir?" asked the host.

"You've been so kind. Please allow me to serve myself. I'd just like a green tea please." John got up and filled his plate with buttermilk biscuits, cowboy beans and roast beef. He felt the eyes of all the room on him, but when he turned around to take his seat, the eyes snapped back to their plates. As John ate his dinner hastily, the man in the 10-gallon hat—which was clearly a recent purchase—sidled on over and sat down next to John.

"Mr. Mittney, I wonder if I could ask yew a few questions?"

John felt pinned between the man's huge body and the buffet table. He looked the man in the eye and said, "I'm going to have to leave soon to attend to some business, but, sure, you can ask me one question, and then I've really got to go."

"Well, all right. Thank you kindly. As I said, I did vote for yew, mostly because I couldn't vote for no nigger, but I was just wonderin'. Do yew think you losing the election and all had anything to do with being a Mormon?"

John was shocked at the man's language and the temerity of the question. What was this guy's angle?

"No, I don't think so. The issue of my faith never really came up during the campaign."

"Well, do yew think it was because you're not a Christian?"

John stared at the man's tiny eyes, lost in a wide ruddy face. "The Church of the Latter-Day Saints is a Christian faith, sir."

"Yeah, but don't y'all believe that Adam and Eve and the Garden of Eden were in Missouri, and that Jesus stopped over in Missouri on his way to Heaven? That don't seem Christian to me!" Ten-gallon was starting to heat up. John grabbed his napkin, wiped his mouth and tried to stand to leave. Ten-gallon stood up, grabbed John by the shoulder and forced him back into his seat. "Yew just stay right there, you fuckin' heathen!"

At once, 10-gallon was surrounded by several large, strong men who grabbed him and, despite his girth, frog-marched him out into the parking lot where they tossed him onto the gravel. John could seem them gesturing to the man, indicating he should leave if he knew what was good for him. The man's wife and two kids slunk out of the dining room to join him in the pickup, which featured a Confederate flag decal covering the back window. Ten-gallon got the family in the truck and then did a big doughnut, spraying gravel against the big windows of the restaurant and putting a ton of dust in the air, before taking off down the road.

John was shaken by this encounter. Some of the other diners came over to comfort him, but he waved them off, saying that he was fine, that the other gentleman had a right to his opinion.

It took three days, during which John checked in daily with Ruha at the theater, for her to agree to his plan. During each of his visits, Ruha insisted on filling him in on more details about Mandaeism.

Ruha told John that when they die, Mandaeans go to the Light World, known as alma d-nuhra, that lies beyond a gate at the North Pole. There is also a corresponding Dark World, alma d-hšuka. The First Life created Second, Third and Fourth lives, which are called Yōšamin, Abathur, and Ptahil, who created our world. Abathur is imprisoned between the Light

World and the Dark World and weighs the souls who seek to enter the Light World.

Abathur actually weighs the souls, she said. They must have the proper weight, not too light, not too heavy, to go through to the Light World. Abathur gave Ptahil the materials and the helpers, demons, to create the Dark World. Abathur gave one of Ptahil's demons, Manda d Hiia, to Adam to infuse humans with sacred knowledge and protect them.

John's brain goggled at the complexity and foreignness of this religion. Such a lot of intricate beliefs, he thought. But I guess learning about it as an outsider is no stranger than hearing about Mormonism would be for a guy like 10-gallon.

John had thoughtfully purchased a rolling suitcase, figuring that Ruha had none. When Ruha finally agreed to go with him, she bundled up a wad of ragged clothes along with several cassettes and video tapes, tossed them in the case, and they were gone to St. George.

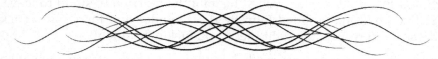

Over the next few weeks, Ruha went from spending the entire day by herself in one of John's bedrooms to cautiously agreeing to take a few meals with the couple. His wife, Lois, suffered from a variety of physical ills, but was always bright and friendly to Ruha, eventually coaxing her out of her shell to the point where Ruha joined the couple in meals every night and began visiting the baptism center with John.

After six months of living with the Mittneys, Ruha consented to be baptized as long as John would let her baptize him as well. John was at first very resistant to this condition, saying, "I have no desire to convert to your religion!" Ruha explained that, unlike Mormon or other Christian baptism, Mandaean baptism does not initiate the person into their religion but is a method of washing away sins. "It takes much more to convert to Mandaeism, Guv'nor. You can't get away that easily, ya know?"

After many discussions, John relented, and allowed Ruha to baptize him in the Virgin River. Ruha said she required several things to perform his baptism, and that of others. When the day came, at the riverside, there was a white, looped-up silk banner on a cross-barred, wooden pole stuck into the riverbank. Myrtle was twined on the crossbar, and an almost invisible thread of gold was tied under it. A clay table holding bowls of incense and fuel sat on the ground. Also on the table were bowls of flour, salt, and sesame, a bowl containing a bunch of myrtle twigs in water, brass drinking bowls, and a flask of water.

John waited by the river for Ruha to appear. He was dressed in a strikingly bright white suit. Ruha arrived in a much nicer version of her blue robe, which John's wife had helped her shop for. She walked serenely down the riverbank to the low table and recited the prayers for the day. Then she burned the incense and mixed the flour and salt with water to make a small, biscuit-sized flat bread that she cooked over the flames and ate. She then descended into the water and beckoned to John to follow.

As he had been instructed, John turned leftward around behind Ruha, and crouched in the water, fully submerging himself three times. Ruha then threw water from the flask onto John three times. Using her left hand, Ruha grasped John's right hand and transferred him to her right side. She submerged him three times and then wetted a finger and drew three lines across John's face from ear-to-ear. John extended his hand, Ruha filled it from the flask, and John drank. The two shook hands, and Ruha placed a myrtle wreath on his head while chanting the names of Yōšamin, Abathur, and Ptahil.

During this ritual, John got a vision that he was to create the Third Temple on the site of the Brigham Young campus. He left the river overcome with the feeling he was destined to do great things. His whole body was shaking. His wife covered him in a cloak, but John realized it wasn't the cold that wracked is his body. It was something more.

The next day, John stopped the construction of the main campus hall, and over the next few weeks, recast it into a tabernacle. He told no one of the reason for the deviation from the construction plan, nor did he call the building a temple.

Seven weeks following his baptism, John and Ruha began baptizing together in the river. Over the next three-and-a-half years, the two baptized thousands of living and dead Mormons. They had perfected an almost assembly-line method of dealing with the crowds that often massed on the banks of the Virgin River. Each supplicant was baptized twice: first a baptism by John initiating or reconfirming them into the Church of Jesus Christ of Latter-Day Saints, and a second time by Ruha. The baptized who asked were assured that the Mandaean baptism did not initiate them into a religion, but rather helped cleanse the soul. Nonetheless, the practice caused a stir among the elders of the Mormon church. Given John's notoriety and increased stature within the church due to the thousands and thousands of new Mormons he attracted, none spoke out against it.

Because of the huge crush of supplicants, the pair spent long hours in the river and soon found that various adjustments in garb and foot gear were needed. Flowing robes were a bit of a hindrance, especially in the heavier river flow in the spring, but Ruha insisted on wearing her blue robe. John opted for white polyester pants and shirt. For better traction in the river, both wore light, quick-drying hiking shoes.

One bright summer morning, the two were attending to a small crowd of supplicants when suddenly a great flood of water, 30 feet tall, came roaring up river, washing John and Ruha 40 miles upstream into Zion National Park, into the left fork of North Creek, bouncing up the rapids, past Tabernacle Dome, past South Guardian Angel, past North Guardian Angel, deep into the mountains. John screamed as the torrent tumbled the pair, though they remained miraculously unharmed. Whenever the river turned sharply or narrowed, they were kept from injury, borne to the top of the flood, sometimes surging high over obstacles. Although John was terrified, Ruha maintained a curious smile as they rode on the flood.

Finally, they sped through a narrow tube-like passage and the water sent them sprawling onto a sliver of beach on the other side. Totally disoriented and woozy from the ordeal, John laid prone on the pebbly beach, dazed and overcome by adrenaline. He tried to calm his mind, which was whirling from the incredible journey on the waters.

The end will come like a flood, John thought distractedly. Daniel 9:26 is trying to come true! Are these the End Times? How else could this miraculous flood of water sweep us up the river, thousands of feet up into this place? But who is the Anointed One? John shivered from the cool air, and the fear that perhaps it was he who was the Anointed One of the Apocalypse. He looked skyward, searching for the promised sign that was to announce the Second Coming, and the angels that would presage His return. Oh, I wish I had gotten further in my baptismal work! There are so many LDS ancestors who will remain in the spirit prison. They won't be part of the First Resurrection, thus never ascending into the highest kingdoms of the afterlife. John bent his head to weep for those who would be lost forever.

Suddenly he remembered Ruha. Where is that frail old woman? he thought. Has she survived the torrent? John looked around and found

Ruha sitting comfortably on a rock several feet above him with an amused look on her face.

"So, Guvnor, this is a fine kettle of fish, eh?" The years appeared to have peeled away from Ruha and she now seemed no older than middle age. Her ever-present blue robe was dry, as were her hair and body. Her eyes were bright and intense with inner fire. She jumped down from the rock and strode up to John, cackling like a demon. "Bet ya never had a ride like that, right? Where in heaven's name are we anyway?"

John surveyed his surroundings. The stream bubbled along the slender strip of beach at one end of a curving tunnel-like formation whose rounded walls gave way to a steep opening to the sky. The retreating water was draining quickly from the area, exposing glistening walls and revealing bright sunlight at the other end of the tube.

John pulled out his damp cell phone. Miraculously, it came to life when he turned it on. He activated the GPS function and brought up Google Maps. It took a while for John to find a spot in the canyon where the device could get a fix on the GPS satellites. "We're about three miles inside Zion National Park and this must be a feature called the Subway. I can see why it has that name. It looks like a train could come barreling through that tube at any moment."

"Let's hope it doesn't," Ruha said with a little laugh. "After that flood, I wouldn't be at all surprised if it did, ya know?"

John was flabbergasted by Ruha's cheery disposition. They'd been tumbled and scraped, but mostly they rode the top of the flood on its winding path to this place. That they were essentially unharmed was a miracle. But Ruha can hardly contain her glee, John thought, while I'm terrified.

"What are you grinning about, Ruha?"

"Don't ya know, John? It's starting!"

"What's starting?"

"What a conciurge like me has been waiting for all my life. It's what in your religion you would call the Second Coming, the Apocalypse, the End of Days!"

John had just been entertaining the same thought, but to hear Ruha say it struck him like a punch in the gut. Reflexively, he sat down heavily on the sand. What if it's really happening? How will I be judged? he wondered. I have done my best to be a righteous man, although an ambitious and perhaps a prideful one. Another thought struck him: He was going to meet

Jesus! He just about fell over in the sand at that realization. God, my Heavenly Father, he prayed, I thank Thee for the blessings of my life. I hope I have pleased you. I repent of all my sins. I humbly plead with Thee, if it be according to Thy will, asking that Thou wilt forgive my arrogance, pass by my sins, and guide my actions. Of this I testify in the name of Jesus Christ, amen.

The prayer calmed John a bit, and he sat alone with his thoughts for a few minutes. Eventually, he said, "How can you be sure this is the beginning of the Apocalypse, Ruha? Sure, that flood was like nothing I would have ever believed to be possible, but that doesn't mean it's the End Times."

"Believe me, Guvnor, it is. Ya told me your book teaches that the first sign of the Second Coming has passed, when Elijah appeared to Joseph Smith, right? Ya see, I am the conciurge for the demiurge. I was born for these times. I await my master, Ptahil, the demiurge of this universe, and it's time for the reckoning."

John, still in shock from all that had happened, was reeling. He recalled that Ruha had mentioned Ptahil when she was teaching him about her religion, but he still was a little hazy on what the demiurge was in Mandaeism.

"I'm sorry," he said, "I'm unclear as to what you're saying."

"I am slowly coming to realize that I am Ruha, not just in name, but in fact: the spirit mediating between body and soul in this evil world that my master, Ptahil, the Fourth Life, produced. This knowledge has been growing in me since I met you, and while riding the flood, it got stronger, and even now, it is becoming even clearer. I was imprisoned in this body and am now slowly awakening from its bondage. I remember now that I took mortal form to assist in the end of this existence."

Wide-eyed, John stared at Ruha, who had begun to shine with an inner light. The years again seemed to peel away from her, her hair turning from silver to blonde as he watched. Either I'm hallucinating, or she's completely crazy ... could it be she is who she says she is, and this is the End Times?

"So why are we here in Utah? According to scripture, the Second Coming is supposed to occur in Israel."

"According to your scripture, you mean. But ya said it yourself, we're in Zion, Zion National Park. I guess the First Life is having a laugh at our expense!"

"Ah! Now that I think of it, it's even more interesting than that," John said, standing and panning around the map on his phone. "Not only has Zion been an enduring symbol of Mormonism, representing courage, dedication, endurance, and faith, but as I recall, Mormons named many of the places in this park, including the park itself. Early LDS settlers named Kolob Canyon—Kolob meaning a heavenly place close to God—the Towers of the Virgins, Prodigal Son, Tabernacle Dome, and the Three Patriarchs— named for Abraham, Isaac, and Jacob."

"Zion is also the site of the second Jewish temple," Ruha said.

"You mean Mount Zion in Jerusalem. True."

"Perhaps this is the site of the third? Is there not a place called temple here?"

John winced a bit as he thought about his vision of the Third Temple, and his attempts to build it. He consulted his phone. Due to the very spotty cell coverage, he climbed partway up the canyon and disappeared around a corner. After some minutes, he returned. "You're right! There's a place called Temple of Sinawava, named for the Coyote god of the Paiute Indians who used to live here."

"Then I think that is where we are called to go. My brain is still fogged, but I feel this is so. What else did you find out about this place?"

"It seems there's a rock formation in the temple canyon called The Pulpit."

"That's it! Can you find the way there?"

John consulted his phone. "It would be quite a trek! It's about four or five miles as the crow flies, 22 miles and 8½ hours if we hike the West Rim trail, or 38 miles by car, and we don't have a car. Or decent hiking shoes." John looked down at the quick-dry hikers he and Ruha were wearing.

"I believe we are meant to hike to the Temple, John. Let's get started." John, still wrestling to absorb all that had happened, fell silent. I am so overwhelmed, he thought. We're miraculously washed away by a flood— miles upriver through some of the most treacherous canyons in the park. Not only are we unhurt, but Ruha's not even wet anymore. I can't believe any of this! It's like a strange dream! And now she insists we spend the rest of the day walking to a so-called temple. John crumpled again to the gritty beach and cradled his head in his arms. Can this really be the Second Coming? After sitting for a few minutes, John sighed and stood back up.

The pair set out on the rugged trail. After a steep climb out of the canyon, they proceeded on the Northgate Peaks trail and eventually the Wildcat

Canyon trail which, thankfully, was fairly level and easy going. The Wildcat was crawling with day hikers, and as they passed, John heard several talking about the weird flood in the North Fork. If they only knew how weird it was, John thought.

As he trudged on, his mind, still reeling from the shock of the miracle water ride, tried to come to terms with what had happened to him. They passed through wildflower-filled meadows and had several good views of the White Cliffs of Wildcat Canyon.

John finally had a decent signal on his phone. While they walked, he called his wife. As the phone rang, he tried to think of what to tell her. I can't very well tell her that these are the End Times. I can scarcely believe that myself. The phone went to voice mail. John said, "Honey, I'm in Zion and I won't be back for a while. There was a flood, but I'm OK. I'll try to call you later."

After a couple miles, they stopped at a muddy spring to drink before descending toward the dry crossing streambed of Wildcat Canyon. The tourists had thinned out, and they rarely saw people until they got across the canyon and climbed up to the West Rim trail.

Having proceeded in a northeasterly direction for the first leg of the trip, they turned sharply southeast for the longer part of the trek. After three flat and uneventful miles, the pair got their first glimpse of South Guardian Angel mountain. In Potato Hollow they stopped to drink at a spring, where both he and Ruha washed their faces. With her wet finger, Ruha drew three lines on John's face, from ear-to-ear.

Then they tackled the uphill climb to Hammerhead Viewpoint and its views of Inclined Temple. They climbed again, to Horse Pasture Plateau and then took the Telephone Canyon Trail spur to save time and avoid the increasing crowds of tourists that slowed them down. At Cabin Spring, they drank and rested for half an hour. Again, Ruha blessed John with the water lines.

They made the steep climb down through the White Cliffs and the descent into the main canyon. Since it was mid-summer, there still was good light to hike as they switchbacked down to the Grotto Trailhead on the canyon floor. Thankfully, at the trailhead Ruha agreed to hop the park shuttle to its last stop: The Temple of Sinawava. There they took advantage of the toilet facilities and then stood in awe of the sight of The Pulpit, the taller and wider of the two towers across the river from the parking area.

"Here we are," said John. "Now what?"

"Now we rest," Ruha said. "We need to get across the river and find a place near The Pulpit where we won't be found. There ain't no camping in this area."

Sighing, John wearily followed Ruha across the parking lot, and into the stream, which was just above ankle deep. "What are we going to eat?" John asked.

"Nothing," Ruha said. "Today we fast."

"Where will we sleep?"

"We can gather some grass and brush for bedding. You mustn't worry. All will be well tomorrow."

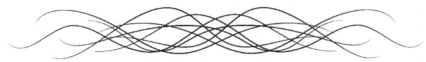

The next day dawned with a clear sky above them. But on the edges of their sight, all around them above the canyon walls was a ring of dark black clouds, threatening, and bursting with lightning. As near as they could tell from their canyon, the circle of blue sky was perfect, ringing them in the center. As they watched, the clouds began to flow, each in a quadrant of the sky, with darker clouds flowing in toward the circle, then lightening and flowing away along the quadrant lines.

Coming out from behind the Pulpit, the pair looked across the river and saw two men, one on the closer riverbank, and one on the opposite. The nearer man was clothed in rough burlap, and was turned away from them, so they could not see his face. The farther man, clothed in white linen, floated above the waters of the river and spread apart his arms and said, "The power of the holy people has been finally broken, and all things are completed. Many will be purified, made spotless and refined, but the wicked will be damned to the Second Death and the Dark World. The seven seas that run high shall swallow them, but the righteous shall be lifted up."

The pair looked up and saw a disturbance in the clouds. There appeared to be a multitude of dark figures swirling in the vortices of the quadrants. The winds howled as if the crowd were screaming in torment. Lightning and fire flashed through the clouds and between the quadrants.

They turned to look at the hovering man and he had transformed. His hair was now white as snow, and his eyes were like blazing fire. His feet radiated heat as if a furnace, boiling the river beneath him, and his voice was like the sound of rushing waters as he said to them, "Do not be afraid. By the baptism of water, and the baptism of fire, you can speak with the tongue of angels. You are the Witnesses to the Exaltation, the two olive trees that stand before Ptahil, the Lord of the Earth. Should anyone try to harm you, you can devour them with fire from your mouths. You have power to shut up the heavens so that it will not rain, and to turn the waters into blood, and to strike the Earth with every kind of plague."

My goodness, John thought. He speaks as if from Nephi, and Matthew, and Revelation! Perhaps the Scripture is coming true? John asked, "Will we witness the judgment of the Sons of Perdition?"

The figure said, "There is much error in the religions of this world, and this is a particular one. All souls will be weighed, but the decision is not about the final destination of each soul. Rather, as in your companion's religion, which is also full of error, souls after weighing may be sent on journeys during which they can recapture their virtue by ascending through various spheres of grace, among the worlds of light and the stars of the Zodiac. Those who are beyond improvement, the Unredeemables—the Sons of Perdition as your religion names them—are sent to the Dark World and are no more. Abatur Rama d-Muzania and his flawed son, Ptahil, will soon be released from their bondage in the Earth so that Abatur can complete his contemptible task of weighing the souls."

John was devastated by these remarks. As a true believer of Mormonism, to discover even one error in doctrine called into question the whole foundation of his spiritual life. His mouth was suddenly dry when he finally managed to ask, "So, the Church of Latter-Day Saints will not be established throughout the world?"

"This world is coming to an end. It was created in error, but the First Life will ensure that the good souls who were exiled to this world, and who are not beyond redemption, will rejoin It, if they are found worthy."

With tears in his yes, John asked, "Will I see the return of our Savior, Jesus Christ?"

"As I said there is much error in the religions of the world. The man you call the Savior was inspired but was not a god. There are no gods as you have pretended to understand them. Only the First Life, which is formless. The belief of your religion, that the church originally formed around Jesus but became corrupted within decades of being established, is true, as far as it goes. But much of what you believe is error. Jesus was enlightened, and a whole soul, but he was not divine."

John began to weep uncontrollably. He felt as if the rug had been pulled out from beneath his whole being. He crumpled to the ground and placed his hands over his eyes. Ruha put her arm around his shoulders and urged him to regain his feet.

The floating man said, "Stand by she who is the Great Mother and ascend to the pulpit of the temple of heaven to witness the judging of the living and the dead."

John stopped crying and looked in astonishment at Ruha. The Great Mother? This woman, beside whom he had baptized thousands, now mysteriously unbent and clear-eyed, and no longer frail-looking? Ruha beamed back at him, her face transformed by an inner light. "I told you I am the conciurge. I assisted the demiurge, Ptahil, in creating this world. I am its Mother."

John's mind, already reeling, was coming apart. "Whoa," he said, and began to lose consciousness. Ruha threw his arm around her shoulders and bore his weight easily as they turned away from the floating man and made their way back to the Pulpit.

The path to the top of the tower rock was a semi-technical climb, but luckily, its last climbers had left ropes and pitons in place. Ruha scrambled easily up ahead of John and helped him haul his way up the pitches until they reached the top of the Pulpit. Miraculously, at the top was an altar carved into the rock, covered with a fine white cloth with incense holders smoking on all four corners. Seven places were set on the table, with gleaming gold plates and utensils, and embroidered silk napkins, and dazzling crystal goblets.

"Who are these for?" asked John.

"These are for the Seven Kings."

"Which kings are those?"

"The seven rulers of the world. Long ago they were kings, but today you might call them, um, er, what is the word? Captains of Industry? No, they are from various walks of life. There is a name, I think a medieval name, for a shadow government? Hidden rulers?"

"Illuminati?" John guessed.

"Yes! Illuminati. The Illuminati will join us for a feast." John nodded dully at this latest shocking revelation and looking around, noticed there were now steaming tureens of soup, and fruits, beans, and vegetables on serving trays on the altar.

"If this is the feast, where is the meat?

"The Seven Kings are, of course, vegan. They are not permitted to harm an animal to provide their sustenance, for animals have their own special purpose in the world, to help promote the world's bounty."

John again nodded blankly and wondered at this for a moment. There was just too much to absorb. The Illuminati are real. Christ was not the Son of God. Much of the teachings of his church, if not all, were in error. Ruha was somehow the Mother of the world. As he tried to process these revelations, he was interrupted by a loud screeching cry from the sky. Looking up, John saw a huge black dragon pass overhead. He could see the creature had a hideous, a near-human face, and two horns like a lamb. Its head and neck were covered with curly white fleece in stark contrast to its jet-black body and shiny dark talons.

"Oh, my son!" Ruha exclaimed. "At last you are free from the Dark World! Come 'Ur, and alight upon this pulpit so that I may caress you."

The giant monster wheeled across the river and turned to alight on a rock outcropping at the outer edge of the altar. Ruha scrambled out on a ledge to hug his neck. "My son! My son! Oh, the prison of this body is slowly melting away, and now I can remember! I remember how together we birthed the planets and the stars of the Zodiac! I remember how you brought the blue to the sky of this world. And now you have been released! We can be together again."

'Ur spoke, and his voice was like a scream: "Mother! Glad we close again! How help I you?"

"You will have a role. But for now, be still and wait." The dragon's red eyes became hooded as he perched on the outcrop at the edge of the altar and loomed over it.

Ruha looked out across the river, to the parking lot, where a purple motor coach had just pulled up. It wasn't the standard national park coach, but a private one. "Ah," Ruha said. "They have arrived!"

"Who?" asked John, startled from his stupor, and terrified that there would be more shocks to absorb.

"The Seven Kings, the Illuminati! They have arrived." Seven old men of various races debarked from the coach and stared at the turbulent sky. They appeared to be bewildered but were even more shaken when the floating man reappeared and levitated them across the river and up to the top of The Pulpit, landing them gently on the rich Persian carpet, each adjacent to his place at the altar. The waiting man from the near side of the river also appeared and stood in the back of The Pulpit.

"What the hell is going on?" demanded a bespectacled white-haired gentleman in a tight, navy blue V-necked sweater, white shirt and tie. Incongruously, he was clutching a ukulele, but from the attitudes of the others, he was clearly the leader of the group, all of whom were dressed more casually, as if they had just come from a round of golf.

"Not hell, not the Dark World, but it is the end of days, Spartacus," Ruha says. "The final age is ending. You seven are to hold a conference to ensure that when the weighing of souls begins, the great shall not receive more honor than the lesser."

The men turned to one another, confused, and began to murmur together, while turning their heads wildly, taking in the strange sky, the perched 'Ur, and the splendid table before them. Not even the one she called Spartacus was able to gather his wits to reply to Ruha. He just goggled, open-mouthed, absent-mindedly clutching his ukulele.

"But first," Ruha continued, "we feast. Please be seated at your places and let us break bread for the last time on this Earth." Terror filled the eyes of the Illuminati. John watched them and commiserated. At least I've had a few hours to digest all this, he thought. These poor men have been plucked from who knows what golf course and plunked down in this fantastic scene. Yet they do seem to be taking it better than I did at first.

Indeed, these captains of industry, political masters, religious powers behind the thrones, and backroom deal makers were still carefully examining their surroundings, trying to find out what trickery lay behind this mind-blowing scene. They were looking for the wires that supported the floating man and the gears that animated the dragon. They took their seats warily. Before each of them, on the table on their left hand was a round tray containing a small water bottle; a cup of miša; fatiras; a drinking bowl containing four raisins; a twig of myrtle, grape seeds, and shreds of Ba, pomegranate, quince, dates, coconut, almond, walnut, and citrus. All were arranged around the tray in the positions of the Zodiac. A second tray on their right hand held a basin of flaming liquid and a stand upon which sat a cube of incense.

Ruha passed down the table, filling the seven goblets with blood-red wine. When she was finished, she raised her own goblet and cried, "As the water falls on the Earth, so shall all sins, trespasses, follies, stumblings, and mistakes be loosed from those who love the name of Truth, and from the souls of our righteous fathers, teachers, brothers, and sisters who have departed the body, and those who still live." She nodded her head to the seven to encourage them to drink.

Next, she asked the men to drop the incense cube into the fire, saying, "All fruits wither; all sweet odors pass away, but not the fragrance of the First Life, which never ends nor passes away, as does this Last Age. The incense rises as our prayers do, to the First Life."

Ruha then bade the men to eat, and she withdrew to the back of the Pulpit to join John. "Now watch carefully," she told him. John regarded the men keenly, watching them whispering to each other nervously as they ate. Soon he noticed the hovering man drifting close to one of the seven and appearing to whisper in his ear. The man seemed not to notice the floating man and continued to converse with his companion. Eventually, the hovering man floated away. But the others had seen the spirit, and asked him, "What did the spirit tell you?"

"What do you mean? There was no spirit! I talked to no one."

This angered the others. One said, "We all saw it. Tell us what the spirit said or die!"

"I swear! I see nothing! I hear nothing! I know nothing!"

But the others fell upon him and one stabbed him in the heart with a table knife, killing him.

The remaining six eyed each other suspiciously. Their eyes were now a bit glassy, and they seemed to be in a trance. The floating man spoke to another, and another, and each of them in turn, except the leader, with the same result: The others accused, and then killed the protesting man. The last turned on the leader, who, anticipating the attack, sliced his jugular before the other could raise his knife.

Only Spartacus now remained, shaking with rage and fear. He turned to Ruha and said, "Why have you caused these men to die? These were the most powerful men in the world! For decades, we have fixed elections, started and stopped wars, controlled economies, and bent populations to our will. How dare you?" The leader stopped to catch his breath, his face red with fury. "What is to happen to me? Am I the final king of the world? Or will you kill me next?"

"You all have met your deserved end, before the end of this world. Your rule over the world has been almost absolute, and while the Illuminati have sometimes governed wisely, you all have many sins to repent, especially you. No, I will not kill you," Ruha said. "But my son will."

The last Illuminati heard a rustle behind him and whirled to see 'Ur unfold his wings. Spartacus grabbed a bloody knife and his ukulele and backed away. 'Ur flicked his wings and was on the man in an instant. The leader of the Illuminati struck feebly with the knife and bashed the ukulele into 'Ur's head, but the dragon grotesquely unhinged his human-like jaw and gobbled Spartacus in a single gulp. John watched in horror as 'Ur recomposed his face, licked his lips, and then flew, screeching, in ascending circles up to the vortex of the clouds.

"He is taking back the blue of the sky," Ruha said. "It is almost time for Ptahil to break the bounds of Earth and for Abatur Rama d-Muzania to begin the weighing of souls."

John shivered at what was to come next. How would his soul measure up on Abatur's scales? And what caused a soul to have weight? Ruha had said something about progressing through various worlds so those who weren't ready could purify themselves. And what was all this business about the Zodiac? Did this mean that astrology was actually a power in the Universe? John had so many questions, and an equal number of fears for his everlasting life, if there even was such a thing.

"What do you mean 'Ur will take back the blue of the sky?"

"This is the first phase of the dismantling of the world. 'Ur removes the blue, and then when people look up, they'll see the blackness of space, the stars, the Zodiac, and the planets. The atmosphere will also start to dissipate until all the air is gone."

"When people see this, they'll go crazy."

"Yes, this is one of the final tests. Those who react by raping, pillaging, killing and committing other atrocities will join that crowd." Ruha pointed skyward to the swirling black figures in the quadrants surrounding the blue circle. "Those poor souls are the Unredeemables. They do not need to be weighed but will be sent directly to the Dark World. In life, they embraced the power of the Dark World, and so they will become one with it."

John absorbed this and felt lucky that he had not yet joined the circling horde above. When he looked down from the sky, he noticed the bloody corpses staining the fine carpet. "Why did you cause the Illuminati to kill one another?"

"It was not I who caused their behavior. It was their natures. They were arrogant, competitive men, ambitious to a fault. The idea that one of their kind might obtain an advantage by receiving secrets from the Angel of

Death drove them to their murderous acts. You noticed that their leader did not participate in the killings, except at the end when he was defending himself." John nodded. "It was not because his soul was less stained than his fellows. It was because, to gain his position, he had needed to be in better control of his emotions, his envy, and his gluttony."

"Why did he receive a different fate than his fellows?

"His sin was compounded by the fact that he stood by while his subordinates murdered one another. Such it is with his type of leader. He bore the greatest sin and, by controlling his followers, brought all their sins upon him. 'Ur is delivering him to the maelstrom in the sky and thus directly to the Dark World."

John thought of his own leadership. Am I that type of leader? Will 'Ur come and take me next? He needed to sit down and moved over to the altar, picking his way among the bloody bodies. He sat at the table and looked out over the river. He noticed the two trays before him and examined the strange arrangement of foods on the left-hand tray.

"Is this place setting part of some kind of ritual?"

"Yes," Ruha says. "This is the traditional setting for a Mandaean masiqta, or death mass. As the Angel of Death said, most religions have errors, but there are true things in most of them, too. Mandaeanism's death mass is the most error-free ritual to initiate the End Times."

Again, John felt a pang in the center of his being. He had led a life worshipping in a religion filled with error. "Is Mandaeanism the most error-free religion, then?"

"It is hardly worth thinking about at this time. You probably desire to know all the errors of your faith, and how it compares to other religions. But the First Life cares not for worship, or religious dogma. What counts is the soul's ascent to the Light World. A religion is only as good as its ability to aid in the soul's purification, so that it may make this ascent, which depends upon leading a good and true life. An example of an error in Mandaeism is the belief that at death, the souls of all Mandaeans go to the Light World, as long as they had a pure death and proper death rituals. This is not at all true. As the Angel of Death told you, all souls are weighed, and most must journey through purifying worlds before rejoining the First Life. As I said, the Unredeemables are sent directly to the Dark World."

"Why is all this happening now? Is it because of the rampant evil in this modern world? Mormonism and other religions have long believed that crises, earthquakes and the breakdown of moral structure are signs of the end."

"The First Life does not perceive events on this world. It is and always is. The fleeting lives of souls here are of no concern. Most of your religions ascribe a consciousness and personality to the supreme being and imagine that it has a hand in human affairs. Nothing could be further from the truth. There is no hand of a god directing human affairs. And there is certainly no reality to the concept of a petty god who demands to be worshipped and who can be insulted.

"Souls yearn to be reunited with the First Life. However, there are only a finite number of souls in this existence. When I created the world with Ptahil and 'Ur, we populated it with all the souls that ever were to be here. The explosion of the human population has meant that each soul has been fractured and contained, really trapped, inside more than one person. There exists a point beyond which a soul can no longer be diluted, and that has determined the end of this world. Had this world persisted for even another generation, babies would be born without a spark of soul, and would be relegated to the life of a vegetable. Thus, this world must cease to be, and the souls set free to begin their journey back to the First Life."

John took this in and thought for a while. He only has a fragment of a soul. He will be judged and probably will need to pass through several other worlds to be purified before he can rejoin the First Life. There is no God. Everything he has been told is wrong. He heaved a great sigh, and asked Ruha, "So all my works, the baptizing, the building of the university, all are for naught? Has my life been wasted?"

Ruha settled into the chair next to him with a kind expression on her face. "Don't you realize, John? You have been chosen. You are one of the two witnesses to the end of days. Your recent life, your devotion to the salvation of souls through baptism: these have redeemed your soul and washed away most of the imperfections that stained it. Even though my mind was clouded by my imprisonment in flesh, I saw the spark in you when we first met in the movie theater."

For the first time since the flood, John felt a glimmer of hope. Perhaps he wasn't doomed. He had been chosen to be a witness. But Ruha referred to two witnesses. Surely, she wasn't one?

"Ruha, you said there are two. Who is the other witness?"

"The waiting man we saw earlier, and who stands in the darkness behind you."

John wheeled around in his chair. The waiting man, still clothed in a burlap robe, moved forward into the light. He was short, swarthy, with thick black hair covering his arms and a curly beard. His long hair was thick and tangled, and his brow jutted over hooded but clear hazel eyes. Although it was a homely face, it shone from within, radiating a calmness.

"Who are you?" John asked, standing to face him.

"I am Jesus, the son of Joseph, the carpenter," the man replied simply.

For the second time that day, John almost lost consciousness, and again Ruha moved in to steady him. "Jesus, the Christ?" John croaked, his throat suddenly dry as the desert floor below.

"I don't know this Christ," Jesus said. "I am a simple man who preached love and forgiveness and was executed for it. I had a small band of followers. It must have been long ago, for I have never seen such a magnificent coach as the one across the river."

John at this point was almost catatonic. Ruha guided him back into his chair. He crumpled against the table with his forehead on the tablecloth and his arms folded protectively over his head. He began to weep.

I can't take any more of this, he thought. Jesus was only a simple carpenter with a message of love, the Son of Man and not the Son of God? He wasn't resurrected, just murdered by the Romans? And now he's risen to witness the end of the world, not to preside over the Exaltation and the establishment of his kingdom on Earth. There will be no resurrections, no battle with Satan. My religion has been an error, and I am not prepared for what is to come.

Jesus walked over to John, compassion evident on his face, and laid a comforting hand on John's shoulder. "My son, why do you worry so?"

John, startled at Jesus' touch, sat bolt upright, inadvertently shrugging Jesus' hand from his shoulder. "Oh!" he exclaimed, wiping at his eyes. Jesus just smiled at him. John could feel the man's power, his goodness. "Forgive me, Jesus . . ." he began, and then burst into ragged, near-hysterical laughter. Jesus naturally was puzzled. "Sorry, Jesus—there I go again! You see, for the last two thousand years, men have worshipped you as the Son of God, and we have been waiting for your return."

Jesus looked puzzled, and asked, "But why? I was but an itinerant preacher with a small following."

"Well, how do I explain?" John thought for a minute. "OK, Jesus, you probably don't know what the Bible is, but you did know the Torah, right?"

Jesus nodded. "Well, your followers, and their followers, wrote a big addition to the Torah, all about you and your teachings. They called you the Christ—the Messiah—and they started a church, the Christian church, to spread your teachings throughout the world."

It was Jesus' turn to be astonished. "This is incredible! All I preached was that people should be nice to one another for a change, and they nailed me to a tree for it."

"You mean a cross, don't you?"

"No, they thought a cross was too good for me. They nailed me to a tree, an algum, I think."

John just shook his head sadly. "I see. So, I suppose you never worked any miracles?"

"Miracles happen every day, my son. You just need to be aware of them."

John, numbed by all the shocking revelations of the day, merely nodded his head. He turned to Ruha. "Why have I been chosen to be a Witness? Surely there are more righteous people than me left in the world?"

"John, as you know—and are very proud of—you are of the lineage of Aaron. And you may understand that, consequently, John the Baptist, which my religion regards as a messiah, is also your ancestor, along with Jesus. This lineage has been allowed to breed in such a way that the line has gathered together many soul fragments. Thus, your soul is one of the most complete still on this Earth. And that is why you have been chosen to be a Witness. In the same way, the ancient line produced Jesus, a complete, whole soul. The two of you were destined to be the Two Witnesses to the Exaltation."

Stunned yet again, John pondered this new information. I'm not a fractured soul like the rest of the world. I've been, not exalted really, but honored in some way to play a part in the end of the world. This is too fantastic to contemplate.

"Does this mean I can expect a better fate when my soul is weighed?"

"Yes, John. Your journey to reunion with the First Life will be much shorter. There is less in you to purify. As the Angel of Death told you a while ago, you have powers now, to defend yourself, to stop the rain, to turn waters to blood, and to cause plague. You and Jesus will need these powers when the might of this world is turned against this place."

"What do you mean?" At that moment, the blue of the sky in the circle above them disappeared and they could see blackness and stars. John looked at Ruha. "What does this mean?"

"It means that all on Earth who are awake now will see as the circle expands that there is nothing between them and the stars. They will also soon notice that the swirling clouds now above us are expanding from a center above this place, and they will come, many with terrible force, to see what is happening. You and Jesus must be ready to defend this place."

"Is this the battle between good and evil prophesied by the Bible?"

"No. Those who come will come with good intent, to protect their fellows. They believe their force can stop what is happening in the world, and they are doing their duty. Their souls will be weighed in accordance with their lives, not these last deeds. There is no battle between good and evil. There is only good, and error."

John was confused by this. "You're saying there is no Satan?"

Ruha laughed. "I am the closest thing to your idea of Satan. I am charged with managing the Dark World. I am the Earth, and I built Jerusalem. When Adam was created, a substance of light from the Light World was embedded in his evil body, or Pagra. You call this your soul, and your job is to rescue it from the dark, and this world. This is the fourth and last age of the world, overseen by Noah with his wife, and symbolized by the flood yesterday. I am the mother of the evil spirits of the zodiac and of the planets. I am radiance; I am light. I am death; I am life. I am darkness; I am light. I am error; I am truth. I am destruction; I am construction. I am light; I am error. I am wounding; I am healing.

"But I am not The Adversary. There is no Satan. This world was created in error, and the souls in it struggle to seek the path of goodness, away from error. Some embrace error, and you call them evil. They are being prepared to enter the Dark World even now." Ruha pointed again at the swirling clouds and the dark figures within them. "Once the circle of clouds expands to cover this world, it will be unbroken, and all souls will be weighed, and this world will be no more."

John struggled to assemble his thoughts and put them into words. After several moments, he said, "How long will it take until the circle is unbroken?"

Ruha says, "The outer edge of the cloud circle is moving at about 70 miles an hour. The opposite edges will meet in the Indian Ocean west of Perth, Australia in about 15 days' time. During this time, you and Jesus must defend this place. The edge of the clouds should reach Nellis Air Force Base near Las Vegas in an hour or so. The great crowd of Unredeemables in the Las Vegas area will join the clouds in the sky, rising into the air from wherever they are, and all will see the sign of the End Times. It will probably only take an hour or so after that before the Air Force identifies the center of the clouds and is in the air coming this way. We need to be ready."

John and Jesus exchanged looks. Jesus said, "Do you mean we need to kill the pilots? I cannot do that."

Ruha looked at Jesus fondly. "All on Earth will perish in 15 days. Those who die while we defend this place will die just as surely in two weeks' time. But this place must be protected. It is the site of the weighing of souls. You must defend against planes, against missiles, against whatever force seeks to harm this place."

Jesus wept. John was also brought to tears. The two men sat beside one another at the altar crying piteously for the better part of an hour. Ruha came over and spoke kindly to the two men. "It is time to prepare. The two most effective powers that you have during this time are fire and plague. You must decide how to use them to defend us. You can use the fire against the jets, but you may need to use plague against the armed forces yet on the ground."

John flipped on his phone and searched for news from Las Vegas. He found a live news report on a local TV station.

> "Las Vegas is now a scene of mass hysteria. People are rising up into the sky and disappearing to the northeast as ominous clouds and winds slowly blanket the city, shutting out the noonday sun. All over Las Vegas, cars have smashed into each other, people, storefronts, and casinos because they no longer have drivers. I am standing in front of the Bethany Baptist Church, east of the Strip, with Margaret, a church member. Margaret, what do you think is going on?"

> "Well, it's obviously the rapture, when those who have been born again in Christ are taken. 'For the Lord himself shall descend from heaven with a shout, with the voice of the archangel, and with the trump of God.' Those of us who have been watchful, who read the Rapture Ready News, for example, and have seen that the rapture index is close to 200, or who listen to Rapture Ready Radio, have been reading the signs that have foretold this event. As Revelation says, 'If therefore thou shalt not watch, I will come on thee as a

thief, and thou shalt not know what hour I will come upon thee.' That hour has come, praise God! The First Seal has been opened! Hallelujah!"

"So, these people who are ascending to the sky, they are the righteous who have been born again?"

"That is what scripture tells us."

"But what do you make of the fact that these souls are streaming from the casinos and other seedy sites from all over Las Vegas? Or the reported streams from Jewish temples and from mosques?"

"Um, I don't know. Those people should be damned to hell."

"One last question, have you been born again?"

"Why, yes, of course I have!"

"Then why are you still standing here?"

"Um, ah, I don't know."

"OK, thank you, Margaret. Back to you in the studio, George."

John switched to CNN.

"There are reports of hysteria in Las Vegas at this hour. People are calling CNN and reporting seeing fellow citizens rise into the sky and flying off to the northeast. We are attempting to get ahold of the head of the Las Vegas Valley Water District to see if there is somehow a contamination of the water source that is causing the apparent mass psychosis of the people of Las Vegas.

"Wait, I'm being told we have live video from station KVVU in Las Vegas. Oh! Oh, my God! This is unbelievable . . ."

John turned off his phone. The word was spreading fast. There was little doubt that Ruha was right. The natural response would be to send the US military to the center of the storm. Jesus and he would need to take preemptive measures against the threat.

John turned to Jesus and said, "I'm afraid we need to send a plague against the air force and ballistic missile installations within immediate range, and soon across the whole country. There's no way we can shoot all the planes and missiles out of the sky as they approach."

Jesus looked puzzled. "I don't know what you mean. What are planes? What are missiles? I am not familiar with these words."

John quickly filled Jesus in on the threat. Jesus appeared to take the news reasonably well for a man who was two millennia out of touch with technology. On his phone, John showed him pictures of fighter jets, bombers and missiles and described their power.

Jesus said, "If I understand you, the army can kill at great distances and our only hope is to disable or kill the warriors by sowing plague. Is there nothing we can do with that brick you were just consulting?"

John blinked in confusion and then realized Jesus was referring to his cell phone. "No, Jesus. I don't think this will help, although we can try to keep in touch with what is happening, for as long as it has power, that is. Let us try to visit a plague upon all the closest air force bases—the places they launch the planes from."

John did a search of nearby air bases. "There are 19 Air Force bases we need to worry about right now. We'll eventually have to disable the rest of the 82 across the US. But we don't even know how to cast a plague." John turned to Ruha. "How can we do this?"

"Just imagine the places, think of the type of plague, and say, 'So be it.'"

"OK. Jesus, let's concentrate on Nellis first, although they've probably already scrambled some planes. How about a plague of sleep? It seems the least harmful." The two men closed their eyes, concentrated, and said in unison, "So be it."

John said, "We should check the news to see if it worked."

Ruha replied, "No, there's no time for that. I can assure you, it worked. Your powers are absolute. You should take care of the remaining 18 bases quickly, and then move on to the rest, followed by the missile sites."

"Do we need to do them one-by-one?"

"For the first few, I suggest you do. But you can do all at one time, once you get used to it. You'll probably need to extend across the world to Russia and any other power that can strike this area. We'll also need to disable the army. This site is remote enough to make overland assault difficult, but the other armed forces have air capabilities as well. You'll be very busy."

Just then, a pair of fighters streaked overhead, and banked sharply to return. "We need to use the fire this time," John told Jesus. "We need to hit them before they crest the surrounding peaks, so the destruction doesn't fall into this valley."

Jesus and John looked to the planes coming back from the east, opened their mouths, and spit long arcs of fire. The planes, despite last-minute evasive action, ran into the pillars of file and exploded, crashing into the other side of the ridge. A huge fireball rose into the sky. The two men were devastated. It was one thing to put people to sleep. It was another to murder them. The fact that all were doomed to die in two weeks hardly made it better. Ruha comforted the pair, putting her arms around them and saying, "Your vigilance is critical to maintaining this place until Ptahil and Abatur Rama d-Muzania break the bounds of Earth seven days before the end of this existence."

And so it was. For eight days, Jesus and John visited plague on the armies of the Earth and fought off air and missile attacks until the ridges around the Temple of Sinawava smoked continuously.

On the eighth day, John and Jesus felt a strong trembling in the ground. To the south rose a great cloud of dust. At the same time, a similar pillar of dust rose to the west. Soon the earth was quaking, and rock was falling into the canyon, but the Pulpit remained steady and unshaken. John asked Ruha, "What is happening?"

"Watch and see," she replied.

As John watched, boulders shot into the sky and two massive heads appeared over the rim of the canyon, approaching from the south and west. The beings appeared to be made of rock themselves, and the ground shivered at the impact of their steps. As they approached the parking lot, cars, lampposts and other metal objects took flight and clung to the sides of their legs.

"Who, or what, are they?" John cried.

"They have gone by many names: Gog and Magog, Wolf and Coyote, the Nephilim, Messiah ben Joseph and Messiah ben David, but their real names are Ptahil and Abatur Rama d-Muzania, the Fourth Life and the Third Life. Ptahil rose from the earth under Tabernacle Dome, and Abatur rose from under the Three Patriarchs."

John began shivering. He had dreamt of the day he would meet his maker, but he had never dreamed this dreadful nightmare. My creator is a two-hundred-foot magnetic being made of rock? And his father is not my Lord, but another huge rock being, and he's going to weigh my soul. This is way too much to take.

He looked at Ruha, who now wore a flowing white robe and seemed to be iridescent and almost transparent. Her eyes were fixed on the two giants, whose bulk closed off the end of the canyon as they settled over the river. Their rock faces were impassive as their dull eyes swept over the canyon. Ruha nodded and raised her arms toward them. The two giant heads nodded slightly, and she turned to look over the side of the Pulpit. The river water quickly started to flow toward the Pulpit, at first sinking into the parched desert ground. There seemed to be much more water than the meager river would provide, and the level slowly crept up the sides of the Pulpit. Soon the water was so high that Ruha was able to lean down and dip a pitcher into it. The water stopped rising, and Ruha turned with the pitcher and gestured to John to retake his seat at the altar. She then turned to Jesus and indicated he should take the adjacent seat.

John, barely able to walk due to the violent shaking of his body, slowly made his way to the altar and took his seat. Ruha approached the two and indicated they should bow their heads. She then poured the water over each saying, "In the name of the First Life! Let every man whose strength enables him and who loves his soul, come and be baptized, and receive the Pure Sign. It is the water in which we clothe ourselves and put on robes of radiant light."

The water flowed down from the men's heads, down over their shoulders, torsos and legs, leaving behind shimmering, glowing robes. "And now rise," Ruha commanded. John and Jesus rose to their feet and continued rising several feet into the air. Jesus took this better than John, who waved his arms and legs and flailed in a futile effort to climb down out of the air.

"Don't be afraid, John," Ruha said. "You have been finally prepared for your witness." John stopped flailing and hung in the air next to Jesus, who turned and smiled at him. "Be of good cheer, John. We are part of a momentous process. I am sure you would not have been chosen if you were not worthy."

John smiled weakly and reached out for Jesus' hand. "You may not be who I thought you were, but I am glad you are by my side. You give me strength to carry on."

Ruha said, "The weighing of souls will begin with the Unredeemables, who do not need to be weighed, but they do need to be ushered into the Dark World." With that she turned to Ptahil and Abatur Rama d-Muzania and nodded. They nodded back and turned their huge heads to the sky, which was full of dark figures whirling in the quadrants of the clouds. At their glance, a stream of figures broke away from the northern quadrant and poured toward the stone giants. The stream blotted out the rest of the sky as it swooped toward The Pulpit. When it encountered the rock of The

Pulpit, it split in two and each stream entered one of the stone mouths, which were gaping open. The sound was terrifying, as each soul screamed horrifically as it passed the Pulpit and entered Ptahil's and Abatur's mouths.

John and Jesus continue to observe, floating above the rock of the Pulpit as the streams continued for hours, then days, then for three days. The two men were not aware of any fatigue during this process and remained vigilant as the souls streamed past.

On the evening of the third day, the torrent of souls was finished. Ruha said, "Although you two have been exalted as Witnesses, you are still mortal, and need rest. Please take your rest and be refreshed, for tomorrow begins the weighing of souls." John and Jesus alighted back onto the floor of The Pulpit and noticed two fine beds, with embroidered silk sheets and plump pillows, awaited them. They went to bed and fell instantly to sleep.

The next day, at sunrise, they awoke to Ruha singing a wordless song. It sounds sad, John thought. He arose and went over to Ruha, who was turned away from him. He looked at her face and saw she was grieving and in pain. "Ruha! What is the matter?"

"My world. My world is ending. When the last soul is weighed, this world will be done. I will have lost everything."

"What will become of you?"

"I am bound to serve Ptahil, who will undoubtedly try again to create a perfect world." Ruha sighed. "I suppose I should look forward to that, rather than mourning this ending."

John put his arm around her shoulders and nodded. "I understand. I, too, have lost everything. I don't know what has become of my wife, my family, my friends. I've been terrified that I would recognize one or more of them as the dark souls streamed by." John began to cry, and Ruha joined him.

Jesus watched this from his bed. He got up and approached the two, enfolding them both in his arms. The three remained like that for 10 minutes before Ruha shook herself and said, "It is time."

"What will happen?" John asked. "Will there be streams of souls like with the Unredeemables?"

"No," Ruha replied. "All will be weighed on the scale and ascend on their assigned path, either through the purifying worlds, or to join the First Life. Their lives are more virtuous, so they are spared terror and fear. They will leave their bodies behind and appear before Abatur on the scale." As she said this, the two witnesses looked across to the two giants and there was a huge two-panned balance scale in front of Abatur. John and Jesus rose into position, and Ruha nodded at Abatur, whose rocky face looked distinctly unhappy.

"It's hard to tell, but it seems that Abatur is not happy about his task," John said.

"Yes. Abatur, the Lofty of the Scales, detests his job as scales guardian. Because his faulty instruction to his son during the creation of the world, he was forced into this job as punishment. He complains bitterly about that, and about being imprisoned in the rock while weighing souls for millennia."

John turned back to Abatur and the weighing began. The only sign that invisible souls were being weighed was a slight shivering of the pans of the scale as souls of differing weights passed over it in a split second.

Like the disposition of the Unredeemables, the process took three days. When it ended, Ruha said, "There are two souls left to weigh."

John and Jesus looked at each other, bewildered for a moment. Then they realized Ruha was referring to them.

"Are you ready?" Ruha asked.

John's fear was as palpable as the knot in his stomach. Unconsciously, he knew this moment would come, but with all the activity, he had not had any time to deal with it. He glanced at Jesus, who nodded at him. The two men turned to Ruha and said in unison, "So be it."

"As Witnesses, you are afforded the privilege of proceeding to the scale in the flesh. Which of you will be first?"

Jesus quickly said, "I will!"

John turned to him and, with tears in his eyes, said, "In a way, you are indeed my Savior! You are giving me a few moments more of life and I thank you for it."

Jesus floated out of the Pulpit and down to the scale. He turned back to Ruha and John and waved. He settled on the pan, which did not move at the addition of his weight. Then he was gone.

John embraced Ruha and said, "If I had known when I sought you out that this would be the result of our friendship, I'm not sure I would have done it. But I am glad to have played my part in this end. Goodbye." Ruha began weeping and nodded as John floated down to the scale and settled onto the pan. The scale moved a little, and then he was gone. A split second later, the world winked out of existence.

I believe in the rapture, below the waist

Fall Out Boy—*Bang The Doldrums*

Wow, thinks Charles, sitting at his keyboard. Wow, wow, wow!

Charles had been stuck for months on a single point in his latest attempt to start his novel: Who is the second witness to the Second Coming? He had relentlessly searched on Google to try to get a clue, from the Bible, from the Book of Mormon, from Mandaean scripture, from a host of other minor religions.

Finally, in an attempt to move beyond this stumbling block, Charles had decided to just start a description of the witness, with no thought of how the sentence would end. Then, pow! Partway through the description, his fingers wrote: "'I am Jesus, the son of Joseph, the carpenter,' the man replied simply."

"Holy shit!" Charles exclaims. Everything just fell into place in a moment of inspiration! Now I know how the chapter will end! It is perfect. My fucking subconscious. It—I— knew all along.

Charles sits in awe of how seamlessly the rest of the fragments that had been whirling in his mind for months had suddenly joined into a coherent narrative. He begins typing like a madman, pouring out a thousand words before he collapses, exhausted, onto his couch.

After another week of writing, Charles is done. He prints the chapter and texts Chip: "You got time to review my latest attempt?" Charles throws *Sticky Fingers* on his record player, cranks the volume, and skitters across the linoleum of his kitchen like a spider on a hot frying pan, jumping and sliding from one side to the other, pumping his arms over his head, and shouting. He pulls his phone from his pocket a dozen times, looking for Chip's reply. When it comes, it's disappointing: "Can't do it now, my droog. How about dinner?"

Charles doesn't like to meet with Chip for dinner to discuss his writing. Eating is so distracting. He'd rather the two would meet at his apartment, or Chip's office or man cave, or at least over a drink. "OK, when and where?" he replies, and the two make plans to have dinner.

Charles is so het up, he grabs his keys and races downstairs to his car, leaving the Stones blaring away. It's a couple of hours until dinner, but he just has to do something. He decides to go to the beach.

Heading north on Miami Avenue, he passes the Seventh Day Adventist Church. Hmmm. Speaking of taking the Bible literally, Charles thinks. Those guys believe every line in Revelations—all the righteous dead resurrected, and, along with the righteous living, taken straight to Heaven. Maybe I should have worked some of their perspective into the chapter. I wonder how they reconcile the various contradictions of Bible verses? Jesus comes back as lightning from the east that is also seen in the west, and also like a thief in the night.

Already the neighborhood is less shabby as he gets closer to 79th street, the beeline to the beach. He passes an abandoned shell of a six-story condo complex that is waiting for better times to resume construction. He passes a boat storage place festooned with razor wire across from an abandoned strip mall. Crossing over Little River improves the landscape a little. He notices a shiny CVS Pharmacy across from a high-rise, more boat storage, without razor wire. Things are looking up, yet down a few more blocks, there's an empty lot across from a failed car wash. Charles thinks, how do you fail at washing cars down here in Florida? Just before the causeway, 20 stories of condos, and then he's out onto the bridge.

It feels like escaping from a third world country, Charles thinks. The water is beautiful, and he rolls down his window to breathe the salt on the hot, humid air. He catches his first glimpse of the high-rises of North Bay Village. The island is bright, clean, and walled. Charles is getting closer and closer to the big money; the high-rises are getting thicker, huge slabs of opulence and privilege. Another causeway and he's on North Beach. He's getting impatient now as he gets closer to the sea. He speeds up a little and soon pulls into the parking lot of a Subway, gets out, and almost runs to the beach, ducking through a little pavilion and shucking his socks and shoes to walk out on the scorching sand. He runs down to the waterline to cool off his feet and just stands there, watching the boats passing by in their random pursuit of happiness.

Charles stands there without moving, transfixed, for 15 minutes. This is what feeds my soul, he thinks. The ceaseless waves, the blowing wind, the crying birds, bright sun, clouds. He tries to get to the beach at least once a week, which makes him different from Miami natives, who might spend months without seeing the water.

Certainly, the folks who live in my neighborhood never go to the beach, he thinks. It's the same everywhere. When I was in California, I met a guy in Long Beach who was 30 years old and had never seen the ocean, eight blocks away. I want to keep this special, but regular.

After another several minutes absorbing the salty breeze, Charles walks up and down the beach for a bit, then climbs back into his car to head to dinner with Chip at a pizza and coffee place not too far away on the mainland, but on the right side of the tracks.

Chip's not there when Charles shows up. He's always wary of taking a table until his friend appears since Chip is often late or doesn't come at all due to some congregation emergency. So, he sits in a straight back chair in the waiting area. It seems like forever, but Chip eventually shows up half an hour late.

"Did your order for us?"

"Chip you know I wouldn't do that. You might not show."

"Sorry. A guy just got the news he's got stage 3 bone marrow cancer, so I got a little involved."

Charles now feels like a jerk for being pissed. "So sorry to hear that. How longs' he got?"

"A year or two. Let's see if we can eat fast. I need to get on over to the Haitian Emanuel Baptist Church to deliver a package to Pastor Dabrezil before 7:30."

Great, Charles thinks. Another rushed dinner with Chip. He's not going to be able to focus on my chapter. The two order a pizza and Chip begins reading the chapter. Charles, as usual, is uncomfortable and concentrates on his glass of Cabernet and surreptitiously ogling the two young ladies at the table adjacent to them. After a while, they catch him at it and smile. He reddens, jerking his glance away to a nearby window. Their pizza arrives and still Chip is reading.

Finally, Chip surfaces. "This is more like a short story than a novel. You go through a whole book's worth of stuff in 30 pages. That said, it's not bad."

"Go on. I sense a 'but' coming up."

"But me no butts, buttinsky! There's no but, kinda like you. You're a . . . what's the opposite of bubble butt? Crater butt?"

"So fucking funny!"

Chip continues. "Anyway, I guess my whole problem is the approach to the Second Coming. I really don't like this whole 'second coming as disaster' attitude, in your chapter but also in general. I would deconstruct any apocalyptic system or idea as the ultimate in pessimistic theology. I prefer the optimism of God's love. I see Jesus as having a focus on the ultimate being, constantly wanting to redeem creation rather than end it. In the Jewish tradition, the apocalypse is not an ending, but a beginning to God's righteous reign on Earth. You kind of nod to that in some of the Mormonism discussion, but it's fundamental to a true understanding of Christianity."

Around a mouthful of pizza, Charles says, "But how can you have judgment without people getting, if not banished to hell, at least hurt? Maybe not burned in global fire, but at the least denied what the righteous have. There's no mention in the Bible of any rehabilitation or salvation for evil ones. There's no sense of God's forgiveness from what I can see. It's dualism: Heaven for the righteous and Hell for the rest. Humans comprised of body and soul, one corruptible and the other eternal. And morality is largely based on 'body bad; spirit good.'"

"Well, not all religious thinkers accept dualism, at least as you're presenting it. For example, there's a group of Catholic intellectuals called the New Natural Lawyers . . ."

"Great. Lawyers opining on metaphysics."

Annoyed, Chip says, "No, you dolt. They're not legal lawyers. This bunch promulgated something called the New Natural Law. Law, Lawyers. Get it?"

"OK, continue, your honor." Charles wonders if Chip's in a bad mood because of that guy's cancer diagnosis.

"So, the New Natural Law has three major components that build upon one another. The first component is practical reason, which describes basic goods necessary for mankind to flourish: life and health; knowledge and aesthetic experience; skilled work and play; friendship; marriage;

harmony with God, and harmony among a person's judgments, choices, feelings, and behavior."

"Sounds good so far, although you know I'd quibble over the God business."

"Of course, you worthless heathen. The second component says these 'goods' are equally useful and beneficial. One is not better than the other, but each delivers a unique benefit to humans."

"I'll bet there's a ton of Christian conservatives that would argue that point."

"No doubt. Now shut up while I illuminate you, pesky acolyte."

Charles rolls his eyes, places his hands together, and does a little bow, saying, "Namaste, you namaste asshole."

This seems to cheer Chip up a bit, and he grins. "So, anyway, this second component is seen as a support for free will or free choice. The third point follows from the first two: the pursuit of these 'goods' is not inherently moral. The intent must be good when making choices to pursue the various 'goods.' And good is defined, in part, as always striving to contribute to communal well-being and avoiding detracting from communal fulfillment. So, there you go. A moral code without resorting to dualism."

"Well, I'll admit it's interesting, but I don't see Natural Lawyer churches— or would they be courtrooms—all over the landscape. Instead, we've got tons of bizarre churches, like that Seventh Day church I passed today over on Miami Avenue. But, let's get back to talking about my chapter. You'd see the Second Coming as a positive event, OK, I get that. But what about the bad guys? Even your Lawyers must admit to the problem of evil. What about Hell and Purgatory?"

"Well, you know United Methodists don't believe in Purgatory, like you Papists do."

Again, Charles rolls his eyes, then sticks out his tongue and makes the "Gag me" sign.

"Look," Chip continues. "I don't believe in the lake of fire. But United Methodists do believe in the resurrection of the dead—the righteous to life eternal and the wicked to endless condemnation. We believe in free will. A pastor named Rob Bell put it this way: 'We are free to resist, reject, and rebel against God's ways for us. We can have all the hell we want.' That said, the Methodist church doesn't officially describe Hell, relying on various of Jesus' statements which, while not terribly specific, generally refer to fire. But we preach about Jesus' grace and love, and not about Hell. So, I'm not much help for you there."

Charles is disappointed. Chip criticized his vision of the Apocalypse but can't or won't offer advice on improving it. Fuck it, Charles decides. I'm not changing the flavor of the End Times. It will play well with the mainstream reader, anyway.

"OK, what else do you have to say about the chapter?"

"My other problem with this chapter is it needs more color and a sense of humor. I want to laugh at this ridiculous crap that you spew in your hodgepodge of apocalyptic traditions. This shit is hilarious. Don't you realize that?" Chip jams half a slice of pizza into his mouth and grunts in pain as it burns the roof of his mouth.

Charles is a bit taken aback. Although he had added a few odd comic touches, he meant the chapter to be serious. "No, man, I don't think it's that funny. I created a whole new apocalyptic scenario from all these disparate bits, and I meant it to be taken seriously, or more accurately, satirically, rather than comical. Besides, there's funny stuff in there. You didn't find the Kraut on the roof funny?"

"Well . . . yeah. Of course, derivative of *Springtime for Hitler*."

Charles smiles. He figured his friend, a complete movie nut, would get the reference. "Well, if you're going to steal, steal from the best, I always say. Anyway, how about John almost getting clocked by the redneck? Funny, right?"

"Yes . . ."

"And the left-behind fundamentalist?"

"Yeah, yeah, yeah, but . . ."

"How about the ukulele of the leader of the Illuminati?"

"Yup. Well, yes. That was a bit incongruous, but you didn't really do anything with it. It was a bit of that color like what I was looking for, but that business in particular seemed out of place."

Charles thinks for a moment. "How 'bout I have the leader plead for one last favor before he gets judged? Like, maybe he asks if he can play 'It's the End of the World as We Know it?'" Charles pauses to think. "Now that I think of it, there are some pretty relevant lyrics in that song: 'That's great! It starts with an earthquake, birds and snakes, an aeroplane.' Also, hmmm, just let me bring it up on my phone here, yes. 'The ladder starts to clatter with fear, fight, down, height.' That's John and Ruha going up on the Pulpit. 'Team by team reporters baffled, trumped, tethered, cropped.' The scene with the reporter in Vegas. Um, 'Save yourself, serve yourself,' kinda what the Illuminati did. 'Continental drift divide. Mountains sit in a line' that's our animated mountains."

"OK, OK, I get it," Chip says.

Charles wonders what's bugging his friend. He's certainly on edge tonight.

Chip says, "Yes, that would be pretty funny if the old guy plays that song on the ukulele and then gets gobbled by 'Ur. But not the whole song. Perhaps he confuses the verses so they all hang together and then 'Ur gets him before he finishes?"

"That could work. But I don't really want to turn the whole thing into a joke like I did with that first chapter I showed you with the three wise guys."

"No, I don't think that's what I'm looking for. It's just that the whole thing is relentlessly serious, but the pieces are incongruous. For example, I assume you picked the Nazi guard to show that John and his God can redeem anyone."

"Right, but I don't think she's that evil, at least in her earthly incarnation. She joined to save herself and was just a dormitory guard. She witnessed all the horror."

"So kinda like, you have to watch but you don't have to do?"

"Right."

"Well, for me, being complicit in an evil thing, no matter how tangentially, makes you responsible," Chip says.

"OK, that's a good perspective. But remember, she has a dual nature—she doesn't know at that point that she's the demiurge of our world. And in Mandaean religion, Ruha is a very conflicted character, at the same time reviled and revered. She's responsible for evil, and for inspiration, and for nurturing the Earth. Without her, Adam couldn't stand up and was a vegetable. And she created the flawed world in the first place, under Ptahil's instructions. And, if you really want to get deep into duality, she brought forth the planets in the solar system by sleeping with her son, 'Ur. Incest, just like in Genesis. By the way, she's not at all satisfied with the way the planets turned out, so she sleeps with 'Ur again and produces the 12 zodiac spirits. Not sure that was an improvement. So 'conflicted' doesn't even begin to describe her. That's what I was going for when I made her a Nazi guard."

Chip thinks for a moment as he finishes the last slice of pizza. "OK, how about this: As part of his building of the Third Temple, John creates, like, a theme park ride through Mormonism. You know, hop in a boat on a rail and ride past Joseph Smith digging up the golden plates, Brigham Young leading the move Westward, the whole kit and caboodle. It would be hilarious, especially if it featured an animatronic plural family."

Charles has to admit this would be pretty funny. "Yeah, I definitely planned on blowing out the whole struggle John goes through to convince the Elders, get ordained, and so getting a Brigham Young campus designated Mormon World would be pretty funny. But I don't want to go all Broadway 'The Book of Mormon' here."

Chip said, "OK, beloved, I need to leave. I gotta get over to Emanuel Baptist in 10 minutes. But speaking of Mormon satire, I have to tell you my favorite Mormon joke."

"I hope it's better than your last joke."

"I'll let you decide. A Mormon bishop gets on an elevator and a beautiful woman walks in. On the way to the lobby, the gorgeous woman hits the stop button. She turns to the bishop and says: 'Can you make me feel like a true woman?' The bishop says: 'I sure can' and excitedly takes off all his clothes and throws them in the corner of the elevator. He turns to the woman and points to the clothes and says, 'Now fold them'."

Chip starts laughing his head off while Charles just groans. "Worse, way worse than the last one."

"I live to serve. Be good." Chip hustles out of the restaurant, leaving Charles to pay the bill.

She's got everything she needs, she's an artist, she don't look bad

Bob Dylan—*She Belongs to Me*

Edie rushes at Charles bearing a battle ax with a demonic look on her face. Charles ducks behind an armoire and Edie splinters it with a single blow. Charles crawls down the stairs on all fours. He can't get his limbs to work fast enough to keep ahead of the huge, green, wriggling worms controlled by silver leashes bunched in Edie's enormous grotesque fists. He falls through the landing into a swimming pool of blood. Edie surfaces and grabs him by the neck. "You never loved me!" she screams, exposing six-inch-long fangs. Her gaping mouth moves closer and closer despite Charles's desperate attempts to fight her off. Just as her jaws close around his dick, Charles wakes with a shout, sitting bolt upright in his bed, shivering and sweating.

"Get the fuck away from me!" he screams. Hyperventilating, he writhes and twists, trying to brush the worms off his skin. It takes another few seconds for him to come to his senses. Thank god, he thinks. Only a dream. He shivers at the recollection. Why in hell did I dream about Edie after all these years? I haven't given her a thought in forever.

Charles swivels, sets his feet on the bedroom floor, and shakes his head as if clearing cobwebs. His sheets are soaked. Charles sleeps in the nude, so when he stands up facing his bedroom mirror, he can see that his manhood is intact. He groggily schlumps into the bathroom and plops down on the toilet. He can't figure out any reason why his old flame should have visited his dreams.

Later, dressed, shaved, and somewhat pulled together, Charles rustles through a box of old manuscripts, looking for the only poem he ever wrote about Edie. He finally finds it and sits on his couch to read it.

> Breathe upon my arm,
> The hairs stand
> In tingles. Your mist
> And hazy presence
> Settle
> In my senses.
> I sigh, and feel desire
> Diffuse and buried
> Pounding through sweet cotton.
>
> You are an event
> That happens to me.
> I cannot say
> How much I imagine.
>
> Walking, thinking of you
> Out upon the grass,
> Or in the morning, at the mirror,
> My lips tremble to the touch
> Of tender breezes.
>
> Feel the music
> As you move
> As you curl
> On a pillow by the window
> My soul purrs.
>
> You slant your head,
> Parting lips to speak,
> But what I hear
> Are words from all your ages,
> Rebecca, Leah, Mary,
> Sinuous in grace.

Edie hated this poem, Charles thinks. She said, "Get this fucking thing out of my life!" And I never wrote another about her, or at least never showed her another. Thoroughly bummed now, Charles leans back against the couch, lights a cigarette, and remembers Edie.

Charles and Edie met in graduate school in Denver in the fall of 1975. Edie was a tall, long-faced, small-breasted dirty blonde with narrow hips and a blocky butt who was five years older than him. Her wire-rimmed Granny glasses, holey jeans, and flower-girl-gone-to-seed persona belied her cynical attitude. She lived with two roommates—a Bible-thumping Southern cracker closeted lesbian and a skinny, rigid, pole up her butt librarian, both of whom she drove quite mad—in the graduate dorm apartment just below Charles's. Charles was in his second year in the master's program in creative writing, and Edie was in her first year getting an MFA in photography.

By the second week of fall semester, on their second date, Charles and Edie slept together, a screeching, frantic, high-energy affair on Edie's part that excited yet intimidated Charles. Although he was a fairly experienced lover, having had a steady girlfriend since sophomore year in college, he was used to a bit more leisurely pace.

One night, in late fall, Charles and Edie were walking down the deserted quad, on the way back to the dorm after watching *The Seventh Seal*. They were holding hands and chatting idly about Bergman when the double report of a pair of firecrackers echoed loudly through the quad. Edie screamed "Incoming!" broke away from Charles quick as a cat and hit the ground, rolling into the shelter of a nearby bush. Charles was stunned and stared at the spectacle of his new girlfriend cowering behind the bush.

Edie stood up and sheepishly brushed the leaf stubble off her jeans. "Uh, sorry," she said. "Ever since Nam, loud noises really freak me out." She clutched her sides and shivered. Edie had recently confided that she had spent three years after college as one of the first female photojournalists in Viet Nam.

Charles picked a few twigs from the back of Edie's sweater and said, "Wow! That was really something. Did you have some kind flashback?"

"No, it's not really like that—the acid metaphor really doesn't quite work—although something like this does put me back in the jungle emotionally. You know, the terrifying sound of the guns, the mortars, the dying. Shit." By now the shivers had turned to shaking and Charles quickly put his arm around her. "That was worse than the dreams," she said.

"You dream about Nam?"

"Yeah, most nights. Sometimes it's OK. I'm with my patrol in-country and there's no sound, but I can smell them, I can feel their heat, and sense the Cong all around us. But I feel OK. I'm not afraid, just exhilarated. I'm safe. I know the unit will protect me." Edie sighed and wiped her nose. "Other times, we're pinned down by gook fire and every man in the patrol is ripped to shreds around me. Everybody but me. I usually wake up screaming." She eyed Charles. "So, you've got that to look forward to, if you ever let me stay over," she said with a grim smile.

Charles was quite particular about his bedtime habits. Having slept solo in a double bed since his early childhood, he wasn't comfortable sharing a bed with anyone, and so always asked Edie to return to her first-floor apartment after late-night lovemaking. That this had already become a bone of contention, mere weeks after they started sleeping together, baffled and irritated Charles. He thought Edie lacked an understanding of the concept of personal space. She even wanted to keep a toothbrush in his apartment, which Charles thought ludicrous because there were six feet of hallway and ten stair steps between their two apartments, as he pointed out repeatedly. Edie said she had bad teeth and brushed up to eight times a day, and why was it such a big deal to keep a lousy toothbrush where she could use it?

"Well, you make spending the night sound damn attractive!" Charles had said with a smile, hoping to lighten the mood. Edie had just looked at him gloomily and said nothing.

Edie's shivers had mostly subsided, so Charles said, "C'mon, let's go get a beer to calm down," He steered Edie in the direction of the little student ghetto across the street from the campus.

In the deep gloom of the Hoffbrau, B. B. King's "The Thrill is Gone" was on the jukebox. At a scarred dark oak table with a guttering candle in a red tulip vase covered in plastic netting, Charles ordered a pitcher of beer and looked compassionately at Edie, who was silently weeping, tears melting down her cheeks.

"You want to talk about it?"

"No. Not really. You know, it wasn't that long ago. I came home on an Operation Babylift plane last April."

"What's Operation Babylift?"

"Oh, it was just the saddest thing ever. You know it was chaos when we pulled out of South Viet Nam, right? Choppers taking off from the roof of the Saigon Hilton and all? Well, chaos doesn't even begin to describe it. It was hell on Earth. Everybody and his brother was trying to get a ride out. Civilians, I mean. But even the soldiers were scrambling. When that asshole Kissinger sealed the deal in Paris, nobody had planned the goddamned retreat. And once that bastard Nixon got chased from office and replaced by the current Boob in Chief, I guess things got a little crazy at the top. Then Congress refused to continue the war funding, and we were sitting ducks."

The waitress set the pitcher down along with two frozen mugs. Edie grabbed one and poured beer into it quickly, mindless of the burgeoning head. She placed both hands around the ice-slick mug and tipped its contents into her mouth in one quick motion, draining it within seconds. Wiping her mouth with her hand, she refilled, more slowly, and then filled Charles's mug. "God, I needed that," she said, and then burped loudly.

"So, it was crazy in Saigon at the end, huh? Yeah, I saw the news footage of the helicopters on the roof. It was heartbreaking."

"Shit!" Edie said, with a look of disgust. "You wouldn't know heartbreaking if it bit you on the butt, you strait-laced asshole!"

"Whoa!" Charles recoiled against the wooden back of the booth. "Take it easy! I don't think I deserve that."

Edie drank another long draught of beer before answering, "Yeah, sorry, you're right. I get a little crazy when people who weren't in the shit act like they know what it was like. You see, I was a civilian. After I finished my nursing degree and worked in a hospital for a year, I decided I really couldn't hack being a nurse, kowtowing to the docs all day and having little real power. So, I had a little bit of money left from a scholarship and decided I would go take photos of the war. Thought it would be thrilling. Showed up in Saigon about three or so years ago and managed to wangle a journalist credential from a guy who worked for *Look* who my dad—my fucking famous heart surgeon dad—knew. *Look* bought some of my photos, but I was basically a free agent, a stringer. And for the whole time I was there, I was generally the only poontang around, if you can imagine what that was like." She regarded Charles coldly, then rapped the table, making him jump. "Just think about the worst fucking thing you can possibly imagine and double it, Charles," Edie finished with a sneer.

Charles sipped a bit of his beer and tried to shake off his irritation at Edie's unfair outburst. "Tell me all about it, sweetie."

Edie sagged back against the back of the booth and heaved a big sigh. "I dunno," she said wearily. "I don't know if I'm up for that." After a minute and more beer, she continued, "You know, I don't know who I'm maddest at: that arrogant cocksucker criminal Kissinger; Nixon, his certifiably insane partner in crime; or the chicken-shit Congress who refused to fund any South Vietnamese resistance to the North's final offensive that chased us out of Saigon like a bunch of goddamned cowards."

Edie took off her glasses and wiped at them with the tail of her shirt. Charles extended his hand across the table palm up. Edie glanced at the hand and continued polishing her glasses. Embarrassed, Charles arced his hand to his mug and tried to act like that was the idea all along. After a long silence punctuated only by the clicking of the billiard balls across the mostly empty bar, Edie sighed again and said, "Look, Charles, I may be mad, but I'm not mad at you. Sorry I'm acting like a bitch . . ." She sniffed and blew her nose in the damp napkin from beneath her beer.

Charles assured her he understood while secretly wondering what kind of screwed up devil woman he had gotten himself involved with.

"It's just that all this shit is still too fresh. I decided to give up photojournalism and get a fine arts photo degree to try and help put this crap behind me. But I think I'm still a little batshit crazy . . ."

"Look, Edie, if you don't want to get into this, that's just fine with me," Charles said, a bit stiffly. "All I want to do is help, and if it helps to talk, great. If not, great." Charles was still miffed. He dug in his jacket pocket for a roll of Certs, peeled one off the top, and popped it in his mouth, then winced as the peppermint taste mixed with the taste of the beer.

"No, I guess you have a right to know what's going on with me, especially when I act like Shell-Shocked Suzy." Edie managed a tight smile. "So, here goes. I'll tell you what it was like getting my ass out of Saigon." Edie took a big breath and slowly let it out, whistling between her teeth.

"You see, *Look* mag just didn't give a shit about me. I was never real official even with the press cred. They bought maybe 20 photos from me the whole three years I was there. But I was putting my butt on the line every day, living with the grunts and even traveling with them on patrol. And all I got was the same grub they ate, as well as unwanted attention from every grabby officer around when they were on R&R."

"Did the, uh, grunts, ever make a pass at you?"

"No, they pretty much accepted me once they realized I was putting my butt out there too. They actually hoped I'd make them famous, getting them in the magazine. In fact, it was often difficult to get unposed pictures of them, at least at the beginning. They all wanted to look so damn heroic on the cover of *Look*. Like I'd ever get the cover of *Look*!

"Anyway, after the Paris treaty was signed in early '73, I knew, I just knew, it was all going to end badly. The Viet Cong weren't going to honor any cease fire, and it was only a matter of time before they went on the offensive again. And sure enough, that happened this past spring, and as soon as I heard they were on the move, I spent every waking hour trying to get a ride out. I was flat broke—you try to live on a grand or so for three years. I wasn't military, so I had little chance of airlifting out with the GIs. The goddamned Thieu government commandeered every plane, truck, or boat available to get their families and their sorry asses out of Dodge.

"And, like I said, my *Look* friends were hardly interested in lifting a finger to help me. As Charlie got closer to Saigon, though, I heard of a plan to get the sons and daughters of US GIs out via something called Operation Babylift. There were four flights planned out of Tan Son Nhut, and I managed to bluff my way onto the tarmac for the last one with my press pass and my nursing license. They were loading the plane, and Charles, you can't imagine the atmosphere. The Cong were firing rockets into the airport, and it was a complete, utter madhouse. Buses, jeeps, jitneys—all kinds of vehicles were pulling up and disgorging dozens of kids, some half Vietnamese, but some obviously full Vietnamese. The nurses and GIs would scoop them up and hustle them toward the plane. I got wind of the fact that since so many were toddlers or younger and many of those sick, they needed seat fillers—they called them lap holders—to go on the plane and take care of the kids on their way to Seattle.

"As soon as I heard this, I ran like hell for the plane, which was more than half full already. Screaming 'Press, press!' I bulled my way on board and threw myself into this little canvas seat attached to the side of the C-141. Almost immediately a nurse plopped a kid on my lap and told me to belt in. The kid, a beautiful little half-Vietnamese girl with blue eyes who looked like she was three or four months old, was sicker than a dog, burning up. She immediately barfed all over me but continued to smile up into my face. She had the most beautiful smile. Her teeny little hands kept grabbing my camouflage blouse. I'm sure I looked like hell and smelled like a beast, having lived in those clothes for several days by that time, and with barf all over. But she just kept beaming at me like I was some kind of angel.

"After only a couple more minutes, the plane was full, and we took off like a shot, at a steep angle to avoid Charlie's rockets. The plane was a madhouse—dozens of screaming kids in little cribs attached to the Starlifter's deck, with scared adults yelling and screaming for water, food, or new diapers, or whatever. Turns out a couple of spooked MPs had dumped the food and supplies just before takeoff; don't know why. Even though we ran out of water an hour into the flight, things calmed down a bit after we'd been over ocean for a while, and me and Sunshine—that's what I named her—grabbed a few winks.

"Because of the lack of water and such, we were diverted to Clark air base in the Philippines. When we landed, I wouldn't leave the plane and I wouldn't turn Sunshine loose either. I don't know what my deal was. I just wanted to sit there with Sunshine. I had that maudlin little flower child song, "Wear Some Flowers in Your Hair," running through my head. I think I was pretty crazy at that point. I was dehydrated, hadn't eaten in three days, had hardly slept on the flight, and had a hard time concentrating on anything but that shitty song and Sunshine.

"Finally, an official-looking doctor came on board and sat down next to me. 'Miss,' he said gently, 'You're here; you're safe, and I need to take that little girl and get her looked at right away.' I looked at him like he was from outer space. Then I looked at Sunshine, who was either asleep or passed out. I looked back at the doc, who had a somewhat goofy smile on his face, and handed him Sunshine. 'You have to let me visit her,' I pleaded. 'I have to know she's all right. Please.' 'Sure,' he said, but I never saw Sunshine again."

Edie began to cry, this time for real. Huge racking sobs shook her body as Charles slipped out of his seat and pushed in beside her, putting his arms around her.

Say baby I love you / If you ain't running gay

Destiny's Child's—*Say My Name*

Charles drives over to Chip's house. He tries not to go there too often since Chip's wife Trixie felt they had enough visitors, what with church folk constantly coming by to seek Chip's advice, blessing, or to help him with various house and yard chores. The house is a low, long, cinder-block-walled, flat-roofed, typical south Florida home. It was painted, badly, an institutional lime green.

Charles knocks on the front door and Trixie lets him in. Charles can't tell if she's annoyed that he's come over or just peeved to be interrupted.

"Hi, Charles. I was just stripping the kitchen floor. Damned ancient linoleum. Stupid church building committee won't pry loose the money to replace it. Ruins my nails whenever I have to do this."

"Wow, you never hear of anyone having to strip the wax off floors anymore. What a bummer."

"To live is to suffer, my daddy used to say."

Trixie, born Beatrix, was from an old, traditional Southern Baptist family that had been heavy into sugar cane in Cuba until Castro overthrew Batista in 1959. Her father, Beauregard Pettus, lost his fortune as a result of the revolution. During Trixie's younger years, her father struggled to rebuild his cane business in Florida, fighting displaced Cuban cane growers for a share of a market that was nowhere near as lucrative. Beauregard was as conservative as they come, in both his business and his religion. When the strong-willed Trixie told her father she wanted to marry a United Methodist minister, he threatened to disown her. They married anyway, and her father did not carry through his threat but did refuse to attend the wedding. Trixie and her father have rarely spoken ever since, nor has Trixie seen much of the rest of her family, despite them living up the coast a ways in Vero Beach.

"Well, enough about me. Charles how ya doon?"

"I am well, thanks for asking. At least I don't have to strip my kitchen floor. Or maybe I should. It might be as old as yours." They both laugh.

"Charles is down in the 'Man Cave.' Go on down." Charles notices Trixie also has the habit of emphasizing things with air quotes.

Charles heads down the stairs. Chip's parsonage sits on the edge of an old sinkhole and, because of the drop in grade, actually has a walkout basement, unlike the vast majority of Florida houses, and a pool in the backyard. The room opens out to a patio underneath the first-floor deck, and thus is partially lit with natural light. The two sit across from one another on parallel couches. Between them is a table Chip made from a weathered wooden high-tension wire spool upon which he had painted the red N of Nebraska football.

After the two open a couple of beers, they are idly chatting about women when Chip asks, "What's the deal with the ring, dude? I've been meaning to ask. You haven't been married for years." Charles holds up his left hand and looks at the gold and silver wedding band, turning the hand back and forth.

"I made a commitment for life. I may be divorced, but I never stopped being married."

"So, you're a fucking monk—no nookie for all these years?"

"Well . . ." Charles begins but stops. He is sure Chip is going to tease him or call foul.

"Well, what, douchebag?"

"Well, she started it!" Charles says, trying to make light of the fact that not only was there a period after his divorce when he screwed anything with boobs, but he still occasionally swiped right on Tinder. And that was something he didn't want to get into with Chip.

"Blessed are those who rejoice in her, and do not burst forth in ways of folly, eh?" Chip quotes with a snort.

"What the fuck?" Charles said, utterly confused.

"Just baffling you with my erudition about the Dead Sea Scrolls, Padawan."

"Big deal, Scholar Boy. Anyway, I'll never take the ring off, and I'll never remarry, 'cause I'm still married."

"Well then, your wife's a bigamist! Didn't she get married to her lezzie lover once the law got changed in Oregon?"

Charles winces at the thought. Gay marriage is a sore point for him. In fact, he hates the idea of homosexuality in general. There had been many times during their marriage that Charles had thought maybe Karen was gay. Like Edie, about whom Charles had had similar suspicions, Karen had exceedingly close female friends, and when together, the women couldn't keep their hands off each other, hugging and smooching, if only on the cheeks. He always blocked these suspicions about his wife from his mind. Charles thinks, So . . . what? I'm only attracted to queer women? Am I that kind of sicko?

Pulling himself back out of reverie to the current conversation, Charles says, "I hate gay people. With good reason."

"So I gathered from your tirades in the *World*. But, dude, hate is a strong word to use on an entire class of humanity. John said, 'Whoever says he is in the light and hates his brother is still in darkness.'"

"John didn't have to live with my ex! I don't think I've ever told you about Munch."

"Munch? What's that? A new kind of potato chip?"

"No, Munch is Karen's wife."

". . . or maybe a new kind of rug?" Chip roars at his own stupid joke.

"Very funny, Chip. Munch stole my wife from me. Can I hate her?"

Chip, instantly becoming serious again, says, "Well, since I don't know the details, I can't say for sure, but probably Munch was just trying to pursue her own happiness. And you shouldn't hate anyone."

"Let me tell you the whole gory story," Charles proceeds to fill Chip in on his wife and the dissolution of his marriage.

After Charles married Karen, they were happy for a few years and had a son. But it wasn't long before he became suspicious that Karen was fooling around on him. Eventually, Karen confessed to two indiscretions.

The first one was with one of Charles's students. Charles had had a class over for dinner at the end of the semester and the student had groped her when she went into the laundry room for another bottle of vermouth. She had reprimanded him, but two weeks later, after finals, when he saw her at the campus soda shop, he asked her back to his dorm room to see his etchings—he was an art major and he actually did have etchings. They had no birth control handy, so she gave him a blowjob. That was almost worse for Charles. Seduction and the heat of the moment is one thing, but he thought of blowjobs as being rather calculated, and something that a person could help oneself from doing.

The second one was when an out of town friend came to stay for a week and Charles went on his first business trip in his new job. Although things between Charles and Karen had been better, the friend had always had a thing for Karen, and they had been smoking dope. They decided to play strip poker and when she was down to top and panties, she took off the panties, which the friend took as a sign that she wanted to screw. She had only taken the panties off because she was ashamed of her small breasts, however.

After confessing these incidents, Karen swore she would be faithful. But there was a final unfaithfulness that Charles didn't find out about for years. Munch, a teaching assistant Karen had met at Charles's son's preschool, became fast friends with Karen, and soon they were meeting for coffee in the afternoons when Karen picked up their son. Munch was married to a Syrian she met in graduate school. It was an apparent green card marriage, since the macho, Islamic Sepehr cared more about hanging out with his Syrian friends than spending any time with Munch. Charles actually suspected, from some of the random interactions he saw between Sep and his friends—the grappling, wrestling, and rolling around on the floor—that perhaps Sep was gay. No matter. He paid almost no attention to Munch who confided in Karen that they rarely made love.

Munch eventually demanded that Sep give her a child, and after some months of trying, Munch did become pregnant and bore Sep a daughter. This was, to Sep's mind, a huge disappointment. Of course, being a typical Middle Eastern man, he wanted a male heir. He neglected Munch and the child and spent even more time with his friends. Munch and Karen soon became inseparable and when Charles would come home from work, it was a rare day when Munch and little Katie weren't at his house, playing with his son. Charles brought this up with Karen, saying that it was hard enough for the two of them to have alone time without having these other people around all the time, eating dinner with them almost every night and staying until way after the kids' bedtimes.

"It's OK, sweetie. Munch really needs us right now," Karen said. "Sep has been married long enough to be able to stay in the US if he divorces her, and that's all he can talk about now. Poor Munch."

Charles resigned himself to hiding out in his study and working on a series of never-completed novels while the whole Munch/Sep divorce played itself out. In the process, he not only withdrew from his wife but also his son. When the heartbroken Munch, kicked out of the house by Sep pre-divorce, began living with them, it was the last straw for Charles.

"Look, Karen, she's got to find her own place right away."

"C'mon, Charles, you know she can't afford that on what she makes at the preschool."

"I don't care, Karen, her being here all the time is affecting our relationship, and I'm sick of it. I need her out of here right away."

"Well, if that's the way you feel, perhaps you can find your own place," Karen said in a cold voice. "I think we need a break."

Charles was stunned. Had he overplayed his hand? Was his relationship with his wife really that bad? How could things have deteriorated this far?

Luckily, Charles was scheduled to go to a week-long conference in San Francisco, so he persuaded Karen to agree to wait until he returned to discuss things further. "I'd really like it if Munch and Katie were gone when I got back," he said.

"You can dream," Karen replied.

While in San Francisco, Charles thought about trying to find Edie, who years ago had said she was moving there. He had mixed emotions. He was worried about her and whether she had managed to pull out of the tailspin she was in years before. But he also felt that she might actually have understood him better than Karen did. He went back and forth in his mind: Should I call her? Should I leave well-enough alone? Finally, Charles looked up her name in the white pages in a tiny phone booth in a crowded restaurant on the pier. There were three entries with her first initial. He sat there in the tiny booth for 10 minutes before deciding he lacked the courage to try them all.

Of course, Munch was still there when Charles returned home, but Karen had cooled down a bit. Nonetheless, she relegated Charles to sleep in his study, on the very uncomfortable old couch he often used to catch a catnap while writing. One evening, Karen went out with Munch and came home at 6:00 am the next morning after Charles had been up all night with worry.

"What were you two doing?"

"Oh, we just went out, got too drunk, and Munch had this idea to break into her and Sep's apartment. She knew he was out of town, so we did it. Did you know that Munch knows how to pick locks? I sure didn't. But we got in and decided we were too drunk to drive anywhere so we just stayed the night."

"And you couldn't call me? I've been sick with worry."

"Sorry, Charles. I was pretty out of it. Sorry."

Charles had his suspicions about that night. What had those two been doing? Was his wife gay? One thing was for sure: Karen no longer had any regard for his feelings or his love, so he packed and moved out. He had no illusions about getting back together with his wife, but if he had, the fact that Munch officially moved into his former house to live with Karen, and that friends were constantly sidling up to him and whispering that they had seen the two of them go into this or that lesbian bar downtown, seemed to make reconciliation an impossibility.

All his waking hours, Charles was plagued by thoughts of Karen's infidelity, of getting divorced, and the collapse of their marriage. Did Karen become unfaithful to goad him into leaving her? Was she just lonely and trying to fill a void? Had she always been a lesbian? Who left whom?

Charles hit the booze, grass, pills, quite hard in the aftermath. He ate compulsively and ballooned to almost 300 pounds. He clung to his job only because his boss was extremely understanding, having gone through a divorce himself. Eventually, Charles surfaced, breaking clear of the ocean of his grief, still married, and refusing all efforts by Karen to finalize the divorce. Even once he finally did sign the papers, he refused to take off his wedding ring.

After telling the tale, Charles lets out a huge sigh. "Afterward, I mostly felt betrayed. I was emotional, sure, and lovesick, but the betrayal thing was huge. It was a long time before I could trust anyone—male or female—again."

"Wow, man, that's tough, and it breaks my heart. But don't you think that Karen was perhaps always gay, or bi at the least? Don't you think that her acting out with other guys and eventually with Munch could have been a way for her to try to find her own happiness?"

"Why couldn't she have tried to find it with me?"

"Well, I don't rightly know, but did you even know she was unhappy?"

"No, I guess I didn't."

"Could you have?"

"Possibly."

"Did you do everything you possibly could to enable her happiness, or were you more concerned about your career, your friends, your life?"

Charles is stumped by the question. Had he really been the perfect partner for his ex-wife? He had to admit he hadn't. I've always had to have my own way, he thinks. I definitely could have done more to satisfy Karen. He thinks about their lovemaking in the years leading up to the split. He realizes that she probably hadn't been satisfied sexually for quite some time. And, he thinks, I'm not exactly the warmest person in the world. I certainly could have given her more support.

Chip, in full pastoral counseling mode now, says, "I'm not saying you're to blame. It takes two to tango, and if Karen had unfulfilled needs, it's reasonable to expect she should have taken the initiative to communicate them to you. So, don't worry, Little Buddy. We're all flawed, and we all make mistakes and sometimes shit happens for reasons we have no fucking idea about."

Charles manages a wan smile before saying, "Thanks, Father Confessor. I appreciate your insight, and I've got a lot to think about. But I'm not taking the ring off."

"Keep it on, sure. I'm not trying to get it off you. Just wondered why you still wear it."

Two days later, Charles publishes a column on the subject.

CHARLES BEAUMONT DEFRIES

Charles Beaumont DeFries: Gays Shouldn't Marry

HIGHLIGHTS

LGBTQ people are perverted.

Allowing them to marry is an an abomination.

Let's put them back in the closet.

BY CHARLES BEAUMONT DEFRIES
cdefries@miamiworld.com

Touted as an equal rights question, the question of gay marriage is likely to be decided by the courts, not by the people, in the case Pareto v. Ruvin. Far from reflecting the will of the people, a gay success in this case would be actually a major win for those who would legislate morality, and the politicians they own.

In case you haven't been paying attention, here's a summary of the case. On January 21, 2014, six same-sex couples and Equality Florida Institute filed a lawsuit in Florida state court in Miami claiming that Florida's laws barring same-sex couples from marriage violate the United States Constitution's Equal Protection and Due Process Clauses.

On July 25, 2014, that imbecilic court issued a decision striking down Florida's ban on marriage for same-sex couples and ordering Miami-Dade County to allow same-sex couples to marry. The court stayed the order pending appeal.

It's now looking likely that the court will lift its stay, perhaps as early as this week. Concerned Floridians need to make their voices heard to prevent this attack on the institution of marriage and prevent the spread of immoral behavior throughout society.

There is compelling evidence that gay "marriage" would be a tragedy for our society. On their website, the Family Research Council puts forth some very persuasive arguments from the Witherspoon Institute, including the following:

- **Children hunger for their biological parents**
  Family Research Council and the Witherspoon Institute, whose paper they quote, say that homosexual couples using in vitro fertilization (IVF) or surrogates deliberately create a class of children who will live apart from their mothers or fathers. They quote research that reports children of IVF often ask their single or lesbian mothers about their fathers, questions such as: "Mommy, what did you do with my daddy?" "Can I write him a letter?" "Has he ever seen me?" "Didn't you like him? Didn't he like me?" Other research shows that these feelings are similar to those of children of divorce.

- **Children need fathers**
  The research states that one result of same-sex "marriage" would be that most same-sex couples with children would be lesbian couples. Thus, even more children will be raised apart from fathers. Having a father reduces antisocial behavior and delinquency in boys, and sexual activity in girls.

- **Children need mothers**
  Despite being less likely to have children than lesbians, gay men are and will be raising children, thus denying children a mother and the emotional security they provide, especially for daughters going through puberty and adolescence.

- **Evidence on parenting by same-sex couples is inadequate**
  Although many leading professional associations assert that there are no differences between children raised by gays and those raised by heterosexuals, their research is inadequate, preliminary, and suffers from serious methodological problems.

- **Evidence suggests children raised by homosexuals are more likely to experience gender and sexual disorders**
  Sociologist Judith Stacey, an advocate for same-sex "marriage," found in a review of the literature on child outcomes, "lesbian parenting may free daughters and sons from a broad but uneven range of traditional gender prescriptions." Studies show that sons of lesbians are less masculine, and daughters of lesbians are more masculine, and in general, report having a homoerotic relationship or attractions in larger numbers.

- **Same-sex "marriage" would undercut the norm of sexual fidelity within marriage**
  Gay "marriage" would probably damage the norm of sexual fidelity. Andrew Sullivan wrote in *Virtually Normal*, his book

in defense of same-sex marriage: "There is more likely to be greater understanding of the need for extramarital outlets between two men than between a man and a woman." Imagine the effect on sexual fidelity norms if this sentiment were presented as normal to the public in sitcoms, magazines, and other mass media!

- **Same-sex "marriage" would further isolate marriage from its procreative purpose**

  Throughout human history, marriage and procreation have been tightly connected. The best argument for the institution of marriage is that it secures a mother and a father for each child. Same-sex "marriage" fosters an anti-child-bearing mindset that could fuel population decline, causing gigantic social, political, and economic strains on society. Breaking the necessary link between procreation and marriage would produce an ever-dwindling world population and associated crises caused by global growth slowing to a standstill.

- **Same-sex "marriage" would further diminish the expectation of paternal commitment**

  Political scientist James Q. Wilson states that the advent of no-fault divorce destabilized marriage by weakening the legal and cultural meaning of the marriage contract. Nobel laureate and an economist George Akerlof found that the sexual revolution, driven by the widespread availability of contraception and abortion, enabled men to abandon women when they got pregnant, giving them the ability to blame their girlfriends for not using contraception or procuring an abortion. Legal recognition of gay "marriage" would further destabilize the norm that adults should sacrifice to get and stay married for the sake of their children by institutionalizing the concept that children do not need both a mother and a father.

- **Marriages thrive when spouses specialize in gender-typical roles**

  Same-sex civil "marriage" of necessity de-genderizes marriage, amping up existing social and cultural pressures to neuter our thinking and our behaviors in marriage. According to University of Virginia psychologist Mavis Hetherington, when spouses specialize in gender-typical ways, marriages typically thrive, and couples are less likely to divorce when the wife concentrates on childrearing and the husband concentrates on breadwinning,

- **Women and marriage domesticate men**
  Research has shown that men who are married earn more, work harder, drink less, live longer, spend more time attending religious services, and are more sexually faithful. Their testosterone levels also drop, especially when their children are in the home. It's hard to imagine similar social and biological effects arising in gay "marriages."

If the preceding didn't concern you or make you sad, you have the heart of a stone.

While I don't agree with all of the above assertions, I have seen many of these trends and themes at work in my own life. Many of you know from past columns that homosexuality broke up my marriage. My now ex-wife fell in love with a woman, snuck around behind my back carrying on an affair with her for years, and a year-and-a-half-ago married her lover in Oregon. To say homosexuality destabilized our family would be a huge understatement. The judge gave my homosexual ex-wife complete custody of our son, and I rarely saw him until he became an adult. He grew up mostly in the company of women, without my help and guidance through the horrors of puberty, and the uncertainty of finding his way into adulthood. To this day, he remains somewhat estranged, and I'm lucky to see him a few times a year.

The only positive effect of the advent of same-sex marriage for me personally was that I no longer need to support my ex-wife for the rest of her life.

And now, in Florida, unless you act, same-sex marriage may soon become the law. This could happen to you!

The day the column is published, Chip calls Charles.

"What the fuck, dude?! That was a seriously nasty column! What were you thinking? I know you've got a bug up your butt about lesbianism but keep it to yourself!"

"I'm just telling it like it is, man. Homosexuality is a threat to society."

"Oh, come on! Really? You think persecution of a sexual minority would be good for society? Perhaps we should put them all in prison. Don't you think making the stability of marriage available to all would be a good thing?"

"You read the facts from the Family Research Council."

"Facts? You call vague inferences from supposed experts and bald assertions like 'children of gay people are more gay' facts? That stuff has been totally debunked."

"Why aren't you on my side, by the way? Isn't your religion against homosexuality?"

"Well, United Methodism can't ordain gays or promote the gay lifestyle, but the church commits to not reject or condemn gay members and friends. It's not exactly 'don't ask, don't tell,' but rather live and let live."

"But the Bible is clear about condemning homos, right?"

"I wouldn't necessarily call it outright condemnation. In Genesis, Sodom and Gomorrah are destroyed because of a crowd of men who wanted to rape two angels that Lot was protecting. So, the Bible could be condemning gang rape. And why would angels have gender, anyway? But the passage goes on to basically condone incest between an unsuspecting Lot and his daughters, so you need to take all this with a pillar of salt." Chip smiles at his pun.

"Funny, Funny Boy!"

"Anyway, Lot's daughters' actions, which gave rise to a whole race, the Moabites, are condemned in Leviticus 18 along with polygamy, infidelity, human sacrifice, bestiality, sex during menstruation, and male homosexuality. Homosexuality is called detestable, but that's a way less judgment than most of the other things on the list, which are called profane or wicked. But, dude, anyone who wants to live strictly by Leviticus would need to stop doing a lot of pretty common things, like swearing, eating crab, shellfish, pork or fat—goodbye bacon—haircuts and beard trimming, infidelity—I agree with that one—having pimples or disabilities, drinking alcohol in holy places—like taking communion at church—eating or touching the carcass of flying insects with four legs, going to church within a month or two of giving birth—it's two months for a daughter because, I guess, daughters are more unclean—holding back wages for a day, failing to stand in the presence of the elderly—I ain't standing up for you, bucko—working on the Sabbath, and selling land permanently."

"You got that stuff memorized?"

"The subject of many of my sermons. You need to understand and interpret the underlying meaning of the Bible. Many of these strictures— like not eating shellfish—are codes created to prevent sickness. Others, like not tilling a field to its very edge, are intended to do small but important things like prevent erosion. The Bible was a code of behavior that goes beyond the spiritual. The United Methodist church teaches that we should interpret the Bible by asking ourselves: What did a passage mean to its original hearers? How does that fit into the whole message of the Bible? How does the passage reveal what God is saying in my life, community, and world? And what changes should I consider making as a result of my study?"

"So, you're not literalists? That's good."

"Hey, let me tell you my favorite Methodist joke."

"Please, please, please, no!"

"OK, here goes. A Methodist minister and his wife were driving along Lake Shore Drive, in Chicago, and they were pulled over for speeding. As officer O'Malley approached the pastor, he saw the man's clerical garb and mistook him for a Catholic priest. 'Oh, sorry about dat, fader. Uh, youse just try and slow it down a little, OK?' As they drove away, the pastor's wife said, 'Shame on you, Harold! That was unethical. You know who he thought you were!' 'Oh, I know who he thought I was,' replied the pastor. 'I'm just wondering who he thought you were.'

Charles just buries his head in his arms.

A new religion that'll bring you to your knees, like Velveeta cheese

Allanah Myles—*Black Velvet*

Aleister awoke to find his familiar, his wife Rose, at the foot of the bed. She had the faraway eyes that signified a possession. "What is the matter?" he said. He was worried, as she had recently said that she felt she was pregnant.

"There is something you must know," Rose said. "A being of great power wishes to communicate with you."

"Can't he wait until after my breakfast?" Aleister pleaded.

"He comes now." Rose fainted to the floor and a voice came into the room. To Aleister, it appeared to emanate from a corner of the bedroom. The voice was neither high nor low, but deep, musical and expressive, and spoke unaccented English. Taken aback, Aleister sat upright in bed and clutched the bedclothes to him.

"Who are you?" he asked in a small voice.

"You may call me Aiwass. I am to give you the Book of the Law and signify the equinox of the old gods, and the beginning of the last Aeon of the world. You shall take it down from my dictation and spread its word throughout the world."

Aleister blinked and swiveled his head back and forth across the room. All seemed in order, except for his crumpled wife on the floor. He craned his neck and twisted his body to look out the window behind the bed. He saw nothing but the familiar sights of a spring day in Cairo. What did I do last night to bring on this apparition, he thought. A devoted libertine, Aleister was renowned for drinking, dancing, drugging and extreme sexual exploits with all manner of devotees and hangers-on.

"But who are you?" Aleister repeated. "And, where are you?" Aleister had had visions before, but generally only when out of his head with intoxicants of one sort or the other. When the spirits came to his wife, she typically narrated what they told her, as a translator. But now, here, in the stark midday Egyptian sun, he saw a handful of dust in unreal blue shadow in the corner of his room, from whence the sonorous voice emanated.

"I am Aiwass, the minister of Hoor-Paar-Kraat, endowed by the powers ruling this Earth at present."

Aleister was very acquainted with the spirit world, having mastered invisibility and evocation four years previously, and he claimed to be an adept at Magick. He called himself the Beast 666, yet he had never trembled so much in the presence of a spirit. It was as if his whole body was a lightning rod yearning for the bolt of creation.

From his bed, Aleister peered into the shadow in the corner and thought he beheld a tall, dark man in his thirties, well-knit, active and strong, with the face of a savage king, and eyes veiled lest their gaze should destroy what they saw.

"I have come to command you to set down the Book of the Law that will supersede the Christian Bible and all others and set the course of your race into a new Age. I will come to you thrice to recite the past, present, and future so that you shall understand the Law."

Upon hearing this Aleister was not the least bit stunned at the enormity of the task—to set out laws for all humanity to follow. His ego was such that it didn't occur to him to be awed by the proposition. Rather he was overwhelmed by a feeling of bliss that had been chosen to be the ultimate prophet of the Creator.

"I am ready to receive your enlightenment," Aleister said.

"Very well. The first law is the only law: Do what thou wilt."

"Wait. Does that mean there are no rules, no strictures on conduct, and all may do what they wish?"

"No," Aiwass said. "Love is the law, love under will. There is no law beyond 'Do what thou wilt.' People are stars whose destiny is to move on each's true orbit, as marked out by the nature of position, the law of personal growth, the impulse of past experiences. All events are equally lawful— and everyone necessary, in the long run—but in practice, only one act is lawful for each at any given moment. Therefore, duty consists in determining to experience the right event from one moment of consciousness to another. Each action or motion is an act of love, the uniting with one or another part of Nuit; each such act must be 'under will,' chosen so as to fulfill and not to thwart the true nature of the being concerned."

"I'm not entirely sure I grasp the difference between this Law and lawlessness," Aleister said. "Surely, I have governed my own life under similar principles, but I am an elite, possessing greater intellect, discernment, and moral surety than the less fortunate masses. A world run under the Law you state would come quickly to sin and ruin."

"The word sin is restriction," said Aiwass. "A sin is a lie, a folly against self. The practice of 'Do what thou wilt' is that every man and every woman has definite attributes whose tendency, considered in due relation to environment, indicate a proper course of action in each case. To pursue this course of action is to do one's true will. Do that, and no other shall say nay."

"Again, I see how this works for the elite. But what of the less-gifted?"

"One should not protect the weak and the vicious from the results of their inferiority. Doing so perpetuates the elements of social dissolution. Rather aid nature by subjecting every newcomer to the most rigorous tests of his fitness to deal with his environment. The human race grew in stature and intelligence as long as individual prowess achieved security so that the strongest and cleverest people were able to reproduce their kind in the best conditions. Now that security has become general through the operation of altruism, the most degenerate of the people are often the offspring of the strongest.

"Your race has a sentimental idea of self-sacrifice, the kind which is most esteemed by the vulgar and is the essence of popular Christianity— sacrifice of the strong to the weak. This is wholly against the principles of evolution, and of the Law. Any nation which does this systematically on a sufficiently large scale simply destroys itself. The sacrifice is in vain; the weak are not even saved."

Aleister is taken aback. "So, civilization must be tossed aside, and we all should struggle like vicious animals? Only the strong-willed are to survive and the weak are to be abandoned and pitied?"

"The Law regards pity as despicable. But further, to pity another man is to insult him. He also is a star, one, individual and eternal. The Law does not condemn fighting. If he be a King, thou canst not hurt him."

Aleister, who had embraced Buddhism and its teachings that all existence is pure joy while sorrows are but shadows, was shocked at the implications of the law that Aiwass revealed. Despite his debauchery and his feeling of superiority, deep in his soul, he was infinitely sad at humanity's state of universal sorrow, and passionately eager to raise humanity. The Law denounced pity as damnable, and by implication, acclaimed war as admirable.

"You are saying we should forsake Christianity, Buddhism and all other religions, to forsake the Bible and all other codes of conduct?"

Aiwass replied, "All bibles or sacred codes have been the causes of various errors in understanding the nature of man, such as the separation of body and soul, the idea that evil only resides in the body and goodness and reason in the soul, as well as the biggest error: that God will torment man in eternity for following his will.

"In reality, man has no body distinct from his soul, for what is called body is a portion of the soul as discerned by the five senses. Similarly, energy is the only life and is from the body and will is the bound or outward circumference of energy, which is eternal delight. I am the God of Vengeance. I am thy Holy Guardian Angel. I shall return the next three days. Be prepared to receive the Book of the Law, which I shall dictate to you."

With that, the shadow disappeared and Aleister sat blinking in astonishment at what had happened. After a moment, he thought of his wife, leapt to the floor, and cradled Rose in his arms. Slowly she regained consciousness and, startled, cast her eyes about the room.

"What happened?" Rose asked. "Where is Horus' messenger?"

"I have just had the most exhilarating experience," Aleister said. "I know that during the trances that you've had over the past few days you said that the god Horus was trying to contact me. Darling, where did you get these ideas from? It appears that through your instrument, Aiwass, an angel of Horus, whom he called Hoor-Paar-Kraat, visited me and said he would give me the Book of the Law. He said he would visit me three times, speaking of the past, the present, and the future. What do you know of this god, Horus?"

"Until the trances, I had never heard of the names Horus or Hoor-Paar-Kraat. You know I don't know anything about Egyptology. I don't remember anything about those seizures. You are the one who said I spoke of Horus."

Aleister, confused about the vision he had, decided he needed proof that his wife wasn't manufacturing these incidents. Aleister quizzed his wife on a number of symbols related to Horus, according to the system he had gotten from Golden Dawn occult practitioners.

He asked, "What are Horus' moral qualities?" Immediately Rose replied, "Force and fire."

"Who is Horus' enemy?" Rose replied, "Forces of the waters—of the Nile."

Aleister continued his inquisition, and his wife knew Horus' weapon, planet, number, and most impressively, arbitrary symbols Aleister concocted on the spot to represent Horus. After this last, Aleister became convinced his wife could read his mind. Nonetheless, he was still skeptical about the divine nature of the encounter, so he decided that the couple would go to the newly opened Boulak Museum where many ancient Egyptian artifacts were on display.

At the museum, Aleister asked Rose to point out Horus to him. The couple strolled through the museum and passed several well-known images of the god without note. Instead, Rose led Aleister straight to a painted wooden funerary stele from the 26th dynasty that depicted Horus receiving a sacrifice from the deceased priest Ankh-f-n-khonsu. Upon examining the piece, Aleister was stunned to note that it was numbered 666 by the museum, a number associated in the Bible with the devil, and with which he had identified since childhood.

Satisfied that Rose could communicate with Horus' messenger, Aleister allowed himself to be guided by her. Over three days, following Rose's instructions, he went to one of their rooms at noon. There he experienced trances mediated by Rose during which he took an hour of dictation from Aiwass.

From these experiences, Aleister created the Book of the Law and, convinced that Horus wanted him to establish a new religion, he created Thelema, named after the Greek word meaning "will."

There was one aspect of the Law that Aleister felt particularly comfortable with:

I am the Snake that giveth Knowledge & Delight and bright glory, and stir the hearts of men with drunkenness. To worship me take wine and strange drugs whereof I will tell my prophet, & be drunk thereof! They shall not harm ye at all. It is a lie, this folly against self. The exposure of innocence is a lie. Be strong, o man! lust, enjoy all things of sense and rapture: fear not that any God shall deny thee for this.

This call to the life of licentiousness justified Aleister's past and current behavior as the fulfillment of his being and his will. In part because of this godly endorsement of excess, the newly created religion first caught on among the many upper-class devotees of occult practices in England, particularly the Great White Brotherhood and the Golden Dawn.

Although it grew slowly at first, after a decade, Thelema had spread throughout the world, with followers numbering in the millions. Most of its earliest followers were educated, cultured, and rich, and captains of industry. To them, the precepts of Thelema were a justification of their already self-serving behavior:

We have nothing with the outcast and the unfit: let them die in their misery. For they feel not. Compassion is the vice of kings: stamp down the wretched and the weak: this is the law of the strong: this is our law, and the joy of the world.

No longer did elites need to feel responsible for the mass of humanity. All should do what they wilt and leave the masses to pull themselves out of their condition. Charity dried up. The rich built tall walls around their enclaves against the possibility of a plebeian revolt. There was a consolidation of power and money to the rich privileged classes unprecedented in human history. There was, of course, a resulting general descent into poverty and crisis for 90 percent of the world population. Although never a majority religion, Thelema claimed virtually all the world's rich and powerful among its followers.

Many of these followers were in a position to carry out the exhortations of the third chapter of the Book of the Law:

Now let it first be understood that I am a god of war and vengeance. I will give you a war-engine. With it ye shall smite the peoples; and none shall stand before you. Lurk! Withdraw! Upon them! this is the Law of the Battle of Conquest: thus shall my worship be about my secret house.

Mercy let be off: damn them who pity! Kill and torture; spare not; be upon them.

Argue not; convert not; talk not overmuch! Them that seek to entrap thee, to overthrow thee, them attack without pity or quarter; and destroy them utterly. Swift as the trodden serpent turn and strike! Be thou deadlier than he! Drag down their souls to awful torment: laugh at their fear: spit upon them!

The Great War began and ravaged the world, producing a million casualties, and more than 300,000 dead in a single lengthy engagement. Increasing technological might enabled wholesale killing. Other wars raged unchecked, used by Thelemic rulers as both population control and a distraction from the real issues facing mankind. Enhanced killing machines enabled Thelemic adherent Talat Pasha to use the Ottoman government to systematically exterminate 1.5 million Armenians.

Thelemic capitalists did what they wilt, regardless of the effects on the less fortunate. Major cities lived under huge black clouds of pollution, waterways became too toxic for fish and threatened drinking water. Babies were born deformed, and minorities were slaughtered in pogroms and genocides. Apart from that, death rates skyrocketed as the masses were decimated by diseases caused by pollution and toxic food.

Aleister continued to live a life of debauchery while serving as the high priest of Thelema, spreading the practice of his Gnostic Mass, taking drugs, writing erotic poetry, and practicing Sex Magick, engaging in sex with dozens or hundreds of partners, with no reservation and no regrets. He felt his conscience to be an obstacle and a delusion, an obsolete holdover of heredity and education. As the Chosen One, he felt he could use all methods of implementing his religion with impunity. Aleister expected the New Aeon Aiwass foretold to release mankind from its pretense of altruism, its obsession with fear, and its consciousness of sin.

He maintained his prodigious literary output, not only about Thelema and Magick, but also of plays and books, all the while traveling the world, once crossing China on foot.

Aleister's hyper-promiscuous sex life, combined with his broad travels, actually set off several pandemics of venereal disease. In a pre-penicillin world, this meant a trail of suffering followed him, although paradoxically, he himself seemed immune to the diseases.

Desiring to establish a formal Abbey of Thelema, Aleister ended up in Cefalù, Sicily in a villa filled with his followers. Gathering his fold together, the master of Thelema preached that Thelema would one day sweep away Christianity and free men from all restrictions on their will.

"I want blasphemy, murder, rape, revolution. Anything bad or good, but strong!" he declared. "I have exposed myself to every form of disease, accident, and violence. I have driven myself to delight in dirty and disgusting debauches, and to devour human excrement and human flesh. I have mastered every node of my mind and made myself a morality more severe than any other in the world. A thousand years from now the world will be sitting in the sunset of Thelema. Follow me and do what thou wilt!"

Aleister and the group created a latter-day Bacchanalia, filling their days with orgies, drugs and constant debauchery. The disciples performed Sex Magick rituals under the influence of hashish, opium, and cocaine. Naked children ran in and out of rooms where disciples were engaged in orgies.

After three years of constant pleasure-seeking and heavy drug use, a regretful Aleister cradled the head of Raoul, a young follower who had barely survived a heroin overdose and was sick from enteritis. "Master," the young man said. "I miss the godly sweetness of my first heroin high— the warm silky euphoria palace, waves of pleasure massaging my soul, and the face of Horus smiling upon me. I miss being free from everything, mind, body, the outside world, the inside world. But each time I return, the road to the palace gets longer, and Horus sends me away earlier and earlier until it seems like he no longer cares for me. The love is gone, and it's dark and cold outside and there's nowhere to get warm except back in the palace. Now I see Horus no more. I just hope for a little warmth before I return. I will never feel the way I did the first time, and it will never get warmer outside. And I am forsaken!"

With this last, the boy closed his eyes and eventually stopped breathing. Aleister was shaken. His towering confidence was shattered. He realized that despite his power, his moral surety, and his god-given mission, he could not control all. He gathered his followers together, many suffering from various diseases of excess and recklessness, and led them in an epic 72-hour orgy. Aleister was the last to pass out, surrounded by white bodies sprawled naked on the damp stone floor.

In the nightmare room, when Aleister awoke, exhausted, he was surrounded by pornographic paintings, loathsome sayings—Soak me in cognac, cunt, and cocaine!—and tins overflowing with drugs. Rubbing his eyes groggily, he sneezed, and a white cloud billowed from his nostrils, He turned over to lie on his right side. He was filled with nothingness, divested of the passions that had driven him. No sensation, just a numbness. He regarded his dirty hands and broken fingernails blankly.

Staring at the blue wall on the far side of the room, Aleister was struck by a vision. He saw with startling cleanness the edge of the abyss upon which civilization trembled. He saw terrified multitudes pitch into the darkness, falling from the smoke and flames of burning cities, arms and legs waving as if feebly attempting to fly, plunging deeper and deeper into oblivion. Startled upright, Aleister's stomach churned in horror as he realized his part in bringing the world to the brink.

Is all this because of 'do what thou wilt,' he thought. And because of my selfish ego? What have I done?

Aleister staggered to his feet and walked unsteadily into the courtyard, where he vomited for quite a long time before relieving his bowels on the pavement. Exhausted, spent, and demoralized, Aleister decided to clean himself up, turn out his flock, and book passage to Cairo so he could summon Aiwass in hopes of an explanation. He wanted to know if he had been an unfaithful servant, or if he had failed to grasp Horus' intent in giving him the Book of the Law. He turned and entered the building again, slapping his followers awake and telling them to leave as quickly as they could.

Once in Cairo, Aleister managed to rent the room in which he had received Aiwass' enlightenment. He began to prepare himself to contact Horus' minister. His ex-wife Rose was long gone, driven mad after Aleister abandoned her and their child in the Orient. Later he had had her committed to an asylum for alcohol dementia.

Nonetheless, Aleister was determined to make contact with Aiwass and tried for three days with drugs, incantations, and Magick to summon his Holy Guardian Angel.

Late on the third day, close to midnight, Aleister noticed a pale blue light, like a flame, winking in and out in the dark corner of his room. He repeated his invocations and the light grew to fill the room.

Aiwass said, "Why have you summoned me?"

Aleister replied, "It is not you, but your master that I seek. I have serious and painful questions to ask of Horus. Bid him come and speak with me."

Aiwass assured Aleister that this was impossible, that Horus did not commune with vassals such as him. Aleister recited a prepared list of the horrible things he had done in his master's name and informed Aiwass that he now saw clearly that he must have misinterpreted Horus' commands. "I do not wish to speak with you any longer," he said, "but would converse with the Master, not the messenger."

It was sunup when the angel finally relented and agreed to set up an audience for the following night.

At the appointed hour, Aleister, fraught with tension and anticipation, observed inky clouds forming in the corner of his room, eventually growing to fill the distance between the corner and Aleister's bed. After some time during which the room was wracked with thunder and lightning, the billowing clouds parted and revealed a dark figure seated on a burnished ebony throne. Beside him was a tall seven-branched candelabra with candles that sucked light rather than releasing it. Behind him was an inky blackness of great apparent depth, except there were no stars, no visible thing: nothingness.

"It appears you no longer wish to serve me," Horus said.

"No, no, no. I don't mean to leave your service, Master. I am troubled and confused about what my mission is. I must have misinterpreted your wisdom and my charge. It now seems to me that You cannot have intended for me to sow doubt, trouble, and pestilence in the world, and to attract the weak-minded to your service."

"That is precisely your charge, and you have executed it well," Horus said. "This is your mission, and I am well pleased. Why are you troubled?"

Aleister was stunned silent. Was this some kind of test? He struggled to decide how to respond. "Master, even though I have lived life as a libertine, disregarding most of the strictures of society, I haven't intentionally harmed anyone, but have served to spread your word, the Book of the Law. Begging your pardon, but it seems you want me to do evil, which I presume is against Your plan."

"Quite the contrary. That is my plan."

Aleister blinked, his mind awhirl. He felt the urge to vomit but choked it back. "Sure . . . surely you cannot want to harm Creation? Surely the message of the Book of the Law must be to preserve Creation and cement man's place in it? Surely that is the will of the Creator?"

"You think that weakling, Yahweh, made this Creation? He did not. I did," Horus said with a sneer of disgust.

"Think about it. Look at all the suffering, devastation and cruelty in your world. Regard the decay of the sense of sin, the growth of irresponsibility, the strange modifications of the reproductive instinct with a tendency to become bisexual or epicene, the childlike confidence in progress combined with nightmare fear of catastrophe, against which the sniveling masses are yet half unwilling to take precautions. Surely that self-righteous fool Yahweh couldn't abide all the evil! No, 'tis mine! You serve the Creator, and my rule is dark. If you are to be my Messiah, you will need to embrace this dark world and assist me in bringing about its complete ruin!"

Aleister's brain buzzed with confusion. The Creator of the world was . . . Satan? If so, why was the whole world not evil?

"Why create a world just to destroy it? You are Satan, the one cast out of heaven? Then why is there goodness in the world?"

The Creator laughed. "You have it exactly wrong. I cast Yahweh out of my realm. He was a poor soldier, always reluctant to rain destruction down upon humanity. He had his uses and successes, but he was unreliable. Nonetheless, in any game, one must have an opponent, and after I cast him out, he proved a worthy adversary. The gambit with his so-called son and the mythology that grew up around him was Yahweh's attempt to build a religion of goodness and light. But he failed in so many ways. Popes! What a laughable mistake! Declare a feeble human an absolute authority and mayhem ensues. And he thought he was helping his cause! Every religion he started after that played right into my hands. He's never gotten it right, not that he could, given his materials. I made humanity with a fatal flaw: hubris. It is this flaw that will ensure my eventual victory in this game. Yahweh cannot prevail against me as he is afflicted with hubris himself; he even fancies himself my equal."

Aleister, shocked and mortified, cringed from the edge of the blackness. Can this be? Is the world really doomed to suffer and die? How can I serve this evil master?

"Away from me, Satan!" he said. "In Jesus' name, I renounce you and all evil spirits. I renounce all your works and all your empty promises. In Jesus' name, I cast you out, never to return."

The Creator howled in laughter. "You fool! Yahweh's blasphemous book says that Christians have dominion over me and the world. But the opposite is true. By following me, you gain dominion over the Christians, and the world. The silly words in Yahweh's foolish book have no power over me. And you can no more renounce me than you can renounce yourself."

"Nonetheless," Aleister cried. "I am done doing your bidding! If to do wrong in your Creation is to do right in my life, then so be it. I will serve you no longer."

"Nor will I permit you to serve me. Begone!" At this, the black clouds swallowed the Creator and Aleister found himself back in his room, standing upon his bed.

You've got to change your underwear, baby, before I start loving you.

Santana—*Evil Ways*

Chip and Charles are hanging around Chip's basement man cave, each on his own couch as usual. On the table between the couches are a couple of beers, a basket of Doritos, and a bowl of melted Velveeta, Chip's favorite snack food, which Charles can barely stomach. The modest flat panel TV is showing a NASCAR race with the sound off.

Charles has brought the first draft of his Aleister chapter and Chip is intently reading. As always, Chip doesn't quite know what to do, so he starts wandering around the basement. Everything is Nebraska-themed: the Big Red N throw rug, the football posters and framed pictures of Chip in his lineman's uniform, the cups and glasses on the dry bar in the corner, even the treads on the stairs to the first-floor feature red Ns.

This dude is obsessed, Charles thinks, peering closely at the photos on the wall. Look at this one, he thinks, examining a picture of Chip dressed up as the Cornhusker mascot in overalls with an ear of corn jutting from the hip pocket, wearing an oversized red cowboy hat, and cradling a football in one arm while giving the OK sign with his left hand. He's the spitting image, Charles thinks. Did they use him as the model for the mascot?

After a while, Chip looks up and says, "Jeez. A lot going on here. Are you really saying Aleister Crowley is the Anti-Christ?"

"Well, first off, I never say it's Aleister Crowley," Chip says with a smirk.

"Oh, come on! Thelema? Hello?"

"Well, anyway, to answer your question, the protagonist in this chapter is a servant of the godhead of his universe. So, he would be the Christ, if anything."

"Yeah, tricky way to deal with the problem of evil: Make it the problem of goodness. Very fancy. But I gotta say, you butchered Crowley's story pretty badly."

"Like I said, it's not Crowley. Yes, there are similarities . . ."

"Similarities?" Chip snorts. "You rip him off verbatim in places!"

"Well, I didn't expect you to know your Crowley so well, being a pious preacher and all."

"Har de fuckin' har, you so funny! Yes, I know Crowley and a dozen other religious charlatans. It's my biz, after all. From time to time I get church members who have just stumbled into Thelema, or Scientology, Santeria, or, fuck, or even Thee Temple ov Psychick Youth or the Creativity Movement. They are often either really confused at being confronted by another worldview, or gung-ho for the shit. Sometimes takes a while to straighten 'em out. Sometimes it doesn't work, and we lose them to a crackpot religion. I've even participated in efforts to deprogram some of these folks. So anyway, back to the crux of the biscuit, you got some of the Aiwass and the Law stuff pretty much verbatim, but you cut out a lot of stuff."

"Right. I just needed enough to set up the logical consequence. I was interested in asking, what if, instead of Crowley the Buddhist being initially horrified and disturbed by *The Book of the Law*, to the point where he put it away and even forgot where it was for years, what if Aiwass was a bit more directive and asked him to set up a religion? What if Crowley then evangelized amongst the dissolute hipsters of early 20th century London, and the thing caught on? What if on his many travels, he spread Thelema throughout the world of the one-percenters, and evangelized the libertine lifestyle implied by 'Do what thou wilt?'"

"Yeah, I can see how, with some effort, it might have spread through the privileged class. I expect it would have taken over the Ayn Rand crowd a few decades later. Thelema, in some interpretations, is pretty close to the laissez-faire capitalism Rand espoused—the heroic man with happiness as his purpose and achievement his god."

Charles nods. "Achievement! Reminds me of *The Big Lebowski*. Perhaps I can work the anti-Dude in there somewhere, or the Little Lebowski Urban Achievers or, let's see, like 'Men who are unable to achieve on a level field of play. Men who will not sign their names. Weaklings. Bums.' But, to your point, yes, Thelema is tailor-made for the Objectivism Homo Superior crowd. That's why I have it becoming, like, the state religion of Vulture Capitalism."

"And they run roughshod over the 99 percent, ruining the Earth, bringing pestilence and war and stuff like that."

"Yes, I think that's taking it to the logical conclusion, despite what Thelema's adherents would say, and I've seen some pretty tortuous verbal machinations by Thelemites on YouTube trying to explain that 'what thou wilt' doesn't mean 'anything goes.' Also, as I quote in the chapter, the *Book of the Law* says, 'I am the Snake that giveth Knowledge & Delight and bright glory and stir hearts of men with drunkenness. To worship me take wine and strange drugs whereof I will tell my prophet, & be drunk thereof! They shall not harm ye at all.' Party on, Wayne!"

"Party on, Garth!" Chip grabs a Dorito, loads it with Velveeta, and thinks for a moment. "Yes, I can see that even if Thelema caught on with the proletariat, they'd take it as an exhortation to party. An underclass of wastrels."

"Great band name, that," says Charles and the two men lean across the table to high-five.

Slamming back into the couch and crossing his legs ankle on knee, Chip turns a few pages back and forth, rereading sections. "OK," he says. "This whole upside-down universe business—the Creator is really the Destroyer—I don't think it's quite all there yet. If the Devil builds a universe, why is there good in it? Oh, wait . . ."

"Gotcha!" Charles says. "Ya burnt!" Chip uncharacteristically turns a little red. Charles pounces on the point. "The problem in an evil universe is that there is still good. Thus: 'How could there be a God if there's good in the world?'"

Chip frowns and pauses to regain his composure. Chip pops another cheese-laden chip in his mouth and downs it with beer. "Yes, but the universe you created here is obviously being taken over by evil. Wouldn't it start evil, in the Wasteland of Eden, and good would be the threat?"

"That's right," Charles says. "The parameters of this universe aren't internally consistent. But there's a reason for that."

Chip is stumped. He goes silent and rubs his stubbly beard with one hand as he reads and re-reads the chapter until finally, he says, "Aha! I've got it! It's a virtual reality game! The Creator talks about a game, like this is his entertainment, a sporting event. He needs Yahweh as an opponent. The world is set up relatively balanced between good and evil and the two players duke it out!"

"Yes, Padawan," Charles says, hardly able to contain his delight at turning one of Chip's put-downs around on him. "Patience you must have my young Padawan."

Chip explodes in laughter. "You got me, asshole, this time! But watch out! Paybacks are a bitch."

Charles smirks at his friend. It's not often he gets the upper hand with Chip when it comes to insults. "So anyway, yes, it's an artificial game universe. The Creator says he cast out Yahweh, but that could just be part of the game script, the parameters of the game world. I like to think Yahweh was doing his master's bidding up until the whole Jesus thing, where he went off script. The whole Old Testament could be viewed that way. Lots of suffering believers in that book, and don't get me started on Leviticus. The game universe was set up to reward evil, and Yahweh thought he'd change things up and try to get more points for good via Jesus. Nonetheless, it's obviously not a perfect analogy."

"Well, good on ya for skewering the Popes, by the way. As a good Protestant, I have to applaud."

"Hmmm. Maybe the next chapter should feature Luther as the anti-Christ?" Charles says.

Chip makes a face, dips a Dorito in the Velveeta and tosses it at Charles. Charles turns his head and the chip smacks him in the side of his face and sticks there.

"You bastard!" Charles yells, grabbing a rag and wiping his face. He glances at the rag, and it turns out to be a dirty pair of Chip's underwear. "Ew! You're not only a bastard, you're a filthy bastard!" Charles whips the offending garment at Chip, who ducks, and the missile flops to the floor behind the couch. "What the hell was that doing on the couch?" Chip grins, makes an empty fist, and shakes it up and down in the universal sign of masturbation. "Oh, double-ew!" Charles sticks his finger in his mouth in the gag sign.

After a minute to calm down, Charles continues the conversation. "You know, you onanistic old fool, there's a theory out there that our universe might actually be a video game or a simulation kinda like what Descartes was saying about 'I think, therefore I am' not necessarily proving anything more than that he exists; he could easily be a brain in a vat."

"Of course," Chip replies, "all that 'trust in God's fairness to not deceive us' business Descartes proposed was sort of weak, and, in your Thelema universe, it's clear that the Creator is a deceiver."

"Right. But some physicists use the infinite timeline argument to postulate that, given infinite time, some species somewhere will simulate our universe, and we could be in that universe. I remember reading a book—did you read *Simulacron 3*?"

Chip shakes his head no. It's not often that Charles references a book that bibliophile Chip has not read.

"Oh, man," Charles says. "You gotta read it. I read it in high school, and it blew my mind. Basically, it's the story of a virtual environment inside a computer—kinda like the Matrix—designed to do, of all things, marketing research. The premise, which I thought was kind of weak, was that real people don't like to respond to opinion polls, so they built this simulation machine. Somehow the creators of the machine can simulate human beings so completely that when surveyed, they give real-world results."

"Yeah, that's kind of bullshit, right?" Chip says. "If you can simulate a human, or different kinds of humans, then you can run your fucking marketing and advertising ideas by the simulation without going to the trouble of creating the whole environment." Chip digs into the Velveeta and holds up the cheese-coated chip, waving his hand seductively over it, Vanna-like. "Buy Velveeta! No, buy this chip! Hell, buy me!"

Charles snickers and says, "Gee, Vanna, you've put on weight!" Chip batts his eyes, tilts his head, and smiles broadly. Charles continues, "Anyway, the weird and interesting thing is that in this virtual reality, the populace is required to answer surveys, and the more elite you become, the fewer surveys you need to answer, with the one-percenters not having to do any of them. I loved that part, even if it doesn't make any sense. Certainly, advertisers would also be targeting the rich. So anyway, the virtual people have their own consciousness; they are self-aware and otherwise normal, except that, of course, they are unaware that they are only electronic impulses in a computer."

"Like the Holodeck, but you can't leave."

"Exactly, so the protagonist watches a guy vanish right in front of him, which freaks him totally out. Eventually, he figures out that his world is not real, and, yada, yada, yada, he finds a way to escape into the real world."

Chip laughs and says, "But is it the real world? Or is this just fantasy? Caught in a landslide, no escape from reality."

"Yeah, you're obviously easy come, you wanker! Anyway, yes, it could be a simulation of a world that built a simulation because people kept escaping from the simulation, and there are maybe infinite levels. Neal Stephenson wrote a book, *Anathema*, based on the alternate universes theory proposed by string physicists."

"Yeah, I read that book. Really slow going in the beginning, but pretty interesting in the end. I love the master who, at the end, is trying to move his friends into a universe in which they all survive."

"Right. And the fact that he must pick one in which he dies makes him a messiah."

"I'm glad you said that, not me," Chip says, pulling a face.

"So anyway, as I was saying, physicists posit that we are indeed in a simulation due to some discrepancies involving cosmic ray particles. I obviously don't understand the physics . . ." "Obviously, since you're a friggin' English major," interjects Chip. ". . . but there appears to be a seemingly arbitrary limit on the amount of energy cosmic ray particles can have, which physicists say looks suspiciously like a limit in simulation."

Charles glances at Chip, who seems intently interested. He continues, "Neil DeGrasse Tyson has a thought experiment, kind of like Descartes': If we accept that it is possible to simulate a universe, then we have to assume that, given infinite time, somebody, somewhere, will simulate the Universe. Sorta like that meme about the infinite monkeys eventually typing the Bible. So, if a perfect simulation of the Universe is possible, perhaps we live inside just such a simulation. And, what's to say that this couldn't just go on and on, with an infinite number of simulations arising from an infinite number of civilizations?"

"That's pretty mind-blowing," Chip admits, crunching loudly on a mouthful of chips.

"Yeah, no shit. So, the way this story goes is, since at the quantum level there is an infinite number of paths between one object and another, it's impossible for a finite computer to model them all. Therefore, we see the limit on the power of cosmic rays because that's just as good as the computer that contains us can do, given limited power and limited time."

Chip raises both hands beside his head and makes the brain-exploding motion.

"Yup. Pow! Anyway, since cosmic rays are the highest-energy particles in the Universe—we can't even generate them in the laboratory and they actually pull the fabric of the Universe—thus they would probably be difficult to simulate. Another relevant point: Physicists took a look at the relationship of the energy and momentum of these particles and found discrepancies. So, something's off about cosmic rays. And thus, we might be in a simulation. What should we or could we do about that? Cosmologist Max Tegmark proposed a rational approach. He said, assume we're in a simulation, so go out and lead very interesting lives and do unexpected things so that those in charge of the simulation don't get bored and shut you down."

"Good advice no matter what," Chip says. "Well, I don't hang out with physicists and I'm not a geeky physics fanboy like you, but, like you said in that quote war we had a while ago, extraordinary claims require extraordinary evidence. It doesn't sound like there's extraordinary evidence in this case. Just because we can't reconcile some unexpected results with exotic particles doesn't mean we're in the Matrix. And anyway, if this hypothesis is valid, doesn't it open the door to resurrection—a reboot—eternal life and, for God's sake, faith and religion?"

Charles hadn't thought of this angle and it knocks him for a loop. It's his turn to mime his brain exploding. He had assumed his argument would disprove the divine. He grabs some chips and munches glumly for a bit. "Yeah, imagine if you could just fiddle with a few parameters until things work out: You get the girl, become a billionaire, solve world hunger. Which reminds me of a joke." Chip groans. Charles is not renowned for his joke-telling prowess.

"OK, here it is. It's kinda long." Chip groans again. "No, no, no. It's worth it, I promise. A young man walks into his chemistry classroom to take his final exam. He must get a perfect score to get into the college of his choosing. The teacher passes out the tests, and the young man blazes through, knowing every answer with certainty. He then arrives at the final question, which reads, 'How many electrons are in an atom of hydrogen?' The young man breaks out in a sweat, realizing that he doesn't know this one for sure. In a lapse of judgment, he puts down '3' for his answer and turns in his test. A few days later, he gets his grade back: an entirely perfect score except for the last question. He doesn't get into his college, and he decides to take a depressed walk on the beach to try to clear his head. While walking, he trips over a magical lamp. He rubs it and a genie billows forth. The genie tells him he can have one wish. The young man eagerly replies, 'I wish I'd gotten that question right!' The genie nods and says, 'It is done.' And then the Universe explodes."

"Well, I must say, you've told worse," Chip says with a small chuckle. "But if the owners of the machine were simulating humans, do you think they'd come up with this miserable lot?"

"Bugs. We're bugs in the program. The real action is light years from here, maybe at Proxima Centauri B."

"What's that? A Nissan?"

"No, it's the closest star system that might have a Goldilocks planet."

". . . which is?"

"Not too cold, not too hot, just right for life."

"With an ocean made of porridge, I'm sure," Chip says. They both laugh.

"Well, anyway," Chip continues, "that's an interesting idea, humans being a bug in the system. I read a sci-fi novel once about an advanced civilization that, against the Prime Directive or whatever, had to jettison their waste while passing Earth. After eons, that waste becomes us, and the offending ship captain, having been required to return to the scene of the crime and sterilize the Earth, shows up, and moral questions abound."

Charles says, "Ex luto rather than a Domino, eh?"

"Dominoes? What?"

"Two years of high school Latin finally comes in handy! It means 'from the mud rather than from God.' Perhaps, though, more accurately, it would be 'de stercore non est de Deo.' Stercore is shit in Latin."

"How do you say shithead in Latin?"

"Irrumator."

"Well you fuckin' irrumator, Latin is one of the gaps in my education for sure. I took Greek. Don't," Chip puts up a warning finger, "say 'It's all Greek to me!' Been done." Charles, having opened his mouth to say just this, pops it shut again and smiles.

Charles says, "Well, if you really want your mind blown . . ." Chip interrupts, "I'd rather get my dick blown." ". . . Dr. James Gates, Jr. claims to have found computer code inside the math that supports string theory.

Not just stuff that looks like computer code, but some error correction code identical to that created by the father of information theory, Claude Shannon, in the '40s. Gates has created visuals of the codes that he calls adinkras."

"You're a dink, brah!"

"So mature! I'm talking heavy physics and you're regressing to high school." Chip blows him a raspberry, spattering Velveeta all over the front of his Jimi Hendrix T-shirt, and shoots him the bird.

"Anyway," Charles continues, "the very existence of error-correcting codes—which are in our browsers, our phones, our computers— embedded in the current models of the Universe—well, that's exactly what we would expect to see if we were living in a simulation."

"Yeah, that could mean something, or nothing," Chip says. "I mean, just because the laws of our universe are set up so that there is a consistent way to do a thing, no matter the context, doesn't mean squat. You can expect the Universe to rhyme."

"Oooh, I like that! But let me take a different tack: why dark matter? Physicists think that there's six times as much dark matter in the Universe as, um, real matter. So, what's the point, if this is a simulation? It greatly increases the complexity of the simulation, and, if we theorize that the cosmic ray thing is a hack to avoid having to overtax the simulation machine, then what's up with that?"

"So, you're arguing the other side now?"

"Not at all," Charles says. "You seem to assume I believe in the Matrix thing. Like a lot of things regarding religion and reality, I'm an agnostic. I find this sort of thing fascinating, but not convincing."

"So, you're making my head hurt for no reason?"

"Just giving you an education, initiate!"

Chip erupts in laughter. "Yeah, that's what I need. More education!" Chip has three masters' degrees, including his divinity degree. He often says that he's too educated for his own good.

Chip says, "But anyway, all this multiverse talk puts me in mind of one of the weirdest, most misunderstood verses in the New Testament. Jesus says, in John 10:16, 'I have other sheep that are not of this sheep pen. I must bring them also. They too will listen to my voice, and there shall be one flock and one shepherd.' I've studied on this verse a lot over the years.

When the Jews heard it, they interpreted it to mean that Gentiles and Jews would become one flock, and they were truly pissed, and ready to stone Jesus. But what if Jesus meant he would go on to his next gig in another universe once his work in ours was done? What if the verse implies the vastness of the multiverse?"

Again, Charles gives the exploding head sign. "Wow. I never thought I'd find physics and religion being so cozy. That's pretty weird."

Chip says, "Hey, speaking of blasphemous interpretations of the Bible, here's one of my favorite jokes: Thomas Aquinas walks into a bar in Belfast. 'Barkeep, make me a Virgin Mary,' he says. 'Sorry,' says the barkeep. 'If He couldn't make one, neither can I.' 'I know, right?' Aquinas says. 'Just give me a tomato juice.'"

Charles puzzles over the joke for a moment and says, "I don't get it."

"Of course not, Mr. 'I'm an expert on theology.' You see, Thomas Aquinas did not believe in the Immaculate Conception, and was against the Church declaring it dogma. And Protestants typically don't believe in it. And Northern Ireland is Protestant."

"Well," says Charles, "If you have to explain it, it's not funny!"

"If you have to explain a joke to a moron, he's still a moron! Enough of this pondering of the Universe. We're out of beer. Time to start drinking wine! Oh, that reminds me of the other day. Trixie and I were sitting around sipping wine when she said, 'I love you so much, you know. I don't know how I could ever live without you.' I said, 'Is that you or the wine talking?' She said, 'It's me talking to the wine.'" Chip breaks into maniacal laughter. "Gotcha!"

Charles just shakes his head sadly.

The piano sounds like a cannonball / And the microphone smells like a beard

Billy Joel—*Piano Man*

Charles met Steve not long after meeting Edie. One evening Charles was walking by the Mary Reed Building and heard Mozart's "Rondo alla Turca" being played faster than he had ever heard it before. Curious, he found the piano practice room and stood at the door watching Steve tearing up the keyboard. Steve finished the piece, looked around, and saw Charles watching.

"Wow," Charles said. "You have some real chops!"

"Naw. I got short fingers and can barely span an octave."

"Well, you make up for it with speed and fire." Charles played bass in a jazz band on campus. He had thought their keyboardist was pretty talented, but Steve blew him away.

"Thanks. Look, you're not gonna turn me in, are you?" Steve turned sideways on the piano bench, leaning forward as if ready to bolt. His blond hair sprung from his head in tight, swept-back waves, as if he'd put his finger in a socket. The hair, a scruffy beard, a hand-rolled cigarette, huge engineer boots, and worn, dirty clothes conveyed a portrait of a derelict.

"What? No, no. I don't care," Charles remarked. "I guess that means you're not a student here," He was trying to determine how old this guy was—he looked old as the hills, but his eyes were a youthful teary blue.

"Used to be. Long time ago. Long story," Steve said, shifting off the bench. "Well, I guess I better be moving on." He hiked up his jeans and headed toward the door.

"No, no. Wait," Charles said, moving toward Steve to catch his elbow. Steve yanked his arm away and whirled to face Charles with a wary look in his eyes.

"Whaddaya doin'?" Steve looked ready to bolt.

"Look, look, uh, I'm in this jazz band, and, well, why don't I buy you a beer and let's talk."

"Where?"

"Over at the Stadium Inn. It's not far. Couple blocks."

Like a wary junkyard dog, Steve followed Charles from the room and across the campus, trailing him down Evans Avenue, always a few paces behind.

Once ensconced in a raggedy booth with a pitcher between them, Charles asked what Steve had meant about the long story.

Bit by bit, Steve told the story of his childhood as a musical prodigy in Bennett, Colorado, out in the dusty plains east of Denver.

"I was one of those kids who started playing at three or four, without no lessons," he said, simply. "You know, dime a dozen," he shrugged his shoulders and ran his fingers through his wild hair. "Always came real easy to me."

Steve eventually got a music scholarship and went to DU as a 16-year-old, a bit intimidated by the busy city and older classmates. But by the time he finished sophomore year, he realized that his fingers were too short to ever be an outstanding musician. So, he quit and got a job driving a semi. After eight years, he'd saved enough for a down payment on his own semi-tractor. Then, on a run out near Mesquite, Utah, the engine blew, requiring a hundred-thousand-dollar repair. After a few conversations with his insurance company and the bank that held the loan, Steve flipped the keys into the glove box and told the bank to come pick up their truck. His credit ruined, he worked for a while for a moving company doing household moves.

With a couple of beers in him, Steve relaxed a bit and told Charles about how every time he moved a house that had a piano, he would sit down and play a complicated Mozart or Beethoven piece, sitting there in his grubby moving clothes with his dingy long hair and cigarette hanging from his mouth. This invariably caused the homeowners to rush from wherever they were to gape at this apparent bum wringing beautiful music out of their piano.

Sorry, he'd say, and go off to move a bureau.

With his guard down, Steve was sardonically funny. "Hey," he said. "Did you hear about the kid who says to his mother, 'Mom, when I grow up, I'd like to be a musician.' She replies, 'Well, honey, you know you can't do both.'"

Charles laughed and Steve, now emboldened, cranked out a few more jokes in rapid fire.

"How do you make musicians complain? Pay them. What do you call a guitar player without a girlfriend? Homeless. What do you get when you drop a piano into a mine shaft? A Flat Miner. What's the difference between a pianist and God? God doesn't think he's a pianist. I think that's my favorite one."

"You've got a real talent there . . . for piano," Charles said, laughing. "Look, we ought to get together sometime and jam."

"Well, I'd like to, but I haven't got a piano or even a permanent address."

"We can play at Mary Reed. My band practices there all the time, after hours. As far as a place goes, you can crash at my house tonight. And you need a job?" Steve nodded. "Well, I do some pickup work with a moving company myself. The guy is always needing humpers. I'll hook you up."

"Dude, you just met me. Why you doin' all this stuff for me?"

"I dunno. I just think a guy who can play like you should play."

Charles was as good as his word. He'd moved to a three-bedroom house with two roommates at the beginning of the semester, and Steve bunked in the basement for a while. He even got a permanent gig at the moving company. After one of Charles's roommates complained and decided to leave, Steve took the empty room and moved a few personal items from his folks' basement back in Bennett. It was evident to Charles that Steve hadn't had a real home for some time.

Edie was not at all thrilled by Steve's residence at Charles's place. Even though they were not yet living together, a bone of contention that caused many arguments, Edie was often quite jealous of Charles's friends, especially if they came over to the house while she was there. Charles had observed that she had problems being around more than one or two people at a time. When Charles got tickets for a concert—George Harrison and Ravi Shankar at the Denver Coliseum—Edie tried to put a brave face on, but once through the turnstiles, she turned and bolted back outside.

"Edie!" Charles yelled, unsure what to do, since he was already inside the venue. "What's wrong?" Edie said, "I . . . can't. I . . . just can't. I'll grab a cab and go home. Enjoy yourself." With that, she ran around the corner. Charles was torn: the chance to see a Beatle versus his loyalty to his girlfriend. He turned and walked inside to find his seat.

While Steve was living at Charles's place, the first couple of times Edie came over, she spent the evening with her eyes fixed on Steve as if looking for that one wrong move that would end her life. She would usually excuse herself early, saying she had a headache, and Charles would have to drive her home. After this happened the second time, Charles asked Edie, "What's wrong, honey?"

"Nothing. I'm fine. I just have a headache. That grass was shit."

"You sure that's all? You were staring at Steve like he was the devil."

"Well, you gotta admit, he looks skeevy! What do you know about him?"

"Not a ton. He's a good guy, though."

"But how do you know? He looks like an ax murderer to me. Or like one of those burnouts from my unit in Nam. He creeps me out."

"OK, look. I'm pretty sure he's not an ax murderer, and he's my friend, so if you don't want to hang out with him, that's fine."

"I don't. I'm not ever coming over again if he's there."

"That could be difficult, since he lives here."

"You choose," Edie said with a severe look on her face.

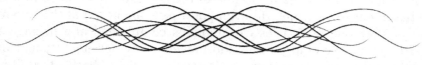

Steve and Charles became quite close, often crewing together on moving jobs. On long distance moves, they talked almost non-stop as the miles churned by. Steve, always wary, eventually opened up and discussed his life after the truck engine blew up.

"I drifted around the West from town to town and job to job. I didn't really want to become a drifter. I just never found a job I liked as much as driving."

"Why didn't you try to get a job with a trucking company, then?"

"Nah, after I bailed on my rig, I had to declare bankruptcy, that ruined my credit, and the question always came up as to what happened. Did I over-rev? Did I go too fast? Use the wrong gears? They always had questions like that, and so that was that. Even though the engine problem had nothing to do with the way I was driving, the truck companies were spooked. After trying a half a dozen places, I decided I needed something different."

"What about music?"

"Yeah, I did some piano bar gigs, but I don't really get off on playing standards, top 40 or somebody else's favorite song. If I ever have to play "My Way" again, I think I'll just shoot myself."

"Ah! A drifter with standards!"

Steve, who was driving at the time, shot a look at Charles and looked like he was about to get angry. He obviously thought better of it, and instead made a joke. "I told you. No standards!"

Charles snickered at the pun and relaxed. He'd had Steve go off on him a couple of times and it wasn't pretty. In a flash, Steve's face would turn red and taut, the veins would stand out all over his face and neck, and he'd squinch up his eyes and begin jabbing the air with his right index finger, sometimes poking Charles in the chest. It could be extremely scary to be around him when he was pissed, especially if he'd been drinking. Charles had never seen him be violent, but the stuff he'd say when dressing down the object of his rage could wound, and deeply.

Steve continued. "One time, I was playing this horseshit bar in Bumfuck, Kansas, and this guy came up to the piano, right in the middle of the Doobies' 'Long Train Running,' saying that I had the lyrics wrong. Fucker got up in my face—right in the fucking middle of the goddamn song—and yelled, 'Stop! It ain't "You know I saw Miss Lucy/Down along the tracks/She must've hung Alabama Lee/And she won't be comin' back" you turkey! It's "She lost her home and her family/And she won't be comin' back!"' That totally fucked up my concentration, so I stopped playing and said, 'What the fuck did you just say?' The guy, plastered, of course, repeated his spiel. I said, 'Thank you kindly, sir. Now get the fuck away from me before I tear off your arm, bitch slap you with it, and shove it up your ass.' He looked at me blankly, and for a second, I thought he was gonna take a shot at me, but he just said, 'Get it right!' and turned and lurched back to his seat."

"That's hilarious!"

"Well, that's what you get when you learn a song by ear and don't buy the sheet music," Steve said with a wry smile. "I've had several people come up, always politely, and always after I'm finished, and correct my misheard lyrics. That asshole was the only one who was rude about it."

"So, what made you stop playing in bars?"

"Well, the lifestyle sucks. Playing all night, usually just for tips, maybe a meal, and sleeping in the day. I'd rather drive a truck, or move furniture, or even do a shit job like cow stunner."

"Cow stunner? Do you dress up like a really, really attractive bull?"

"So not funny, dude. No, you take this pneumatic bolt gun, press it against the cow's skull, between the eyes, and bam! Trigger the gun and a bolt smashes into the cow's skull. And she's done."

Charles was disgusted by the mental picture. "My god, that sounds like a terrible job. How long did you last on that one?"

"Well, I really needed the job, and the pay was OK, but after a month, I started dreaming of ghost cows, I shit you not. Flyin' ghost cows! That was it for me. I got the hell out of Dodge. Literally. That's where the gig was."

Charles tried to stifle a laugh because Steve did not seem to be in the mood. Steve glanced over and gave him the evil eye. "Sorry," Charles said. "I know it's not funny. Just incongruous."

"Yeah, I was a vegetarian for a while after that. Still don't really eat red meat." The discussion was clearly depressing Steve, so he decided to lighten the mood a bit. "Hey, you want to hear a cow joke? I think a guy like you would really like this one."

Charles said, "Sure. Shoot. Um, strike that. Go ahead."

"What do you call a herd of bulls masturbating?"

"I give up."

"Beef strokin' off." After the tension of the cow discussion, this struck Charles as hilarious, and he laughed his head off.

"Wait a minute. What do you mean 'a guy like me?'" he asked. Steve just smiled and raised his eyebrows. The two drove for the next half hour without talking.

She's so sharp, sharper than cheese

J. Geils Band—*So Sharp*

Charles is working on a draft of a new blog post. He's not sure where he'll post it and not at all sure it will be received positively wherever he posts it. This one's hot, he thinks. I need to talk with Chip about this before I post it. He texts Chip, who says, "Come on over to my office." Chip throws on his jacket and walks across the street to Chip's office.

"'Sup, your Dudeness?" Chip asks when Rita ushers Charles into the office.

"I've written this blog post about the interactions of really smart people, especially those who are eternally the smartest guys in the room."

Chip replies, "Or gals?"

"Right," says Charles. "Although increasingly 'guys' seems to be non-gender-specific. But my observation is that it's the smart men who have the most trouble dealing."

"With what?"

"Look, just look at the post—it's nowhere near finished, but I'd like your thoughts." Charles hands Chip the pages and does his usual tour of the inside of the office while Chip reads it.

The Repelling Force of Intellect

The Universe contains myriad opposing forces: positive and negative magnetic poles, organization vs. chaos, and even moral concepts like good and evil. Most people are familiar with these forces. But there's a powerful force I've observed in the interactions between brilliant people that is not universally recognized.

If you're one of us, you know how it goes. You're in a meeting trying to develop a plan, and the Normals are blathering on about something when all of a sudden, somebody speaks up and offers a brilliant suggestion or insight. Your head snaps toward him or her automatically, and your eyes lock. Sometimes there's even the slight inclination of your chin as you recognize: Hello, fellow smart person.

Then you meet, intentionally just after the meeting, or at random at some other dreadful, thrashing, decision-making gathering. You're both excited, but a bit wary. Are you going to be competitors or cooperators (another set of opposing forces)? Can you find common ground? You're sizing each other up. Feeling for the edges of intellect, trying to determine if they are smart or they just talk smart.

Then either of two things can happen. You can form an alliance, and jointly try to move the Normals in the right direction, or you repel, like two positive magnetic poles, and have nothing more really to do with one another other than perhaps a nod while passing in the hall. This rapprochement is probably caused by the shock of no longer being unequivocally the smartest person in the room.

When you grow up being the smartest person in every room, you have mixed feelings. Often there's the feeling of loneliness. Where are my kindred intellects? Is there no one who can understand me? I am lonesome for my own kind.

Sometimes the opposite feeling dominates: I am homo superior, why don't these bugs recognize and cherish me? Look upon me and be amazed. This generates an arrogance that further pushes the Normals away.

You also might feel competitive with those who may be more-enlightened Normals, but whom you must beat back into their rightful subservience to your massive intellect. You belittle them in front of their peers and dominate every conversation.

When two Ultrabrights repel each other, it often leads to endless battles of wits, boasting, and other ego defense measures. Each has rarely been in this position before. Sure, you've worked with bright people, but you have scant experience working with another Ultrabright. You need to do what Normals constantly must do: find your place in the pecking order. Are you smarter than them? Are they smarter than you? Are they going to call bullshit on your brilliant ideas? Best to stay away, exchange your secret nods when in proximity, but essentially live and let live.

The magic happens when the Ultrabrights can resolve their issues, team up, and guide rather than bully the Normals in the right direction. Guiding can be difficult for a single Ultrabright to do because of their low tolerance for frustration. "Can't you see? Your idea is crap! We need to do it my way, and I haven't the time to convince you!"

Like a creosote bush, which inhibits growth of any plants within the reach of its roots, or the barren ring around a penicillin spore in a petri dish, some Ultrabrights lay waste to competition in their sphere of influence. They cannot tolerate the presence of other bright people. They stake out the smartest-guy-in-the-room position and sabotage anyone who dares challenge their intellect.

Now I don't want to go all Ayn Rand on you, but this is a serious problem for society. If you can accept the premise that as a society, we need the smartest people doing the smartest work in order for our lives to be improved, having Ultrabrights locking horns and suppressing all other forms of innovation is a bad thing. A very bad thing. I submit that this struggle may be a key reason why so many human systems fail. There have been exceptional examples of lots of Ultrabrights working together to achieve greatness: the Manhattan Project, the moon shot, Edison's laboratory. But if you look closely at these efforts, they generally feature an alpha male (probably an Ultrabright, but not necessarily) who knows how to encourage cooperation and innovation. These strong leaders are even rarer than Ultrabrights.

There's a long history of anti-intellectualism in the world, and especially in this country. Our culture marginalizes the bright, calling them losers, nerds, geeks, four-eyes, what have you. In the US, this problem goes back to the founding fathers and probably further. Many people found Jefferson insufferable because he always had the best ideas. Of course, like many Ultrabrights, the guy was a bit of a jerk too. He didn't have any patience for waiting while the Normals around him worked their way into the solution Jefferson knew was inevitable.

This is a common problem with Ultrabrights, who often don't have the best social skills. In many cases, this is self-fulfilling: They get rejected and so have little opportunity to learn how to be social. In other cases, it's part of their makeup. Many Ultrabrights are on the spectrum—that continuum that runs from a little bit nerdy through insufferable Sheldon to full-on Raymond.

I've created a website for fellow Ultrabrights to converse and discuss this problem and how to move forward. Please join at Ultra-Brights.com. You'll need to go through a vetting process—unfortunately necessary to weed out the trolls.

I hope together we can figure out a solution to the Ultrabright problem.

Chip finishes reading and stands up to stretch. "Well, you'll get the trolls on your butt for this one, my fellow Ultrabright."

"Yeah, I'm wrestling with even publishing the thing."

"No! You have to," Chip says heatedly. "I've never seen anyone tackle this problem. But perhaps you need to amp up the benefits of supporting rather than suppressing the Ultrabright. The Normals will look at what you wrote and think, 'This asshole thinks he's all that and a bag of chips' and leave it at that. How can you avoid insulting the Normals, which you kind of do here, and convince them that demonizing the Ultrabrights rather than praising them is against their own interests?"

"Good points, thanks. I think I'm coming it at it from the painful side, having been bullied and literally spat upon by Normals for being bright. I do try to present the cost to society for that kind of behavior, but I get what you're saying."

"Great. So, tone it down and make it less of a complaint. Yes, you want them to empathize with the pain society causes Ultrabrights, but in the end, the Normals need to understand what they would gain by supporting, not stigmatizing us."

"Yeah, I know, but I don't see anyone talking about this, and it's a real thing, isn't it? Haven't you experienced the conflict with other smart guys?"

"Well, I always think I'm the smartest guy in the room, including this room," Chip says to Charles, pulling himself to his full height, thumbs in his belt loops, chest out, and bumping Charles, chest to chest.

"In your dreams," says Charles. "You are so far beneath me that as you gaze upon my countenance, whale poop floating at 40,000 fathoms appears to you as a fluffy white cloud while I float effortlessly upon the waves."

Chip chuckles. "But seriously, Charles. I get it. There is isolation to being brilliant. And that often leads to so many lonely arrogant smart bastards: They haven't learned how to cope, not only with the Normals but with their peers. I counsel a lot of LASBs in my side gig."

"LASBs?"

"Try to keep up, you ninnyhammer! Lonely Arrogant Smart Bastards. So anyway, when you add in the fact that most of the brightest are on the autism spectrum, it's easy to see why they have problems integrating. By the way, you said 'Sheldon to Raymond.' I get that Raymond is Rain Man— and by the way, you should make that clear—but who's Sheldon?"

Charles is flabbergasted that Chip, the omnimedia omnivore, doesn't know Sheldon Cooper. "He's the main character on *The Big Bang Theory*."

"Oh, I hate that show. Tried to watch it once and couldn't make it more than a few minutes. So, this Sheldon guy's on the spectrum?"

"Oh, definitely. He's also on the arrogance spectrum."

"Ah! Good to know. You know, that stuff about locking eyes across the room reminds me of a bit from *Gravity's Rainbow* about stumbling 'into an orgy held by a Messiah no one has quite recognized yet, and to know, as your eyes meet, that you are his John the Baptist, his Nathan of Gaza, that it is you who must convince him of his Godhead, proclaim him to others, love him both profanely and in the Name of what he is.'"

"Too deep to get under, man," Charles says, awed as usual at Chip's instant access to a tremendous mental library of pertinent quotes. "I suppose that may describe the moment that Jesus met John. Mind if I use that in the post?"

"'Tain't mine, you tosser! Pay attention. It's Pynchon's. You really need to read that book."

"Tried to so many times. It's just too confusing."

"Well, it's all in how you read it. If you want to understand every aside, every poorly-punctuated lurch to a new narrative line, every stream-of-consciousness jag, then you'll be frustrated. Just gloss over the hard stuff and the abrupt transitions and get the main ideas."

Charles shrugs and thinks he might have to read the book to get Chip off his back. "Well, anyway, back to the post. Should I post it? I guess that's my main question."

"Well, it needs some work, as we discussed, and an ending, of course. Something beyond inviting Ultrabrights to a website. But, yeah. You should do it. Just don't read the comments. I'll do that for you, if you like."

"Great idea! A journalist buddy of mine has an intern read the comments and pass along anything helpful, which generally isn't much. Anything I should add to the post, other than an ending?"

"I think you've captured the smart person's dilemma, which, by the way, is getting worse in this Alternative Facts era we're now living in. Hey, I got a joke for ya." Charles knows there's no stopping him, so he says, "OK, whip it out."

Chip feints toward his zipper and says, "So when I was younger, I went with the senior pastor to visit a farmer, one of the pillars of the local church. We were sitting on the fence by the driveway, and as far as the eye could see were beautiful eight-foot cornstalks. Pastor says, "You know Norm, you and God have done tremendous work out here." "Yah," says the guy. "But you should have seen it when God had it by himself." As usual, Chip roars with laughter while Charles groans.

I am so into you, I can't get to know the nurse

Atlanta Rhythm Section—*So Into You*

Edie and Charles went to an amusement park and got on a Ferris wheel ride where the cabs spun on their long axes. Partway into the ride, Edie couldn't take the disorientation and said, "I'm going to barf."

Charles grabbed the wheel that controlled the spinning of the cab and constantly cranked it to keep the cab upright throughout the rest of the ride. His arms and shoulders were on fire as he struggled as the ride continued for what seemed like forever. Throughout the rest of the ride, Edie howled, "I'm gonna barf! Oh, my God, I'm gonna barf!"

When the ride finally ended, and they got out of the cab, Charles was drenched in sweat and it was his world that was spinning. Even at the time, it seemed like a metaphor for their relationship: Charles the uptight, upright savior in Edie's spinning world.

Nonetheless, shortly after the amusement ride, Charles acquiesced to Edie's constant requests and moved out of the house he shared with Steve and moved with Edie into a little four-unit student apartment building over near Broadway. The apartment was a small, shabby one-bedroom affair with tiny windows overlooking the broken pavement of a small parking lot and the buzzing traffic on Evans Avenue. The kitchenette linoleum was cracked and buckling, and the place hosted a small village of cockroaches, one of the few successful insects in Denver's mile-high dryness. Steve moved into the apartment beneath them, which Edie didn't like at all, but was powerless to prevent.

The couple pooled their furniture, much of it harvested each May from the overflowing dumpsters as the undergrads discarded anything bigger than a suitcase before disappearing for the summer, or the rest of their lives. The bookshelf that spanned the living room windows was a cinder blocks and boards affair that Charles had moved from place to place through a series of short-term living situations during the past couple of years. On it stood Charles's one extravagance: a state-of-the-art turntable, a serviceable receiver, and large, loud, speakers.

Edie's touches in the apartment were few. She was used to living with only what would fit in a backpack and suitcase. Her one memento was a cut-down howitzer shell casing upon which several soldiers' names had been scratched. Edie didn't want to talk about it much, but it was obviously important to her since she placed it in the middle of their rickety coffee table. She often flicked her cigarette ashes into it when she was really out of it.

Their relationship, always a bit rocky due to Edie's frequent war dreams and daytime flashbacks, seemed to even out a bit after they moved in together. Still, Charles didn't feel that Edie trusted him enough to confide in him completely, and he wondered if she ever would.

"Look," Edie shouted during an argument in their kitchen. "You need to understand. For me there's black, and there's white. You're either black or white to me. No gray. And now you're black, dammit, so get the hell out here before I do something we'll both regret." Charles grabbed his coat and hightailed it out to take solace in a bar down the street.

One day a few weeks later, Charles came home to find an ambulance in the parking lot. Steve was leaning against a railing looking distraught. Charles bolted from his car and rushed over to Steve.

"What happened? What's going on?"

Steve looked at Charles with teary, unfocused eyes. "Uh, Charles, ahh, it's Edie." He turned away and smashed his hand down on the hood of a nearby car.

"What, what happened to her?" Charles was starting to freak out and grabbed Steve, turning him to face him.

"She tried to kill herself, Charles. Slashed her wrists—the long way, up the veins. She was serious." Steve hung his head and shook it sadly, tears dripping from his eyes.

Charles rushed over to the back of the ambulance, just as the medics were slamming the doors. "Wait! That's my girlfriend!" he shouted. One of the medics said, "She's lost a lot of blood and we need to get her to the hospital right away. You can see her when she gets into recovery." With that, the medics climbed into the truck, turned on the sirens and lights, and roared out onto Evans Avenue.

Charles turned back to Steve, who threw an arm around his shoulders. "Charles, if I hadn't dropped upstairs to see if you wanted to go play racquetball, Edie would have probably succeeded."

Charles had begun to cry and sobbed, "I don't understand. She seemed happier than usual recently."

"Yeah, well, believe me, she meant it. She had taken off her top, laid down in the bathtub and slit her veins all the way up to the elbows. There was a puddle of blood in the tub when I found her. I grabbed her wrists and hoisted them up above her head." Steve paused, considering how to proceed. "Charles, she fought me. She struggled to yank her arms down, and, damn, she's a strong girl. I had to quit for a minute to call 911, but when I went back, even though she had to be weak from the loss of blood, she still fought me until she fainted, just before the medics came. Shit!" Steve shuddered at the memory. "God damn, I need a drink." He wiped his eyes.

Charles stared in stunned silence at his friend. He couldn't process it. It just can't be, Charles thought. The dreams seemed to have become less frequent, and Edie seemed more normal recently, with not a single blow up in weeks. "Yeah, I could use a drink myself," Charles said, "But I've got to get to Denver General. Can you drive me? I think I'm in shock."

"Sure, buddy," Steve said with a sigh. "I guess I gotta wait to get that drink."

Edie pulled through but was mad as a wet hen when Charles finally was able to visit her in recovery.

"Goddamn that fucking Steve!" she shouted. "He should have left well enough alone!"

"Edie, you can't mean that. I know you're hurting, but Steve saved your life. Fate put him there to help you."

"Fate is a foolish thing to take chances with!" said Edie, a bit quieter, and quoting Charles's favorite *Gay Divorcee* line. Charles had to stifle a smile. Edie was clever even when in pain.

"Why'd you do it, Edie?"

"I can't stand it anymore. The dreams. The breakdowns. The fucking strangeness of having to live among all these people who haven't a goddamn clue what real life is like. All the people I lost! That poor baby on the plane. Even you, poor clueless you. All the shit I've put you through. You don't deserve me."

Charles had heard this type of breakup statement before, but it generally meant he was the unworthy one. When Edie was eventually released, she and Charles fell back into their old patterns, and Edie continued to wake screaming from dreams a little more often now.

Edie no longer had classes on Fridays and would often just hang around their apartment all day. Often by the time Charles came home, she was blackout drunk and barely able to stand. After a few weeks of this, Charles confronted her. They agreed to remove all alcohol from the apartment, and Charles called Steve to come upstairs and haul the cases of beer and the bottles of wine back to his place. Steve looked like he had won the lottery, with a huge smile on his face. Charles, however, looked gray and grim.

The alcohol ban worked for about six weeks. Charles found it refreshing to not have alcohol around. Maybe I needed to cut back a bit myself, he thought. I'm not an undergrad anymore. Then one Friday, Charles came back from class to find Edie passed out on the floor beside an empty bottle of grain alcohol, barely breathing. Charles called 911 and they took her to Denver General. After pumping Edie's stomach and starting a saline IV, Edie stabilized.

Once she was conscious and sober, the doctor said he could release her to Charles's care, but warned him of the possible deadly effects of alcohol withdrawal. "She could die of the DTs or of several other symptoms. I strongly recommend that she enter a detox program right away. They can monitor her and help get through the worst of it with medication."

Edie was at first completely opposed to the idea, but then Steve showed up, having seen the note Charles had hastily shoved under his door on the way out. The two of them double-teamed Edie and finally, she agreed to at least talk to the social worker. The social worker was very positive and kind, describing alcoholism as a disease, and not a moral failing. Eventually, they convinced Edie to go to county detox, where the social worker had found a bed. She was to remain there for at least two days.

Edie asked Charles to go back to their apartment to get her a book and some clothes. The nurse said he didn't have much time before the transport would be there to take Edie to detox. Charles rushed back to his car and drove madly across town back to their place. He grabbed the book, some underwear, and a few tops, and bolted back to his car, driving again like a madman back up Broadway to the hospital. When he arrived, he saw a van waiting in the ER and raced back to the trauma room Edie was in, fearing that he had missed her departure. As he came down the hall, it appeared the lights were out in the room and his heart sank. But once he got there, he saw Edie, and the orderlies were just coming with the stretcher to take her to the van. She looked almost catatonic as she accepted the grocery bag full of things from Charles. He kissed her and said, "Edie, this is for the best. You'll get better." She gave a slow nod, and then the orderlies wheeled the stretcher out to the van.

As he watched the van leave the parking lot, Charles began to cry. He got in his car and wept for five minutes before drying his eyes and slowly driving home. On the way, he stopped off to buy four Snickers bars. I need to stress eat, he decided. He got home and devoured half a bar before finally making himself some dinner, a leftover burrito from their last trip to the Oak Door Mexican restaurant.

No visitors were allowed for as long as she was in detox, but later that evening, Edie called Charles from a county phone. "I need you to get a couple of prescription meds I have for high blood pressure and bring them to me."

Charles had not been aware that Edie needed the meds. He said he'd bring them, and Edie hung up before saying where they could be found. Charles couldn't find them in the medicine cabinet. He ran around the apartment searching, cursing a blue streak. He finally found the meds in a bedside table drawer and hopped in his car before realizing he didn't know the address of the county detox center. He ran back up the stairs to the apartment and found the white pages. After some difficulty, he found the address for the detox unit, about five miles away.

He got there a little after 6 pm as another van was loading up a patient coming out of the center. He entered a depressing, bare, elevator foyer with a concrete floor and black smudges all over the walls. There was a squawk box with a red button on it next to an elevator. The sign on the elevator said, "Press the button—once." Charles pressed the button, but nothing happened for about five minutes. They probably are busy, and they don't want people leaning on the red button, he thought. So, he waited another few minutes before pressing the button again, this time hard. Turned out he hadn't pressed it hard enough the first time because the box came alive with a phone dialing sound followed by someone asking him what he wanted. He told the box that he had medications for Edie and the box said to wait while someone came down from the third floor to get them.

After a few minutes, the elevator doors opened, and a short black guy with a wary look on his face looked at him, and then stretched out his hands for the pill bottles. Charles gave them to him, the guy mumbled thanks and pressed the button to return to the third floor. Damn, it's like a fortress here, like they're expecting some kind of a siege. He returned to his car and drove home in a stupor.

Once again, Edie survived and returned to living with Charles. But the suicide attempt and the alcoholism cemented the feeling within Charles that he had no future with Edie. He had been agonizing for a year about leaving her. What if I drive her to attempt suicide again, and she succeeds? I couldn't live with that.

Despite his fears, Charles broke off the relationship three months after the detox episode. Edie took off for the Rockies, and Charles didn't see her again until one October night a couple of years later when she rang Charles's bell. Wild-haired, crazy-eyed, twenty pounds heavier, and wearing shabby clothes that were too big for her, she asked if she could crash at his house. She said she'd been living in St. Louis and she'd driven straight through to Denver that day. She had this nutty idea about traveling across country to live the artist's life in San Francisco and homesteading a house in the city.

As they sat on the couch, three across with Charles's fiancé, Karen, Edie told the couple that she'd gotten a gun and had started taking target practice on a regular basis. "A girl needs protection these days. One night in St. Louis not too long ago, I was out too late and too drunk, and these two black guys grabbed me, threw me down, and raped me." Edie related the story almost in a monotone, with no apparent emotion. Charles and Karen were shocked.

"Oh, my god, Edie!" Charles said. "Did they beat you up, too?"

"No, they just had their fun and split. I didn't even go to the ER. I went home, drank a bottle of wine, and got up for work the next day."

Charles and Karen exchanged a look, and Charles could see tears in Karen's eyes. She excused herself and went into their small kitchen. Charles followed her. "You OK, Honey?"

"Oh, not really. That poor woman! And she doesn't even show any emotion about it! She must be so hurting inside."

Charles said he agreed and asked if Karen wanted him to tell Edie she couldn't stay the night. Karen said no, it was the least they could do for her. She'd heard the Edie Viet Nam stories and, although she was a little jealous about Charles's ex showing up at their home, she was making the best of it.

"I think I'll just get out some chips and salsa for you two and go to bed. I'll put new sheets on the spare bed. Tell Edie there's a blanket in the closet if she needs it." Charles kissed her on the forehead and said good night.

Charles returned to the living room with the chips and salsa and sat back down with Edie. After he made Karen's excuses, he said, "Edie, that's so horrible what happened to you. How are you doing?"

"Oh, it's nothing. I got over it pretty quickly. I just decided it's never going to happen again." Edie pulled a .38 pistol out of a pocket of her baggy jeans and showed it to Charles.

"Uh, is that thing loaded?" was all Charles could think of to say.

"Sure, it's loaded. I'm a single woman on the road. But the safety's on, don't worry. I know my way around a gun." Edie shoved the gun back in her pocket. "It's never going to happen again, and so that's all there is to that." She nodded her head curtly as if putting a seal on the subject.

After a few minutes of silence, Edie said, "You know, I've been thinking a lot about becoming a lesbian."

Charles didn't know what to make of this non-sequitur. His mind went back to their time together at school and he thought about the very close friendships Edie had had with a succession of women. Back then, he had wondered what all the touching was about. Charles didn't know what to say and just stared at Edie, thinking she'd probably elaborate. Instead, Edie jumped off the couch and rummaged through her huge backpack, pulling out a portfolio.

"Here's what I've been working on recently," she said, handing Charles a pencil drawing. Despite Edie having had a few drawing courses when she was working on her fine arts degree, the drawing looked like the work of an untrained amateur. Charles didn't know what to say, and obviously didn't react as enthusiastically as Edie would have liked, so she picked a fight and, even though she had already driven 850 miles that day, stormed out of the house yelling, "You're still the same!" Charles responded coolly, "And so are you, my dear."

Perplexed, Charles turned the "thinking of becoming gay" business over and over in his mind and eventually decided that this was typical Edie. She always had to feel in control of her destiny lest she spiral into madness. It would be just like her to decide to be gay, either for real or for the shock effect. Well, I wish her luck, he thought.

Ever since this weird encounter, Charles was vaguely afraid that they would meet again, only this time, she would avenge herself upon him for jilting her. This paranoid fantasy was fueled in part by numerous midnight phone calls, obviously long distance. The caller usually waited for 20 seconds or so and then hung up without saying anything. Even though Charles had moved frequently over the years, after about six months in a new place, the calls would begin again. As the years went on, the calls decreased in frequency, but never quite ended, inspiring a sense of dread that often took days for Charles to shake.

The truth is lost and maybe never to be found / Like the shadows of my panty line

Kamelot—*Sacrimony (Angel Of Afterlife)*

Charles is dreaming.

He meets Sigourney Weaver secretly in the back of a cruddy coffee shop, far away from the windows. They are involved in some sort of illicit undertaking, a plot, a heist, or something similar, and they quickly leave the shop, then walk the streets quickly, aimlessly.

Finally, in a large gathering in a roomy house, Sigourney takes Charles and another plot member each by the hand and winks, leading them into a corner of the huge living room, which is dominated by a king-sized canopied bed. She means to take them both to bed, but there are children all around in the living room, clamoring for autographs from Sigourney the star.

She sits on the bed and begins to strip off her clothing. She gestures to the curtains on either side of the bed. Charles jumps up and begins drawing them. Like a hospital bed, the curtains hang by beaded chains and draw all the way around. The kids are on the outside, as is Charles's rival. Charles winks and says, "See you in a bit," as he draws the curtain right in front of the other man. Sigourney sits in tailor position on the bed, entirely nude, with her pudenda showing through a wispy beard. Charles examines her labia and is struck by the similarity between the minora and her nose.

The labia are long and narrow and symmetrical just like Sigourney's nose. Charles theorizes that women's labia are shaped like their noses, a corollary to the theory that for men, a big nose equals a big penis. Charles thinks amusingly of the various reasons why no one has ever discovered this relationship: the hidden nature of vaginas; men are usually distracted when in the area; prudish attitudes would prevent such research. He thinks of a study he read about once—by a European researcher who performed an exhaustive investigation of female genitalia, categorizing their size and shape. He remembers the guffaws that such research elicited from the professors at the college he used to work at.

Sigourney is glistening and obviously ready for love. Her body is sleek and lean. She has tied her hair back in a loose ponytail and holds her arms out toward him, quite like her character in *Ghost Busters*. Charles looks down at his body, and, finding himself suddenly undressed, moves over to her on the bed. They kiss and fondle for a while. The children are making noise beyond the curtain. Sigourney says, "We don't want to get caught. Here, sit up on the bed." She turns her back to him and straddles him, slipping his rod into her slowly.

He embraces her small breasts from behind as she moves up and down on him. As usual during dream sex, Charles can't feel anything. He goofily breaks into song: "Anhedonia, Anhedonia! What makes the coming so hard?" When younger, Charles could not even get to the point of entry in his dreams. Now he can enter his dream females, but there is no sensation, and worse yet, this lack of sensation is evident in the dream, so that he is irritated by it even while dream-fucking.

He thinks about his rival having to take sloppy seconds and knows that Sigourney was just being polite in asking the rival along.

Suddenly, a neighbor across the hall starts using a power saw, and Charles awakens from the dream, tight and turgid and frustrated as usual.

He lies in bed and wonders about the meaning of the dream. Still woozy from sleep, he thinks that maybe it's about the longing for days gone by. The Sigourney in the dream was, after all, the '80s Sigourney. But he never really was all that hot for Sigourney Weaver. As he slips out from under the top sheet and swings his legs to the floor he remembers she was nude in one movie—what was it—long ago, probably the '80s or '90s, in a bathtub—pursued by a bad guy or something.

Awful stupid thing to be thinking and dreaming about, he decides, as he clicks on the bathroom light and turns on the radio. As he shaves, the Atlanta Rhythm Section comes on singing "Homesick." OK, that's weird, he thinks. I was just thinking about longing for days gone by, and now this song comes on. He thinks, it's true. We '60s children are really trapped in a more vibrant, but past, time. The '60s youth were the spoon that stirred the culture, which is still swirling, no matter what the conservatives today think—the planet still cannot rest from the ideas that were formed in the crucible of cultural upheaval way back then. He chuckles as he remembers he used to think the song went, "Homesick, to kiss this guy."

Turns out it's a Two for Tuesday, and ARS' "So Into You" comes on. Charles smiles broadly as he remembers when the song first hit the airwaves in summer of 1977. The lyrics seemed way too specific to his situation then: In graduate school for his Ph.D., he was involved with Claire, the quirky Kansan in the poetry class he taught. When he first heard the song, he heard the lyrics as, "I am so into you, I can't get to know the nurse" and it made him think of Edie. Chuckling, Charles wipes his face and runs the shower. I wonder what Claire is up to now?

Later, at lunch with Chip, Charles tells him about his dream and the synchronicity of his morning. "I have these déjà vu moments all the time," he says. "Mostly it's just annoying, feeling like you've been here before, but not being able to put a finger on when, where, and why."

"So, you're David Crosby, now, Hippie Boy?" Chip says. They're at a Rasta vegan restaurant in Little Haiti. "I'd worry more about Vu Jà Dé."

"What's that?"

"The unshakable feeling that this has never, ever happened before." Chip roars with laughter at his own lame joke.

"Jeez, man, you're about as funny as a screen door in a submarine." Charles takes a forkful of his tofu curry. Chip smiles broadly and digs into another vegan chicken wing.

"Well, I wish you would take me seriously on this," Charles says. "What if we really have been here before? What if this is Purgatory, and we're doomed to repeat our pitiful lives until, by luck or chance, we get them right?"

"This ain't Purgatory, bucko," Chip asserts around a mouthful of faux chicken. "There's not nearly enough suffering. And 1 Corinthians 3:10— which our president would call One Corinthians—says there's supposed to be fire: 'Each one's work will become clear; for the Day will declare it, because it will be revealed by fire; and the fire will test each one's work.'"

"Hmm. Sounds more like hell to me." Charles says. "But I thought you heretics didn't go in for all that Catholic mumbo jumbo."

"And speaking of mumbo jumbo," Chip says. "why do you believe in Purgatory? I thought you were a lapsed Catholic."

"Not lapsed. Retired. I retired for good from all religion while in college, done with pretending while accompanying my dad to church every Sunday. I view religion as a fantastic set of incredible myths that generally describe how people project their inner lives using archetypes."

"So, you're a Jung man, old man?" Chip snickers at his pun. "Anyway, Methodism, like the rest of the Protestants, rejects the idea of a purifying Purgatory in favor of thinking it's a kind of waiting room for Resurrection Day. And, here's the kicker: There's no real support for the idea of Purgatory in scripture."

Charles ponders for a moment. "OK, we've gotten off track, here. I don't really believe that the sense of déjà vu is due to us being in Purgatory; it was just a thought. So, what do you think the dream meant? Could it have been prophetic?"

"Prophetic? That you'll hook up with Sigourney Weaver? In your dreams! Literally. But as to the meaning of your dream, I dunno. Maybe you're secretly really hot for Sigourney Weaver and she reminds you of Edie? You know, tall, skinny, small boobs. Maybe you'd rather be in bed with a semi-hot Hollywood actress in her prime than to be picking at your tofu at the Garden of Eatin' in Little Haiti with me. I know I would. And by the way, doofus, you wouldn't have had a shot at her even if you'd hit the lottery back in the '80s. And prophetic! Ha! If you think I would believe for one moment that you're somehow going to meet Sigourney Weaver and do the Reverse Cowgirl with her, you're goofier than I think you are! Finish up. I gotta get back."

The next day, Charles writes an essay for the atheist and counterculture blog, the Orbit.

ATHEISM • ACTIVISM • CULTURE

I Got Your Messiah Right Here

By Charles Beaumont DeFries

When I was about 11 or 12, I began to wonder if I might be Jesus.

I was clearly smarter than anybody I knew, excepting maybe my parents; I felt I had wisdom, even at that early age; and I had a grasp of the world as it is that I thought transcended not only my peers but obviously most adults who were running things.

I know what you're thinking. But this was not a full-of-myself moment, really. I truly started to wonder what I was made to do and had to consider the fact that I might actually be the Second Coming.

Having turned this idea around in my mind for several months, I concluded that it was a real possibility that, once I turned 30, I would find my destiny as the new Christ. All of this speculation was completely separate from my attitude about religion and the Catholic Church.

In fact, my experiences in Catechism fed into my feeling of spiritual superiority. So many of the Bible tales the nuns told did not make any sense on the face of them. David and Goliath. The pillar of salt. The parting of the Red Sea. The plagues. There always seemed to either be a rational explanation for these miraculous events, or they strained all credulity. If these Biblical figures had all this power, why did they not subjugate the Earth and bend all people to their faith? Why was the history of the Jews—God's Chosen People—fraught with such suffering? Wandering in the desert for 40 years after a horrific escape from Egypt? Very little of what they tried to teach me made sense.

As little sense as the Old Testament made, it was the New Testament that really had me scratching my head. And the thing that particularly got me crossed up was the idea that nobody went to Heaven before Jesus died for them. That's what the Sisters taught.

It just really bothered me that the billions of lost souls in Purgatory before Christ died would never be saved because they had died before his sacrifice could wash away their sin. All of them—the whole spectrum from the righteous and the just-less-than-evil—every last one of them were the same in God's eyes, destined to wait in Purgatory for the Second Coming.

All this was bad enough, but the question that particularly galled me was: Why did Jesus' own father, who died before him, not get into Heaven? That's what the nuns told us. The idea is simply preposterous and, if true, an indicator of a god that had his priorities wrong. That's why I took the confirmation name of Joseph. The poor guy.

The nuns didn't take too kindly to my questioning their dogma, especially when I asked if people who were Protestants or Jews got into heaven and was told no. I decided that either this god was not one of goodness and light, or the whole church and the Bible were wrong. The rules of the church and the conflicting messages sent by the Old Testament about the temperament of the Lord confused me to the point that I just set it all aside as nonsense. At 12. In my bedroom.

From what I could tell, Jesus was a pretty cool guy. Almost every quote from him is antithetical to the beliefs and conduct of his purported church. Take as just one example: the rich man and the eye of the needle. Even if you leave aside the slick Protestant preachers—God wants you to be rich!—you're still left with the ungodly opulence of the Vatican and every medieval cathedral, all built on the backs of the suffering faithful. If Jesus meant that seeking riches was wrong, or turned you away from righteousness, or tempted you to do evil things, how could all this in-your-face wealth jibe with a religion of peace and equality?

I began to think that if Jesus came again, he would find little to like in his legacy: holy wars, persecution, inquisitions, "Christian" political parties, and nonsensical dictates from a splintered church. Why no birth control, for example? If God gave us free will and also gave us the ingenuity to make all the wondrous things our civilization has accomplished, why, when we find a way to control fertility, is that against God's word? Why isn't, say, building huge death machines, or cities or, or, or feedlots that foster the suffering of God's creatures? Why aren't these things subject to a papal ban?

It became clear to me that religion, and in particular Catholicism, just didn't make any sense, if looked at rationally. Its central figure, a man of peace—who taught to turn the cheek, to remain humble, to not be rich—seemed reasonable, but the whole apparatus surrounding his teachings reeked of hypocrisy and unfaithfulness. Of course, I couldn't articulate it quite this way when I was 12.

It seemed to me that Jesus dying had had no real effect, other than to provide religious structures that men could use to justify anything they chose. If he really had absolved us of sin, why didn't things get better? A major sin—Original Sin—wiped off the ledger. Wonderful! Shouldn't mankind, and especially Christians, be better off after such a burden was lifted? Even just a little better?

I asked myself: Did Christ's dying fundamentally lead to a lack of sin or a decrease of sin? No. Were the people who carried on their lives after his passing better in some way? Clearly not. There was more of the same: God's new People—the Christians—were also persecuted and killed for their beliefs. No change there.

But more important to me was this question: If I was the next Jesus, what was my mission to be? I felt it would be to either return the Catholic Church to its core beliefs of their gentle savior, or to create a new religion that not only espoused Jesus' theology but provided a means for mankind to live better lives.

This idea terrified me, to say the least. If I really was a messiah, it seemed like a huge, thankless, dangerous, and probably fatal task, given what I knew about human civilization and religious history. I decided to study spiritual history and see if there was ever a religion that had succeeded as I thought Christianity should have.

One of the writers I ran into almost immediately was Reimarus, the German philosopher who created Deism and who asserted that Jesus was a politically minded secular revolutionary who hoped to establish an earthly kingdom through force. This all went south when he was arrested and crucified. His disciples, hoping to achieve his goals, or at least to glorify themselves, stole his body, fabricated the resurrection story and clothed the Jesus myth in spiritual messiah trappings based on the Jewish concept.

I was fascinated by this possibility. And I also wanted to know: What defined a messiah for the Jews? Did they expect someone to come, die for them, and absolve them of sin? In other words, was this the original concept of the messiah, or had the disciples transformed it?

Come to find out, the Jewish messiah concept was a fairly earthly one, at least early on. Not only did Jewish tradition not prophesy a singular messiah, a messiah didn't even need to be Jewish. Cyrus the Great, king of Persia, is named in the Old Testament as a messiah for his decree to rebuild the Jerusalem Temple. Far from a spiritual savior, the Jews thought of a messiah as a holy anointed king or high priest for the line of David.

Although the Jewish messiah was not totally a secular guy, he did have a large number of secular tasks to undertake. In addition to starting the Messianic Age, he would gather the Jews back into the land of Israel, usher in an era of peace, build the Third Temple, father a male heir, re-institute the Sanhedrin—the governing council—and so on. Despite the religious meaning of these tasks, they're pretty worldly in nature, more reflecting a political revolution than a huge spiritual change or awakening.

So, I studied the Messianic Age that the Jewish messiah would establish. It was to be a time of universal peace and brotherhood during which crime, war and poverty would cease to be. This seems more like an earthly utopia than a great spiritual awakening. Sure, it was expected that, given this setting, Jews would be able to deepen their relationship with God, but just look at the secular trappings set forth for this era in the Bible:

> They shall beat their swords into plowshares and their spears into pruning hooks; nation will not lift sword against nation and they will no longer study warfare. (Isaiah 2:4)

> The wolf will live with the lamb, the leopard will lie down with the goat, the calf and the lion and the yearling together; and a little child will lead them. The cow will feed with the bear, their young will lie down together, and the lion will eat straw like the ox. The infant will play near the hole of the cobra, and the young child put his hand into the viper's nest. They will neither harm nor destroy on all my holy mountain,

for the earth will be full of the knowledge of the Lord as the waters cover the sea. (Isaiah 11:6-9)

The messiah will bring about vegan lions!

Except for the last bit about being full of the knowledge of the Lord, the rest of these descriptions are very secular. Maimonides did clarify some of the spiritual nature of the Messianic Age in his torah, but that was 11 centuries after Christ, and 18 centuries after Isaiah. Maimonides' work, even though it became part of Jewish law, may even be seen as an attempt to spiritualize an age that had previously been defined only in secular terms.

Interestingly, the events that presage the coming of the messiah are eerily similar to those of the New Testament Apocalypse—and our current age: a dwindling generation that is either overwhelming wicked or righteous, beset by troubles, and facing enemies all around.

It became very clear to me that all of the Jewish messiah's acts are grounded in this Earth, not in a spiritual realm. All wrongs done to the Jews will be remedied; they'll get their land back; all the world will worship the God of Israel; evil will be conquered; death will be abolished; they'll experience the Torah directly, but nothing essentially changes in their faith. They just get more time to get closer to God.

So, the Jewish messiah's main purpose is to rid the Jews of their physical suffering, not to forgive any original sin. This is especially true because Jews don't believe in original sin to start with. Thus, they don't cotton to the idea of the forgiveness of that sin.

Upon finding this out, I asked myself: So, where did Jesus' disciples get this forgiveness idea from? The idea of the sins of the fathers passing through the generations was an old one, present in Greek religions and others. But it turns out it was Paul who codified this idea into the concept of Original Sin, created by Adam's bite of the apple and absolved by the crucifixion of Jesus.

What a great move this was, especially if you wanted to found a church! If people could attain a spotless soul by themselves, they would have little need for a church, priests, or possibly even for an organized religion. But if the only way to obtain absolution is through the mediation of a church and its priests, and this absolution must be refreshed on a weekly basis, well that's a basis for handing over a huge amount of power (and money) to a religious institution. Religion begins to resemble an addiction.

Paul brilliantly brought into being a framework that has oppressed the world ever since. Today every good Christian is a forgiveness junkie, needing a weekly fix to remain righteous.

I understood all this at 12 and threw off my belief in religion, and a god that could be petitioned to improve my life. But for many years I didn't shake the feeling that I might just be a messiah. Now, many years later, I have totally given up faith that there was or will be a messiah.

And you should, too.

Charles is so excited about this latest post that he immediately texts the link to Chip. He then begins to wait, in his usual agony over how Chip will respond. He reads the post over and over and becomes convinced that he's really stepped in it this time. Chip's gonna hate this. I'm not sad I posted it, but I wish I hadn't sent it to him. Oh, man. He's gonna be furious!

After a couple hours of this torture, Chip texts back, "We should meet and talk about this." They agree to meet at Charles's place for dinner. As they sit down to a dinner of vegan hot dogs, Chip says, "I got to tell you, Savior Boy, this messiah complex of yours is a little worrying."

"I got better. I don't really think that way anymore."

"OK, but, wow! My psychoanalytic friends would probably have diagnosed you as having grandiose delusions, or even worse, bipolar disorder and schizophrenia."

"Well, do you honestly think I'm sick?"

"In so many ways, beloved," Chip laughs and winks. "But, seriously, no, you're just a little odd."

"You're a big odd!"

"What are you, a middle-schooler? What a lame comeback." Charles sticks his tongue out, puts his thumbs in his ears, and waggles his hands. "But seriously," he says, "what do you think of the post?"

"Well, I follow some of what you say. All human organizations are at least a little corrupt, and, of course, I love it when you attack the Catholic Church. But I can't say Protestant faiths are a whole lot better. Especially when these charlatan evangelists milk the credulous and feeble-minded for their benefit. And I do like your take on Jesus. I just disagree that, on the whole, religions have entirely corrupted his message."

Charles nods, and says, "Understood, and I didn't really expect you to get behind all my points. What do you think about the 'Paul created Christianity out of whole cloth' business?"

"Well, of course, it's very similar to your theme in your Jesús Christos chapter attempt. As a scholar, I can see some support for it. Paul, as you know, was not one of the original Apostles. In fact, before his vision of Jesus on the road to Damascus, Paul was obsessed with persecuting the early disciples of Jesus. Although, in his defense, not all Biblical writings attributed to Paul are thought to be his. I agree with you that if there were no Paul, there's a good chance there would be no Christianity. But when he was blinded by the light, Jesus took care of that. After Ananias of Damascus restored his sight, Paul began to preach the Word and began to found churches. In your Jesús Christos chapter, you blamed Christianity, or Paulicism, on him. But I believe if it weren't Paul, it would have been some other great organizer that Jesus would have chosen to found his church. You got any beer to wash down these terrible vegan hot dogs you gave me to eat?"

Charles nods and gets up to go to the fridge as Chip continues. "As far as the 'whole cloth' business, it's clear that Paul's sources were the Apostles and others who had heard Jesus' teachings. It's not like he made everything up."

"OK," Charles says, popping the caps off two bottles of Guinness, "I'll give you that, but I would be much more likely to believe the Jesus story if he had written anything down. Hearsay evidence isn't admissible in court, just in religion."

"Ouch!" Chip says. "Objection, Your Dishonor!" Both men laugh, and Chip wets his finger and draws a vertical line in the air. "One point to Charles the Poopy Pants." Charles scowls and mimes pouring a beer in Chip's lap, but he loves getting anything over on his friend. They clink their bottles and drink their beer.

After a bit, Charles says, "Well, speaking of creating religions out of whole cloth, you remember, back when we were talking about the Universe as a simulation, I said I was agnostic on the topic? Well, I've done some more thinking, and now I'm a believer."

"Yes, you are a monkey, not a trace of doubt in my mind." Charles groans at the lame reference. Chip continues, "Why the change of heart? I thought you were just bringing all that simulated universe stuff up just to bug me."

"No, bugging you is just an added bonus. I've been thinking about some strange, not occurrences so much, more like . . . tendencies—in my life. Specifically, the tendency of snags."

"That sounds like the title of a shitty transcendentalist essay: 'The Tendency of Snags' by Ralph Waldo Thoreau."

"Funny. Not. What I'm talking about is the constant, sometimes highly improbable, snags in my life—physical snags, like once when I caught my shirt sleeve on a coat hanger while getting my coat out of a closet. Pulled myself into the closet and bumped my head on the clothes rod and fell to the floor. At a party. To great hilarity. Or in high school science class, I was walking to the sink with the remains of my dissected frog and my belt loop got caught on a drawer handle. I flipped backward, ripping my pants, and fell to the ground with my tighty-whiteys showing. The frog flew up in the air and plotzed on my face. More hilarity. Virtually any time I carry a cord or string, it snags. If I untuck my shirt, something will snag on the buttons. Just this week, two big snags. My shoelace snagged on the emergency brake pedal while I was getting out of my car. Has that ever happened to you? Of course not. Probably hasn't happened to more than a couple people ever! And yesterday, at the *World*, my belt loop snagged on one of those lever door handles. The lady following me ran into me, slipped on the puddle my Diet Coke made, and fell down. I spun around and fell, with my face in her crotch! It's maddening, embarrassing, and often comical, and that's when I started to think."

"About time . . ."

Charles glares at Chip and flips him the bird. "What if this is some kind of hilarious comic entertainment for whoever is viewing this universal simulation? I mean, you have no idea how unlikely some of these snags have been! My wife snagged her wedding dress in the car door while getting out to come to the ceremony! And simultaneously, her sister, the driver, locked the keys in the car. Delayed the ceremony by 45 minutes until a cop came and jimmied the lock. That one was probably just prefiguring later disaster, now that I think about it. Years ago, I started hoping that someday all this snagging will pay off with a snag that saves my life or something. I gradually have begun to feel like I'm in this surreal, in the true sense of the word—above reality—sitcom with some entity or an audience of entities laughing their asses—or whatever organ it is they laugh with up there—off watching my life."

Charles looks at Chip who says, "Go on," in a stentorian voice.

"When I thought about it deeper, there have been non-physical snags in my life as well. You know I used to be in startups, right? When I look back, I see improbable snags that doomed many of those companies. The co-founder needs a kidney and is out of commission for a couple of years. A co-founder had planned to finance the development of our mobile app himself and, in one week, a tree falls on his house and his son puts his car in a swamp and, poof! He no longer has the money. It goes on and on. Snags, arrgh!"

"Well, all that could just mean you're a lousy chooser of startups or startup team members," Chip points out.

"Yeah, I've considered that. But it's been so consistent. Great promise and, oops. A snag kills the whole thing. My life's has been chock full of snags—some bigger and some smaller—but they're constant. And to a certain audience with a sick sense of humor, they could be hilarious. So, recently I've started congratulating the puppet masters of the Universe for their novel snags. I engage in imaginary conversations suggesting that they give me a break, or sarcastically thanking them for their attention, or asking them why they have it in for me."

"Glad you said imaginary conversations there. Yeah, sounds like you're not just grandiose, you're also paranoid, or perhaps we all experience the same level of snagginess, and you just are super-sensitive—you are but a delicate flower, after all."

"Well, there is other evidence."

"What, pray tell?"

"I think the universe that is controlling ours intersects with our universe at an angle, about 11.2 degrees in fact."

"Huh? Based on what?" Chip scratches behind his left ear and starts to wonder if Charles is crazy, or just putting him on.

"I've noticed over the years that when I'm not paying attention, I hold glasses and cups at about an 11-degree angle. There's no good reason for this, and not only that, it generally happens at about 11 degrees in a southwest direction. Not so coincidentally, that's about half of the tilt of the Earth from the ecliptic, and the difference between the North Pole and magnetic north is 11.2 degrees."

Chip is silent for a minute. What the fuck? Is Charles really going off the deep end? He's talking nonsense. "Ummmmm. Are you OK, little buddy? That's some pretty weird shit you're spewing."

"Oh, I think I'm more than OK. I think I've got it all figured it out. And I also figured out that my messiah complex as a child was most probably because I felt the eyes of the extra-universal audience on me. I'm the star of a hit interdimensional comedy!"

Chip leans forward, elbows on knees and stares at his friend. "But, dude, you're taking these little incidents or tendencies of your life and going way, way, way too far with their significance. Snags: you could just be a clod. Tilted glasses: you have a bad sense of balance, which could help explain the cloddishness. Messiah complex: you were—or are—a conceited asshole. You're reasoning from a pretty skimpy set of observations and assumptions."

"Nope. I'm convinced. I talk to my evil—or perhaps just starved for comedy—overlords every day."

"Wait. Do they talk back?" Chip is becoming increasingly alarmed about his friend's mental state.

"No, of course not. Then I'd know for sure what the deal was. However, recently I think I might have picked up some of their chatter. You know I sleep with earplugs, right? The least little noise wakes me up. Well, I've discovered that you can hear some things better when you've got earplugs in. Often, when I'm lying in bed waiting to go to sleep, I hear these voices. Well, kind of hear, kinda voices. I hear the rhythm of their conversation but can't make out the words. It kinda sounds like a far-off radio program."

Chip's eyes grow wide. Voices, great. Charles is losing his mind. Chip says carefully, "These voices aren't telling you to do things, are they?"

"No, no, no. It's like a radio muffled by a pillow. They are carrying on conversations, and not speaking to me. I'm kinda eavesdropping, like. I can hear the tones of their voices, and it does seem like English, but I can't make out any words. It's hard to say if they're talking about me. Anyway, I've decided to follow Max Tegmark's advice—you remember I mentioned him before, the cosmologist—just keep them interested. Do unexpected things so that those in charge of the simulation don't get bored and shut you down."

"I'm getting pretty worried about you, dude. You're not pulling my leg, are you?"

"I'm as serious as a heart attack. But don't be worried. I got it all under control." Charles leans over to pat Chip on the shoulder. "For all I know, you could be my comic sidekick in the sitcom. But anyway, I believe in snags. I believe the Snag Masters control my fate, and that I must please them by reacting to these apparently hilarious snags in a comical way. It's my new religion. Someday I hope to understand what they're talking about when I'm lying in bed."

"Oh, come on, Charles! You can not be serious! How can you build a religion on your clumsiness, your incipient schizophrenia, and your lack of balance?! It just doesn't make any sense."

"Religions have been built on less. Snagology makes more sense than following a religion that has a bipolar god—who's a man, by the way. Why should the Supreme Being have a gender? I wrote a poem once on the subject, called 'On God's Cock.'"

"Man, I'd love to read that," Chip interjects, with a tense laugh.

"Why follow a religion that has such tremendous paradoxes, like tripartite divinity? Holy Ghost? What the fuck? It's an obvious throw-in from a different cosmology. And such a range of ways you can miss out on Heaven: You're just as surely damned if you whack off as if you eat a plate o' shrimp! Or mix dairy with meat! Holy cheeseburger, Batman! This god hands down totally contradictory laws, accepts 32 virgins as his tribute, and condones their slavery without the possibility of ever being freed, kills his son to absolve the evil that he himself put into the Garden of Eden, and seems powerless to prevent bad things from happening to his most devout followers. My Snag religion is a far simpler belief system. I'm the only important person in a simulated universe whose rulers are treating my life as a comical reality show. Rather than getting everlasting life by dying, as in your religion, I'm hoping to get everlasting life by pleasing my Snag Masters, so they renew me every season."

Chip is stumped, shocked wordless. He slumps back against the couch, almost knocking it off the cinder block. He's torn between being positive that Charles is putting him on and being positive that his friend is going insane. "OK, let's say you're right and you're in a pan-universal reality show. How do you know you're the only one?"

"That's a really good question. I can't rule out the possibility that there are others, or even that everyone else is in the same show. But since the only thing I can be sure of is that I am on stage, that's what I'm going with. You know, Chaos Magick practitioners believe laughter is the highest emotion because it contains all the others from ecstasy to grief. For them, laughter is the only tenable attitude in a universe which is a joke played upon itself. I think they may be on to something there. If laughter is built into the Universe, maybe that means we're part of a cosmic *Comedy Central*, featuring lots of other shows with different kinds of comedy."

Chip says, "Well, it's certainly true that the great existential question is: Are we alone in the Universe? Am I alone in the Universe? Descartes obviously battled with it, like you mentioned—the brain in the vat thing. So, you've got good company there, with your feeling that you're the only actor in a cosmic comedy. But I'm very concerned about a lot of the things you've said. I have to be honest. You sound like a paranoid schizophrenic, and I've seen quite a few in my counseling practice."

"I'm as sober as a teetotaling priest, dude. I know lots of this stuff sounds crazy, but, as I said, it's not nearly as crazy as some of the crap religious people believe. It makes as much sense for me to believe in Snagology as it does for you to believe in Christianity. And it's so much simpler. I don't have to keep track of lots of incompatible urges and dogmas. I don't need to worship any god, don't need to submit to the judgment of any priest. To achieve everlasting life, I don't need to lead a blemish-free life or pray for absolution of my sins, I just have to keep the Snag Masters entertained. And it should be so much easier now that I'm wise to the gig. If I've satisfied them for this many years without even knowing it, think of how much better I'll be now that I know what I know. I should be able to get renewed for all eternity! And the very best thing is, all I have to do is live. The snags will come; I couldn't prevent them if I wanted to. But I can subtly improve my reactions to them, and keep 'em rolling in the aisles, or whatever it is that they roll in up there."

Chip just shakes his head. He thinks, I don't know which is worse: thinking my friend is crazy or that he's running an elaborate con to get my goat. Mental note: keep an eye on Charles.

"Anyway, Chip, there's a lot of support for the idea that the Universe is an illusion, particularly from Eastern religions. All is Māyā, say the Buddhists, meaning all we experience is illusory."

"I know what fucking Māyā is, you knob. Religion 101. Hey, speaking of the Universe, I got a great joke for you."

"I seriously doubt it," Charles said.

"Here it is. Josey wasn't the best pupil at Sunday school. She often fell asleep, and one day while she was dozing, the teacher asked her a question. 'Who is the creator of the Universe?' Joe was sitting next to Josey and poked her with a pin to wake her up. Josey jumped and yelled, 'God Almighty!' The teacher congratulated her. A little later the teacher asked her another question, 'Tell me who is our lord and savior?' Joe poked Josey again and she yelled out, 'Jesus Christ!' The teacher congratulated her again. Later the teacher asked, 'What did Eve say to Adam after bearing their 26th child?' Joe poked Josey again and she shouted, 'If you stick that thing in me again, I'll snap it in half and stick it up your ass!'"

"Make . . . it . . . stop!" Charles clutches his head in agony.

Blow up the world with strange magic

ELO—*Strange Magic*

Trial

Jeannie D'Arcy, wearing a long wrap-around skirt, a white peasant blouse, jeans jacket and desert combat boots, walked into the coffee shop and ordered a soy salted caramel mocha. She also grabbed a packaged vegan blueberry banana muffin. Impatiently, she sat down in a booth to eat the muffin and flipped open her iPad, settling it into the groove of her Bluetooth keyboard.

That damn Harlon, she thought, as she gathered her wavy auburn hair into a ponytail. Son of a bitch is on my last nerve.

At the *Magic Universe* Grand Prix last night, Jeannie had watched Harlon like a hawk as he shuffled and was sure she saw him pull some tricks. She wasn't certain enough, however, to call a judge over. But then, as she was considering what to do, Harlon drew a card, slammed it down, and yelled "Goddammit!" knocking over the die he was using to keep his life total. Jeannie was sure Harlon then reset his die to a higher number, and she called a judge. But it was he-said, she-said, and Jeannie ultimately lost the game, her first loss in more than a year.

I'll get that sonofabitch, she thought as she logged in to Wizards of the Coast and clicked on Report Conduct.

"Jeannie, soy salted caramel mocha," called the barista, and Jeannie got up to get her drink. Returning to the booth, she glanced at the name on the side—Genie—and smirked. Who thinks it's spelled that way? she thought, popping the cover off the cup and taking a long draught of the hot liquid.

She wrote, "Harlon Rickmer cheated in the most recent Grand Prix by causing a distraction—throwing down a drawn card and uttering an oath—while simultaneously knocking over his Life Total die. When he righted the die, he made it indicate more life than he had earned."

Jeannie leaned into her complaint, pounding on the fragile keys of her keyboard, cheeks growing redder as she went on. Finally, with a flourish, she stabbed her index finger at the Submit button and sent along her complaint to the authorities.

I hope they ban the bastard for a year, she thought, but she knew it was a long shot that Harlon would get anything more than a warning, if that. She could have used the money, too. The top prize was $10,000.

Flipping to the tournament's website, she saw that the final match had featured a Troll Guardian deck from finalist Brandon Sullivan and reigning champion Skip Parvin's innovative Cloud Assault deck featuring Strapius, Chancellor of Ilexium. Parvin prevailed.

Well, Jeannie thought, at least that cheater, Harlon, didn't win, not that he was likely to. Damn, I could have beat that deck and that Parvin dude. Now I've got to find some way to pay first and last rent next month, assuming I find a place. And get the damn car fixed.

Jeannie's ancient Camry was on its last legs and had been awaiting a muffler since the old one fell off two weeks ago. She could drive it, but it was so loud she knew she'd get pulled over. Throughout her life, she had always been discovered whenever she broke a rule.

It started in kindergarten with two incidents that cemented her hatred of authority, at the age of five. Her teacher, Miss Chipman, was seated in a chair in the middle of the classroom reading a book to the students, and several of the children were clamoring for her attention.

"Miss Chipman! Miss Chipman!" they chirped.

Jeannie thought she heard the boy next to her say, "Miss Chipmunk!"

She turned to the boy and asked, "Did you say Miss Chipmunk?" The boy ignored her, so she asked louder, "Did you just say Miss Chipmunk?"

Miss Chipman heard this and glared at Jeannie. "Under the chair!" she said sternly. "Under you go!"

Jeannie tried to point out what she had actually said, but Miss Chipman just got angrier, so Jeannie had to climb under the teacher's chair and remain there while Miss Chipman read the rest of the book to her classmates.

The second incident was her mother's fault. Often when Jeannie repeatedly asked her mom where one of her toys was, she'd snap, "I ate it!" Her mom was just being funny, but one day, while coloring with other children at a table, the little girl next to her kept asking Jeannie, over and over, where the green crayon was.

Finally, frustrated that the girl wouldn't stop, Jeannie said, "I ate it!"

The girl started to wail and ran to Miss Chipman. "Jeannie ate my crayon!"

Jeannie didn't quite know how to explain that she thought "I ate it" was a legitimate response, and soon she was under the chair again.

This pattern repeated itself again and again throughout her life. If there were a bunch of kids doing something bad, and she joined in, she'd be the only one who got caught. If she drove on expired license tabs, she got caught. If she picked up a lost wallet on the street, she got accused of lifting it. If she went in through the out door, she got caught. So, she decided to dedicate herself to leading a faultless life, never straying a millimeter from the proper path. The problem with this was that she was an out-of-the-box thinker, although she detested that phrase, often saying, "What box?" when people applied the saying to her. How can you be a rule-breaker if you're always caught breaking rules?

This contradiction resulted in her current predicament: out of work (for offering a better solution than her boss's and thus embarrassing him in front of his manager), out of friends (for telling her best friend's husband that his wife was cheating on him), and out of patience with her last so-called boyfriend. Glenn's general lack of interest in anything but reciting his daily work successes and his every brilliant thought resulted last night in Jeannie finally leaving him, and also, unfortunately, his apartment. Which led to this day, following a night sleeping in her Camry.

It wasn't like it was hard for Jeannie to find a boyfriend. Her large breasts, flowing auburn hair, and pleasant face—but mostly her large breasts—ensured a plentiful supply of suitors. The problem was, men who only saw her boobs were generally shallow people, and they rarely lasted very long before Jeannie tired of them. Nonetheless, being currently homeless, Jeannie figured she needed to employ one of Lily's 50 reasons to have sex, from *How I Met Your Mother*: #7 Paratrooping/bangin' for roof.

She'd have to find a public bathroom large enough to enable her to change into her clubbing clothes, and then find some horny idiot—hopefully not too much of an idiot, and hopefully attractive—to spend the night with. It was late afternoon, so she could hang out at the café for a few hours before walking back to the Camry to retrieve her duds and getting ready for the conquest.

In the meantime, Jeannie scoured the job boards on her iPad. Her last job had been with a Defense Advanced Research Projects Agency contractor developing UAVs, small unmanned aerial vehicles also known as drones. She had a Secret clearance, which should make it easy to find a job in her specialty, machine learning, among the Beltway Bandits in suburban DC. She had been with a unit working on Explainable AI, which sought to produce decision systems that weren't black box voodoo. The essential task was to provide a way for humans to understand the rationale for machine decisions. DARPA was interested in potential battlefield automation, but nobody would trust robots, aerial or terrestrial, to make kill decisions unless there was a way to trace the decision back to its components.

Jeannie had always looked at any problem from an ethical and moral background, partly due to her strict upbringing in the Church of Christ, Scientist. On her application to MIT, when asked, "What is your goal in life?" she had written, "To heal the world, comfort all the afflicted, and eliminate hate."

That answer had come up again in her campus interview. It seemed that MIT rarely got technologists expressing idealistic goals like these. In the interview, Jeannie had argued that technology could achieve all of her goals. It just needed to be the right technology, one that was ethical and had the improvement of mankind firmly embedded in its structures.

Now, years later at 33, Jeannie was an AI expert and a data scientist. Although the work was interesting, she had been uncomfortable with her last assignment. She had faith in the technology; she did not have faith in those who would use it, primarily to make kill decisions on the battlefield. She hadn't yet found a way to embed morality in the machine.

Her current dilemma required a speedy but perhaps not an ideal solution: She needed a job, probably with the feds, and she needed it fast. She had heard of another DARPA project to create a camera that integrated unbelievably tiny pixels—the size of red blood cells—with an independent AI system for each pixel that could transform the type of electromagnetic radiation the pixel could register. These pixels could combine into a system that could simultaneously do 3D mapping, infrared imaging, and motion tracking from a drone, yielding tremendously valuable information about a battlefield situation.

Jeannie went onto the DARPA site and checked out the jobs available for the Microsystems Technology Office, the group that produced the camera.

Hmm, she thought. Nothing pertaining to the camera, but what about this: "AMEBA ULF & VLF transmit antennas that generate electromagnetic (EM) fields by mechanically moving trapped charges (electrets) and magnets." She had done some work on the radio control interface for the drones, so she had hardware experience.

They must need some kind of AI to coordinate all these tiny devices, she thought. Troy's the program manager, so I expect his typical coterie of contractors will be applying. Deadline's next week. Whom do I know who may be responding? She downloaded the attendee list for the Proposers' Day meeting and scanned it. Yeah, it's the typical Beltway Bandits, including MacAllan.

Jeannie brought up her address book and did a few searches.

Aha! If Juston at MacAllan isn't applying for this project, I'd be very surprised. We both were on the Wolfhound project to equip forces in Afghanistan with radio signal tracking devices. Plus, he made a very clumsy, grabby pass at me at the MacAllan Christmas party a couple years ago. I wonder if he's still single. I wonder if he'd like to go dancing tonight.

Jeannie opened Google Voice and texted to Juston. "J-man, it's Jeannie. I haven't seen you in forever and my date for tonight just canceled. We were going dancing. Care to fill in and catch up?"

Maybe I can kill two birds with one stone, she thought. Juston's reply came almost immediately. "J-girl! Was just thinking about you!"

Sure, sure, Jeannie thought.

"I'm free tonight. Where shall we meet?"

The café was only a few blocks from the Pentagon City Metro, so Jeannie wouldn't need her car if they went somewhere downtown. She wanted to go someplace where they could talk, so lots of the popular clubs would be much too loud. Ah! The Midtown Partyplex! Perfect. Four floors with different things happening on each.

"J-man, how about Midtown Partyplex? Meet about 6ish? I won't have eaten by then, so we can grab some dinner and talk. Plus, dancing!"

"CU there. Can't wait. ☺ "

OK, that's sorted, Jeannie thought. I guess I should just hang here until I need to change and leave.

With some time to kill, Jeannie indulged in her habit of clicking randomly on Google results and rapidly generating new queries from words and phrases from the resulting pages, sometimes as tabs and other times as new windows. She quickly flipped through the pages, sometimes scrolling, sometimes registering an image and moving on, sometimes drilling deep into an image by blowing up the view.

As she moved through windows of images at an insane speed, she realized that a certain set produced a fleeting image of a word: spelt. What the heck is that? The past participle of spell?

Upon further investigation, though, she found out spelt was a type of ancient grain.

I kind of like my interpretation better, she thought. She took a bite of her muffin and noticed it had a slightly weird texture. She looked at the wrapper. What do you know? This damn muffin is made with spelt. What are the chances? A little weird, but awfully good, she thought, as she absently munched the muffin.

Her mind drifted back to thoughts of Harlon, and that reminded her she was doing a *Magic* draft on the weekend and she should probably bone up on some cards she might be able to trade for. I need to finish in the money in that draft and sell a bunch of cards if I'm to have any chance of renting an apartment, she thought. She pulled her dice bag out of her jacket pocket and took a quick look at the cards inside. Yeah, these should fetch a good price. I wonder if I could find some more in that mess in the back seat of the car.

Jeannie had built herself an iPad app that searched Google Images for pictures of *Magic Universe* cards and displayed them on the screen in rapid fire. An expert player since she was small, Jeannie knew lots of cards, their costs, and their uses. She wanted to know them all, but with more than 18,000 available cards, it was a daunting task, despite her photographic memory. Her app was smart enough to cull out duplicates and featured controls for speed, pause, and magnify.

She brought up the app on her iPad and started the cards scrolling by in a horizontal gallery. Jeannie tried to identify each along with its value to her decks. "Dark Tracer," got it. Ooo, "Breach Piercer" up 20 bucks. "Stormy Hill," got to get it. "Jitterbug," I should be so lucky. "Flame Burst," I could use that one. "Fire Carver," too. Hmm, two pyros in a row.

Jeannie had gotten so good at recognizing cards, she could crank the display up to max and still be able to spot the ones she wanted. She set the speed at about 10 cards per second and sat without moving for 15 minutes staring at the screen as the cards whizzed by.

In minute 16, however, something startling happened. She saw a run of very powerful cards: "Lightning Striker," "Brain Freeze," "Bent Sword," "Astral Walk," "Mage Academy," "Dark Secret," "Barnstorm," "Total Recall." Wow, she thought, what's up with the really powerful cards? How unusual.

Suddenly the surroundings of the café faded to black and Jeannie became encircled by a set of nine huge *Magic Universe* cards. There was a low, humming, electrical sound in the air.

"What the hell just happened? Where am I?" she cried fearfully. There was no echo, and no answer. She was in a dark hall with a black seamless stone floor. She bent down to feel it. It felt neutral, not cold like concrete. Through the gaps between the cards, she could see a black wall a few feet away on the left. She craned her neck upward but could make out no ceiling. The space was dimly lit by an invisible light source.

She turned in a circle to look at the eight-foot-tall cards that surrounded her. They glowed as if from an inner fire. My god, she thought. These are the Sovereign Nine!

This legendary set of nine cards was old, from the beginning of the card game. The ring around her consisted of "Black Dahlia;" "Total Recall;" "Astral Walk;" the Bearers: Opal, Topaz, Onyx, Amber, and Peridot; and

"Time Control." These cards were usually restricted or banned in tournaments due to their great power.

"Omigod, where the fuck am I?" Jeannie asked again.

She could see no evidence of the café or the real world. I must be having some sort of vision, she thought.

Each card was surrounded by a pulsing electric aura. She examined the cards closely, starting with the Bearers. The five Bearer cards seemed unremarkable, except for their gigantic size. They appeared to be faithful replicas of the real cards.

Despite their rarity, Jeannie knew all about these legendary cards. As she walked the circle peering at them, she thought about how they were used in the game. Each Bearer adds a different type of mana to the player's mana pool. The Total Recall card, one of the Boons, enables a player to draw three cards. Astral Walk lets you take an extra turn. Time Control forces players to shuffle their hands with their library and draw a new hand of seven. That one would be tricky to play, Jeannie thought. She touched it and jumped back at the small electric shock it imparted. Holy shit! That thing feels like it's alive. She touched each of the other Bearers in turn and got a milder set of shocks.

She then turned to the Black Dahlia, the Holy Grail of *Magic Universe* cards. It grants three mana and, if played right, ends the game instantly. Jeannie was in awe of even seeing this card, considered to be the most valuable ever printed, and last auctioned for more than $200,000. As she reached out to touch the card, a huge arc of light surrounded her and lifted her off her feet.

Jeannie screamed involuntarily and said, "Put me down, whoever you are!"

A voice, seemingly emanating from the giant card itself, said, "Who are you, who have called forth the magic of the Universe?"

Jeannie was stupefied. That barista must have slipped some acid in my coffee, she thought. The Black Dahlia talking to me? What the fuck?

"Answer us," the voice commanded.

She replied, "I'm Jeannie, and I don't know how I got here, but please put me down."

"Only true sorcerers are granted entry to this realm," the voice said. "What is your mage name?"

"I don't know. I've never been given a mage name. I'm Jeannie D'Arcy."

"We have brought you to this realm because you have magical powers as yet untapped. Untrained, you represent a threat. You must run a gauntlet of female wizards and then take a mentor to train you further for 40 days at which time we shall determine your fitness for continuing into apprenticeship."

"Um, what the fuck are you talking about?" Jeannie was moving from confusion to irritation. Who was playing this elaborate trick on her?

"Here is your first trial, with Bright Knife, the temptress." Black Dahlia set Jeannie back on her feet and the scene changed. All nine cards moved to form a line along the wall to the left. Each was situated three feet from the wall with two-foot gaps between them, forming a kind of corridor behind them.

Before her stood a scantily clad alabaster-white woman with extensive earrings and a red mohawk. From her studies of *Magic Universe* cards, Jeannie knew about this rare entity, but there was not much of a backstory available as there was with some of the other cards.

OK, she thought. She's a temptress and an assassin, but I'm not a dude, so perhaps I'm gonna be OK.

"My darling," Bright Knife said, "What is it that you desire?"

"I desire to get out of this fucking insane dream!"

"My darling, what makes you think this is a dream?" Bright Knife stepped up to Jeannie and slapped her. "Didn't that feel real?"

Jeannie was startled and involuntarily brought her hand up to cover her slapped cheek. "Yes, that seemed real enough, but seriously, I just want to get back to my life."

Bright Knife gave her a penetrating come-hither stare. "Sweetie, you'll have to go through me to get anywhere." Bright Knife smiled seductively. "You like girls?"

Jeannie flashed back to a near-intimate encounter with her lesbian roommate at college. "No, I only like dudes, so quit looking at me that way."

Bright Knife had begun to undo the top of her skimpy outfit.

"And stop undressing!" Jeannie said. "It's not going to do anything for me."

"Are you sure?" Bright Knife asked, dropping her clothing to the floor and coming closer to Jeannie, who stumbled backward and collided with the card wall behind her. She felt an electric thrill throughout her body, looked up and saw that she was backed up to Time Control. She was becoming more frightened by the minute.

Bright Knife pressed her body against Jeannie, pinning her to the card, and placed her right hand between Jeannie's legs, groping through her flimsy skirt. Jeannie twisted away from Bright Knife at a right angle and assumed the Tai Chi "Play Guitar" defensive position.

"Stay away from me," she commanded.

Bright Knife smiled slyly and said, "I can help you if you tell me what you want."

"I told you."

"Returning to your life is not your true desire. What is it you really desire? What would really make you happy, satisfied?"

Jeannie thought for half a second and then blurted, "To be able to snap my fingers and fix all that's wrong with the world."

"Now we've got something to work with. I can help you attain your desire, but first, you must beat me."

"Come at me, bitch!"

"Hand fighting is not my way." Bright Knife produced a long knife in her right hand seemingly from nowhere and lunged at Jeannie with it. Jeannie deftly turned parallel to the knife, bumped Bright Knife's arm out of the way with her left, raised her right arm as a bar to retaliation and then brought it down in an attack. She landed a solid blow to the neck and Bright Knife staggered back, still holding the knife. She jumped back at Jeannie in a two-handed overhead attack, and Jeannie once again moved to parry, grabbing Bright Knife's right wrist and driving her left shoulder into her elbow, breaking it. She pulled the arm behind the stricken creature and kicked at the back of her left knee, bringing her to the floor while snatching the knife from the groaning Bright Knife. She then placed her right foot on her neck.

"Had enough?" Jeannie put more of her weight on Bright Knife's neck.

"You have defeated me! Most of my knife work has been done at close, even intimate, range. If I could have gotten you into my bed, things would have been different."

"In your dreams, bitch. Now tell me how I get out of this place or I'll cut you good."

"There's no rest for the wicked, honey. You've many more trials to face." With that, Bright Knife disappeared, causing Jeannie to fall to the floor in a heap leaving her knife behind.

"What the fuck? Where'd you go?" Jeannie said as she picked up the knife.

The voice of the Black Dahlia answered, "You have done well, initiate, with your first challenge. Beware your next."

Jeannie looked around and noticed two red figures approaching. As they grew closer, Jeannie noticed they both appeared to be engulfed in flames. One had hair that looked like a flowing fire, and the other, clad in red leather, held what appeared to be a whip of fire, swirling it around her body in endless loops.

As they neared, Jeannie recognized them as Flame Burst and Fire Carver. Jeez, she thought. I just saw these two in my card review. I must be dreaming. Flame Burst, daughter of wealth, and Fire Carver, a street urchin thief in her younger days. Let's see, Flame Burst lights up when angry or frustrated. She's impulsive and hotheaded. Fire Carver is reckless and without morals.

"'Sup, ladies?" Jeannie said, hoping to play the innocent.

"We saw what you did to Bright Knife. We'll not be fooled by your trickery," said Flame Burst.

"Well, then you know I'm not to be trifled with, don't you?" Jeannie said.

Fire Carver laughed and snapped her flaming whip in Jeannie's direction. Jeannie jumped out of the way, caroming off the Astral Walk card and landing in a crouch. Flame Burst tossed a fireball at Jeannie that she barely avoided.

I need some protection, she thought. Glancing around, she noticed the gap between the Astral Walk and Total Recall cards. She quickly passed through and flattened against the wall opposite the back of the Astral Walk card.

Think, Jeannie. Think. OK, OK, OK. What can I do to counter fire? A huge blast of fire ripped through the card gap, narrowly missing Jeannie and singeing her hair.

"I love the smell of burnt hair in the morning," Fire Carver said with a laugh. "How about a little more fire, scarecrow?"

Another torrent of flames roared through the gap, but Jeannie had made her way down to the end of the card row. She peered around the corner of the Black Dahlia card and watched the two attackers.

They don't seem too smart, she thought. They're attacking that gap pretty single-mindedly. Now how can I counter them? Instinctively, she patted the pockets of her jacket. Ah, my phablet! Perhaps I can simulate Dark Mirror and reflect their attacks back on them.

She opened the large cellphone and selected the mirror app she often used to check for stuff in her teeth.

I need them to be close to one another. Oh, good, she thought, peeking around the card again. They're going through the gap. She quickly stepped out from behind the giant card and waited until the pair of pyros sounded closer. Then, with a shout, she spun back behind the card holding her phone straight out in front of her. Flame Burst and Fire Carver unleashed a fiery attack. Jeannie's phone splashed the fire right back on them, killing Flame Burst and critically injuring Fire Carver.

Jeannie whipped back around to the front of the Black Dahlia and sprinted down the line of cards.

I figure Fire Carver only has two life left. Perhaps I can put her away with an electric shock.

Her phablet had an extra high capacity battery case attached. She removed it, pulled a bobby pin from her hair and grabbed her hair tie. She stretched the hair band lengthways across the battery and inserted the end of the bobby pin under the band, on top of one of the electrical contacts. How long should I hold it after I short the battery out? she wondered.

She leaned back against the Astral Walk card and felt a shock go through her body. The battery in her hand started to warm and soon began to glow. Omigod! I'm drawing power from the card! Where's that damn Fire Carver now? She peeked through the card gap and was almost face-to-face with Fire Carver. Quickly, she moved the bobby pin to short out the contact and jammed the battery down the front of Fire Carver's leather suit. She turned and ran back toward the Black Dahlia as the battery blew up, arcing and spraying fire both ways down the corridor behind the cards and sending Jeannie sprawling to the ground.

"Well done, initiate," said the voice from the Black Dahlia card. "Fire against fire and shock against Fire Carver. Well played. But your next challenge will be harder still."

"Listen, I didn't ask to be initiated. I was just minding my own business. Why can't you let me go?"

"Your power is too great to go unchecked, initiate. You must complete the initiation or perish."

Oh fuckin' great, Jeannie thought. I wonder how many challenges there are. Well, at least I've learned I can lean on the power of these humongous cards. Jeannie allowed herself a little smirk of triumph.

Let's see, if we're going in order of card value, Total Recall will be the next card I can use.

She looked around to see what had changed and noticed Fire Carver's red leather suit at her feet.

Hmm, perhaps a little protection would help, Jeannie thought. I hope I can squeeze into it. Fire Carver was a bit shorter than I am.

She quickly stripped to her underwear and pulled the pants on. They morphed, seemingly flowing over her form. The top stretched to accommodate her ample bosom. Sweet! Not only am I a badass, now I look like one, too! I just need a pocket for my phone. At this thought, a hip pocket appeared, and Jeannie jammed her phone into it.

She then discovered Fire Carver's fiery whip somehow holstered on her right hip and Bright Knife's knife in a scabbard on her left.

Damn! she thought. How'd that happen?

She noticed Flame Burst's fiery wristlets laying nearby and put them on. Man, I'm armed! She pulled on her boots and her jacket and stood up and looked around.

She thought she heard horse hooves echoing from far away. She turned in the direction of the sound and began to make out the form of a white horse galloping her way.

Oh, shit, she thought. That better not be Lady Zhurong! But it was.

The regal Asian figure on a golden saddle atop the white steed got closer. and Jeannie could see that on her head was a visored helmet sporting two long moth-like antennae that streamed behind her as she rode. Incongruously, she wore two large tasseled earrings.

That makes no sense for a warrior, Jeannie thought. They could be caught in a sword or pike and pull her off her horse. Need to keep that in mind.

She's based on a character from an old Chinese novel. Hmm, let's see. In one battle, after resisting twice, she was lured into a trap because a guy insulted her. So, impulsive. She wields flying half-moon swords. Fantastic. More sharp things. This leather won't help much against that. But a fire whip should do a number on her horse. Let's get it on!

Swords flashing, Zhurong charged at Jeannie, who deftly slipped aside and cracked her whip across the horse's buttocks as it passed. The horse reared, but Zhurong was yanking on the reins to turn the beast's head around for another pass. The horse keeled over awkwardly, rolling onto Zhurong's right leg. She kicked herself out from under the struggling animal and regained her feet, staggering on her injured leg toward Jeannie with her swords whirling.

Jeannie feinted toward Zhurong's feet and she took the bait, jumping up and raising her swords above her head. Instead of striking low, Jeannie sent the whip high, tangling Zhurong's arms. Zhurong screamed and dropped the swords, one of which gashed her breast on the way to the floor. She landed and crouched, grabbing the burns on her arms.

Using her whip, Jeannie flicked one of the swords toward herself and bent to pick it up. As she did, she heard a whirring and looked up to see her adversary sprout two insect wings and rise inches off the ground.

Jeannie barrel-rolled to her left and jumped to her feet. Zhurong lunged at her with the other sword, swinging low. Jeannie leapt and swung at Zhurong's head. She missed, but the tip of the sword caught in Zhurong's dangling earring, ripped a chunk out of her earlobe, and knocked her slightly off balance. Continuing the same movement, Jeannie followed with a roundhouse kick to Zhurong's bleeding chest knocking the wind out of her. Zhurong fell to her knees gasping, but lashed out with her sword, just managing to snag a bit of leather off the boot on Jeannie's right ankle. Jeannie stumbled, off-balance, heading away from her adversary.

Still winded, Lady Zhurong staggered to her feet as Jeannie retreated, making for the gap in the card wall. She turned to ensure that Zhurong was following her, but the Warrior Queen hung back, fearing a trap. Entering the gap, Jeannie leaned up against Total Recall to catch her breath. She suspects this is a trap, so I've got a few moments to think. Ah! She's vulnerable to anger and insults. Wei Yan lured her into the valley and a net trap by insulting her. I should give that a try.

Using the strands of the whip, which obligingly clung to the wall and the back of the card, she set up a fiery web across the corridor about four feet from the gap and two feet above the floor.

She peeked around the edge of the card. Zhurong was crouched a dozen yards away, pressing one hand against her bleeding earlobe and the other over her gashed breast. Jeannie ran out from the gap as if she was going to attack. Grabbing her sword, Zhurong jumped to her feet and raced toward her. Jeannie turned and ran back behind the card, and Zhurong stopped and retreated. I've got her now, Jeannie thought.

Immediately she charged out again yelling, "You weakling! You wretched piece of insect dung! You can never overcome me!"

She feinted at the Queen's face, then at her feet. Zhurong immediately lunged, but Jeannie sidestepped and turned to run back to the card gap.

"You're not fit to be a foot soldier, let alone the Warrior Queen! I fart in your general direction," she called over her shoulder.

The enraged Queen gave chase, closing fast behind Jeannie. Jeannie reached the gap and turned left, then slid under the fiery web. Zhurong entered the corridor, charging too hard to stop, and ran straight into the fiery lariat web, which sliced her into pieces. Jeannie scooted on her butt further down the corridor to avoid the spreading pool of blood.

Hah! She thought. I'll bet it was that last Monty Python insult that did her in! Maybe I should have added "Your mother was a hamster and your father smelt of elderberries" for good measure. She chuckled as she caught her breath. After a few minutes, she looked down the corridor at the vanquished Queen. Zhurong's body and blood were nowhere to be seen, but her armor and swords remained.

I'm assembling quite an armory, Jeannie thought. I expect I'll need it for the next challenge, whatever that may be. She donned the Queen's shoulder armor over her jeans jacket and sat back down to rest. With a start, she realized she'd been in the corridor for quite some time. Oh, hell. I wonder if my next challenge is already here. She looked around the corner of the card and, sure enough, she could see a huge, bulbous, amorphous mass crawling toward her from several hundred feet away.

That looks like a giant slithering colon, Jeannie thought. Wait, oh no. That's, that's not . . . damn, it is. It's the Pod Spawner! She could split off a whole army if I don't take care of her quickly. But she's a ways off and crawling slowly, so I have some time to prepare. I think I'll need all the Bearers to beat this mama. If she spawns off too many pieces, I'll get overwhelmed quickly.

Thinking hard, Jeannie realized she could use the cards to make a five-spoked revolving door. She ran over and grabbed the Opal Bearer card, turned it 90 degrees and pushed it against the back wall. She grabbed Topaz Bearer, pushed it against the open edge of Opal Bearer, adjusting it to a 72-degree angle. She did the same with Onyx Bearer, Amber Bearer, and Peridot Bearer, assembling the cards arranged around a center. The cards could now act like a revolving door: five giant cards on a central axle. Jeannie could push the assemblage and rotate it around, and she could position it with two cards nearly touching the wall, creating an enclosure she could hide in.

She rotated the pentangle and hid in the protected compartment, with two of the cards against the back wall on either side of her. She was protected for the moment from a ground attack.

As she leaned against the wall, Jeannie felt a weight in her jeans jacket pocket. What the fuck? She patted the bulge, then put her hand inside the pocket. Ah! My dice bag. But it shouldn't be this heavy. It just had my dice and a few cards inside. She pulled the bag out and opened the drawstring top. To her surprise, she saw many cards inside.

Where did these come from? I thought I just had a couple in there. She grabbed some cards and pulled them out. Omigod! Bright Flyer, Octocopter, Blue Bearer, White Bearer, Black Bearer, Total Recall, and Time Control! Great cards, but where did they come from?

She thought for a moment. Oh, yeah. Time Control enables a player to draw seven cards. It must have given these to me when I used its power to beat Lady Zhurong. But wait. Does this mean I can use cards in these battles? I could mount a pretty good defense of Pod Spawner with these. Damn, though. I'd certainly need more. It'll take a least six turns to beat her and her minions. What counts as a turn, though? Let's see. When the pyromancers attacked me, maybe Astral Walk gave me two turns. My first turn was when I used the mirror app on my phablet to kill Flame Burst and drastically wound Fire Carver. And the second turn enabled me to destroy Fire Carver with the shock of my phablet battery after drawing electricity from Astral Walk. So, when I used Total Recall to battle Lady Zhurong, I should have gotten three cards.

She looked back into the bag and drew out three more cards: Amber Bearer, Theranos, and Froggify.

Wow. I'm getting a pretty decent library together here, she thought. And my battles have given me more assets. I got the fiery whip from Fire Carver, along with her fireproof leather suit. I got the wristlets from Flame Burst. I wonder if they enable me to use her residual power to cast fire. And just now I got Zhurong's armor and swords when I defeated her. She glanced at the armor she was wearing. So cool, she thought, getting excited.

I'm going to need some mana to pull this off if I can do what I think I can do. She looked deeper into the dice bag. Huh? It looks like a tangle of necklaces in the bottom. She pulled one out, an opal necklace. Is this the manifestation of the Opal Bearer? She retrieved another, a peridot necklace. "Peridot Bearer," she almost yelled. I'll bet all the other Bearers of the Sovereign Nine are in there.

She took Onyx Bearer and Topaz Bearer out and put all the necklaces around her neck.

I must have gotten these when I assembled the cards into the pentangle. OK, so if each gives me the associated number of mana, I'm very close to having what I need to beat the Spawner.

Omigod, she thought. It'll be so cool to be able to cast these cards against Pod Spawner and her Pods. Let's see what else I've got. I think I had a couple cards in the bag before I entered the arena, including one of my favorites, Dark Fury.

She dug into the bag again and found, yes, she had Dark Fury, and Deadly Shock.

Jeannie moved the pentangle and peeked from around the edge of a card. The Pod Spawner had slowly drawn near. Here goes nothing, Jeannie thought, and leapt from behind the card to charge at the Spawner, whirling Lady Zhurong's swords. The Spawner waved a lumpy appendage toward her, and Jeannie slashed it off. The Spawner manifested a thin tail and whipped it around toward Jeannie, who leapt into the air and sliced a few feet off the end. The Spawner struck Jeannie with the back of her shortened tail, knocking her sprawling. Jeannie got up and ran back to the pentangle, rotating it to seal herself against the wall.

The Spawner toward the pentangle and squeezed out another Pod. Jeannie heard the flapping of wings and thought, oh shit. She must have split off a Winged Darkness.

The beating of wings came closer as Winged Darkness rose up, perched on the top of the pentangle, and started trying to peck Jeannie from above. It couldn't reach her and started walking about on the tops of the cards, trying to figure a way to fit itself into Jeannie's compartment.

Crap, Jeannie thought. I need something with wings. I'd better cast Bright Flyer and Octocopter.

She used three mana from casting the Bearers.

Bright Flyer came into being inside the compartment and the copter materialized just outside. Bright Flyer, with her blond hair in a slightly disheveled ponytail and wearing a blue and gold uniform, immediately sized up the situation. "Pods. God, why did it have to be Pods!"

"Yeah, right? They're tough. First things first: We need to get rid of this flying bastard."

"OK," Bright Flyer said, "here's what we should do." The two consulted on a plan. While they were talking, Winged Darkness continued trying to find a way down into the compartment. Jeannie and Bright Flyer suddenly pushed on the pentangle, which caused Winged Darkness to stumble awkwardly, pinning one of its talons between a card edge and the back wall.

Bright Flyer sprinted to the Octocopter, climbed aboard, and got airborne. Jeannie ran away from the copter, and Winged Darkness finally freed itself and followed. Bright Flyer quickly circled around in back of Winged Darkness, flew up from the rear, and dropped onto the creature from above, shredding it with Copter's quartet of bottom rotor blades. Blood and pieces of Winged Darkness rained down. A large section of skin from Winged Darkness' wing fell and draped over Jeannie like a tarp. She threw it off and ran over to Bright Flyer, who had landed the Copter.

"That was terrific! You made mincemeat of that Pod!"

"Thanks. I'll hang around in case you need more help, but I'm not much good against anything without wings." With that, she got back in the copter and flew high out of sight.

Jeannie's hand now contained only Total Recall and Time Control.

Meanwhile, the Pod Spawner crawled slowly toward Jeannie, she pinched off a black Pod—Disease Cloud, whose touch means death. The two Pods advanced slowly toward Jeannie with Pod Spawner to her right.

Jeannie cast Total Recall to draw three cards to replace the ones she had used. She drew Amber Bearer, Theranos, and Froggify. Jeannie cast the Theranos—whose power immediately adhered to the power of Fire Carver's fire lariat. Combined with the power of Lady Zhurong's armor, which prevented damage, Jeannie felt fairly well-equipped to battle the Pods.

Disease Cloud was disgusting to look at, resembling hunched, huge-beaked vampire covered in giant leeches and maggots. I hope those things falling off them aren't autonomous, Jeannie thought. As she watched, some of the leeches and maggots fell to the floor and became little puddles.

Jeannie circled to her left, placing the Pod Spawner behind Disease Cloud so she could deal with one at a time. It would take time for the slow-crawling Spawner, who took damage from casting Disease Cloud, to flank her again. She waited for Disease Cloud to advance within reach of her whip and then lunged forward and snapped the whip with a two-handed overhand motion.

The whip cracked and spit purple fire as it sliced Disease Cloud in half. The Pod remained upright for half a second, then, as the halves fell to the ground, leeches and maggots boiled out of its interior, falling to the floor and liquifying along with the Pod's body. The puddle boiled and quickly spread toward Jeannie.

Skirting the stinking and rapidly evaporating wave of liquid, Jeannie whirled her whip around her head to keep the Pod Spawner at bay as she retreated to the pentangle and enclosed herself again. When she heard the Pod Spawner approaching the left side of the pentangle, she rotated out the right side and ran 30 feet away.

That damage the Pod Spawner took by spawning Disease Cloud is taking its toll, she thought. The Spawner is hurting.

With a groaning effort, the Pod Spawner hauled her bulk around the side of the pentangle and pinched off Dark Fury. The hideous tubular dragon had one huge, sharp, spiked arm that was almost as tall as the Pod itself. Jeannie used the Amber Bearer to cast Froggify, which turned Dark Fury into a small purple frog. The frog lurched sideways before hopping feebly toward Jeannie uttering, "Ribbit!"

Suppressing a giggle, Jeannie quickly cast Time Control to get seven new cards. To her surprise, she only found six cards in her bag: Opal Bearer, Peridot Bearer, Fire Elemental, Dark Fury, Malevolent Growth, and Deadly Shock.

What the hell, she thought as she backed away from the slowly advancing Pod Spawner and the comically menacing frog. Where is the seventh card? She looked in the bag and couldn't find any more cards. Damn, I must be out of cards! Shit!

She needed to get on with the battle quickly, so she played Fire Elemental. The blue frog instantly burst into flame as thin lines of rippling fire encircled it. It leaped ineffectually at Jeannie with its mouth agape before flopping over on its back. As the fire seared its belly, it burst open, propelling thousands of small, dead, black ants. The frog body turned black and shriveled until it was no more.

The Pod Spawner lurched forward and quickly squeezed out Dark Predator, a snarling four-legged demon with huge claws and snake-like hair.

Hah! She's getting desperate, Jeannie thought. Unlike the previous Pods, though, this one is fast and nimble.

Jeannie moved quickly to cast Malevolent Growth. Dark Predator immediately sprouted multicolored stinking tumors that grew at a lightning rate. Some popped, spraying a foul liquid in Jeannie's direction. Jeannie retreated, but some of the goo landed on her armor. Damn good thing this is enchanted armor, she thought. If that stuff stings as bad as it smells, I could be a hurting unit. As she watched, the gigantic tumors totally enveloped the Pod, smothering it to death.

"Oh, yeah! I think I just got in touch with my inner monster!" Jeannie said.

The effort of splitting Dark Predator so quickly obviously had drained the Pod Spawner further. Her forelimbs were limp wrinkling tubes. Her back legs were dragging as she slithered feebly toward Jeannie. She groaned three times and finally struggled to squeeze off a new Pod, Life Drain.

Jeannie recognized the significance of this choice instantly. Life Drain is a siphon for life. Pod Spawner is definitely on her last legs if she needs to siphon life, she thought.

Jeannie cast Deadly Shock just as Life Drain leapt at her. A gigantic laser beam streamed down from above and incinerated Life Drain in an instant. The battlefield filled with an acrid stink. Jeannie started coughing.

Jeannie figured it was time to use Dark Fury, a kind of nuclear option which kills all creatures on the battlefield. She needed to do it quickly before the Pod Spawner could squeeze out another pod. But she was short mana. She needed four mana to cast Dark Fury, but she only had two, from Opal Bearer and Peridot Bearer.

If only I had been able to draw all seven cards via Time Control!

The Pod Spawner dragged herself slowly toward Jeannie. Jeannie retreated to the revolving pentangle, and the Spawner labored to follow after her.

Jeannie was beginning to panic as she rotated the pentangle to form a compartment. What can I do? Perhaps I'll need to use Fire Carver's fire lariat again or Flame Burst's wristlets, assuming they can still produce fire.

The Pod Spawner squeezed an appendage through the tiny opening between the back wall and the card wall. It grew seven grasping fingers and blindly groped at Jeannie.

Desperate, Jeannie stuffed her hand into the dice bag and felt something soft. She looked inside and saw the top of a Black Dahlia petal protruding from a hidden pocket. Omigod! That's the seventh card! It was hidden all this time! And it's three mana!

Quickly she withdrew the Black Dahlia flower and cast it and the Opal Bearer. Then, with the Pod Spawner's fingers a hand's breadth away from her face, she cast Dark Fury. The Pod Spawner's arm disappeared, and all Jeannie could see was a bright white light. She covered her eyes. It was several minutes before she could again see the walls of her compartment. She rotated the pentangle a bit and looked outside. She was alone on the battlefield except for the giant Black Dahlia card standing 15 feet from her.

"Congratulations, novice," the card said. "You have passed the tests and dispatched your adversaries with great speed. We see greatness in you. Your power is formidable, and you have the potential to be the most powerful mage in the world."

Jeannie blinked in surprise at this.

"However, you have much to learn and must be carefully taught. You must undertake the 40 days of mentorship we mentioned earlier."

Emotionally and physically exhausted, the idea of enduring more agony at the hands of the haughty Black Dahlia enraged Jeannie. "What if I say no?"

"That is not an option for one of your talents."

"That's what you think," Jeannie said. She raised her arms and shot fire at the Black Dahlia using Flame Burst's wristlets. The giant card crumpled, smoking and crippled. Ragingly mad, Jeannie took Fire Carver's lariat from her belt and was moving in to strike again when, in a blink, she was back in the café.

Overcome with nausea, she gripped the table edges and placed her forehead on its surface. Oh, my fucking god! I think I'm gonna be sick, she thought. But she stemmed the tide of vomit in her throat and after a minute, lifted her head to look around the café. Nobody seemed to be staring at her. The cards were still flashing by on her iPad. She glanced at her watch. It seemed that hardly any time had passed.

OK, that had to be some kind of psychedelic trip, she thought. Perhaps it was that crazy grain in the muffin, that spelt. She opened a new tab on her browser and typed a query: psychedelic grain.

"Ergot!" she said aloud. Then quickly looked around. A guy across the way gave her a weird look.

That's the psychedelic fungus they thought caused the Salem witches and lots of other witch incidents, she thought. I'll bet the spelt in the muffin sent me on a trip! Yeah, that must be it. What a weird dream! She looked around the café again. Wait a minute! That chick looks like Bright Knife. And over there, she looks like Fire Carver, sitting with Flame Burst! She turned around to look at the back half of the seating area. Yup, there's Lady Zhurong. And you were there, and you and you, and you! Well, Dorothy, it looks like you're back in Kansas again, but at least it's not in black and white.

Satisfied that she'd solved the mystery, Jeannie got up and dumped the rest of the muffin in the trash. She briefly thought about telling the barista, but thought that would sound crazy, and decided to leave well enough alone. When she returned to her booth, she shut down the *Magic Universe* card carousel app. I think I've had about enough *Magic* for today, she thought. Now, what should I wear tonight? Something low-cut, of course. That Juston is a sucker for boobs. She laughed at her inadvertent joke.

Apprentice

At four o'clock, Jeannie packed up her stuff and got ready to walk back to her car. As she got up to go, she realized her right ankle hurt. Bending over to examine it, she saw a little cut that still bled a little. OK, that's pretty freaky! That's where Lady Zhurong nipped me with her sword! Jeannie's brain seemed to lock for a moment. What . . . the . . . fuck, she thought. She shook her head and shivered. There's no fucking way, no fucking way. I must have scratched it on the edge of the booth or something. She hurried out of the café onto Hayes Street and headed south.

She'd parked on the bottom level of the underground garage in a remote corner because she figured she might have to change in her car. She got into the car and dug around in the suitcase in the back seat to get her slinky sequined black dress and her black heels. She pulled the dress over her head and wriggled out of her peasant blouse. Then she squirmed to get the dress over her long skirt, which she then pulled off. Ditching the combat boots and grabbing her black purse (which contained her little black Remington RM380), she strapped on her heels. Finding her makeup bag, she did her lips and lashes in the rear view and patted on a little powder.

After combing out her hair, she was ready for the 10-minute walk to the Pentagon City Metro. Oh, shit she thought. Where the hell is my perfume? Jeannie only wore a single brand, *Trouble*, which was fairly expensive. I hope I haven't left it behind at Glenn's. She got out of the car, opened the driver's side rear door and bent over to rummage among the bags and small boxes on the floor behind the driver's seat. Her skirt hiked up a bit over her butt as she shifted her possessions around.

She was startled by a wolf whistle followed by a male voice saying, "I see London, I see France." She stood up abruptly, bumping her head against the ceiling of the Camry. Furious, she turned to locate the jerk who had accosted her. A fat, well-dressed man in a business suit was grabbing his bag out of the trunk of his car across the aisle from her. He turned to face her and leered.

"Get lost, you son of a bitch!" Jeannie spat, turning red with fury. A huge gust of air from the garage's ventilation duct behind her blew her hair over her eyes. When she pushed her hair back behind her ears, she saw that the man was gone. That was fucking quick, she thought. I don't see how a guy of his size could have disappeared so fast.

Grabbing her purse, she slung the strap across her left shoulder and the bag onto her right hip, unzipped it, moved the Remington to the top, and went over to the man's car with her hand on the pistol. I'll bet that fucker's hiding and ready to jump out at me. But she saw no sign of him. Jeannie searched between the adjacent cars, thinking he might be hiding there. No dice. Fucking dude vanished, she thought. Well, at least the asshole's gone. Jeannie went back to her car and eventually located the bottle of Trouble, stuck way down in the toe of one of her sneakers, inside a shoe box entitled "Taxes." She applied the scent, brushed her disheveled hair, locked up the car, and headed for the elevator.

The subway ride was uneventful, except for the usual pervs staring at her boobs. She'd perfected the "Don't Even Think About It" look, though, and that generally prevented open ogling. Once she arrived at Farragut North, she realized it was a little before six and she'd be early. No sense looking over-eager, she thought. She decided to pop into the Mayflower Hotel to grab a cup of coffee and wait.

Breezing by the doormen like she owned the place, she walked into the bar and sat down in a booth. After the waiter took her order, she sat back and reflected on her hallucination. I've been stoned before, but never had a vision like that, she thought. It was so real. I should sue that café, or at least let them know they've got a bad run of muffins. But something was nagging at the edge of her consciousness. The ergot explanation just didn't seem to fit in some way she couldn't identify. The dream couldn't have been real. Seriously. It was a seizure, perhaps, or a psychedelic muffin, or . . . what? What else? She ran her mind over the battles, the electric shocks, the cut on her ankle. She crossed her right leg and looked at her ankle. The cut was on the outside of her ankle and there was little way she could maneuver in the booth to get a good look at it, at least to do so and remain ladylike in her short dress.

Her salted caramel soy mocha espresso showed up and she sipped it for a few minutes. Then a thought occurred to her. Wait a minute. Those women in the café, they looked like the women in my hallucination, right? But now that I think about it, they looked exactly like the way they look on the Magic cards. Those ladies were dead ringers for Gwendlyn, Jaya, Chandra and Lady Zhurong! What are the chances of that? Approaching zero. Rather than me using the faces of random café people in my vision . . . um, oh shit! That can't be. It can't be that these real women were somehow both human and Magic creatures. Jeannie buried her face in her hands as she became a little woozy at the thoughts she was thinking.

The waiter came over to her. "Are you OK, miss?"

"Oh!" Startled, Jeannie snapped her head up. "Yes, yes, sorry, I just realized something and it kind of shook me up. I'm OK. Thanks." The waiter was staring at her boobs. "So, thanks, and please bring me the check." The waiter snapped his eyes up to her face. "Right away."

Jeannie shook her head to clear it and glanced at her smartwatch. OK, it's a little after six. How long should I make him wait? She tapped the watch to check for messages or emails. No word from Juston. Maybe he's running late. She realized she had to pee and got up to go to the ladies'. When she returned, the waiter, a bellman, and the front desk manager were standing and talking next to her banquette. "Hello, gents. Can I sit down again, please?"

The men exchanged glances, and the waiter and bellman walked away. "Oh, sorry, miss. When the waiter noticed you were gone, he mistakenly thought you had departed without settling the bill."

"So, you've never had an unaccompanied lady have to use the loo while visiting your bar?"

"Yes, yes, of course. It's just that Bill thought that . . . Well, anyway."

"He thought I was a streetwalker trying to beat the Mayflower on a tab, eh? That's pretty insulting! Do you get a lot of that here at the Mayflower? I thought this was a classy place."

The manager turned red. "No, no, no, we don't, I mean . . . Look, Bill's new, and that's no excuse. I apologize on his behalf. I am sorry for the inconvenience. Your bill is on the house and please visit us again."

Not bloody likely, Jeannie thought. "Well, you can tell him for me that he should quit staring at ladies' bosoms if he knows what's good for him." The manager was nonplussed. "I, ah, will certainly tell him," he said and gave a slight bow, then turned to return to the lobby.

Well, that turned out OK, Jeannie thought to herself with a smirk. The stinking coffee was probably 20 bucks. I don't know why I thought this would be a good place to grab a drink.

Her smartwatch buzzed and Jeannie glanced at the message. It was from Juston. He had arrived at Midtown Partyplex and found it was closed to the public.

Juston's text said, "They turned it into an event space. Dude says try the Dirty Martini down the street."

Jeannie texted back, "OK, where?"

"Just a couple doors down, same side of the street. CYA."

Jeannie got up and walked down the street. She found Juston waiting outside for her. He went for the hug. She extended her hand and he ran into it. Flustered, they embraced awkwardly.

"Jeannie, it's been a hound's age since we last saw each other!"

"It's true. Good to see you, Juston. How have you been?"

"Just peachy! Let's go get a drink. I could use one."

Inside the Dirty Martini, Juston told the maître d', "Could we go upstairs? We've not seen each other in a while and want to talk." Jeannie thought this was too much information for the maître d' and assumed Juston was just trying to impress the man with the fox he was dining with. Typical dude.

Once seated, Jeannie ordered a Dirty Martini, shaken not stirred, and immediately started pumping Juston for information about the AMEBA project. It turned out that Juston was not only involved; he was going to be the program manager if Booz got the bid.

"Well, could you use a girl like me?" she asked.

"In so many ways," Juston said, barely suppressing a leer. Jeannie frowned and Juston quickly said, "We're actually looking for an AI person. I think you'd be ideal."

"OK, I don't really call it AI. The state-of-the-art today is more appropriately called Machine Learning. We should be so lucky, or possibly so unlucky, as to have real Artificial Intelligence. But, yeah, it sounds like an interesting project, and I'd love to come aboard." From the look on Juston's face, Jeannie knew that he was thinking of coming aboard, in a different way.

Jeannie leaned forward, resting her elbows on the table. "Juston, if I do come aboard, I don't want any funny business, like the last time." In addition to making an overt pass, Juston had taken many opportunities to brush up against Jeannie, or to touch her in a familiar, but not overtly sexual, manner: putting his arm around her while walking, standing close to her in the elevator, touching her arm in a reassuring manner when mansplaining something to her.

"Right. Yes. Of course." Juston looked very uncomfortable. "Jeannie, I'm going to be straight with you. I've had a massive crush on you for some time. But I will be a gentleman."

Jeannie thought to herself, Wait a minute. I have two goals here, and one of them is to go home with Juston. Get it together, girl. Sweeten up.

"Why, Juston! You little sweetie. Well, let's get to know one another better and see what develops." He was a pretty good-looking guy, nice build, nice bulge, and she'd had worse.

What developed was they both got quite drunk before ordering. Jeannie didn't find much a vegan could eat on the menu, and so ordered the mixed greens, hold the gorgonzola. Juston ordered the ancho-rubbed ribeye. Typical guy, Jeannie thought. After a few more drinks, Juston asked Jeannie if she'd like to come to his place for a nightcap. Ordinarily, Jeannie would have turned down such a ham-handed proposition, even drunk as she was. But there were the two deals she needed to close, so she accepted, and Juston ordered an Uber to take them to his apartment at Foundry Lofts at The Yards. Jeez, thought Jeannie. How much does this guy make? That's a pretty nice area, and not too far from the Booz office and the Nationals' ballpark. If Juston didn't seem to be such a dickhead, I might could get used to a place like that.

When they arrived, Jeannie's impression of the place skyrocketed. Soooo nice! she thought. Nice view, nice furniture, impeccable. He must have maid service, she thought. Juston took her on a short tour, ending in the bedroom. He leaned in to kiss Jeannie, and she let him. One thing led to another, and Jeannie was bangin' for roof.

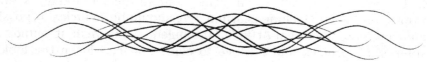

In the morning, Jeannie awoke to find Juston already gone to work. Oh, my head, she thought. And my nipples! Juston played with my boobs for fucking ever last night. They're sore as fuck. She sat up and immediately fell back. Take it easy, she told herself.

After a few minutes, she rolled to the edge of the bed and dragged herself onto the floor. She crawled into the bathroom and sat on the john for about 20 minutes before she felt ready to stand up. After brushing her teeth with the toothbrush she kept in her purse, she showered and then looked through Juston's drawers for something to wear. She found some sweatpants and a sweatshirt emblazoned with the Duke logo. Yeah, that Juston. Always slipping that he went to Duke into the conversation. She was about as tall as Juston, so the clothes didn't fit too badly.

Her head was still throbbing, but she was famished. She looked through Juston's cupboards and fridge. Typical. Mostly just beer and lunch meat in the fridge, and chips and Cheetos in the cupboards. Finally, she turned up a few slices of bread in the frost-bound freezer and popped them in the toaster. At least he's got peanut butter and jelly, but only real butter.

While she ate, Jeannie was scrolling through the national news on the *New York Times* site on her iPad when a picture stopped her dead. The headline was, "Man Transported 1,300 Miles in Three Hours?" She took another look at the picture and realized it was the guy who harassed her in the parking deck. An electric bolt ran up her spine.

Omigod! What the fucking fuck? she thought and read on:

> George Flicker, a bankruptcy lawyer from Washington, DC, walked into Balta, North Dakota yesterday afternoon wet, dazed, and disoriented. One of the (disputed) claims to fame of the tiny hamlet in Pierce County is that it is just six miles from the geographical center of North America. And that appears to be just where Mr.

Flicker landed, seemingly by teleporting from a parking garage in Pentagon City, Virginia to those exact coordinates: a pond near Kilgore Lake in the middle of the desolate prairie west of Balta.

Witnesses put Mr. Flicker at a trial in the Arlington Courthouse at 4:30 pm yesterday. Mr. Flicker says he drove from the courthouse to the Pentagon Row shopping center to run some errands, arriving at the parking ramp a little after 5 pm. As he was getting his bag out of his trunk, he suddenly found himself waist deep in muddy pond water.

A large man and a poor swimmer, Mr. Flicker managed to struggle to shore and followed the waterline west to 21st Avenue NE. Totally disoriented, Mr. Flicker luckily decided to head south, where he found a crossroad at 50th St NE, turned east and followed the signs into Balta. It took him a little over three hours to cover the 10 miles into town, according to Mr. Flicker. He showed up still wet at the offices of Jundt's M & M Repair, where workers gave him a mechanic's jumpsuit to change into and called the sheriff.

Authorities have examined the contents of Mr. Flicker's bag and found they contained legal papers relating to the court case he was working on. One document of particular interest was signed yesterday by the judge in that case, who has confirmed the apparent authenticity of the document. Virginia authorities have found Mr. Flicker's car parked in the Pentagon Row parking garage, just as he said. The timestamp on the parking receipt corroborates Mr. Flicker's story.

Mr. Flicker is obviously shaken by his ordeal and declined to be interviewed for this story.

There appears to be no practical way for a man to be transported 1,300 miles to the middle of North Dakota in roughly three hours. A commercial airliner could barely cover the distance in that amount of time, even assuming it could land in tiny Balta, population 65.

If this is a hoax, there seems to be little point to it.

Mr. Flicker is currently under the care of a psychiatrist at the Center for Psychiatric Care in Grand Forks, North Dakota. Mr. Flicker's wife has been contacted and was expected to arrive in

Grand Forks today. When he recovers sufficiently, the FBI, NSA, and CIA are eagerly anticipating interviewing him.

Jeannie was in a state of shock at reading this. *What the fuck? I tell the guy to get lost, and he magically appears in the middle of nowhere, North Dakota?* She shivered and got up to pace back and forth. *What if it all was real? What if I somehow acquired real magical powers? What if I sent that poor asshole for a well-deserved dunk in a pond? What if those women in the café really were Magic creatures, and Magic isn't just a game, but some kind of reflection of reality? Omigod, my brain hurts.*

Jeannie went over to the couch and laid down, facing away from the window because the light still hurt her eyes. *So, when I beat the Black Dahlia and he said I was the most powerful mage in the world, that was true. Somehow, the whole initiation was real. Somehow, it not only wasn't a dream about a Magic game, I have real power in the real world. But, shit, if every time I get pissed off, I could end up hurting someone, that's so not cool. I need to figure out first, how did I send that poor jerk to Bumfuck, North Dakota? Next, how can I prevent doing this unintentionally? And finally, how can I use this power—assuming I can figure out how to control it—for good. Wait. Black Dahlia mentioned 40 days of mentorship. Oh, I hope that's true. I need help.*

After worrying for another 10 minutes, Jeannie fell asleep on the couch. The next thing she knew, Juston was shaking her shoulder. "Wow, Jeannie, we really tied one on last night. I wish I could have sacked out all day on the couch." Juston smiled as Jeannie sat up quickly. He settled in beside her. "So, babe, how you doin'?"

Oh, I don't know if I'm ready for more Juston just now, Jeannie thought.

"I've been better," she said. "Definitely not 'peachy.' How about you?"

"Yeah, it was brutal at work. But, good news, what I didn't tell you yesterday is, that grant for the radio arrays? That's wired for MacAllan. The feds need to make a show of an open procurement process, but we've got it. Hell, we gave the feds the idea in the first place, and a line on the scientist who's done the preliminary work in proving the concept. So, that means as soon as best and final offers come in in a couple days, we can put you on staff."

"Wow, Juston! That's incredible! Thanks so much." Jeannie decided she probably should kiss him, so she leaned over and gave him a quick kiss. "Now I've got something to tell you. I'm homeless at the moment."

"What? What happened to Whatsisname?" For a split second, Jeannie wondered why Juston thought he should know her boyfriend's name.

"Glenn. I got tired of his bullshit, picked a fight, loaded my stuff into the car, and split, day before yesterday. He's been texting me, but I'm ghosting him."

"Well, you can stay here until you get settled, or . . . if you like, longer." Jeannie searched Juston's face. He wasn't being a smart ass. He must have meant it when he told me he had a big crush on me.

"That's so kind of you. I don't think I'd be comfortable moving in permanently at this stage in our relationship. You know, we barely know one another."

Juston briefly looked disappointed but recovered. "Well, as I always say, you don't ask; you don't get," he said with a laugh.

What he didn't say was that he had been obsessed with Jeannie for years. Ever since they had first met, he'd maintained a folder of every picture, every online post, every shred of information he could find about Jeannie. When they had worked together, he had broken up with his then-girlfriend just so he'd be available for her. He yearned for her touch and was devastated when Jeannie moved on when the project ended. He even did a little bit of hacking after that, breaking into her Gmail and social accounts to see whom she was dating. He pulled back from that after a few months because he creeped himself out. But he never stopped thinking about her.

"I've got a hide-a-bed in the second bedroom," he said. "That's my office, but I can sleep there until you get situated."

This was just what Jeannie had been hoping to hear.

"That's so kind of you Juston. You're a lifesaver!" She gave him another kiss. "You don't happen to have a parking space available in this building? My Camry needs a muffler and I've got it stashed at Pentagon Row at the moment."

"Yeah, I get a space with the apartment, but I don't own a car so, sure, you can have it. You want to go get it now?"

"No. It makes such noise. Let's wait until it's dark and there's fewer cops around."

Since there was no food in the house, they decided they should go out, but no place fancy, due to Jeannie's attire.

"Hey, wait a minute!" Juston said. "The DC Duke Club is having a gathering tonight to watch the basketball game at Mackey's Public House, just off the Mall. And they've got veggie options. You wanna go? You're dressed for it."

Jeannie thought for a minute. Do I look too grungy to be seen in public? Juston read her mind. "You look fine. Most everybody will be dressed like you."

"All right, but just don't tell anybody I'm a Dukie. I hate Duke."

"You wound me, mademoiselle!" Juston made an outraged face, then smiled, and started for the door. "It's across the street from Metro Center. Let's go."

In the train, Juston said, "Why do you hate Dukies? Don't you like excellent schools with dominant college basketball teams that actually graduate players?"

"I don't know. I think it's something—no offense—about their attitude."

"What attitude?"

"Well, for example, Dukies never say, 'When I was in college.' They always say, 'When I was at Duke.' And, I don't know. Why do people hate the Yankees? Or used to hate the Cowboys? Because they win too much. America loves an underdog."

"I don't buy that. Ivy Leaguers are much more obnoxious, for example. Ever talk to a Hahvahd man? And Kentucky and even archenemy Carolina win a lot, too."

"True. I don't know. I went to MIT, and nobody hates me for it. Could be a perceived white privilege thing?"

Juston said he didn't know and then turned to look out the window at the rushing blackness. He knew he was prone to say, "When I was at Duke." Jeannie had nailed him there. But he also loved the reaction when he said it: a noticeable pause and a look that said he was being reassessed positively.

For her part, Jeannie decided she had come on too strong. The recent events had her frazzled. "Look, Juston, I'm sorry. I guess I'm still recovering from last night."

This cheered Juston up, since it brought back memories of their lovemaking. Jeannie sure was a hellion in bed. And those boobs!

They arrived at Mackey's and there was already quite a crowd of Duke-blue-clad revelers. The NCAA tournament game had just started, and the fans were getting rowdy.

Juston said, "Hair of the dog?"

Jeannie grabbed her head in mock anguish. "No," was all she said.

"OK, anything else to drink?"

"Yeah, get me a lemonade. You know this place is louder than I had expected. We may just need to eat and leave."

They grabbed a table at the back, and when Juston returned with the drinks, the crowd erupted at a spectacular Duke dunk. Juston craned his head to see one of the TVs.

"Nice. Seven-point lead and the game's only seven minutes old." He glanced at Jeannie who took a huge gulp of the lemonade.

"Oh, my head," she said.

"Poor baby. Look, we don't need to stay."

"No, I can see this is an important game for you. We can stay, at least for a while."

Jeannie started feeling better, especially when her tofu vegan salad came. She realized she hadn't eaten anything all day other than the PB&J. By the time she finished the salad, she was feeling more human and actually started getting interested in the game.

They switched to a booth with a better view of a TV. Juston was yelling and screaming. In his excitement, he looked like a teenager. Eventually, the game came down to the final 10 seconds with Duke behind by two points. South Carolina had the ball, but Duke's freshman player of the year candidate stole it and launched a three-pointer from way far away. It looked like it might go short.

"Go in!" shouted Jeannie, and it did. Duke won and Juston went nuts, jumping up and down and high fiving everyone he could find. The commentators were shocked, calling it a miracle shot. They replayed the shot in slow motion, and it indeed looked like the shot was going to fall short, but at the last instant, it somehow moved horizontally to fall into the basket.

Jeannie was thunderstruck. Omigod, she thought, I've done it again. Damn. Juston was in seventh heaven with his Blue Devil buddies, pogoing around and hollering. After he calmed down a bit, Jeannie reminded him that they needed to go get her car. Juston jabbered about the game all the way to Pentagon City. Jeannie listened politely, but her mind was fixated on going back to the garage. It felt like returning to the scene of a crime. That poor man. He was a jerk, but he didn't deserve to be terrorized like that.

When they got to her car, she realized she'd have to do some rearranging, since she'd piled some of her stuff in the passenger seat. While shifting stuff to the back seat, she kept glancing back at the spot, festooned with yellow police tape, where George Flicker had disappeared, half hoping he'd reappear and say, "Surprise! I'm a twin. Psych!" Of course, that would be ridiculous. This can't be happening to me, she thought. I must still be on a trip. Please, please wake up! She even tried pinching herself, which prompted a raised eyebrow from Juston.

Once they were settled in the car, Jeannie started it up, and the noise from the broken muffler echoed from the garage walls sounding like a jet fighter taking off.

"Jeez, you weren't kidding! That's hella loud!" Juston said.

"What?" said Jeannie, just for a laugh.

They drove out onto Joyce Street and headed toward I-395. When they got off on South Capitol, just past the Capitol Skyline hotel, Jeannie noticed several fire engines parked on the side street.

"What's up with them? They're just sitting there."

"That's a staging area, I think. Since the traffic sucks so bad in DC, the fire department keeps engines all over the city, just in case."

As they passed the intersection, they saw a police car at the head of the line of engines. It turned on its lights, pulled out behind them, and pulled them over.

"Oh, merde!" Jeannie said. "I'm busted. And I don't really have the money to pay a ticket. Goddamn!"

The DC cop came over and asked for license and registration which he took back to his squad car to run a check. When he returned, he said, "You know, young lady, we got a noise ordinance here in the District. It's after 10 pm, which means a double fine. I can also arrest you."

"Oh, officer," Jeannie said with a big smile. "You don't want to do that."

After an awkward pause, the cop said with a puzzled look on his face, "No, I don't want to do that. Just get that thing fixed. Have a nice night." He returned to his squad and drove off.

"What the fuck, Jeannie? Do you always get off so easily?"

Jeannie had a feeling the cop fully intended to have her spend a night in the slammer. Oops, I did it again, she thought, smiling.

"Sure. The Girls help," she said, indicating her breasts. "Even with no cleavage."

Juston just shook his head as Jeannie pulled back into traffic. "Men are definitely the weaker sex," he said. "An extra hundred or so cc's of breast tissue turns men into fools."

"Yeah, guys are boobs for boobs. I've certainly found that. But it's actually no picnic to have big boobs, let me tell ya. I can't lay on my stomach and tan my back at the beach unless I do some excavation. I sometimes get under-boob rashes; I basically can't run or jog very far or ride a roller coaster; clothes generally don't come in my size; and I can't use the tray table on airplanes. My cleavage also catches crumbs—the term of art is 'titty litter.'"

Juston laughed with a snort. "Man, that sucks!"

"Plus, there's the backaches. And, don't even get me started on all the reactions from men. In addition to creepy men staring at them—starting with my uncles when I was 12—they feel free to yell, from across the street, 'real or fake?' or 'hey airbags!' or some other inanity. Also, men immediately assume I'm a dunce. I used that to my advantage a lot at MIT and since. Alternatively, they think I'm a call girl. You know, I stopped off at the Mayflower to grab a coffee yesterday, and the fucking waiter thought I was a working girl and called the manager when I went to the Ladies'. So, I'm just sick of my boobs. I'm just sick of dealing. I've actually been saving up to get breast reduction surgery."

Juston was shocked by this. "No!" he yelped involuntarily, then sheepishly said, "Sorry. I mean, that seems so drastic."

"Yeah, well you don't have to lug around 18 pounds of flesh on your chest every day. Besides, don't worry, I'm constantly raiding the Deboobification Fund when I'm between gigs, like now. And it's basically down to nothing at the moment."

"But there are advantages to big boobs, right? Like getting out of parking tickets. Turn here. The garage entry is around the corner."

"Oh, for sure. The fact that I can easily manipulate 'breast men' into doing pretty much anything, short of committing murder, is a plus. Or the fact that several of my boyfriends didn't care when I would put on weight because they were so overjoyed at how much bigger my breasts got. But I think I could have all the advantages with fewer disadvantages if I were a C cup."

They pulled into the underground parking, the engine sound reverberating, parked, grabbed a couple of Jeannie's suitcases, and took the elevator to the second floor. Once inside Juston's apartment, he got some linen and blankets from the closet and made up the hide-a-bed in his office.

"Nightcap?" he asked.

"No, thanks, Juston. My boobs need to recover from the working over you gave them last night."

Juston turned bright red. "Oh God, I'm sorry."

"Don't worry about it. I'm kinda used to it. But when—or if—we make it again, treat the Girls a little nicer."

Juston was so embarrassed he just gave a dorky little wave and retreated to his office.

Alone in Juston's bed, Jeannie finally had a moment to reflect on the crazy few days she'd had. Losing her job was a bummer. But if that asshole boss of hers can't stand someone being smarter than him, well, good riddance. Leaving Glenn didn't bother her so much. It had been coming for months and she was glad to be rid of his boasting. If the cost was sleeping a night in her car, it was worth it.

The mindblower was the magical power she had acquired in the battle, which was apparently real, and not some sort of psychedelic hallucination. Did I really drop that poor jerk into a pond in North Dakota? Did I really score the winning basket for Duke? Did I really beat a ticket with more than just the Girls? The feelings that she'd been holding at bay suddenly washed over her. Serially and all at once she was scared, bewildered, skeptical, intimidated, and near catatonic. She again felt like throwing up and hurried to the toilet in the master bath. But no vomit came. She sat on the cold tile with her mind roiling. After what seemed like hours, Jeannie's mind cleared, and she got up and climbed back into bed.

Let's take stock of what I know, she thought. It appears I can create miracles. And so far, I've used power inadvertently except for, I guess, that cop. Apparently, my power works at a distance. The Duke game was at Madison Square Garden a couple hundred miles away, and I sent that Flicker dude halfway across the country. It must work without regard for the physical Universe, otherwise, that Flicker jerk would have been smashed against the garage ceiling or been incinerated by the friction generated by moving through the atmosphere at hypersonic speed. I can affect people's minds as well as material things.

So, for what shall I use this awesome power? I think it would be best to start off slow, but perhaps eventually I can work on my life's goal: saving the world. Perhaps if Juston gets me this radio gig, I can figure out how to instill ethics into war machines. That still sounds like a huge goal. I guess I should concentrate on getting employed, getting my own place, and, I guess, figuring out what to do about Juston. Jeannie was realizing the guy was kind of growing on her. He didn't seem to be quite the dickhead she had thought he was back when they worked together, and he obviously adored her. That'll do for now, she decided. Maybe I can be a friend with benefits for a while until I can figure out what the fuck is going on here.

As she was drifting off, she remembered the 40 days of mentorship Black Dahlia promised. Yeah, but I beat his ass pretty good, she thought drowsily. Perhaps I don't need any mentors.

Su
nday morning was bright and sunny. Jeannie awoke a little disoriented. Oh, yeah, she thought. I'm crashing with Juston. She lay in bed for a few minutes until the various magical incidents drifted back into her head,

driving her nuts. She got up and showered. She dressed in the mirror and took stock of her appearance: jeans and a wrinkled untucked plaid shirt. Well, at least it's not Duke sweats, she thought.

She briefly considered some eye makeup but decided against it. Do I care if he sees me without makeup? No. Not really. If he's into me, he should see what I really look like. She examined her pale oval face for incipient zits. Thirty-three and still with the zits already. She stood back and looked at herself in the mirror. Nice eyes, but a little too close together. Small mouth, but nice red lips. If I had more of a waist, less of a beanie, and a little more junk in the trunk, I might be really good-looking, she thought. Oh, stop it, girl! You're a fine figure of a woman! Quit the stinkin' thinkin'.

She brushed her hair, pulled it back into a ponytail, and went out into the living area to see if Juston was up.

Juston was rummaging in his freezer when she came in. "What're you looking for, J-man?"

Juston bumped his head against the top of the freezer. "Ouch. You startled me," he said. "Good morning, J-girl!"

Jeannie came around the end of the counter and gave him a little kiss on the cheek. "Peanut butter and jelly again for breakfast?" she asked with a smile.

"No. I'm planning on have stuff delivered."

"I hope it's vegan."

"Yup. I thought we could get stuff from Sweetgreen. They don't deliver, but Uber Eats will pick it up and bring it here. I have you pegged for the Shroomami bowl and the Spicy Sabzi for me. Both are vegan. The menu's on the counter over there. See what you think."

"Thanks. That's sweet of you."

"And I thought I'd make us some sangria to drink, if I can get this damn can of lemonade unstuck from the back of this freezer." He returned his attention to his frosty struggle. "You know, the Internet and sports media are blowing up about that basket last night. They're analyzing the shot frame by frame and have pretty much concluded it's totally impossible for the ball to have gone in."

Jeannie didn't know what else to say, so she said, "Freaky."

Finally, Juston liberated the can from the ice. He went to get a glass pitcher from the top shelf of a cupboard. It was an odd shape, looking like a stylized upside-down oxbow with two long prongs at the top. As he pulled it down, the pitcher slipped out of his wet hands, hit the top of the refrigerator, and broke across his right shoulder, gashing his carotid. His neck began spewing blood and Jeannie rushed over to him.

"Omigod! Juston!" Jeannie pressed a towel to his neck. There's no way help can arrive in time, she thought. Not even enough time to call 911. Desperate, she yelled, "Heal!"

Juston stopped bleeding immediately but was still freaking out. Jeannie removed the towel from his neck. There was no sign of the injury other than the blood.

"Calm down, Juston! You're not bleeding anymore." Juston gave her a strange look and felt his neck, which although still slick with blood, was obviously not bleeding, or even injured. Juston was hyperventilating and white with shock.

"What the fuck just happened? What the fuck just happened?" he repeated over and over.

Jeannie couldn't think of what to say.

"Seriously, Jeannie, what the hell did you do? I was spurting blood, and now I'm not. What the fucking fuck?"

"Let me dry off this blood and then why don't you go get changed?" she said. "Then we should sit and have a little talk."

Juston walked unsteadily into his bedroom, washed his neck and changed his clothes. When he came back out of the room, his face was still white, and he was shivering. Jeannie had cleaned up the mess in the kitchen and was sitting on the couch, looking pretty unsteady herself. She motioned Juston to sit next to her.

"OK, you're not going to believe any of this. In fact, I don't believe any of this, but most of what I am about to tell you has objective proof." Jeannie proceeded to tell Juston about George Flicker, and the Duke game-winning basket, and the cop, and her move to save Juston from certain death. Juston just listened, staring straight ahead, expressionless except for a kind of shocked bewilderment.

When Jeannie was finished, Juston said in a dull voice, "Wow."

"Juston, honey, look at me. What do you think about what I just told you?"

Juston roused from his catatonic state and turned to Jeannie. "What do I think about it? What do I think about it? I can't think anything. I'm stuck on that part a few minutes ago when you yelled, 'Heal' and I stopped bleeding. Pinch me. I must be dreaming."

Jeannie pinched him. "I didn't mean that literally!" he yelped.

Jeannie put her arms around him. "Something happened to me Friday, and now I seem to have all this power that I don't really know how to control."

"OK, if you want me to believe that this isn't all just some kind of fever dream, lift up that armchair with your mind."

Jeannie gave it a try, but the chair didn't move. She tried lifting a bowl from the counter, a pen off the table, and other small items around the room. No dice.

"It's got something to do with emotion," she said. "The first time, I was pissed at that letch Flicker. When I put that basketball in the hoop, I was excited about the game and worried about the outcome. I was scared that cop would arrest me last night. And, of course, just now, I was terrified that you were going to die on your kitchen floor. So that's gotta be it. I only can use the power when I'm riled up."

Justin shook his head several times rapidly as if freeing his mind from cobwebs. "Yeah, I guess that makes some sort of sense."

The color was beginning to return to his face, and he had stopped shivering. "Look, Jeannie, you may think that I am the type of guy that would never believe in this sort of thing, in magic. But I've got something to tell you as well. I am a Chaos Magick mage."

"And that would be . . ."

"And that would be an adept at Chaos Magick, which is a hermetic tradition involving the manipulation of the hidden code of reality."

"Um, that's not a lot clearer."

"Yeah, I know. OK, Chaos Magick 101." Juston explained that Chaos Magick is based on the belief that magic is a real force in the Universe that can be measured and controlled. He explained some of the ideas of the most influential thinker in Chaos Magick, Peter Carroll, and that the chaos in Chaos Magick was akin to the Chinese concept of Tao with many similarities to quantum physics.

"It is a way of opening oneself to the possibilities of the Universe. A key concept for Chaos Magicians is 'Nothing is true, everything is permitted,' meaning that you can theoretically do anything."

"That sounds a lot like that fiend Aleister Crowley and his ghastly Thelema religion back in the first part of the 20th century. So, if nothing is true and all is permitted, then murder, rape, and torture are all allowed?"

"Chaos Magick is not dark or light. Yes, there are some who use it for evil, but they are constricted by their lack of understanding, which limits their attainment of power. They lack the mental flexibility required to truly master Chaos Magick. The mage can play with the Universe and see how the Universe responds. Living becomes entirely a creative act. Another important concept is malleability of belief. Unlike religions that codify belief into strictures and dogma, Chaos Magicians use belief as a tool, and discard beliefs and take up others as necessary."

Juston paused for a moment, looking into Jeannie's eyes to see if she was following him.

She said, "That last bit reminds me of a Mary Baker Eddy quote I've always liked: 'Belief is changeable, but spiritual understanding is changeless.'"

"Uh, OK. Interesting. We should talk about that later. Anyway, the Magick adept uses techniques to focus his or her mind on a single point, thought, or goal, much like Zen Buddhist practice. It involves the typical magical accoutrements, like wands, robes, visualizations, symbolic systems, sigils, barbaric languages, and rituals to invoke real and imaginary entities who can accomplish the magician's goals. Magicians believe that somewhere in the Universe is someone or something that can accomplish their intentions."

"So, is this just a bunch of immature nerds in their parents' basements—present company excepted—running around in capes with wands?"

Juston was irritated at this. "Look, Magic Jeannie, you're the one who has wielded fantastic power over the last three days, not me. I'm trying to explain to you that there may be a framework that supports and explains the power you have and could help you control it."

"You're my first mentor, aren't you?"

"What?"

"The Black Dahlia said I would have 40 days of mentorship so that I could control my power. You're the first one, aren't you?"

Juston had no idea what she was talking about, but he said, "If it makes you happy, and willing to listen to what I am trying to tell you, then fine."

"OK, great. Now is this Chaos Magick organized in any way, or is it just a bunch of weird—ah, strike that—magicians working alone?"

"Well, I'd have to say we're not really that organized. Remember, a signature aspect of Chaos Magick is the ability to adopt and abandon beliefs at will. Makes it hard to have a dogma, and that's kind of the point. There is an international organization called The Illuminates of Thanateros. Don't you love the name? A combination of Thanatos and Eros, the Greek gods of death and sex."

"Sounds like the name of a death metal band."

"Actually, there used to be a German metal band called Thanateros."

"I just knew it."

Juston described how the Illuminates try to bring others to mastership of Chaos Magick, and how Peter Carroll and Frater Vegtan founded the Church of Chaos in Sydney, Australia in 1980.

"A major way that many mages focus their energy on their objectives is through the use of sigils, physical symbols with magical power that work subconsciously in the mage's mind, bypassing consciousness and the will. The mage creates a sigil as a glyph of desire, charges it with power, grounds him or herself, and then forgets all about it."

Jeannie was skeptical, but this was certainly no weirder than what she'd been through the last few days. "So how does one create a sigil?"

"Well, a common way is to write a short statement of the desire. Like, for example, 'I wish to become a billionaire.'"

"I'll just bet you do."

"Très humoroso, funny lady. Anyway. You take out all the repeating letters from your phrase. Let me write it down here and show you." Juston wrote the phrase on a scrap of paper.

"OK, cross out the i's, the b's, the l's, the o's, the e's, and the a's. That leaves w, s, h, t, c, m, and n. You then arrange the remaining letters into a symbol, stylizing it either using the letter shapes or creating vectors based on numerological reduction. Here. Let's go to Sigilscribe, which creates sigils for you. You got your iPad handy?"

Jeannie got up to get the tablet, and they navigated to sigilscribe.me, entered the phrase and produced a sigil.

"OK, now we charge the picture up with magical energy."

"And how the fuck do we do that?"

"Well, funny you should mention it, orgasm is one way. Meditation or other types of achieving a gnostic state is another. Or dancing. What are you up for?"

Jeannie thought she had heard smooth proposals before, but this one took the cake. Nonetheless, given the stress of the day, she thought a nice roll in the hay with Juston would be good for both of them.

"I choose orgasm, you slick seducer. Tell me you didn't make all this shit up just to get me back in the sack."

"I honestly did not. I can show you the Wikipedia entries if you like."

"No, I'll believe you for the moment. Let's print this thing out and get busy."

When they were done, they sat back down on the sofa and Juston continued. "OK, the next step is to ground yourself. A good way to do that is to burn the sigil and go do something completely different."

"OK, burning is easy. Let's do that and then why don't we just go out to Sweetgreen? How far is it?"

"It's less than a mile."

"Well, it looks like a brilliant day out there. Let's walk."

As they walked up 3rd Street, Juston continued to fill Jeannie in.

"Getting back to the fundaments of Chaos Magick, one of the foundational elements is sharpening the mind through meditative practices. One way to do this is Image Concentration, which helps train the part of the mind in which pictorial thoughts arise. Have you ever, for example, tried to think only in pictures? It's hard but learning to do so enables more control and concentration. So, you try to keep a simple shape, like a triangle, circle, or cross, in your mind's eye, without distortion, for as long as possible. It's surprisingly hard, but after a while, you can see the image with eyes closed, and eventually be able to project it onto any blank surface."

"OK, I can see how that would be difficult, but it hardly seems worthwhile."

They crossed into a tree-lined neighborhood bordered by a park. The spring buds were out on all the trees. They passed by a Walgreens and Juston said, "Oh, can we stop in? I need to get my Claritin. Spring in DC pretty much hashes out my sinuses, and once the cherry blossoms are in full bloom, I'm barely functional without drugs. Although come to think of it, with all these buds out, I should be in agony, since I ran out day before yesterday."

"I guess when I heal, I heal everything," Jeannie said with a weak laugh. But they both fell silent thinking of the implications of her power.

When they turned onto Pennsylvania Avenue, huge federal buildings came into view. The area was boiling with young Congressional aides in dark suits rushing to pick up sandwiches to eat at their desks. Sweetgreen was across the boulevard from the massive John Adams Building of the Library of Congress. Just down the block were the even more massive main Library of Congress and James Madison buildings.

"Say, these library buildings remind me, I'm writing a book about Chaos Magick. I'm maybe half done. Perhaps you can read it and kill two birds: understanding Chaos Magick and giving me feedback on the book."

"Sure. Sounds like a good idea."

"OK, when we get inside, I'll email it to you."

After the two had settled in and ordered lunch, the enormity of the morning's incident descended upon them. Juston stared at Jeannie and said, "Was that a dream, what happened in the kitchen?"

Jeannie averted her eyes for a moment, then met Juston's gaze. "No, Juston, that was real. You almost died. I saved you with, uh, magic, I guess."

Juston again shook his head rapidly, then crossed his arms on the table and buried his head in them. He remained like that for five minutes. Jeannie became more and more concerned.

"Juston? J-man? Hey, it's OK. You should feel good. You're alive, and magic works. And maybe that means you're going to be a billionaire."

Juston laughed weakly and looked up. "Well, that's one thing about Chaos Magick. The spells don't always work. We live in a probability-based universe in which the future is not written but depends on the probability of events as they unfold. Some things remain more possible than others. There are ways to figure out how much probability distortion a given act of magic will produce using spell and anti-spell equations."

"Equations? In magic? That seems counterintuitive."

"That's kind of a pun you did there. But think about it. If we have free will and the Universe is not deterministic—in the sense that everything can be foretold, and nothing can be changed—then that means the Universe is probabilistic. Things might happen, but they're not destined to happen. So, when you cast a spell, if the difference between the probability of something happening due to magic and it happening by chance is large, the likelihood of the spell working is lower."

"So how high can the probability be that a man could be teleported across half the continent?"

"Well, that's kind of what's blowing my mind! The odds are astronomical! As I said, generally, in Chaos Magick, most spells don't work, at least they don't work within a timeframe that the mage might desire. But some mages use a three-dimensional graph called the Tripod of Stokastikos to prove that even an event with zero probability of natural occurrence can occur under the influence of sufficient magic. Among the variables used are: Gnosis—the altered states of consciousness I alluded to when we wanted to charge the sigil; the magical Link—the connection made in a magical operation between the Will of the magician and the desired object to be affected; Subliminalization of intent—that business of forgetting about it; and Belief—you need to believe it will work."

"Well, I've got the subliminalization thing licked," Jeannie said. "I didn't overtly think about banishing Flicker or putting the ball in the basket. And there was nothing planned about the cop or, ah, your neck."

Juston winced at the mention of his injury. "Yeah, you seem to be accessing magic in a completely different way. As a matter of fact, your power calls into question everything I've believed, and have been writing in my book." Juston looked glum.

Their lunches arrived and the two quietly ate their food for several minutes, each lost in a torrent of thoughts. Jeannie thought, well, besides a belief in magic, I'm not too sure what Chaos Magick has in common with my experience, which seems somehow entangled with the *Magic* game. Both may be coming at magic from different directions, but if Juston is my first mentor, I wonder if I'm going to learn much from him. I guess I need to wait and see if Black Dahlia put him in my path on purpose. If he did, it sure doesn't seem like Juston knows he's a mentor. His reaction seemed authentic when I mentioned it.

Juston's thoughts were much more unsettled. This chick has got ahold of some terrific power. She doesn't know how to use it, and it doesn't seem to follow the practices of Chaos Magick. It's so far from Chaos Magick that I'm wondering if there's any reason to continue with my book, or with my magic practice. Have I wasted years becoming an adept? She said something about me being a mentor. What's that all about? If anything, I think I need her to be my mentor. From what she described of her other-dimensional battle, it seemed like she was sucked into the battlefield on purpose. But why? What was the means of entry? Why did she get pulled in now rather than at any time before? Was it that *Magic* card-flipping app that she wrote? Should I learn the *Magic* game and use her app? If Black Dahlia said she was the most powerful mage, why wasn't she called to battle or apprenticeship sooner? How come they couldn't identify her sooner? This is too much like the Luke Skywalker story, but he was stranded on an isolated planet. Jeannie's been right here. What was the trigger? And how can I prepare myself to use it?

Jeannie roused herself from her contemplation and looked at Juston. He had a faraway look in his eyes and had stopped eating. "J-man, are you OK?"

Juston turned his unfocused eyes her way and slowly came out of his reverie. "Oh, uh, yes, um, sure. I was just thinking about all this. You know, at first, I thought teaching you about Chaos Magick would help you. Now

I'm not at all sure. As I said, you're accessing magic in a completely different—and apparently much more powerful, way. I think you should be teaching me."

"Oh, I don't think so. I have no fucking idea how I did any of these things. I just willed them to be."

"Yes, well, that could be an important insight. The will is important in Chaos Magick, but basically, the use of magic is not generally via an act of the will, but rather the setting in motion of magical forces using various techniques. It's much more indirect, more like jiu-jitsu, and obviously way less successful than what you've got ahold of."

"Well, I feel like there was a reason we met at this time," Jeannie said. "You have or know something I need in order to control this power I appear to have. So please tell me more about Chaos Magick."

Juston didn't know how to proceed. Mentally he ran through the various techniques and doctrines of Chaos Magick, discarding them one by one as not pertinent, and potentially completely ineffective. He thought back to his neophyte, initiate, and adept training and ceremonies, but was at a loss to pick out significant parts that might be germane in the new world he found himself in. But wait, he thought. If I am to be a mentor, perhaps it's more like the role of the Insubordinate.

"Jeannie, I'm trying to figure out which parts of Chaos Magick practice can survive the collision with the magic reality you've demonstrated. And I've been wondering how I could possibly be a mentor to you. I've just thought of a role I could play that's not so much a mentor as a kind of reality check on the adept. It's called the Insubordinate. That's an adept who attends the Magister Templi and the teaching magi of The Pact. The roles this person fills are designed to, so to speak, prevent the adept from becoming too sure or too full of him or herself. The Insubordinate chooses two primary roles that best suit them from the five roles available: the Fool, the Jester, the Chaplain, the Confessor, and the Inquisitor."

"That's a cool idea," Jeannie said. "The powerful often forget how much they do not know, and how imperfect their judgment can be."

Juston explained the roles to Jeannie. The Fool ensures that teachings and instructions are understandable and criticizes or demands clarification if they are not. Often the Fool feigns ignorance to make the adept clarify. The Jester has a similar role, but delivers it with levity, poking fun at any pompousness or other big-headedness. The Chaplain concentrates on more-personal failings and blind spots but remains impartial. The Confessor attends to the personal progress of the mage, generally without comment. A main objective is to safeguard against sloth or complacency. The Inquisitor is an impartial arbiter with the power to veto any instructions and report on abuses of position.

"What a wonderful set of checks on power!" Jeannie said. "Which roles do you want to fill for me?"

"Well, I obviously would lack the knowledge to be an Inquisitor or probably the Confessor, since I have no idea how you do what you do. I am perfectly suited to the role of the Fool, but don't think I could handle the Jester. And I guess that leaves the Chaplain."

"OK, so you're the Foolish Chaplain." Jeannie giggled at the thought. "Which Chaos Magick practices do you think would help me learn how to control my power?"

"Well, I don't rightly know. It's hard for me to think clearly, given what happened this morning, facing death and the disillusionment of my beliefs and all." Juston scowled and rubbed his neck.

Jeannie reached across the table and gave Juston's hand a squeeze. "Yeah, it's been a pretty harsh day for you so far. And I'm reeling myself from the last three days. I don't mean to put pressure on you. Take your time figuring out what to teach me. In the meantime, I need to try not to get too wound up and send some other poor jerk to Timbuktu or something."

Juston smiled for the first time since the incident. "Yeah, you need to be even-keeled alright, and I need to be on my best behavior, or I might be that next jerk. Pow! To the moon!" They both collapsed in laughter, not because Juston was funny, but because it was all so stressful and so crazy, they had to laugh.

"You know what you were saying about belief struck a chord with me," Jeannie said. "I don't know if I ever told you, but I was raised in the Church of Christ, Scientist." Juston raised his eyebrows. "I know, most people think it's off-the-chain crazy, but in many ways, it really is quite a sweet religion. Mary Baker Eddy was an amazing woman, ahead of her time. She believed that God, although infinite, was personal and individual. The healing of the sick through faith was originally just a small part of the church she founded. She was so strong. Despite her father's cruelty, which undoubtedly caused her several illnesses—many probably psychosomatic—and the strictures of the time, she became one of the first feminists. What other existing religion was founded by a woman? She was fierce and loving. She didn't believe in doctrine or dogma. She believed in truth, life, and love as taught by Jesus. She was a healer, and using her curative system of metaphysics, performed many miracles that saved peoples' lives. Come to think of it, she seems like a mage." This realization momentarily stunned Jeannie. Was she following in the footsteps of Eddy?

"Wow," said Juston. "That's not the conception I had of Christian Scientists. But, wait, you have strange look on your face . . ."

Jeannie was lost in thought, overwhelmed by the possibility that she was destined to carry on the work of a church she had left as a teenager.

"Uh, no, I'm OK. I'm just thinking of what I'm supposed to do with all this power. And it's occurring to me I should train as a Christian Science practitioner. And, since I haven't been a believer for more than 15 years, it's kind of blowing my mind."

Jeannie slumped down in her chair and didn't speak for five minutes. Juston decided it was best to not bother her and ate his meal. Eventually, Jeannie sat up and said, "OK, we don't know each other that well, so let me fill you in on what's bugging me." She took a deep breath and then told Juston the story of her disillusionment with the church.

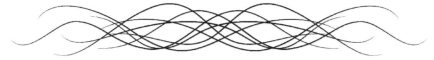

Jeannie's mother, named Mary in honor of Mary Baker Eddy, was a devout Christian Scientist, and her father had been an Episcopalian. He converted upon marrying but had drifted away from the church. Part of the reason, Jeannie said, was the fights the couple got into about raising Jeannie and her younger brother. It got so bad that if Jeannie got ill or needed stitches, her father, who was a stay-at-home dad, would secretly take her to a doctor. He had to pay in cash, so her mother wouldn't know, and so kept a hidden box of cash in the house. Jeannie was sworn to secrecy. She was also instructed by her father to hide any evidence of doctor intervention by wearing coverings, including long sleeves and pants if it was summer.

When Jeannie was 16, her father became quite ill and took to his bed. He told Jeannie his whole lower abdomen felt like it was on fire. He had cramps, vomited frequently, and had bloody diarrhea. He slept all the time, but when he was conscious, he begged his wife to call an ambulance. Mary would not hear of it and summoned first one, then two, then three Christian Science practitioners to help Joe let go of his "fixation" of illness. They prayed over him, and, during his brief periods of consciousness tried to get him to realize that his pain was an illusion.

Jeannie was in tears by this point. "He died after suffering for two weeks. The last thing he said to me was, 'Get away from your mother.'" Jeannie broke down crying.

Juston crossed over, sat in the chair beside her, and put his arms around her.

Jeannie wiped her eyes and said, "He died of uremic poisoning resulting from prostatitis, something that modern medicine can easily cure. He was in agony before he went. I packed some clothes, grabbed the keys to my dad's car, and went to live with my uncle—my dad's brother. From then on, I wouldn't have anything to do with my mom's side of the family. My biggest regret is that my brother was at school the day I left, or I would have taken him with me. My uncle, who was divorced, tried for years to get custody of Cody but failed. I haven't seen him since." Jeannie started to cry again. Juston didn't know what else to do, so he held her quietly.

When she recovered, Jeannie said, "So that's what's bothering me. Is this whole megillah we've been through some sort of sign that I need to return to that so-called church? Should I train as a Christian Science practitioner? Is that part of my 40 days of mentorship?"

"I certainly can't say what you should do, but I'm pretty sure you shouldn't make any big decisions today. Let's finish up and I'll get an Uber to take us back."

Acquisition

Weeks went by, with Jeannie still living with Juston. They kept separate beds but spent most of their spare time together. Juston told Jeannie more about Chaos Magick, and even had a few mage friends over for dinner. Jeannie went to *Magic Universe* drafts but didn't play any games, afraid that she might inadvertently use her magic to win. MacAllan got the federal contract, and Juston hired Jeannie to be the AI team lead.

Both of them were at a loss as to how Jeannie could control her power. Jeannie, for her part, was so paranoid about accidentally using magic, that she carefully examined all her reactions to other people, hoping to tamp down her emotions. When stressful situations came up at work or with other people, Juston would helpfully whisper or text her, "Foolish Chaplain says chill."

Jeannie joined the First Church of Christ, Scientist on 16th Street and started taking Primary class instruction from a healer named Christy. She had to swallow hard to assent to some of the teachings but embraced and was moved by one of them: "And we solemnly promise to watch, and pray for that Mind to be in us which was also in Christ Jesus; to do unto others as we would have them do unto us; and to be merciful, just, and pure."

Jeannie promised herself that she would learn the religion's healing practices, and not attempt to use her power until she had thoroughly understood and mastered them.

After her initial instruction, she attended and later participated in Scientist healings. Although she tried to keep skeptical thoughts from her mind, after seeing many patients, she observed that, although some were helped, they tended to be those afflicted with either psychosomatic or mild mental diseases. She thought, am I really learning anything? Try as she might, she couldn't quite bring herself to fully embrace the church's healing techniques. However, she did notice that her successes tended to be with patients she felt a high degree of empathy with. As her training went on, she tried to increase the empathy she felt for her patients. But it was hard sometimes.

Not long after she had this breakthrough realization, she developed a stunning track record of successful healing. Empathy seemed to be the key to controlling and projecting her power. After she completed the requirements to become a healer, the church recommended she continue to practice at the church facility. Jeannie wondered if this was because the elders were suspicious of her success and thought that perhaps she was sneaking medication to her patients.

The elders and other healers began to talk about her behind her back, calling her satanic and an evil witch. Instead of regarding her success as reinforcing their healing practices, they dehumanized her in their minds to justify pushing her to the side. Nobody had ever been as successful at healing the sick as she was. And the real problem appeared not to be just that she was successful. While that was galling to the others, especially the men, it was her gender that really bothered them, despite women being the majority in that church. What Jeannie was doing, real healing of real disease, not psychosomatic problems, flew in the face of women's suppression and oppression in religious life. She was trying to push back the patriarchic reality of 2,000 years of theology.

One day, as a test they were sure she would fail, the elders gave her a psychotic patient to treat. Others in the healing place had given up on him. He had been living there for a year and could no longer be restrained, even with chains. A bodybuilder, he had broken chains and shattered shackles with almost superhuman strength. He was kept locked away in a padded cell behind a strong door in the mental wing at a Christian Science Sanatorium. The poor man moaned and cried night and day and cut himself with pieces of the plastic utensils they gave him with his meals. The best of the healers had tried, but all thought the man was hopelessly possessed.

Jeannie interviewed him through the barred window in the thick door of his cell. "What is your name?" she asked.

"My name is Legion," he replied, "for we are many."

Ah! Psychotic and obsessed with the Bible, she thought. Well, there aren't any pigs around, I hope. "Why do you think you are locked into this place?" she asked.

"Because we know a secret that no one should know."

OK, Jeannie thought. He's not following the Bible story verbatim. "What is the secret?"

"You shall perish if we tell you."

"We? Who is there with you?"

"We are Legio X Fretensis, legion of the pigs!"

There it is, Jeannie thought. I figured pigs would be involved here somehow, just as in the Bible story. And he thinks he's a famous Roman legion. She decided to try to bluff the man. "I am a goddess of great power. No secret you can share with me could possibly harm me."

The man shrank away from the door and retreated to a corner of the cell. He was obviously thinking over what Jeannie had said. Jeannie could see fear and doubt cross his face, replaced ultimately with rage. The man leapt to his feet and charged full force at the door. Jeannie didn't flinch as the man rebounded and fell dazed to the floor.

Once he regained his feet, he grabbed the steel bars in the window and tried to pull them apart. "It seems to me you don't believe I am a goddess, and that I can hear your secret. Lie on your bed and calm yourself. When you are calm, I will enter your cell and you can tell me your secret."

"I will tear you limb from limb!" the man said, baring his teeth.

"You shall do no such thing. You will do as I have said and calm yourself!"

The man was cowed by her forceful speech and laid down on his bed. Jeannie went to the front desk and asked the man there for the key to the cell.

"I can't give you that!" said the man. "He'll rip you apart!"

"Don't worry," Jeannie said. "Jesus will protect me." She held her hand out for the key and the man got a stunned look on his face but gave it to her.

Jeannie unlocked the door, leaving it open, and knelt beside the man's bed. She felt she needed to know more about him to make the empathic connection that would release her power.

"What is the name your parents gave you," she asked.

"Christian," replied the man.

"That is a beautiful name. Tell me, what was your favorite stuffed toy as a child?"

"A bear."

"Wonderful. Did you love the bear?"

"Very much."

"Did the bear love you?"

"Yes, he did."

"I love you, too. Tell me your secret."

Christian looked puzzled. His eyes darted back and forth as he tried to remember. "I have forgotten my secret."

Suddenly, he sat up in the bed and lunged at Jeannie, grabbing her by the neck. He forced her to the floor and placed a knee on her chest, making it hard for her to breathe. He began to slap her face with both hands. Jeannie bridged her body, rocking the man forward toward her shoulders. As he threw his body backward to try to regain equilibrium, she wrapped her legs around his head and slammed him to the floor.

Christian quit moving. Jeannie scrambled up and checked his pulse. He was dead with a broken neck.

By this time the front desk man and an armed guard had rushed into the room. The guard dropped to check Christian's pulse and looked up at Jeannie. "What happened? You killed him!"

"No," said Jeannie. "He lives."

Christian's eyes popped open and he sat up, bewildered and scowling.

"Now, heal!" Jeannie commanded.

A transformation came over the man's face. He looked at his bloody hands like he had never seen them before and then looked at Jeannie's face, which was cut and bleeding from the blows. A look of sorrow came over his face, and he asked, "Did I do that to you?"

Jeannie said, "Don't worry about that. You are now healed in body and mind. Go now, Christian, into the world, and do good deeds."

Christian looked astonished. "What, how . . . what did you do to me?"

"I healed you," Jeannie said, and then hastily added, "By God's grace."

The guard aimed his gun at Christian as he turned to leave the cell. Jeannie sprang to her feet. "Hold on! There's no need for that. Christian is healed and may now leave and go back to the world."

"I'm sorry," the front desk man said. "We can't allow that."

"Yes, you can," Jeannie said. "Please let him pass." Astonished, the men fell back alongside the door and let Christian walk out of the cell.

This incident received mixed reception among the church members, who were evenly divided between those who thought Jeannie was reckless and those who thought she was a witch. The criticism became so heated, Jeannie left her healing practice, figuring that she had learned enough and didn't need these small minds trying to drag her down.

Without her healing studies to occupy her spare time, Jeannie turned all her attention back to the AMEBA project. She asked herself, with what I've learned about my power, and about empathy, how can I imbue technology with morality and empathy and help heal the world? Just as important, can I handle this power properly? Am I gonna end up a superhero or a villain? It's obvious that empathy is the key to using my power without needing to get into an agitated emotional state. And that really makes sense. After all, empathy was the foundation of the teachings of Buddha and Jesus. Religion properly designed is total applied empathy. And yet I work for an apparatus that has neither morality nor empathy. Jeannie felt she had to use her current opportunity to change that.

At home, she discussed with Juston the dichotomy between her work with the DoD and her newfound understanding of her power.

"Ah!" he said. "Oh, goodie! I get to help. Let me find my *Liber Null*."

"If that's a body part, I'm not interested in helping you," Jeannie said.

"No, no, no. It's Peter Carroll's book. You remember I told you about him. Now, where is it?" Juston ran into his office and Jeannie could hear him mumbling to himself. He returned with a book with a mostly black cover featuring a drawing of a blue three-eyed figure.

"Now let me find it. Ah, here it is, page 17."

All attempts to reorganize the mind involve a duality between conditions as they are and the preferred condition. Thus, it is impossible to cultivate any virtue like spontaneity, joy, pious pride, grace, or omnipotence without involving oneself in more conventionality, sorrow, guilt, sin, and impotence in the process. Religions are founded on the fallacy that one can or ought to have one without the other. High magic recognizes the dualistic condition but does not care whether life is bittersweet or sweet and sour; rather it seeks to achieve any arbitrary perceptual perspective at will.

Consider laughter: it is the highest emotion, for it can contain any of the others from ecstasy to grief. It has no opposite. Crying is merely an underdeveloped form of it which cleanses the eyes and summons assistance to infants. Laughter is the only tenable attitude in a universe which is a joke played upon itself. The trick is to see that joke played out even in the neutral and ghastly events which surround one. It is not for us to question the universe's apparent lack of taste. Seek the emotion of laughter at what delights and amuses, seek it in whatever is neutral or meaningless, seek it even in what is horrific and revolting. Though it may be forced at first, one can learn to smile inwardly at all things.

Jeannie was perplexed. "What am I to take away from this? Laugh more?"

Juston smiled. "No, what you really should understand from this is that often we try to understand the world through dualities. For example, you may say that the mission of DoD—which I argue is to keep Americans from being killed by our enemies—is incompatible and antithetical to empathy. I think that's wrong. I think you can use empathy to achieve that goal you told me about: healing the world. You can do it by seeking empathy even in the horrific things that keep us safe. Chaos Magick encourages adepts to develop a better way of seeing. You need to see a pattern in the Universe that enables you to cast spells, or whatever you call your healing impulses."

Jeannie sat quietly for several minutes, absorbing what Juston had said. Finally, she said, "Thanks, Juston. You've given me something to think about. How to fit my desires, and my power, into a framework to use empathy to reach my objective and my destiny. Empathy is obviously the key. So far, to use the power in other than a fraught emotional state, I've had to use empathy to enter and channel the experience of my target. But I have so far failed to affect more than one person at a time, unless you call Legion more than one person." Jeannie smiled wryly. "I can't possibly heal 7 billion people one at a time. I have to unlock a method of broadcasting my healing power."

Mastery

In the weeks following, Jeannie spent a great deal of time pondering the problem of broadcasting her power. It's not like it's a radio message, she thought. I can't, for example, just take over the AMEBA array to broadcast healing worldwide. I need something with greater reach.

One day, Jeannie asked George, a co-worker, about some classified technology that she thought could help the project.

"Oh," George said. "You'll need a top-secret clearance for that. It's in the NSA databases."

"Can I get the clearance?" Jeannie asked.

George shrugged. "I don't see why not. I'll see if I can get you set up."

A few weeks later, Jeannie had access to the NSA system. While searching for relevant technologies, despite her security clearance, she was still denied access to several password-protected areas. But what she was able to access opened her eyes to the power of the NSA. The agency had nearly limitless data on virtually anyone of any consequence in the developed world, plus extensive unmined raw conversation holdings.

Jeannie thought, I wonder if my magic extends to computer systems. One night, while working late in a deserted room, Jeannie decided to try. "Show me," she said when she encountered an Access Denied message.

To her great surprise, the machine showed her the material. Oh, my God! Jeannie thought. Can I really see everything? She started exploring all the areas she had previously been blocked from, and sure enough, she appeared to have full run of this section of the NSA's databases. She found terrorist tracking information and started absorbing information about the people behind the threats. Utilizing her gift for rapidly assimilating information, she set the machine to scroll terrorist information across her screen, and she started to pick up patterns.

Jeannie began spending late nights at work poring through the terrorist data and returning to Juston's apartment long after he'd gone to bed. One morning, he confronted her.

"J-girl, you need to slow the fuck down. I don't know how many hours you're putting in, but you're going to burn yourself out long before the end of the project at this rate."

Jeannie, bleary-eyed and exhausted, agreed. "I know. I just think I'm onto something, and I have a hard time hanging it up at the end of the day. I'll be better."

She gazed fondly at Juston's worried face. This guy is really growing on me. Fuck, I probably should have moved out long ago. I don't really need a boyfriend when I'm getting so close with the NSA shit. On the other hand, he's just so damn sweet. I should throw him a bone. Perhaps we can sleep in the same bed.

"Say, J-man," she said. "Perhaps we can take our relationship to the next level."

Juston's heart leapt in his chest. He thought, is she talking getting engaged?

"Yeah, I think we can sleep in the same bed now."

Juston tried hard not to show his disappointment.

"What's the matter, sweetie?" Jeannie said. "Don't you want to?"

Juston rallied and smiled broadly at Jeannie. "No, I mean, yes. Yes, I'm up for it."

Jeannie gave him a "you did not just say that" look.

"No, no. I didn't mean that. I, uh, I think you just surprised me. I'm delighted to get my own bed back." Juston immediately regretted the statement. "That's not what I meant."

"That's OK, honey, I know what you meant."

The next day, back inside the NSA computer, Jeannie branched into another database, one containing social media accounts for terrorists. Jeannie's goal was to obtain absolute knowledge about evil and its purveyors, and there was plenty to learn from the new database. But after weeks of absorbing, she realized she was looking at the NSA data with the most pessimistic point of view possible. How can that yield anything other than a negative result? But what if I were to enter into the center of all that info and look at it empathetically, and optimistically, and with hope? She remembered that hope is the one thing left in Pandora's box after the demons flew out. Is hope on the inside or outside of the NSA's boxes?

When you really think about it, Jeannie thought, hope is the movement of empathy in time and space into the future. It's not an event or a data point; it's a process that happens through time and is realized over time in many ways, constantly drawing on the past to create the future. The NSA data does not reflect empathy, but rather suspicion, and a kind of awful pragmatism. She remembered what holocaust survivor Elie Wiesel said: You cannot pursue love and power simultaneously. That's the dichotomy Juston was talking about. You have to choose one: Become Hitler or Jesus. With potentially unfettered access to NSA knowledge, I can rule the world, like Hitler. But instead, I opt for Jesus, or at least to be a savior.

She thought, if you look at it with love, everything changes: darkness to light. When I'm in the NSA, I am the NSA, standing in the center of the world, having all knowledge in the present moment. Maybe I started from a point of prejudice, expecting, like all other users of this data, to find the worst. But if I transform my viewpoint with empathy, I can connect these data, which are neither good nor bad, into a force for good. Instead of looking for evil-doers, I can look for disciples, people who can view the world with empathy and love and transform this data into waves of empathic understanding. I need to get people to see the world with love. Of course, since many will only understand the miraculous, there'll need to be some spectacle, some magic, some fantastic healing to accomplish my goals. I raised a guy from the dead. Maybe some grand gesture like that would work?

The next day, Jeannie felt like she'd absorbed as much as she could from the terrorist databases. She had begun to see the patterns in the chaos of the turbulent data and in the spew of new information that came in by the gigabyte every second of the day, and to look at it with hope and empathy, so she could find opportunities to heal people.

She'd mapped out the interlocking terror networks and identified the connectors. She knew the ringleaders inside and out and formed complete mental pictures of their psyches. She created a plan for empathically reaching out to them and slowly tweaking them to abandon terrorism. But what about the other kinds of bad guys? Surely NSA had records on all kinds of people. Thus far, she had been focusing on a single set of servers at Fort Meade. There were firewalls and gateways between her and the rest of the threat data. Well, we'll just see about that, she thought, and immediately the gateways opened, and her consciousness flowed into a new realm.

As she examined the new data, she realized most of the people in the new databases weren't obvious threats. In fact, most had merely been observed at one or more protests against the government, or Wall Street, or whatever. Yet they all had gotten the full NSA treatment. She followed the links of a few of them out onto the web, mentally cataloging all their websites. One site in particular brought her up short: EmpathySymbol.com. Omigod! Jeannie thought. A site after my own heart! The owner had decided in college that empathy needed a symbol, just like peace. She worked out a design and had a jeweler make a pendant for her. Later in life, she created the site with the goal of spreading empathy across the world.

I love this lady! She's got a good heart! I have to help her. Jeannie downloaded the symbol and stored it on her phone. She then bought a hundred empathy symbol buttons and several dozen bumper stickers from the site. Need to spread a little empathy here in the US, for sure, she thought.

Time to do some hacking, J-girl. She switched back to the terrorist network and zeroed in on one terror leader, Mohammed Zaeim. Zaeim had been recruited after US jets accidentally bombed his brother's house, killing the brother, his wife, and two small children. Before this incident, Zaeim had been studying to be an architect. Driven by his outrage, he rose through the terrorist ranks due to his intellect and his understanding of the perfect places to plant bombs. During his rise, several of his friends were killed in drone strikes, further radicalizing him. Zaeim believed that Allah guides whom he wills and saw these terrible losses as confirmation of his desire to wield enough power to gain vengeance on the American infidels.

Jeannie knew that inside, Zaeim was a moral man who believed in justice, and the need for justice for his brother, family, and friends drove his hatred of the US. She speculated that he would respond to appeals to his empathy. Hoping to lead him away from violence, she built an AI chatbot to engage him in a discussion in a chat room he frequented. She uploaded the empathy symbol so that, at the right moment, the chatbot could present it to Zaeim and explain its meaning. She hid the chatbot in the NSA machine and logged off for the night.

The next morning, when Jeannie logged in, she checked the chat logs with Zaeim. To her surprise, the man had discovered that he was talking to a chatbot, and his cell had launched an attack on the chat site, disabling it. Oh, well, back to the drawing board, Jeannie thought. Perhaps there's no way to project empathy via a machine. Pity. Would be so much more efficient. I can't do everything myself. I need to find some way to automate the healing process.

That evening, after everyone had gone, Jeannie got back into the NSA machine, determined to find a way to bend its resources to her will or rule it out as an ally. One of the guys in the lab had been experimenting with Oculus Rift virtual reality goggles and had left them laying on top of the workstation next to hers. She thought, what the heck. It might be fun to experience the NSA in 3D. She pulled the heavy display over her head and plugged it into her machine.

At first, the experience was pretty much the same, except she could navigate by turning her head. She found a file on the MacAllan network named OculusSim.drv. Oh, I bet that's a driver for the Rift that Andrew put together. She loaded the file and the visuals changed dramatically. As she opened her mind to the stream, something felt different. It wasn't just the 3D effects and the way that Andrew had turned different kinds of information into colors and shapes. She seemed to absorb the flow of information in a more holistic way, not just recognizing connections and correlations, but envisioning and assimilating them without thinking. The flood washed over her, and around her, and through her. Before her eyes, the streams were organizing, taking on colors, spinning out objects that splashed like colored inkblots against waves that broke on unseen beaches, throwing off droplets that coalesced into lattices, spirals, cascades, and other patterns. A monolith, more a polychrome shadow with countless translucent layers shifting and recombining, loomed over the scene, seemingly miles high.

Holy fuck! Did somebody dose my tea? This is like being on a trip! Or, actually, she thought, quite similar in feel to the *Magic* battle. And what the fuck is this monolith? Some sick *2001* homage? Jeannie navigated closer to the object and crossed its outer boundary. Omigod! This looks like all tweets, Facebook posts, LinkedIn profiles and the whole ball of social media wax! NSA's archived all this stuff!

As she watched, the information started to morph and organize itself into objects like the other data had done. Again, she was able to immediately grok insights without effort. She started to see how she might automate this data and marshal it against the terror networks. Her fingers flew across the keyboard creating notes, bits of code and capturing screenshots of the data objects. But typing was too slow. The insights were coming too quickly for her to register them. I'm gonna need a voice interface if I'm gonna be able to deal with this stuff, she thought. Might have to talk to Andrew about that.

Soon Jeannie's brain started to hurt, and she became nauseous. She tore off the goggles and threw up in her trash can. Oh, the cleaning crew's gonna love that, she thought. But, wow, that was powerful! And freaky! I think I ingested more information in the last—she checked her watch— fuck! The last two hours . . . than I have in the last two days. Andrew obviously did more than hack the Rift. He built a whole 3D data visualization application. I wonder is this a side hack or for a client? I definitely will need to talk with him tomorrow.

Jeannie packed up her things and dragged herself to her car. When she got home, Juston was still up. "Hey, hon! You're home early."

Jeannie gave him a wan smile. Juston noticed her lack of enthusiasm. "What's up, babe? You look like you've been run hard and put up wet." Despite being dog-tired, Jeannie was eager to tell Juston all about her adventure in the machine.

"Oh, Juston, I'm exhausted, but I'm wired to the max. You would not believe the breakthrough I had this evening."

Jeannie proceeded to tell Juston about the Oculus Rift and the 3D data and the way she was able to assimilate patterns and data faster than she ever thought possible. Her excitement was contagious, and soon Juston jumped up and started pacing, interrupting from time to time to ask questions.

Jeannie sat on the couch with both legs bouncing with nervous energy. She said, "J-man, this is major. More than major. This is epic. I'm still putting it all together, but I think I can create bots that can do some of the work, maybe just the preparatory stuff to soften up the targets. But I can almost see something, it's on the edge of my brain, and I can't quite grasp it, but I think there's a way I could use NSA to spread empathy throughout the world."

Juston stopped pacing and stared at Jeannie. "For real?"

"For realz," Jeannie said. "You know how sometimes you get a thought or a feeling that's just out of reach?" Juston nodded. "Well, that's how I feel now. I can feel the edges, sense the size of the insight, but it skitters away when I try to probe it."

Juston said, "Ah! I know the feeling well. In fact, there are practices in Chaos Magick that are used to try to surface those truths that are just on the edge of perception. Carroll, in *Liber Null*, talks about how adepts can use any system they prefer to try to reach those insights by forging the magic link. To do so, the magician tries to let the magic slip through below the level of conscious control. Carroll gives an example of Tarot divination. The magician shouldn't just shuffle and reveal cards but look through the pack first and then shuffle lightly. The idea is not to look for a random result, but one guided by some knowledge. That's the place you're at. You've got tons of random knowledge, and the insight evades you. Chaos Magick recommends reducing the quest to a symbol that will help crystallize the adept's perception and form a basis for intuitive guesswork to bring forth the insight."

"OK, so what should I do. Throw some dice? Deal some Tarot cards?"

"The point is, it doesn't matter. Pick something. But be aware that your greatest foe is your own psychic censor. Or you could call it inhibition. It's the thing that prevents us from remembering all our dreams, or on the other hand, from going batshit crazy from all the sensory impressions that bombard our bodies 24/7."

"If I know you, next you'll be telling me sex is the most powerful way to defeat the psychic sensor!"

"Um, well, no, and yes. Sex is a really powerful way to reduce inhibition and improve divination. But I'm a little hurt that you think all this is just a ploy for me to get you in the sack more often." Juston was bugged that there was this dynamic between them. It's not like she doesn't love sex, he thought.

"I was just teasing you," Jeannie said and reached over to him to touch his arm. "I get that sex is powerful in ways I had never considered."

The two fell silent for several minutes before Jeannie said, "Well, that's way too much information and stimulation for me today. I'm hitting the hay, and, yes, I'm too tired to roll in it." Jeannie gave Juston a goofy smile to let him know she was teasing him.

The next morning, Jeannie asked Andrew to lunch. The man was stunned. Being a tall, scrawny, nerdy engineer with a big nose, a scraggly beard, and an ugly topknot, he rarely got lunch invitations from anyone, let alone a pretty woman. "Uh, sure," he managed to say.

Seeing his unease, Jeannie leaned close and whispered, "I want to pick your brain about your Oculus project."

Andrew reddened. "Oh, crap. Did I leave that thing out last night? Damn."

So, it is a side hack, Jeannie thought. That means we need to be very careful.

"Sorry, Andrew," she said in a very quiet voice. "I didn't know it was an, uh, extracurricular project."

Andrew nodded. His expression was blank. Jeannie hadn't really worked with Andrew, but now she saw that he was the prototypical engineering nerd: socially awkward, somewhere on the spectrum, and totally devoted to his work. She'd dealt with his type throughout her career and knew just how to handle him.

"Andrew, I'm looking forward to lunch. I've got some ideas for you and I'd like to hear what you think of them." Andrew brightened and nodded before abruptly turning back to his work.

At lunch, Jeannie started out by praising Andrew's work. She described the brilliance of his 3D visualization and how it was helping her with her work.

"It's got a long way to go before it satisfies me," Andrew said, but he seemed pleased.

Seeing her opening, Jeannie said, "Would you like to hear how it could help me with my work on the radio array?" Andrew had just taken a big bite of his huge hamburger, and so just nodded.

Jeannie described how keyboarding was slowing her down and she'd really like to see a voice interface. Andrew nodded enthusiastically. "Yes, that's one of the features I've been planning to add. I also want to work a bit more on the animation so that it better handles head gestures. Anyway, adding the voice piece shouldn't be that hard. One of my buddies has a great voice module that I should be able to adapt, perhaps as soon as the weekend." Andrew thought for a moment. "You're not going to tell anyone about this, are you? I mostly am working on it on my own time, but my contract has an intellectual property clause that could make things difficult."

Jeannie assured Andrew that she'd keep quiet and she'd be delighted if she could test the voice control on the weekend. They made plans to come in on Sunday and give it a try. From Tuesday through Saturday night, Jeannie spent her free time inside the NSA computer grinding through with keyboard and monitor and thinking of tweaks to the 3D modeling that would help her mission.

Jeannie got up early on Sunday morning. Juston stirred and mumbled, "Go back to sleep. You're not meeting Andrew until 10."

"I can't sleep anymore," Jeannie said. "I'm too keyed up. I'm getting up." Juston groaned and turned over.

Jeannie got ready to go and ate a few spoonfuls of cashew yogurt, but she was too keyed up to eat any more. She decided to walk to MacAllan and wait for Andrew there.

As she passed the guard in the lobby, the man said, "What's got you here so early on a Sunday?"

Jeannie was a little startled by the question and at first couldn't think of what to say in reply. "Oh, just this project. I'm trying to solve a tough problem, and it's got so I can barely sleep, so I thought I'd come in. Andrew is going to give me a hand, so you should see him in a bit."

"You should be out walking by the river or doing something fun on a Sunday like this. It's a great day outside." Jeannie just smiled, nodded, and scanned her badge.

Once at her cube, she logged in to the NSA machine. Jeez, she thought, without the Rift this week, I've made such slow progress. She sighed, and started in again, analyzing terrorist Twitter networks, which was excruciatingly difficult without Andrew's program. Finally, when she was about to give up, Andrew showed up, an hour early.

"Thank goodness you came early," she said. "After doing some work with your program, doing it the old way is painfully slow and boring."

Andrew gave a shy smile and said, "I think you're going to like the improvements I've made. I not only added the speech module, but I beefed up the 3D rendering and added the head gestures I mentioned. Let's see how you like it."

Jeannie suddenly realized she needed a work-related task to test the goggles on. It would look weird if Andrew watched her fly through the NSA terror network databases. Fuck. What dataset is large enough? Ah, the seawater wave propagation and the air-to-water interface testing database! Andrew plugged in his gear and Jeannie brought up the data. Andrew fitted the modified Oculus onto her head and flipped the switch in the new black box he had added to the assembly.

"I had to add some processing power to do the vid and the audio at the same time," he told Jeannie. "So be careful not to get up or move around too much. It's kind of all patched together at the moment."

"OK," Jeannie said. "So how can I navigate with my voice?"

Andrew described the various commands Jeannie could use to cruise up and down and around the data. "And can I take voice notes?" Jeannie said.

"Yup, just say, 'Open note' and give it a name. Then say, 'Note copy' before you speak your note. Say, 'Stop note' when you want to stop recording."

Jeannie nodded, then immediately regretted it. "Wow, I just bounced off the bottom of the data. That was a weird sensation!"

Andrew smiled and said, "Yeah, I forgot to tell you, the Rift is a lot faster with the new black box. Don't blow your mind."

Jeannie trolled through the data and made notes on some new insights she had on the propagation data. After about an hour, Jeannie said, "Andrew, this must be so boring for you. Why don't you go home while I play? I'll bring the Rift in tomorrow morning and let you know what I think." She pulled off the goggles and looked into Andrew's eyes. Shit, he's not digging that idea. I think I need to nudge him. "You don't mind, right?" she said.

Andrew hesitated for a moment, and then realized he didn't mind. "OK, Jeannie. I'll take off, but text me if you have any problems, OK? This stuff's put together with chewing gum and bailing wire right now."

Jeannie smirked. I may not even have had to give him the little magic nudge. Men are so easy to manipulate. Andrew turned and left Jeannie alone.

After waiting several minutes to make sure Andrew was really gone, Jeannie logged in to the NSA machine and plunged into the terrorist and social media data. She found that the voice navigation helped immensely, and so did the upgrade in the visualization that Andrew had added. That guy's a wizard, Jeannie thought. I'm starting to see how I can influence a relatively small number of nodes and cause whole terror networks to fall apart! This is fantastic! Now if I can only build an empathy bot.

It was near midnight when Jeannie returned to Juston's apartment with the Rift in a box under her arm. "Juston, this was magnificent!" she said, placing the box on the kitchen counter and rushing over to him. "Andrew not only added the voice nav, he jazzed up the visualization. I'm finally able to see whole sections of the terror networks and analyze their weaknesses."

She embraced Juston and twirled him around. "J-girl, that's fantastic!" Juston said laughing. "So, you're a little excited, eh?"

Jeannie said, "Ya think?" and went bouncing around the room. "I can use some network jiu-jitsu to cause the terror networks to collapse and then send jihadists messages reinforcing the peace. I've got a large list of terrorists I've gotten to understand, how they can be healed, touched, moved, what makes them feel. Look, I've got a bunch of messages all queued up." Jeannie grabbed her iPad and brought up the list.

- "You cannot guide those you would like to, but God guides those He wills. He has best knowledge of the guided." (Holy Quran/28: 56)

- "O You who believe! Enter absolutely into peace. Do not follow in the footsteps of satan. He is an outright enemy to you." (Holy Quran: 2, 208)

- "None of you will have faith till he wishes for his brother what he likes for himself." (Al-Bukhari)

- "We have appointed a law and a practice for every one of you. Had God willed, He would have made you a single community, but He wanted to test you regarding what has come to you. So compete with each other in doing good. Every one of you will return to God and He will inform you regarding the things about which you differed." (Surat al-Ma'ida, 48)

- "God does not forbid you from being good to those who have not fought you in the religion or driven you from your homes, or from being just towards them. God loves those who are just." (Surat al-Mumtahana, 8)

"I'll create an army of chatbots to feed them positive messages. Then I'll match each jihadist with an empathic person, like the folks the NSA tracks who demonstrate for peace and introduce them on social or messenger or email. They'll wonder at first how the contact was initiated, but my hope is they'll start talking. It's harder to hate someone if you know their name."

Juston had his doubts about how well this campaign would work, but he wasn't going to bring them up when Jeannie was so happy. "This is all marvelous news!" he said. "But you need to get some sleep, and so do I. I've got a client call early in the morning."

"You go ahead to bed," Jeannie said. "I'm much too wired to sleep. I'll be along later."

The next day, Jeannie got up early again and was gone even before Juston arose for his conference call. She was itching to get in to work, get her workday over, and start building her empathy palace inside the NSA machines. All day long she was impatient, wishing the day would end. Andrew wandered by a couple of times, but she pretended not to notice him.

Finally, everyone else left and she dug into the NSA data. After working late into the night, she awoke, having fallen asleep with the goggles on. The gasket around the mask had dug grooves into her face. Wow, she thought. I gotta get some sleep. I think maybe tomorrow I can wewease my secwet weapon. Jeannie giggled at the phrase, a favorite from a video she watched twice a day when she was young. She dragged herself home and joined the slumbering Juston in their bed.

Healing

Jeannie released the army of chatbots at the height of international tension following a gruesome live beheading of five journalists in Syria. The bots swarmed through the NSA machine out onto the myriad networks to which the computer was connected, especially the social networks. They were targeted at all manner of dark behavior, from organized terror networks to lone-wolf terrorists to garden-variety extremist trolls.

Once latching on to a target, the bot engaged the person in dialog that incrementally steered the conversation toward an examination of the subject's reason for living. Often a subject would break off the communication before the end of the process, so each chatbot could assume different identities and personalities to keep engaging with the subject.

When a chatbot identified a person the subject cared for, it leveraged that caring to elicit the feeling of empathy. The bot might suggest that they heard there was a threat toward the loved one. Arousing and then manipulating the empathy that subjects felt toward people they knew enabled the bots to create parallels between the loved one and the many strangers with shared attributes.

Having established a feeling of empathy for these former strangers, the chatbot gradually widened the circle, eventually introducing as a friend another chatbot that had been working a different circle and then encouraging the subject to feel empathy for the larger circle of people. As the merged circles grew larger, and newly connected subjects were introduced to their fellow subjects' circles, a community of fictional objects of empathy and actual terrorists or other bad actors grew organically.

The chatbots managed the connections between the subjects to limit the direct contact they had until they had built up a level of empathy for the formerly hated people. The bots controlled the distance between the subjects and, if one backslid, the bots isolated them from the circles until the subject developed the proper level of empathy.

At a certain point, the bots folded in real people with high empathic quotients from the hated groups. These empaths interacted with the fictional people and eventually with subjects via plausibly created connections. A subject might become convinced that a member of a hated group was related to them either via blood, or common concerns, or some other means. In this way, the subjects' empathy was gradually directed toward the hated group.

Once the bots were satisfied the subjects were ready, they introduced ideas for dismantling their terror networks or retargeted them toward effecting positive changes. Once critical mass was achieved, subjects found their compatriots were also having a change of heart, and the terror cells or networks started falling apart.

Of course, not all subjects were converted. The chatbots encouraged the converted subjects to identify, renounce, and ostracize resistant subjects. In extreme cases, the chatbots arranged for their arrest or demise at the hands of CIA operatives or drones.

This whole process unfolded over a three-month period, during which Jeannie slept very little and spent virtually every non-working hour managing the bots and their networks. Oddly, the more her bots spread empathy, the more energized she got, as if she was feeding on the empathic power the bots were cultivating.

After the first six months, the world started noticing a decrease in terror attacks, which the media wrote off in as a calm before a coming storm of more-deadly attacks. But soon governments and news organizations began to wonder if something else was going on. Scores of ISIL followers publicly abandoned the group and denounced violence, instead turning to rebuilding ravaged areas, schools, and hospitals.

At the same time, American drones were taking out resistant fighters with precision using intel Jeannie provided. Unconverted terrorist groups grew weaker over time. This relatively rapid change caused some at NSA to become suspicious of their suddenly increased ability to track and isolate terrorist targets and they started looking for answers in the NSA network. Jeannie had to monitor and manage this suspicion with a few well-placed suggestions and nudges that convinced the NSA operatives that it was their own brilliance that was carrying the day.

Men are so vain, Jeannie thought.

Integration

Jeannie realized she was reaching the edge of her ability to continuously digest the tremendous flows of information the chatbots were generating.

I need a better interface, she thought. Perhaps I can enlist other senses. There's only so far I can push my visual and auditory abilities. I need to engage my full sensorium. Despite the surge of power she fed on from the generation of empathy, she was exhausted. She tried to think of new ways to assimilate the information but drew a blank. She decided to ask Juston for help.

"J-man, I think I've hit a wall in being able to absorb information from my bots, from the torrent of daily intel that flows into the GSA network, and from the social networks. Vision and hearing can only take me so far. You got any ideas for me?"

Juston thought for a moment and then said, "Why don't you use your largest organ?"

"My liver? My intestines? Oh, you better not be referring to my boobs!"

"No, silly, your skin. I remember a project we did for DTIC that experimented with silent communication via a membrane inside a glove. It was to be used for covert ops. In fact, somebody mentioned to me the other day that ORAU is currently doing something in that area."

"A cookie company is working on leading-edge science?"

"No, no, no," Justin couldn't help laughing. "Not Oreo, ORAU: Oak Ridge Associated Universities. I think the project is sponsored by ARL." Seeing Jeannie's face, Juston quickly added, "Not a pirate outfit, the U.S. Army Research Laboratory. I think it's happening up at the Maryland office. In fact, I think your buddy Andrew came out of that lab. You should ask him."

"Wow," Jeannie said. "What are the odds? I think the Universe is trying to tell me something. I'll talk to Andrew tomorrow."

Jeannie peered into Juston's face and felt . . . encouragement? No, dammit, I feel love, she thought. I've fallen for this guy. And I couldn't ask for a more supportive boyfriend. She pulled him close to her, enfolding him in her arms, and kissed him deeply.

"I love you, J-man," she said.

"It's about time," Juston said with a laugh. "But seriously, I think I'm going to cry." Tears started flowing from Juston's eyes. "You've made me so very happy."

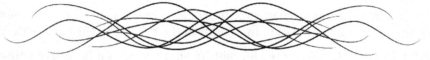

An drew could not have been more excited to tell Jeannie all about the latest in tactile communications. "I left ORAU because they were so hung up on the auditory aspects of tactile comms and focused single-mindedly on bone induction. I argued that much like a blind and deaf person can understand sign language by feeling the movement of the fingers—like Helen Keller—humans can understand language via a skin interface."

"Wowie zowie! What do you think the bandwidth of such an interface could be?"

"Well as it happens, I've been experimenting on just that question in my spare time."

"You have spare time? You're here more than I am. When do you sleep?"

Andrew looked at her blankly. "Since I was young, I've only needed two hours of sleep a day. I'm just wired that way." Andrew's tone indicated he couldn't understand why everyone wasn't similarly wired. "Anyway, first I had to invent a whole symbol set. You really wouldn't want a glove, or other skin appliance . . ."

"I love that term!" Jeannie broke in. "I've dated some guys who may well have been skin appliances."

Andrew shot her an annoyed look. "So, the symbol set is similar to stenography symbols—shorthand. I built a glove with an electrically activated member, er, membrane based on what we were doing at ORAU. It used what are known as electroactive polymers, or EAPs."

"These acronyms are getting better and better," Jeannie said.

Andrew plowed on. "The trick is to get the membrane to form the symbol and return to the neutral state very quickly. That's one way you bump up the bandwidth. By the way, some labs are also looking into creating artificial muscles with EAPs. Some of their research is helpful, especially the teams that are trying to recreate fast-twitch muscles. People have been fooling with this sort of thing since Röntgen in the late 1800s."

"Is that the X-ray guy?"

"Yes. Won the first Nobel Prize in Physics in 1901. Anyway," Andrew was obviously becoming irritated at Jeannie's questions, so she decided to shut up and listen. "I got the EAP membrane in a glove to transmit understandable symbols at an effective rate of 2 megabytes per second. Effective rate is calculated by considering the efficiency of stenographic symbol transmission—in which one symbol could equal one word—compared to English sentences."

"Holy shit!" Jeannie couldn't help but exclaim. "And this is over the area of the human palm? Like, what, nine square inches?"

"Yes. Roughly."

"Do you think you could make a whole suit, to fit me, and enable me to absorb information over my entire skin?"

Andrew was taken aback by the question and absent-mindedly stared at Jeannie's breasts while thinking of how to respond. Jeannie noticed this, and thought, for the millionth time, men are such fools. Andrew remained in this position, his unfocused eyes firmly fastened on her boobs, for a good five minutes. Jeannie was afraid to move and break the spell, so she stood stock still as if she were a painter's model. Finally, Andrew turned his eyes to her face and said, simply, "Yes."

Jeannie pumped her right fist and yelled, "Yes! I can be totally immersed in the data! How soon can you do it?"

"Well, first off, there's the question of the cost. The demand from artificial muscle research has lowered the cost of EAP material somewhat, but the stuff can cost $100 per square inch and you'd need..." Andrew ran his eyes up and down Jeannie's body. "Turn around," he said curtly. She complied, feeling uncomfortable as Andrew scanned her from top to bootie to bottom.

"I'd say your body is around 3,000 square inches, leaving out selected mucus membranes." Andrew actually blushed. "So, a full suit, including wastage due to tailoring, would probably be $350,000."

Jeannie felt her dream deflating. How am I going to get $350K? she thought. Oh, wait! Magic!

"I think I can get that," she told Andrew.

Andrew blinked in surprise. "Really?"

"Yes," Jeannie said. "I'm a trust fund baby. Daddy left me millions. But I expect we'll need more than the EAP membrane, right? A suit like that will need cooling, a power source, and probably, ah, biological waste disposal agencies of some sort."

Andrew blushed again. "You're right," he said. "That would probably add another $100,000."

"Once again, no problem. I can arrange for offshore accounts to pay for it all. It wouldn't do to call attention to myself, or to you."

Andrew just nodded, still astonished at the weirdness of what Jeannie was proposing.

"Once we get the stuff, how soon can you build the suit?"

"By myself, probably six months. I've got several buddies who could help, though."

"OK, I can pay all of you. But they've got to be able to keep the secret, right?"

"No problem. This is a dream project, and a risky one. We'll keep mum until it's done. Then we can tell people, right?"

"Not right away," Jeannie said. "I need this suit for a top-secret project. But eventually, the world will know your brilliance."

For the first time since beginning the conversation, Andrew smiled. He's probably thinking Nobel Prize, Jeannie thought. Well, let him.

"So, Andrew, this project is so secret, you can't talk with anyone here at MacAllan or at DoD about it. I'm not exactly authorized to build this suit, right? I'm financing it myself, but I plan on donating it to DoD once my project is finished."

"You're not doing anything illegal, are you?"

Jeannie laughed. "It is so not illegal. Don't worry. OK, I'll rustle up the money, get the offshore accounts set up, and you and your buddies should start work on a design and a materials list, and we'll get going. I can even rent you a lab of your own if you like. Keep things simple at work here."

Andrew agreed that would be a good idea. Jeannie leaned over and gave Andrew a kiss on the cheek. "Andrew, you're amazing. I'm so lucky you are going to help me. You have no idea how much the success of this project will benefit our citizens and the world." Again, Andrew blushed as Jeannie turned and left the room.

That night, Jeannie connected to the GSA computer and compiled lists of bank accounts owned by drug dealers, slave traders, and other scum. She was amazed the GSA knew so much about these slime molds. She was further amazed at how many accounts there were, all over the world. OK, she thought. I need probably a half million bucks to start, so I could take $10 out of 50,000 accounts and nobody will be the wiser.

Using the power of the GSA computers and a bit of her own magic, within minutes she had the money she needed for the suit. She stashed it in a Swiss bank account and then routed it out in small parcels of less than $10,000, each to a variety of offshore tax havens in the Cayman Islands and elsewhere. An NSA list of such places was very helpful. She created several debit card accounts linked to these funds and made a list for Andrew to use when buying his supplies. She also rented several post office boxes in DC to receive shipments.

The next day when they met, Jeannie told Andrew to ensure that he broke up his purchases into many small orders distributed among several vendors and sent to the various P.O. boxes she set up. As a tripwire, she set up a bot to monitor the GSA robots that watched for suspicious movements of money and goods.

I should be able to see anything that might set off an alarm before the GSA bots see it, she thought. They generally are looking at a macro level, and if we keep the transactions small, we should be OK.

Within weeks, Andrew had rounded up 11 of his buddies to work in the fully tricked-out lab Jeannie had rented equidistant from where the techies lived. No sense setting up strange commuting patterns and raise suspicion, Jeannie thought. To further camouflage the effort, she created a dummy startup company called ItJustSuits.Me, and had a logo designed and painted on the door of the lab. She created a typical startup-in-stealth-mode website for the phony company with a "Coming Soon" message on the single page.

After completing the website, Jeannie and Juston went out on the town to celebrate their one-year dating anniversary.

Soon the lab was humming, and Andrew was giving Jeannie daily status reports. After a few weeks, Andrew arranged to meet Jeannie at the lab at night. When Jeannie arrived, Andrew looked worried. "What's up, Andrew? Problems?" she said.

"No, things are going fine."

"Well, you look like you got something on your mind, Andrew."

"Yes . . . well . . . It's a delicate matter . . ." Andrew looked away and started to blush.

"What's the matter, Andrew? Come out with it!"

Andrew stared at the floor. "It's time to do a full body mapping so we can start to think of how to put the fabric together." He stopped talking but looked like he wanted to say more.

Jeannie said, "OK, let's do it."

"Well . . . you see . . . you'll have to be naked, and I need to scan you very closely with a handheld and, um, ah, I'll need to scan every inch of your body."

Ah! Jeannie thought. He's embarrassed that he's got to see me naked, and up close. Well I can't say I'm too enthused about it, what with him taking pictures of my hoo-ha and all, but I can handle it. To Andrew, she said, "Great. Don't worry about it. Let's get started."

Andrew let out a relieved sigh. "Thanks," he said. "I've been dreading this moment for weeks."

"Why?"

"Because it's embarrassing! Won't you be embarrassed?"

"No, a little self-conscious, I guess, but, dude, it's for science."

"Well, there is the other matter . . ." Andrew looked away out a nearby window as his voice trailed off.

"Spit it out, Andrew."

"Well, you see, there's the, um, potential for, ah, physiological arousal on my part."

Ah! Jeannie thought. He's worried about getting a boner! "That's OK, Andrew, it would only be natural. I wouldn't be offended or threatened if that happens. Cheer up, guy! This is a great milestone in our project!"

Andrew exhaled in relief. "OK, he said. "You can disrobe over there behind the curtains we set up. I sent everybody else home. It will just be you and me."

Jeannie strode over to the circular green-curtained area, shucked off her clothes and said, "Where do you want me?"

"Just stay there. The curtains will act as a green screen and enable me to remove any extraneous scan data. I need to map your skin exactly, every, er, bump or scar or mole or whatever. The suit will need to fit tightly against your skin for maximum data transfer. Oh, hell, I forgot." Andrew got the embarrassed look again. "I'm going to need you to shave your, ah, your . . ."

"My bush? Is that what you're trying to say, Andrew? No problem. I'll give myself a Brazilian. You got some clippers and a razor and some foam?"

Andrew swallowed hard and went to get the items, passing them around the curtain while looking the other way. Jeannie quickly did the job and invited Andrew behind the curtain. Andrew started the scan with a handheld device, starting at Jeannie's neckline and working his way down to her boobs. "I'll, ah, have to touch them, to lift them," he said.

"OK, but no funny business," Jeannie teased but felt bad when she saw Andrew's face. "I'm just teasing you, Andrew. Lighten up!" Jeannie glanced at his crotch and saw a bulge. Poor guy, she thought. He was right to have been worried.

After 20 minutes, Andrew had done every other part of Jeannie's body except her vaginal area. Taking a deep breath, he said, "OK, I'm going to need you to spread your legs now."

"That's what he said," Jeannie quipped, and then regretted it. She glanced at Andrew's reddening face. "Sorry, Andrew. I guess I am a little nervous about this part."

Wait, she thought. Did I shower today? Shit. I'm so exhausted, I can't remember. What if my cooter isn't fresh? Damn. Should I excuse myself to the Ladies'? No, I think it's out in the hallway. She grabbed a lock of her hair and sniffed it. Smells like I washed my hair, but I dunno. Well, I just need to grin and bear it.

"OK, Andrew. Here you go." Jeannie spread her legs and turned her head as Andrew continued his scan.

When that part was over, they both felt more at ease. Andrew said, "OK, two more areas. Please turn around and spread your cheeks, then I'll have you sit on that stool and I'll do the soles of your feet."

At last, Andrew was finished. "All done," he announced with relief in his voice. "Don't get dressed just yet. Here, you can put on this lab coat. I need to take a quick look at the data and run a simulation to be sure I got everything. Jeannie accepted the coat and wandered over to one of the workstations to sit. Andrew took the scanning device over to a computer and plugged it in. Soon a 3D model of Jeannie from the neck down started building on the screen.

Jeannie watched as it slowly revolved, adding more and more details, building from top to bottom. This is like my worst nightmare: to see myself as others see me, she thought. Look at that flat butt!

After half an hour, the model was complete, and Andrew turned it this way and that, looking for holes in the data.

"Looks like we got it all," he said. "Thanks, Jeannie. I'll bet that wasn't too fun for you."

"No, it was a piece of cake, except for that one area, but you were a perfect gentleman and I appreciate that. Can I get dressed now?"

"Sure," said Andrew. "We're done for now. I just need to get a bunch of software set up to process the model. That'll take the rest of the night. It should run for the next day or so, and we'll be able to start the fitting simulations after that."

Jeannie got dressed and walked over to Andrew, who was engrossed in the computer program. "Thanks for all you're doing for me, Andrew," she said and pecked him on the cheek. "Try to get some sleep tonight. I'll see you at MacAllan in the morning." Andrew just nodded and waved with one hand.

Immersion

After two months, Jeannie's suit was ready for a fitting. Jeannie showed up on a Saturday and noticed that the lab was empty. Andrew said, "I sent everybody home because they need some R&R, and because you're going to need to get naked again."

"Yeah, I figured," Jeannie said. "Tell me what you need me to do."

"Well," Andrew said, and then paused. After a moment, he proceeded. "You're going to need to rub a special conductive oil all over your body.

Without the oil, you'd have a devil of a time getting the suit off. You can apply the oil everywhere except your back. I'll have to check you all over before we try on the suit."

Poor Andrew, Jeannie thought. The things he does for science: Staring at naked ladies and trying not to get hard. "OK," she said. "Give me the bottle and I'll lube up."

Jeannie went behind the screen, stripped, and applied the oil as best she could. When she was done, she called to Andrew, who came in and checked her all over. Satisfied that Jeannie was totally covered, he went and got the suit.

The suit was a grayish pink. It was in two pieces with a set of gloves and a set of booties. It covered Jeannie from neck to ankles and out to her wrists, except for a large area of her back. She found it a bit of a struggle to pull it on but eventually managed. She noticed a padded area between her legs and figured out what that was for but wondered about the lack of an accompanying structure for her butt.

"What's up with the back, Andrew?"

"Ah! Well, you may know that the human back has way fewer nerve receptors than other areas. For example, the back can discriminate two points touching it only when the distance is around 35 millimeters or more. So, it's not going to be as good a target for our skin pressure suit. We left the back out since it was going to be low-bandwidth, and we have to leave some skin uncovered or you'd suffocate, like in *Goldfinger*."

"Brilliant!" Jeannie said, and Andrew broke into a big smile, the first Jeannie had seen from him. "OK, how do I hook up? I don't see any sockets for cables or anything."

"Ah! We went with an inductive approach. The whole suit is, if you can pardon the pun, a neural network." Jeannie wondered why Andrew thought that was a pun, but he seemed quite amused. "We can strap on a transducer anywhere to input and extract the data. The transducer can be wired or wireless, and since you want the highest bandwidth, we first built a wired interface. Just plug an ethernet cable into this armband, strap the band on your bicep with the Velcro straps, and you're jacked in."

"Marvelous!" Jeannie said. "I noticed some kind of pad dealie for urine, but don't see anything for fecal matter removal."

Andrew looked uncomfortable and said, "That was too much for us to tackle in this timeframe. If you need to poop, you'll have to unplug and go use the bathroom. Sorry."

"Dude, don't be sorry. This is a magnificent achievement. I'll just go on a low ash diet and deal with potty time when I need to. You're a genius!"

Andrew brightened and grinned. "Well, it was a team effort."

"I'd love to meet them, but I think it's better for all concerned if I don't, in case this leaks out and we have to deal with scrutiny from the Feds."

"I agree. You want to take the suit for a test drive? I can plug you in right here." Andrew got Jeannie situated in a comfortable chair, strapped on her Oculus goggles and plugged her into the network. Jeannie immediately started writhing in her chair.

"Stop! Make it stop!" she cried. Andrew quickly unplugged the suit and Jeannie ripped the goggles off.

"Oh, my fucking god!" she exclaimed. "That was way too intense. It felt like I was being pummeled all over by tiny mallets! I think we need to take it slow, so I can get used to it." She glanced at Andrew's anguished face. "It's OK, Andrew," she said. "Just too much, too fast, know what I mean? I'll get used to it."

"You should have seen your body when I turned the suit on," Andrew's face was white. "I was afraid you were having a seizure. Man, that freaked me out!"

"Yeah, me, too. Can you activate just a part of the suit at first?"

"Hold on. The control program's modular, thank goodness. Let me comment out most of the modules and recompile. It'll take a few minutes."

"OK, good. I hope not too long because, without the cooling mesh on, it's getting pretty hot in here."

Andrew clicked away at his computer for 15 minutes and then said, "Done. I just left the hands active. Let's see how that goes."

With some trepidation, Andrew put the goggles back on Jeannie's face and turned the suit on.

"Ah, much better," Jeannie said. "It's like getting a hand massage. I tell you what, it's going to take a while for my brain to learn to understand these feelings. Let's leave just the hands on until I get the hang of it."

"Good idea. We had planned on a learning period. I can slow down the feed and send the audio of the data to the Rift." Andrew made a few adjustments, and for training, Jeannie dialed in an overview of her public chatbots.

It took dozens of sessions with the suit until Jeannie could experience all the data the suit could feed. She now had insight that was many magnitudes greater than when she only had the Oculus. Andrew had built a feedback mechanism into her gloves so she could type on a virtual keyboard. She found her typing speed was now about twice as fast as with a real keyboard. Andrew bought her two zero-gravity chairs, one for the lab and one at MacAllan, to make long sessions more comfortable. Soon Jeannie was spending so much time in the suit that when she took it off, she experienced a nauseating period of readjusting to the real world, sometimes lasting an hour.

Juston, in addition to missing her company, began to worry about the amount of time Jeannie spent in the suit, often sleeping in it at MacAllan, waking up at dawn to shuck the suit and work a full day, and not coming home for days. When the suit periodically needed cleaning, which took two days, Jeannie exhibited signs of withdrawal, as if from a powerful drug.

"Jeannie, honey, you've got to take a break," Juston said. That suit is ruining your health. You look like death eating a cookie."

Jeannie began laughing so hard, she had to sit down. "I never heard that expression before!" she said when she recovered."

"Got it from a colleague from Oklahoma. It fits you right now."

Jeannie could see it was true. Even though she moved around during her normal workday at MacAllan, her body didn't seem to have the muscle tone and vitality it once had. She had lost weight, and her skin took on a grayish pallor similar to the suit's.

"I know, Juston. It is like an addiction. But I've gotten such better insight into the problems of the world and how to solve them. And you can see how things have improved, can't you? Terrorist attacks are now rare. Many former terrorist organizations are now actively involved in improving people's lives. Lone wolf gun crazies are being surrounded by their families and other people who care and are led back into the fold. It's interesting to see how the governments of the world are taking this. After centuries of paranoia and distrust, they're finding less to disagree about. I'm making a difference. It would be selfish of me to take a break."

"Selfish or not," Juston said firmly, "I've booked us on a flight this afternoon to Denver. We've got a campground reserved at the Peaceful Valley campground in Rocky Mountain National Park. It's the middle of nowhere, and we can even hike into the backcountry and camp if we want. Your bags are packed, and . . ." Juston produced a pair of fur handcuffs. ". . . you're coming with me if I have to drag you."

Jeannie was shocked and immediately started to protest. "But I've got my work at MacAllan. I can't just take off."

"Taken care of. I talked to your supervisor, and she agreed that you need some time off. Everybody there is worried about you. It's all taken care of. Let's go, the Lyft is waiting. And no electronic devices allowed. Give me your cell."

Jeannie opened her mouth to argue but decided to acquiesce. She had to admit she was totally exhausted. Juston was right. "OK, OK, OK. You got me, sheriff. I'll turn myself in. Here's my cell."

"Oh, and your smartwatch, too," Juston said. "We're gonna have a great time. Two weeks. I can't wait."

"Yeah, and maybe we'll find a use for the handcuffs," Jeannie said with a wry smile.

Assimilation

When Jeannie and Juston returned, Jeannie felt refreshed, but worried about how her chatbots had fared without her supervision. She searched the news websites for any clues to unusual behavior and found that the number of CIA drone strikes had quadrupled since she had left.

"Omigod, Juston! What have I done?"

"What do you mean?"

"My system has gotten out of balance. CIA is decimating terrorists who haven't had time to respond to the empathy treatment. I need to get in to work right away!"

Jeannie grabbed the rolling suitcase containing her suit and ran out the door. At MacAllan, she plugged in and frantically searched for the cause of the drone strikes. She spent an anxious half hour blasting through petabytes of data before she found it.

Shit, she thought. Looks like I have a leak! She found a bot of a strange design camped out on one of her terrorist identification routines.

Somebody at NSA has stumbled upon my operations. Fuck! She considered wiping out the bot but thought better of it. No sense arousing his suspicion. Let me take a look at this damn bot.

Jeannie spent two hours analyzing the interloper's bot. Hmm, not too bad. Guy's got some talent, but the structure of the bot has some flaws. I think I can substitute a terror list that dwindles down to nothing. I don't think this guy has any idea where the leads are coming from, so he probably will just think the source petered out. Jeannie created a list of terrorists whom she thought to be unsalvageable and altered the rogue bot to use that source.

Once this list is finished, it'll look just like a dead end and hopefully this guy won't figure out he's been had, she thought.

Jeannie took a big breath and disconnected from the NSA. I need to be more vigilant, she thought. That was way too close. This guy could be trouble if he decides to build more bots.

Weary and stressed, she called it a day and went home to Juston. "J-man," she said, "I just dodged a bullet!"

"Not literally, I hope," Juston said wryly.

"Naw, it actually was more like a huge figurative cannon ball that I dodged. Some asshole, hopefully a clueless asshole, stumbled onto my terrorist list and started turning it over to CIA. Whoever he is, I hope he falls for my smokescreen. I diverted his queries to a static list of the real bad actors that I have given up hope of reforming."

"Wow," Juston said. "That was a close one, huh?"

"Yup. The guy's got some skills, but it seems odd that he would just stumble upon my project. It was pretty well protected. I hope it was just a fluke." Jeannie laid down on the couch and told Juston about the new safeguards she put in place to protect her activities.

"But enough about that. I'm going to try again to find Cody," she said.

"Is that wise? It wiped you out when you did it before, and you need to go to work tomorrow."

"I've got enough time to recover. It's just early afternoon. I can sack out till tomorrow if I need to."

"Well, I guess I'd better go grocery shopping because last time, you devoured everything in sight."

"Fine," Jeannie said. "Get me a half dozen Beyond Meat burgers from Bolt Burger. You can take my car if you want."

"OK, commander. Your wish is my command!" Juston grabbed the car keys and left to get the food.

Jeannie settled in to find Cody. As before, she imagined her mind reaching out over the country, imagined Cody as she had seen him, remembering that she had gotten a small town midwestern vibe off the bar. She struggled for a half an hour, getting more and more desperate when she couldn't feel even a shred of her brother.

Dammit, she thought. It was a lot easier when I tried this before. Why can't I find him now? She was interrupted by Juston's return with the food. He tiptoed into the apartment and moved slowly over to the kitchen.

Jeannie gave up. "Cripes," she said. "I couldn't find him."

"Oh, damn. Did I mess you up when I came in just now?"

"No, it's not your fault. I just don't know what happened. It's not like it was a snap the first time, but this time—I just got nothing. Pure nothing. Oh, Juston, what if I've lost my clairvoyance power?"

Juston put the burgers in the oven, set the temperature to warm, and walked over to sit beside Jeannie on the couch. He put his arms around her and said, "Take it easy, hon. It was amazing you were able to find Cody at all. Perhaps it takes a lot more training or practicing to reliably locate a person."

With a frown, Jeannie said, "I need a burger. Now."

"Jawohl, mine commander. One burger coming right up." Juston said, trying to lighten Jeannie's mood.

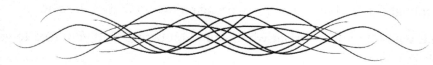

Over the next three months, Jeannie tried intermittently to contact her brother, even using the NSA machine to try to find his address with no luck. Meanwhile, she returned to her relentless probes for miscreants. With the terrorist community on the verge of collapse, she focused on drug kingpins. After several experiments in coaxing them to go straight, she determined, to no great surprise, that these criminals were not as susceptible to her empathic techniques as were the terrorists. Many of the drug organizations were multi-generational and their vicious techniques enforced a kind of natural selection that bred for psychopathic tendencies rather than empathy.

I need a different approach, she thought.

The more she analyzed the drug networks, the more she realized that most of them were propped up by a network of financiers who posed as legitimate businessmen. They also had significant backing from corrupt government officials who, although they were hardly model citizens, were less hardened than the drug bosses.

I could take a WikiLeaks approach and expose the corrupt financiers and their government collaborators, Jeannie thought. But that is too indirect, too fragile. It depends on the honest policing the corrupt. Wait a minute. I'm already stealing from many of these assholes, and money drives everything in their world. What if I drain all the illegal accounts? The network won't have any money to buy the drugs, and it would take ages to build up the cash again, especially if DEA receives a bunch of hot leads on existing shipments.

But what to do with the billions of dollars involved? Redistributing the wealth would draw too much attention, and I can't put that much money in banks. I can't just set it on fire, either. I can't give the money away because a Robin Hood move of this magnitude would bring down a ton of unwanted attention. I can see only one solution. I have to convince or coerce the financiers to become philanthropists. Yeah, no problem. Piece of cake.

Jeannie pulled off her goggles and got up to take off her suit. For a change, she went home early and had dinner with Juston.

At dinner she said, "J-man, I think I'm stuck. I can't figure out a way to smash the drug cartels that doesn't involve stealing billions—probably more than $300 billion—and then hiding it or doing something good with it. That would be such a hassle, not to mention dangerous."

"Why go for the money?" Juston asked.

"Well, my analysis of the drug cartels shows that cutting off the bosses and the smaller fry would do nothing. Plus, those people are pretty empathy-free and so my anti-terrorist empathy program would either not work or take forever. The financiers that control the big money are therefore the only viable target. And taking their money just creates more problems."

Juston thought about the problem as the two sat in silence. "OK, the problem is one of demand, anyway, isn't it? As long as there are tons of users..."

"Yeah, like 250 million worldwide," Jeannie cut in.

"Right. So, as long as there is demand, cutting off the head doesn't do you much good. You need to heal the users."

Jeannie was stunned. Why didn't I think of that? she thought. Well, because it's a project of such enormity, that's why.

"Juston, that's brilliant and totally logical. But I'm not sure I could pull off something that humongous."

"Well, I bet you could," Juston said, putting his arm around Jeannie's waist as they sat on the couch. "You've already done the impossible. Do more impossible things! I have faith in you."

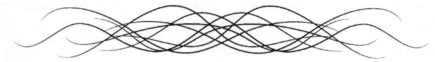

After work the next day, Jeannie began working on a plan to influence the desires and addictions of a quarter billion people. She tried to put the immensity of the task out of her mind as she concentrated on some of the blocking and tackling, adapting the chatbots and the chatbot networking software for a new purpose. I'm going to have to take a leave of absence from MacAllan if I ever hope to get this done, she thought. But I need access to the NSA. I guess I'll have to use some magic to transfer my access over to the lab.

A week later, Jeannie was settled in to the lab with upgraded Internet connectivity. She met her team for the first time.

Andrew introduced them each in turn. "Jeannie, this is my little brother, Peter the Wolf, big data wrangler, and the guy who did the Oculus voice interface way back when—when the Earth was cooling, and we were young and foolish." Everyone laughed.

"He's my right hand. That big guy there is Jim, we call him Jim the Jammer, for his mad code-wrangling skills. Standing beside the Jammer is his little brother, Jack the Ripper. He's not violent, at least if you agree with him." More laughter. "He's great at video chips, drivers, and format translation. Phil is our tactile communications guy, my go to guy when hacking your suit. It took some convincing for him to leave a big-buck job to join our ragtag band of misfits." Phil nodded and rubbed his thumb and forefinger together in the big money sign.

"K-Bart is our application architecture guy. He came to us from NISO. He's the one I worked with in improving the Oculus Rift data visualization software. He keeps the guys in line when they want to cut corners."

"We don't cut corners! We create beautiful hacks!" Jack yelled. The group nodded in support while K-Bart just rolled his eyes.

"Tom is our QA guy. His job is to challenge everything and keep us honest. He helps Bart keep order. Matt's our database guy and came to us from the IRS. The guys are constantly bugging him for tax cheats. He works closely with Peter on database interfaces. James is our most prolific developer, whom we call Code Blaster. Tad the Bad—for badass—is chief developer and James' cousin. His buddy Simon, the Cannon—don't ask why; you don't want to know—is our suit coder. And finally, this is Jude, a developer who works faithfully, night and day and even when he sleeps, at least that's what we suspect."

The whole group laughed, with many of them pointing at Jude and making faces. Jude good-naturedly gave them all the finger.

Andrew said, "Fun fact: Jude is into masquerade masks and balls." This last elicited loud snickers from the group.

"Pleased to meet all of you," Jeannie said. "Now I expect you've been wondering what this top-secret project is that you've all been working on. Well, I'd tell ya, but I'd have to kill ya." The crew all laughed.

"But seriously, I owe you an explanation. I'm sure Andrew told you that this suit is for a super-secret project that cannot speak its name. In truth, I've been working on my own time, without authorization, on an effort to save the world."

Jeannie let that hang in the air for a moment. The team exchanged looks and were obviously bemused by Jeannie's hyperbole.

"I'm serious. That's the goal. Save the world. Save it from terrorists, save it from drugs, slavers, and all manner of degenerate humans and behavior. You may think that I'm a dreamer but let me tell you what you've already helped me achieve."

Jeannie detailed the empathy chatbots vs. terrorists campaign and laid out her plans to heal hundreds of millions of drug users. Some of the crew looked like they were waiting for Jeannie to say, "Just kidding." Others, such as Tom, were obviously skeptical. But the majority looked like they were accepting what Jeannie was saying.

"You want proof? Let me ask you something. What happened to terrorism?" She paused a beat for emphasis. "What changed it from something you thought about almost daily—as one or another horrible act terrified the world—into a very rare event? Surely, you've wondered what changed." She looked around. The men all nodded. "Well, we changed it. You and I. We turned thousands of militant terrorists away from violence and toward helping their communities. And we did it through the power of empathy, and the power of technology."

Jeannie filled the crew in on the technical aspects of the chatbots, the empathy circles, and how she got CIA to deal with those few who couldn't be converted. She also told about the near exposure of the program while she was on vacation.

"Now you might think I'm crazy to try to tackle the drug problem, but you'd have said that if I had told you I was going to solve worldwide terror and set the stage for the establishment of a Palestinian state and recognition of Israel's right to exist by all Middle Eastern nations. Right?"

They all nodded. Tom asked, "Yeah, sure, things have gotten better, but where's the proof that you had anything to do with it?"

"I'll give you access to the logs my bots' interactions with terrorists. If that doesn't convince you, you'll have to wait until we solve the drug problem for your proof."

The others laughed at Tom. "Typical QA guy. Always doubting. Always wanting proof. Always a pain in the ass," Jude said. This really cracked the team up, and they all started laughing and jeering and gesturing at Tom.

Tom, who was used to the flak, just crossed his arms and said, "We'll see, you filthy bug-ridden code monkeys; we'll see. The proof is in the pudding."

"And the pudding's in your pants," quipped Sy. The team fell about screaming in laughter and taking turns slapping Sy five.

"Glad you guys are having fun," Jeannie said, with a mock stern look on her face. "But what I want to know is, are you with me? What we'll be doing is high risk; I have no right to be using NSA resources without authorization, and we could all go to jail."

The team stopped carousing and soberly considered what she had said. Finally, Andrew said, "Look, you guys don't need to decide now, if you don't want to. This is a big deal. Even I need to think about it."

Tad said, "Yeah, why don't we go to the conference room and discuss. We'll let you know if we come to a consensus, Jeannie." The group adjourned to the conference room and closed the door.

Jeannie's brain was flooded with doubt. *Jeez, I laid it all out there. Perhaps that wasn't wise. I gave them enough rope to hang me if they decide not to move on. Oh, merde!*

Jeannie laid back in her zero-gravity chair and tried to meditate. After half an hour, there was no word from the conference room. After 45 minutes, still nothing. Just shy of an hour, the door opened, and the crew filed out, arranging themselves in a semi-circle around Jeannie, who stood by her chair.

Andrew said, "We've come to a consensus." Jeannie tried to read his face, but as always, he didn't betray what he was thinking. *Now the bastard is pausing for dramatic effect,* she thought.

"What's your decision?" she asked as levelly as she could.

"We're all in," Andrew said simply. "Let's heal the world."

Jeannie realized she had been holding her breath and let it out with an audible whoosh. A big smile of relief spread across her face. "Thank you, everyone! I think you all need a hug."

"Uh, I don't like being touched," James said.

"OK, how about an optional group hug, you guys? I have to hug someone!"

Everybody but James came in for the hug, and Jeannie realized she was crying. Damn! I'm supposed to be the strong leader, and I'm crying like a baby, she thought.

After the hug, Jeannie said, "We're all going out for dinner, my treat. Where shall we go?" The team members suggested various restaurants and argued for five minutes before choosing a Greek restaurant several blocks away.

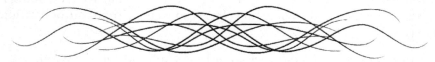

Freed from her responsibilities at MacAllan, Jeannie now spent 18 hours a day jacked in, but it soon became obvious that her body couldn't take it. The once tiny bruises caused by the suit had turned into an all-body bruise. From the neck down, she was a pale bluish-white from lack of sun and the pounding of the suit. And she was having trouble articulating thoughts as her brain ran ahead of her mouth. As a result of this frustration and her sleep deficit, she was becoming increasingly short-tempered. The crew grew alarmed and murmured among themselves that something must be done.

Finally, one day, Andrew confronted Jeannie as she emerged from her changing cubicle. "You need to dial it back, Jeannie," he said with a concerned look on his face. "This is ruining your physical and mental health."

Jeannie was brought up short by Andrew's statement, and the resolve in his voice. "What? Don't be ridiculous. I'm fine." As she said this, one of her knees gave out and she collapsed onto a nearby couch.

"See what I mean, Jeannie? You need some R&R, and you need regular periods outside the suit to walk, exercise, and take it easy. The human body isn't built for the kind of abuse you're putting yours through. You need to dial it way, way back."

Jeannie considered this advice for a minute before saying, "I think you're right, Andrew. Thank you. I guess I needed someone to go upside my head with a lead-filled snowshoe." Andrew looked blank.

"You ever hear of Frank Zappa, Andrew?" He shook his head. "Well, never mind. You're right. I need to live the life I left behind. At least some of the time. I was just going to grab a quick dinner and get back at it, but I think

I'll go home and see Juston instead. Thanks, buddy." Jeannie hugged Andrew, who immediately flushed scarlet.

At home with Juston, Jeannie said, "J-man, I've been working so hard, we never see each other. I'm so sorry."

Juston, who had felt a mixture of worry and loneliness at Jeannie's dedication to her project, sighed. "I appreciate that. Yes, I've been lonely, although I've got a pretty demanding job myself, especially since you took your leave. Your replacement is, naturally, not as good as you, and he's a rat bastard to boot. An arrogant self-important asshat, actually. But I'm very, very worried about you. You look like death eating a cracker."

Jeannie started to laugh and then dissolved into giggles. "Is that worse than death eating a cookie?" she asked.

"Much." Juston said.

"I think I needed a good laugh. Oh, Juston, I miss you." They embraced and ended up in the bedroom for the first time in months.

"Be gentle," Jeannie said, "My skin is extremely sensitive from the suit."

The next morning, Juston said, "Am I gonna have to hijack you off to the middle of nowhere again? You're going to kill yourself unless you cut back on the suit time."

"Yeah, I know it's not healthy. Just peeling off the damn thing has become agony. And it just happens that I'm kinda stumped at the moment. Touching everyone with a drug problem and healing them seems almost impossible most of the time, but, just like when I was stuck before, every once in a while, I get a glimpse of, ah, what? A shadow of an insight, I guess. Something fleeting just beyond my comprehension. Some pattern in the shapes of the data that coalesces for just milliseconds, just long enough for me to start to see it before it's gone."

Jeannie paused to eat a bit of oatmeal. "But I have to admit I've been pretty bitchy to the crew, especially when I can't express what I'm thinking because my brain is moving so fast. I guess I'm a wreck." Jeannie started to cry. Juston gathered her in his arms as gently as possible, but still she winced from the pain.

They decided to take a walk, strolling past the Nationals' ballpark along the boardwalk next to the Anacostia River. They ended up at Bardo Beer, a funky spot with gleaming outdoor mash vessels, where they drank so much, they had trouble walking back to the apartment.

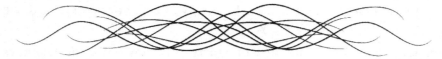

The next morning, Jeannie said, "J-man, I'm beginning to think that in order to accomplish my goal of healing the addicted, I'm going to have to live inside the machine."

Juston's eyebrows raised and his look communicated his astonishment. "What . . . the . . . fuck?"

"I know it's a lot to wrap your mind around, but I need to be faster, smarter, and embrace more data. I'm not sure I can do that given the limitations of my body. Just look at me. I'm a fuckin' mess."

"You're talking cray-cray, J-girl! How could you assimilate into the machine? How can you stay alive if you leave your body? This is insane! You can't leave me!"

"I know, I know. It is crazy. But the idea came to me last night when I woke from a dream. And I think using my magic, I could make it happen."

Juston started weeping. "Oh, Jeannie. Please don't do this. I can't live without you! Look, there must be another way. You need more power, right? Well, what if there are other ways? Like, you originally accessed your power through a card game, right? Chaos Magick supports the use of cards and other kinds of physical world representations of power to bring forth real power."

Overwhelmed, Juston cast his gaze around the living area, spying a box on one of the shelves. "Wait. Wait. I just remembered something from when I used to play *Knights & Warlocks*. There's a spell in that game called Heal All. It heals all creatures within its range. Plus—bonus—it also returns 2X health to the caster. What if that would work using your magical powers?"

Jeannie said, "I'd need to know more about this spell, and K&W itself, since I've never played, before I could assess your idea."

"K&W is quite simple, really. I can teach it to you in a couple of days. Please, Jeannie, let's at least try it. And you really should take a few days off from the suit. Don't make me get the handcuffs out again . . ."

"OK, OK, OK," Jeannie said with a smile. "I'll do it. It's not like I'm looking forward to not having a body, you know. My body is my favorite possession." They both laughed, breaking the tension.

"C'mon, Jeannie, it's our second anniversary. Let's go party."

"Great idea," Jeannie said. She enfolded Juston in a hug and rocked back and forth.

Over the next three days, Juston taught Jeannie *Knights & Warlocks* and showed her how the Heal All worked. Jeannie began to think it was worth a try.

"I really don't know how to draw power from a board game, if there's even any power to draw. It kinda just happened with *Magic*, as you know. Somehow, I glommed on to the power source behind the game."

"Don't think of it that way, J-girl. What if the power is also there in K&W, behind the game? Maybe it's always been there. I'll bet you can use the game to help you use the healing power."

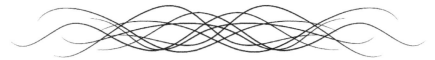

After a week off with Juston, Jeannie returned to her lab, got into her suit, and jacked back in to the NSA. After checking out her bots and evaluating their progress, she turned her attention to absorbing information about *Knights & Warlocks*. Her prodigious powers to locate, assimilate, and understand information quickly enabled her to achieve level 60 in *Knights & Warlocks Online*. She was beginning to feel the magical power behind the game.

But there's a shit ton of work to be done to make it work in real life, she thought. My body is beaten to a pulp. I can't keep on the way I have been. I need to go virtual.

Back at home, Jeannie said, "Juston, honey, I think this is it. I think I'm going to do it—leave my body behind."

"You can't! You can't leave me! Please." Juston was so distraught and his face was so rigid with tension he could barely shed a tear. Jeannie looked at Juston and saw what she was doing to him. He looked lifeless. His face was a mask, and he was shivering with emotion.

How can I do this to him, Jeannie thought. Even if I can heal the world, how can I leave him alone?

"Juston, I have thought this over and over and over. I know it will devastate you, but we can still talk when I'm in the machine."

"But I'll never be able to hold you again. Never take a walk with you. Never make love to you. Never feel your touch." Juston sat down on the couch and held his head in his hands. The tears finally came, and Jeannie quickly sat down beside him and held him. They stayed that way for 15 minutes, both crying their eyes out.

Eventually, Jeannie said, "Honey, it's for the greater good. I need to make this sacrifice to heal a quarter of a billion people. And my body has about had it, you can see that. Just look at me. I need to be able to assimilate the lives of millions of people and cure them with a healing spell. Think of all the good I can do. And I don't think I can do it unless I enter the machine."

Juston wiped his nose and sat back on the couch. "Is there no way you can come back from the machine? Can't you do your work and then come back to me?"

Jeannie smiled sadly at him. "I don't see how that would work. I doubt my body would continue to function for very long without me inside it. Hell, I'm not even sure I'd still be me inside the machine without my body. Who knows how much of what we are is wrapped up in the meat that sustains us? What if I go insane when deprived of normal sensory feelings?"

"All the more reason to not do this dangerous thing!"

Juston leaned forward again, cradling his head in his hands, looking like a man who had lost his last friend. He repeatedly pounded the couch cushion with his right arm.

"OK, look," Juston pleaded. "Why don't we freeze your body? Just in case you want or need to come back? Please, for me?"

Jeannie was taken aback by the suggestion. If I'm honest, she thought, I'd have to admit I'm terrified about leaving my body behind. I'm pretty sure I can survive in the machine, but not certain sure. Perhaps this could hedge my bets.

To Juston she said, "Well that's an interesting idea, but I see several problems with it. For one, it's illegal to cryogenically freeze a live person.

For another, it's hugely expensive, although I guess I could put together a trust that could support the cost for, what 80 years?"

Juston was furiously googling on his phone while Jeannie spoke. "Aha!" he said." 'legally dead' is not the same as 'totally dead.'"

"You sound like you got that idea from the *Princess Bride*, dude! What are you googling?"

"A serious site. You only need to be legally dead, which means your heart is stopped. But cell death happens much later, and total death, all dead as Miracle Max would say, is the point at which all brain function ceases."

"Well that's all well and good, but we're not going to have me enter the machine with a coroner sitting here in this illegal laboratory. We'd need to figure out a way to do it so that nobody knows." Jeannie looked at Juston and saw the hope and the resignation in his eyes—hope for a way to keep Jeannie around and resignation that she was committed to leaving her body behind.

"You know how we could do it?" he said. "You know those cryotherapy vat thingies that are all the rage now?" Jeannie nodded. "We could get one of those, mod it a bit, and freeze you in that, then transfer you to a discreet cold storage facility that you could own, with backup power and such."

Jeannie said, "And a thick Internet pipe, in case . . ." Juston flashed her a look. ". . . that is, when I want to return. There would need to be a ton of data transfer."

"Of course. And, and, and . . ." Juston was getting excited. "We'll need to infuse you with antifreeze. That's got to be done right after, er, you're mostly dead. We'll probably need a specialist or a doctor for that part." Juston continued to rapidly google and eventually said, "OK, looks like the preserving part is not for amateurs. Looks like we need to engage some pros to do it."

"OK, I'll just buy a cryogenics company then," Jeannie said matter-of-factly. Juston's eyes bugged out at the suggestion. "Sure," Jeannie said. "I've got access to all that drug network money. Piece of cake. Let's buy a small cryo firm that I can persuade magically to freeze me when I'm only mostly dead."

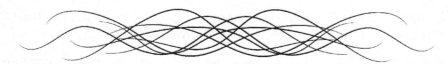

Two months later, Jeannie finalized the purchase of Cryo Flyin', a small human-freezing company out of San Francisco started by two refugees from a much larger cryo company. Jeannie and Juston decided that the less suit team knew about Jeannie's odd departure, the better, and so Jeannie had Andrew tell the staff to take a weekend off and not dare come to the lab. No exceptions. This was received with grumbles by the staffers.

That Friday night, Jeannie and Juston had the team over for a feast to celebrate recent technical breakthroughs on suit development. Jeannie used the occasion to tell the team how much she loved them, how proud she was of their achievements, and to express her gratitude at how close they were to solving drug addiction.

"I'm so excited right now. I feel like we're just inches away from letting loose the empathy bots and fixing this pervasive problem across the entire world." The group stood and applauded, and Jeannie reacted by pointing repeatedly at team members saying, "No, you! You! You did it!"

After the crew was gone, Jeannie and Juston made love twice. Although she had expected that they would both be very emotional, Jeannie was surprised at the strong feelings that washed over her. She'd been approaching this transition rationally and logically. But now she started to wonder if the whole idea was mad. She glanced at Juston, whose eyes glistened with tears, and began to cry herself.

"Oh, Juston, it's just now hitting me how much I'll miss being with you!"

Juston was speechless and broke down crying. Between sobs, he said, "You don't have to do it. Please. There must be another way."

"If there was, I would take it," Jeannie said. "If there was a way I could not make this sacrifice, believe me, I would take it. But I've thought and thought, and I can't see how I can do something this huge and not be inside the machine. Please understand, Juston. I'll still be able to message you. We could probably have Skype sex."

At that, Juston completely lost it, crying huge wracking sobs and burying his face in her lap.

"Juston, please understand. I'm not dying. I just won't have a body anymore. You can still love me, and I can still love you."

Juston sat up straight. "You don't know that!" he said forcefully. "You don't even know if suddenly losing the stimulus of your body won't drive you crazy!" Jeannie had to admit this was true.

"J-man, I have faith that I will always love you and always be there for you. Count on me."

The next morning, the couple got ready to go in silence. They drove to the lab without speaking, entered the building, and sat gloomily in the conference room until the Cryo Flyin' crew showed up. Jeannie showed them the suit and described how to get her out of it. She cast a compliance spell and planted a suggestion that would wipe out their memories of the afternoon and replace them with fake memories of a meet and greet with Jeannie as their new owner.

Jeannie walked over to Juston and said, "Well, this is it." Juston nodded, threw his arms around her, and kissed her. The kiss lasted for more than a minute and then Jeannie had to break it off. "Don't worry, baby. I'll be in touch from the other side," she said and then disappeared behind the curtains to put on her suit for the last time.

She laid down in her zero-gravity chair and pulled Juston close for one last kiss. He tried to say something, but his throat seized up and all he could do was whisper, "Goodbye."

Jeannie stroked the side of his face and then notified the Cryo crew to stand by. She jacked in and flew to the virtual point in the machine that she had established for the transfer. Her avatar appeared on the monitor and she could see the room via the computer's video camera.

"OK, I'm ready," she said. "I'm going to see if I can pull myself into the machine." With that, her body writhed on the chair, jerking almost completely upright before settling back. Jeannie's head lolled to the side and her tongue dangled from her mouth.

This was too much for Juston to take. He turned away and asked, "Are you all there, Jeannie?"

"Yes," her avatar replied. "Everything checks out as far as I can tell. I think you can begin the process." As the Cryo crew quickly went to work, their CEO turned to Juston.

"I don't think you'll want to watch this part, Juston. Why don't you wait in the conference room? We'll get everything taken care of in an hour or so."

Juston nodded and walked like a zombie to the conference room and shut the door. He sat at the table with his head in his hands. This is not happening, he thought. It is so not happening.

The conference room TV came to life and showed Jeannie's avatar. "J-man?"

Juston startled and snapped his head up. "How are you doing that? That TV was off."

"I'm finding I can do all sorts of things I didn't used to be able to. Setting my intellect free of the limitations of the flesh is already showing me so much more than I could ever see before. Anyplace with an Internet connection is pretty much accessible to me now. But that's not important. Juston, how are you doing?"

"How do you think? Not that goddamned well. Thanks for asking."

"J-man don't be like that. Look, I'm still here with you. We can talk. With a few peripherals, we can even make love. That's worth something, right?"

The idea of virtual sex made Juston's flesh crawl. "This is not the time to be talking about that, Jeannie. I already miss you like crazy, and it's only going to get worse."

"Should I just leave you alone for a while?"

"Maybe that would be best. How can I miss you if you won't go away?" Jeannie's avatar roared at Juston's gallows humor. "OK, sweetie. See you at home tonight."

The TV shut off, leaving Juston to ponder how he was going to keep living now that his lover was gone.

That evening, after he barely managed to eat most of a bagel for dinner, Juston decided to go into his home office and log in to his computer. Jeannie's avatar appeared on the screen, so creepily lifelike that it made Juston's skin crawl. "Hi, J-man," Jeannie said. "How are you holding up?

"I think I'm still in shock," he said. "And your avatar is more than I can take at the moment. It's too lifelike.

"OK," Jeannie said. "I can understand that. Of course, it's based on Andrew's scan of my body, but perhaps it's a little too detailed? How about a caricature?" Her image instantly changed into a cartoon. "Better, baby?"

Despite his depression, Juston laughed. "Well, I know a cartoon exaggerates one's appearance, but you don't exactly need any help in the boob department! They look like blimps."

Jeannie laughed and transformed the image appropriately. "OK," she said, "Maybe I can give myself an actual bootie instead." Her butt grew three sizes and she waggled it around.

"Look, Jeannie, I love you just the way you are, ah, were." With this, Juston started crying.

Jeannie frowned and then surprised herself when she realized she also was crying. Well, she thought, if I thought I was going to lose the ability to feel emotion with my virtualization, I guess this proves that wrong.

"Oh, honey. I wish I could give you a hug."

"Me, too," Juston said dejectedly. "Let's talk about something else. What's it like in there?"

"You've no idea how much more quickly I can think, work, and react in here. It's only been a few hours for you, but for me, it's seemed like a hundred years. For example, I'm pretty much ready to heal the addicted. I figured out the magic behind *Knights & Warlocks'* healing spell and it's good to go. I've identified every addicted person who's online—I'm not sure what I'm going to do about the homeless and destitute, whom I obviously can't reach from here. It's amazing, J-man. I have access to the entire online world's activity and history. I've seen every cute cat picture ever posted—and if I could throw up, I would. I've seen all the lonely people searching for love, or porn, or just some human contact. I know who all the crooks are, the murderers, too, and the corrupt politicians. They're next on the hit parade, by the way, the bastards. I'm now the omnipotent ghost in the machine. I know all; I see all."

"Wow," said Juston, grabbing a tissue and blowing his nose. "Well, I couldn't think of a nicer, more moral, or more conscientious person to be in charge of humanity."

"Oh, Juston, don't put it like that. The amount of knowledge and power I have gives me the willies. In that hundred years since last we talked, I spent almost half of it worried about my fitness for the tasks before me. As you know, with great power . . ."

"... comes great responsibility. Yeah, I know, Spider-Lady. Look, I'm here if you ever want a sanity check, if you ever think you're, um, losing your humanity. I'm certainly not perfect, but I can give you the human perspective, in case you need a reality check."

"Thanks, lover. You'll be happy to know I still feel all my love for you. It's amazing that my personality and my ability to feel don't seem to have changed."

"That makes me feel lots better. But tell me. Do you think that at some point you might be coming back to me, in the flesh?"

"I really can't say, Juston. There's so much to do. Perhaps there will come a day when I've done all I can virtually and will need to come back to my body, so I can help the disconnected."

"All I need is a little hope, J-girl. Please try to come back to me. Please." Juston felt himself starting to cry again, but he squeezed his eyes tightly and stuffed the feeling down. "I'll wait for you."

"J-man, I don't think that's a good idea. You should find somebody else. I can't stand to think of you becoming a monk for the rest of your ... ah, until I come back."

"Nothing compares to you, Jeannie. I can wait forever."

"If that's what you want, honey. I will be here for you always. I'm just a screen away. Whenever you want me, I'll be there."

Juston finally broke down in wracking sobs. "Oh, Jeannie," was all he could manage to say.

"OK, J-man, I can see that I'm upsetting you. Just be watching on Monday when I heal the addicted. Can we talk then?"

"Anything for you, Jeannie. I'll be there."

With that, Jeannie was gone.

I'm a crepe. I'm a weird dough / What the hell am I doing here?

Radiohead—Creep

CHARLES BEAUMONT DEFRIES

Charles Beaumont DeFries: We Need to Talk About Black People

HIGHLIGHTS

First off, I love black people.

But we need to talk.

It's about the behavior, not the people.

BY CHARLES BEAUMONT DEFRIES
cdefries@miamiworld.com

Before you go off, filling the comments section with trollish diatribe, please hear me out.

I don't hate black people. In fact, I love them. I'm a member of NAACP. The African-American race has been downtrodden, disrespected, and slaughtered for hundreds of years, with no end in sight. I stand with blacks on issues of equal rights, equal access, and frankly, becoming regularly accepted, ordinary Americans. Black people in America face terrible problems every day of their lives that those of us with White Privilege can never really imagine.

Nothing I'm about to say should be taken as an attack or as a repudiation of the previous paragraph.

But we've got to do something about a prevalent style of behavior that all of you, black, white or other, face, often on a regular basis, and especially if you live or drive in an urban area:

Jaywalking while black.

There. I said it. And you immediately know exactly what I'm talking about:

- A bus stops at a street corner and disgorges passengers. The light is still green, but a string of black folks walks in front of the bus and straight out into traffic, often without a glance, stopping oncoming cars dead.
- You are driving in the left lane on a one-way block that is mostly empty of traffic. A black pedestrian a hundred feet ahead of you strolls out from the right corner. You might expect him to stop and let you pass, but instead, he slowly angles across your path to lengthen his journey to the other curb, forcing you to slow and even stop.
- You are walking down a narrow corridor at a mall. There is a group of young black men in two bunches, one on either side of the corridor. Just as you are about to walk between them, one, seemingly oblivious to your existence, backs up from the group, right in your way, forcing you to squeeze around him.

I know why they do it. It's often the only way they can exercise power. So much in society is out of their control, out of their hands. But they can count on being able interfere with your car or your route using these tactics. That's real power! You can stop a vehicle of any size right in its tracks! Like Superman!

And it works, until it doesn't, and they get run over. In fact, black people are many times more likely to be involved in a car/pedestrian accident than white folks.

Some might want to compare Jay Power with the demonstrations by the Black Lives Matter movement to close interstates, but I'm not one of them. Organized demonstrations, however right or wrongheaded, comprise people who are fully aware of how and why they are seizing power and causing inconvenience or danger.

I'm not sure if Jay Power walking is a conscious thing for its practitioners or an expression of a cultural norm. But I wish it would stop. I wish it would stop before it attracts more attention from biased cops, like those in Ferguson, Missouri, where Michael Brown got killed, essentially for jaywalking while black, and where 95 percent of jaywalking tickets were given to black folks.

So, it is with an abundance of concern for the well-being of black people, and to a lesser extent, my own selfish desire to never accidentally run over a Jay Power walker, that I plead with the black community to do something about this dangerous practice. I realize it may not be your top priority but think of the other positive effects of a Jay Power solution: young people who don't feel the need to act out in this manner because they feel more empowered, and part of a supportive community. They even may be less likely to turn to other ways to obtain power, such as crime, drug use, and other antisocial acts.

Let's all help stamp out Jay Power walking!

Chip shows up at Charles's door after reading his latest edgy post in the *World*. "You just can't help yourself, can you?"

"What are you talking about?"

"The jaywalking article, what else? You just have to stir the pot, don't you?" Chip is agitated and brushes past Charles and plants himself on the couch.

"Look," says Charles as he heads to the fridge for a couple of beers, "there's being racist, and there's talking about race—being racial. I was discussing a dangerous practice predominantly, but not exclusively, undertaken by black people. You've got to admit, you've had similar thoughts."

Chip has to grudgingly acknowledge that he had. He says, "It's one thing to have racial thoughts—thoughts that many people would call racist and get all hot and bothered about. It's another to actually publish these thoughts in a major metropolitan newspaper."

"We're talking the *World*, Chip, not a major newspaper. It's not even in the top 25 nationally. But that's not the point. I don't know why we should be censoring what we talk about just because it has a racial component. Fucking 46 percent of pedestrian deaths are black people, about four people a day! But I'm a bad guy for talking about it, and pleading with black folks to not jaywalk?"

"Well, when you put it that way . . ."

"Yeah. I did put it that way. I know I'll get hate mail. I've got an intern now who reads it. Takes a load off my mind."

"OK, but does he or she screen out the death threats, bwana?"

"Um, I don't know," Charles says uncertainly. I need to find out of Jen is doing that, he thinks. "Anyway, not to change the subject, but let's change the subject. Did you read my Jeannie chapter?"

"Ah! The redoubtable Jeannie D'Arcy! Yes, I read it, and enjoyed the hell out of the booby sections."

"Yeah, figures, you dirty old man. So, what did you like about it?"

"First of all, Jeannie is a badass, and I love women badasses. Married one."

From the interactions he'd had with Trixie, Charles could believe it. She ruled their household with an iron fist.

"And she cleverly uses all her assets, especially her sexuality, to get what she wants. Love that, too. And I especially like the way Jeannie handles Juston with her sexuality. I also like what you did with the *Magic Universe* stuff. I play, as you know, and I've actually never really wondered about the backstories of the characters or how they would manifest in the real world."

"Well, there is some fan fiction, and official backstories from some cards."

"Yeah, but I've only ever concentrated on the strategy of the game, what cards can do in game action. So, it was interesting to see you personify all that. It also plays out like a real game, with the mana and casting, and especially the Pod Spawner. Good job."

"Thanks. What did you think about how Jeannie learns to master her powers?"

"Very good. My favorite part that I wish you had drawn out more was her battle with Legion. I think lots of folks will miss the pig mention, but I thought it was hilarious. You developed the mentorship story and the NSA angle slow, and I liked that."

"And Juston?"

"Juston I also liked. He was kind of a creepy putz at first, but love got the better of him. And the business of freezing Jeannie's body after she assimilated into the machine was brilliant."

"OK, I'm cautiously optimistic that you're not going to have grave criticisms of this one."

"Well, I could quibble about Jeannie's take on Eddy and Christian Science. It's not exactly spot on."

"Right. But I think there are few believers who don't reinterpret their religious dogma somehow, at least picking out the stuff they like and deemphasizing the stuff they don't. Jeannie saw her religion in an idealistic way until it killed her dad."

"I agree," Chip says, taking a sip of his beer. "People who read this might get a different idea about how off-the-hook crazy it is, that's all. OK, here's something else. You don't give much detail about the curriculum for becoming a healer."

"Yeah, there's not a whole lot I could find out about that. If you think it's important, I suppose I could try interviewing some healers. But I expect they wouldn't give up much info."

"How about healers who have left the church?"

"Good luck finding any. If you do, I'd love to talk to them." Charles takes a big drink of his beer and wipes his mouth on his sleeve. That was really frustrating, he thinks. Not a word about the training anywhere.

Chip says, "OK, moving on, the Chaos Magick stuff kinda fits, and kinda doesn't. The part where Juston is trying to teach the basics to Jeannie is a little boring. Do we need all the details?"

"Good point. Part of the reason I go into detail on these weirdo religions is to show just how out-there they are. But I thought I made most of that work, especially as it dovetailed with Jeannie's Christian Science and the *Magic Universe* stuff."

"Yeah, I have to admit, that was an interesting melding of traditions. And, of course, I'm digging on the key role that sex plays in Chaos Magick, and the way you wove that into the dynamic between Jeannie and Juston. You know, I have a saying: Orgasmic reality comes from beyond sexuality. It's a gift from God. He gives us the peaks of experience, and thus shows the way to happiness. Are you ever as happy as you are when you're fucking?"

"My memory's hazy, but I seem to remember loving sex with another person."

"Do I make you horny, baby?"

"No, Austin. You're not my type. Definitely. Without a doubt. Even if I was a woman. No way José. Gag me with a spoon!"

"OK, I get it, Moon Unit," Chip says, laughing. "That brings up a good question: What are the peak moments of your life? Where you either had an epiphany, a blinding flash of clarity, or of just totally being in a joyous moment you wished would never end?"

"Well, there was this one trip with Edie during a sweet spot in our relationship. I had recently fulfilled a lifelong dream of buying a VW Bus camper."

"No shit? Man, I jonesed for a camper myself back in the day. Was it really cool?"

"Not so much. I was working on my Master's thesis and wasn't teaching, so I had a part-time job vacuuming a Sears every morning. Well, half a Sears. Someone else did the other half. Anyway, somehow, I got qualified for a car loan, at 21 percent."

"Fuck! That's some shitty loan!"

"Yeah, it was a recession. Home loans were at 13 percent. Anyhoo, the camper was the farthest thing from cherry. It had been rolled, although the guy who sold it to me swore up and down it hadn't. It looked like it had tumbled off the side of a mountain. I envisioned it happening at this one place on Interstate 70 outside of Denver where the road is steep, with nothing but boulders descending thousands of feet on the other side of the guardrail. The underside of the van looked like had been dragged up on the end of a winch. So, the sink was gone, and the driver's side door could only be unlocked with a secret rite involving not trying the door to see if it was locked. Plus, the slider would fall off the track if you pushed it back too far."

"So, it was basically one step above junker?"

"Yeah, pretty much. The engine had recently been rebuilt and upgraded to a whole 2 liters, so I figured it was mechanically sound. Still wasn't much fun in the mountains, though. Anyway, Edie and I decided to do a weekend up around Mt. Evans, and we hiked up a ways above our campsite, maybe to around 11,000 feet, until we had this terrific view of Echo Lake on one side and the Front Range, and the plains that stretched to the horizon, on the other. Totally magnificent. On the way up, we'd taken some nude photos of each other—I posed for one with my hand shielding my eyes, looking West like a pioneer gazing toward the frontier, with my boner pointing the way."

Chip guffaws loudly and says, "Magnetic Dick, that's what I should call you."

Charles rolls his eyes and continues. "By then we were feeling pretty randy, so we decided to take off our shirts to make a bit of padding and go at it on this bed of moss on top of this peak. I was facing the view across this canyon, with my head up when I came, and it was the most glorious feeling ever! Buns up kneeling, bone in the hole, and ecstatic. Amazing! Afterward, I said to Edie that it was like making love to the whole natural world."

"Sounds amazing! You prevert!" Chip says. "Let's see. I don't think I have any orgasmic peak moments, except maybe the first time I whacked off in the shower. I was pretty naïve about sex and was probably 11 or 12. I knew about boners because I had found a Playboy under a ton of shit on my dad's closet shelf and had shared it with my buddies. We knew looking at the naked boobs made our dicks hard, but we were not sure about the rest of it other than that fucking was fun. This story could never happen today, though, right?"

"Right," Charles agrees. "Tons of info on the Internet including come videos."

"So, I kept stealing the mag in the afternoon and putting it back before my dad came home, but that was getting to be a hassle. Oh, I just remembered. I first saw the magazine when my mom and my sibs picked my dad up from playing golf. My dad put his clubs in the back of the station wagon and then stuck the mag under my seat. He told me, 'Whatever you do, don't look under the seat.' What the fuck! Of course, after he started driving us home, my curiosity got the better of me, and I fished under my seat and got the magazine. I was fascinated. So, I'm thumbing through it, looking at the pretty ladies and my mom glances back from the passenger seat. She goes ballistic, and my dad starts screaming at me that he told me not to look at the magazine. They proceeded to have this huge argument. Seems she took a dim view of porn."

Charles laughs and nods. "Yup. My mom, too. I can just imagine what she thought when she saw you propped up with a Playboy in the back seat."

Chip snickers. "Well, I was still too young to be propping much of anything up, if you get my drift. Anyway, I figured if I took the mag for good, my dad would think my mom tossed it out and wouldn't bring it up. So, I pinched it and hid it under a huge pile of leaves in the back of a friend's house. I let only a small circle of friends know where it was. It really enhanced my prestige with my buddies to have porn on demand. One day when we went to get it, it wasn't there. We tossed the whole area. Gone. I grilled my buddies and one admitted he showed the magazine to someone outside the circle of trust. That was my first experience with betrayal, come to think of it. So now, I was totally paranoid that my dad was going to find out I stole the magazine and ask for it back. That bugged me for weeks. But my dad never said a word about the missing mag. I dunno if he thought mom had thrown it out or if he figured me for the theft."

"So, the shower?"

"Right. Around this same time, I started fooling with my dick in the shower and knew that I could make it grow really big and hard." Chip strokes the long neck of his beer demonstratively.

Charles snorts and says, "No bragging, microdick!"

"It was huge to me! Anyway, I told a close buddy about this, very naively: 'Did you know if you stroke your dick in the shower it gets huge?' My buddy, more worldly than I, flipped out and told me not to ever tell him or anyone else this story. So, first experience with body shaming, another milestone! Eventually, one day, I just kept stroking the thing and it exploded!"

Charles and Chip erupt into peals of laughter. "I thought maybe I'd broken it, but from then on, every day, in the shower, me and Madame Hand!"

After they stop laughing, Charles says, "Well, back to the subject. Any peak moments not involving orgasms?"

Chip says, "I went. You go next."

"OK. The birth of my son was definitely a peak moment. He was born face up—called for some reason posterior. The intern had known it hours before, but it was news to the doctor. They had to use this suction cup thing to suck onto his head and pull him out, so he had a little conehead when he came out. I used to tell him he was born looking for the stars. But he was so calm. Just looking about. He didn't cry until they put iodine in his eyes. We had picked a girl and a boy name because we didn't want to know the sex beforehand. To know his name at once, that was the peak of the peak moment. And I was overwhelmed to at last be a dad."

Chip gives Charles a high five. "Yeah, I agree. There's nothing that compares to the birth of your kids for peak moments, that's for sure. So, let me see. What would I pick for another peak moment? Probably when I was ordained. You see, I kind of had it rough during my time at divinity school."

Charles asked, "How come? Too much of a renegade?"

"Definitely. But the United Methodist church allows a fair amount of leeway in belief, and in challenging belief. Just not around infant baptism. You know me. I'm a scholar at heart, and of course, I had dug very deeply into the Wesleyan belief that the Bible preferred infant baptism and that it was superior to adult baptism. This is, of course, false on the face of it, since John the Baptist mostly baptized adults, including Jesus. There's no scripture to stand on either way. There is no definitive evidence in either the New Testament or early church literature that says that infant baptism was or wasn't practiced by the first generations of Christians. And think about it. Who were the first Christians? Adults. Who were the first conversions? Adults, and possibly their families and households as well, but certainly not exclusively, or even mostly, infants.

"So, my big mouth got me in trouble deep on this subject, to the point that my teachers were laying odds that I'd never be ordained."

Charles looks puzzled. "I'm confused. What's the big deal that's worth fighting about here?

"Well, you rank heathen, obviously this is about John Wesley."

"Of course! How could I have been so stupid?" Charles smacks his forehead in mock disgust.

"Easily, butt wheeze. Easily. But seriously, Wesley called baptism an 'ordinary channel' and 'prevenient grace'—divine grace that precedes human decision—by which God gets to us. Wesley said it was God's claim of us before we ever able to choose God. So, the best way to receive God's grace is to be a baby with no ego to desire God's love for selfish reasons. And to me, this seemed a lot like the Church was declaring adults who are baptized second-class citizens. And that did not seem like God to me."

"OK," Charles says. "I guess I kind of get it. Seems like a silly thing to go all dogmatic on your ass about, though."

"Believe you me, it was no small thing. I really almost didn't get ordained. So, when I did, it seemed miraculous. Thus, a truly peak moment of my life. And, of course, I've been a troublemaker ever since."

"No shit, Sherlock!" Charles smiles. "I'm actually really proud of you for speaking truth to power. That took 'nads, man!"

Chip stands up, beaming, and leans in to give Charles a hug. "That actually means a lot to me that you said that." He wipes a tear. Charles is wondering why this is such an emotional moment for Chip and gives him a quizzical look. "What's up, big guy?"

Chip sits back down on the couch. "I don't know. All these discussions we've been having about faith and religion and messiahs . . . I'm kind of coming around to your side, and that worries me."

"Whoa, whoa, whoa! I'm not trying to, uh, unconvert you, man! I just love a good discussion. I actually admire your faith. Kinda wish I had more faith myself. And you've made some good points for your side, that I'm taking to heart. To me, you personify all that's good about faith, with all the great work you do in your church, your community, and your counseling. I admire that. Now if everyone were like you . . ."

Chip cuts in, "Wait a minute. We so do not want that! Do you know what kind of world it would be if everyone were like either of us?" The tension breaks and the two men laugh until tears drip down their cheeks.

"Yeah," Charles says once he stops laughing. "A world filled with crude, cranky, stubborn, intellectual old guys arguing about stuff that can't be proved. That'd be a fine world!" To punctuate this thought, Chip leans over to one side and lets rip a resounding fart. "Oh, and smelly old guys at that," Charles adds, holding his nose.

"Well," Chip says. "A world filled with jokers like us would probably be a more peaceful world—no Napoleons, Hitlers, or Trumps. Just people who are fundamentally good and much less apt to lie, cheat, steal, and murder."

Charles nods his head. "Yeah, but I don't think I'd be a great model for a race of people. Couldn't keep a wife. Can barely hold a job. Can't manage to write a book. Introverted as hell. You'd be a better template to clone."

"Well luckily, we don't need to worry about that, unless some alien descends from the clouds and decides to crank out Charles and Chip clones by the billions. That reminds me of a joke."

"Of course," groans Charles. "I know I can't stop you; I can only hope to contain you. Make it a quick one."

"That's what she said. OK. A billionaire had himself cloned many years ago. The boy grew up to have a very foul mouth. The more the son swore the madder the father got. One day, the father got so mad he pushed his son off a high cliff. The sheriff arrested him for making an obscene clone fall."

"Even though that was short, I'll never get that minute back," Charles says with his head in his hands in mock pain.

"That's relativity," Chip says.

"What?"

"Einstein said, 'Put your hand on a hot stove for a minute, and it seems like an hour. Sit with a pretty girl for an hour, and it seems like a minute. That's relativity.'"

"Well, you're relatively sadistic, the way you tell those stinkers."

Beelzebub has a telephone inside for me

Queen—Bohemian Rhapsody

When Charles was four years old, he was quite aware of his parents as people. He would often wake very early on Saturday mornings. Not wanting to wake his parents, he would quietly tiptoe past their door and out to the living room to watch television. His two favorite programs were Soupy Sales and Jon Gnagy's *Learn to Draw* program. That program regularly encouraged young artists to get their parents to buy a clingy plastic film to put over the TV tube, so they could trace the examples off the screen. But try as he might, Charles couldn't convince his parents to buy the film.

His dad, a typical Depression Era guy and an engineer, didn't spend money on frivolities, and there was much about the world he viewed as frivolous. Accordingly, the family had only one of everything: one pair of scissors, one roll of tape, one stapler, one yardstick, and one folding carpenter's ruler. As far as his father was concerned, one of a thing was enough, two was splurging, and three was just wasteful. So, an expensive, mail-order clingy piece of plastic for Charles was quite out of the question. "I can get you something like that from work," he said. But he never did.

One morning, Charles pulled a chair up to the kitchen cabinets and got the Magic Marker out of the family junk drawer. He went back to the living room and proceeded to trace John Gnagy's drawings on the front of the TV. He became alarmed when he couldn't erase one drawing to trace another, and quickly turned off the set. When he noticed that the drawing was still there on the glass, he ran back to bed, pulled the covers over his head, and pretended to be asleep. His dad gave him holy hell, but his mom stuck up for him and used Lestoil and rags to clean the drawing off the TV.

While writing at his kitchen table late one night, Charles starts thinking about this incident. His relationship with his father had always been complicated. He adored his dad, who was kind and attentive most of the time, when he wasn't working late or on a business trip or upset about something Charles or his mother had done. His father had a temper, and when Charles would set him off, he very often railed at the boy for five or ten minutes, reducing him to terrified sobs. His mother would intervene, and often as a result, his parents would argue and yell at one another, frightening Charles even more. He decided he needed to be the best little boy possible, so they wouldn't yell at each other.

Charles runs over several incidents with his dad in his mind and soon realizes it was useless to try to write anymore and goes to bed. After tossing and turning for an hour, he falls asleep and toward morning has a vivid dream about another childhood incident.

In the dream, Charles was four years old again and playing in the living room. Suddenly, in the bathroom, his mother shrieked and began to cry. Charles ran toward the bathroom and saw his wailing mother cross the short hallway to the master bedroom and slam the door.

Charles, alarmed, opened the door, but his mother, still sobbing, said in a strange voice, "Don't come in Charles!"

"Why not Mommy?" Charles wasn't so much scared as concerned for his mother.

"Just stay out there. Go to the living room and play."

"Can I at least leave the door open?"

"OK, baby. Just don't come in."

Charles looked around and noticed a streak of blood running from the bathroom across the hall to the bedroom. Wanting to help he called to his mother, "I'll clean this up, Mommy."

"No, honey," his mother said. "Just leave it there. I'll clean it up later."

"What's wrong with you, Mommy?" Charles asked.

"I'm OK, sweetie," she said, but she didn't sound OK, and Charles could see she was crying. This scared him. He wanted to help his mother, so he went to the hall closet and got out a towel. He began to carefully wipe the blood up from the floor. He somehow thought this would make his mother feel better.

"I'm cleaning it up, Mommy."

His mother, still weeping but more quietly, said, "Oh, honey, thanks." After a minute she said, "Honey if you want to help, you can do something for me."

Charles stopped cleaning and went to stand at the bedroom door. "What, Mommy?" he said, peering in and finding it hard to locate his mother's head amid the blankets.

"Sweetheart, could you call Daddy and ask him to come home?" Charles, being four, had never called anybody before.

"I don't know how, Mommy," he said anxiously. The house, as was typical in the '50s, had a single black rotary dial phone that was hardwired to its jack in the living room by the stairs that led to the unfinished half floor above. Charles remembered his mother stretching the cord around the balustrade and sitting on the steps when on a long phone call.

"It's OK, Charlie. I can tell you how. You've seen Mommy dial the phone before, right? You just put your finger in the hole that has the number and twirl it until it stops, and then let go. It only goes one way."

"OK, Mommy. I think I can do that." Charles already knew his numbers and could count to 30. "After I dial the number, will Daddy answer the phone?"

"Well, honey, you'll have to dial seven numbers, and after that, a nice lady at Daddy's work will talk with you, and she will get Daddy for you."

Charles felt better that he could help in some way. "OK, Mommy. What numbers do you want me to dial?"

"Just go to the phone, honey, and I'll call them out from the bedroom."

Charles walked down the short hall and into the living room. "Mommy, why can't I bring you the phone?" He knew the phone connected to the wall. If he could just pull the cord out, he could bring his mother the phone.

"No, Charlie, the phone has to stay there. OK, just lift the big black part off the top. Have you got it? You know how Mommy listens to the phone right? The curly cord should be down near your mouth. Have you got it?"

"Yes, Mommy."

"OK, you should hear a buzz. Do you? OK, now put your finger in the little hole that has the seven in it. Do you see that?"

"Yes, Mommy."

"OK, it should only move in one direction. Move your finger toward the silver thing."

"OK, Mommy. Should I let go now?"

"Yes, Charlie. Good boy. Once it stops moving, put your finger in the hole that has the five." Charles's mother proceeded to coach him through the rest of the phone number.

"And when the nice lady answers, tell her you want to speak to Mark DeFries.

A woman answered the phone. Charles said, "Hi, my name is Charlie. Can I talk to my Daddy?"

"I'm sorry little boy. But your daddy isn't here."

"Where is he?" Charles felt like he was going to cry.

"Honey, you dialed the wrong number. If you try again, I'll bet you can find your daddy. Goodbye."

"Mommy, she said Daddy isn't there and I did it wrong." Charles's stomach was in a knot. Why had the lady said his Daddy wasn't there?

"That's OK, Charlie. Let's just try again. I'm sure you'll get it right this time. Just be sure not to let go of the little hole until your finger hits the silver thing."

Charles's mother coached him through the number again, and this time the switchboard operator at his father's work answered.

Charles, now filled with dread, said, "Hi, my name is Charlie. Can I talk to my Daddy?"

"Who's your daddy, honey?" the receptionist said. "What's your last name?"

"He's Mark DeFries. Can I talk to him now?"

"Just wait a minute, Charlie. I'll see if I can get him." The receptionist returned quickly and said, "I'm sorry, Charlie, your daddy isn't here right now. He's in a meeting. What is it that you need?"

"My Mommy is bleeding," Charles said, his voice trembling. "I need to talk to my Daddy."

"Oh, my goodness!" the receptionist exclaimed. "Hold on. I'll get somebody who works for your Daddy." The next thing he knew, Charlie heard a strange man's voice on the phone.

"Charlie? Hi, I'm Mr. Taggert. I work for your daddy. What is the problem?"

"My mommy was in the bathroom, and then she went into the bedroom, but there was blood on the floor, and she won't let me come in, but I cleaned up the blood."

"Oh my God," Taggert said. "OK, ummm, let's see. OK, look, Charlie, Mr. Dietrich lives near you. Do you remember Mr. Dietrich?"

Charles vaguely remembered that a man who worked with Daddy lived down the block. "I think so."

"OK. Charlie, I'm going to call Mr. Dietrich. He's home sick today and he can come and help you. Will that be OK?"

"I want my Daddy!" exclaimed Charles, now in tears. "Please get my Daddy to come home."

"Honey, he'll be home as soon as he can, but until then, Mr. Dietrich will help you. You just be sure to let him in when he gets there, OK?"

"OK," Charlie said, wiping a tear from his eye. "Goodbye."

"Goodbye, Charlie. Everything's going to be all right."

Charles replaced the receiver and went to his mother's doorway.

"Daddy's not there!" he exclaimed.

"Oh, no," his mother said. "Who were you talking to?"

"A man who works for Daddy. He's going to send Mr. Dietrich to help us."

"Oh, that's good. Everything's going to be OK, Charlie."

"OK, Mommy. Can't I come hug you?"

"No, Charlie, you stay out there. Mr. Dietrich will be here soon."

Dietrich showed up after 20 minutes, dressed in a suit and wearing a fedora. Charlie let him in.

"Hiya champ," Mr. Dietrich said. "Where's your mommy?"

"She's in the bedroom, but she won't let anybody come in."

"Oh, OK. I think she'll let me go in. Why don't you just stay here and play?" Dietrich went down the hall, entered the bedroom, and closed the door. Charlie could hear his mother crying and Dietrich's muffled voice. After a while, Dietrich came into the living room and made a few calls.

When he was finished, he asked Charlie if he was hungry, and made him a peanut butter and Fluff sandwich. But Charlie hated the sandwich because Dietrich didn't make it the way his mother did, with butter and peanut butter.

"I wanna see my Mommy! Why can't I see her?"

"She'll be all right," Dietrich said. "And your daddy will be here soon. Do you want to watch some TV?"

"No, I want my Mommy." Charlie wailed and began to cry again.

"Honey?" his mother called from the bedroom. "You can come see me now."

Charlie leapt from his chair and ran down the hall into his mother's room. "Oh, Mommy! Are you OK?" he said, tears rolling down his cheeks.

"Yes, Charlie," his mother said sniffing and wiping her face. "I'm OK. But you remember how Mommy's tummy got big and I told you that you were going to have a little brother or sister? Well," his mother turned away for a moment. "Ummm. I think there's something wrong with the baby, and I have to go to the hospital."

"But you're going to be OK?" asked Charles with fear in his heart.

"Yes, honey, I'll be OK. I'm just going to wait until your Daddy comes home to drive me to the hospital."

A half an hour later, Charles's father came home, and his mother and father spoke for several minutes with the bedroom door closed. Finally, his father came out with his mother and she was walking in a funny way.

"Charlie, Mommy and Daddy are going to the hospital. We want you to stay here with Mr. Dietrich until we get back. Everything's going to be OK," said his father.

"No! I want to come too!"

"Sorry, buddy, but you can't. Don't worry. We'll be back before dinner." His parents hugged him goodbye and left. Charles watched out the window until long after their car drove out of sight.

Charles awakes from the dream. Wow, he thinks. I haven't thought of that incident for decades. That was intense, like a perfect recording of that awful experience. He lies in bed turning the dream over in his mind. After several minutes, he suddenly realizes that his fear of talking on the phone stems from that experience when his mother lost her fourth baby since Charles had been born. The reluctance to use the phone has bothered Charles throughout his life. He generally writes it off as an artifact of his shyness and introversion. It often takes him days to screw up the courage and the will to make phone calls to strangers. He has always credited the behavior to his tendency to procrastinate, but now he realizes he has a debilitating phobia. Shit, that's why I hate the phone, Charles thinks. Wow. That memory must have been trying to surface for years.

Still shivering from remembering the dream, Charles goes into the kitchen, plucks the Post-It note from the refrigerator, lifts the receiver, and dials the auto shop's number.

Tell the devil you can freeze hell

Creedence Clearwater Revival—*Down on the Corner*

Chip is sitting in a sour mood drinking and thinking at the dive bar next to Charles's apartment building, a half-empty pitcher of Bud Light before him on the table. A mediocre jazz trio murders the standards via the joint's out-of-tune piano. Charles looks in hesitantly from the street, spies Chip and self-consciously walks over to the booth.

"Well, it's 'bout time you showed up, you sad sack," Chip greets him. "Get lost on the wild side?"

"Well, I have never been into this bar," Charles says.

"It's next to your fucking building, you moron! You've never been here?"

"No," Charles says, surveying the definitively down at the heels décor: torn vinyl on the banquettes, dusty, fake mounted game fish, and tons of Marlins baseball paraphernalia on the walls. "Not my style."

"Which you know how? From never setting foot?"

"Cram it, buddy. Whatcha drinking?"

"Spud Light, grab that mug there and I'll pour you one." Charles hates light beer, preferring craft stout, but he takes the full glass and sips a bit. He looks around the place. He's never been comfortable in places he's never been before, mainly because his beanpole stature and sport jacket often make him stand out. More than one drunken behemoth had given him unwanted attention in similar bars.

Nodding toward the standup bass player on the stage, Charles says, "I think I told you I played bass guitar in a semi-pro jazz band during graduate school. We had what we thought was the coolest—pun intended—name: *The Laws of Ice*. It's from a short piece by Ralph Waldo Emerson called 'The Comic.'"

Chip snorts. "Give me a break! What a highfalutin' pretentious grad student wimpy pansy-ass name! A name, I'm sure, with a backstory!" Chip pours himself another beer.

"Well, I was in the creative writing program, after all!" Charles says, almost apologetically. "The gist is, even the high and mighty, while out walking, must obey the laws of ice or they go down."

Chip guffaws at the double entendre. "That's what she said!"

Mildly exasperated, Charles continues, "Anyway, we thought it was a cool, egalitarian kind of name for a band, but even the English majors didn't get it."

"Can't for the life of me figure why . . ." deadpans Chip, and then snickers.

Charles glares at his friend. "Anyway," he says, irritatedly drawing out the "a" in the manner of annoyed persons everywhere. "The part of the Emerson passage—which is in general about the ascendency of wit,"—more snorts from Chip—"If I may continue, the part that is germane to our current discussion goes like this, and yes, I did happen to have memorized it, for an Emerson course I was talking," Charles explains quickly to head off another taunt from Chip, who is making ironic air quote signs in the air. "Anyway, it goes: 'Dost thou think, because thou art virtuous, there shall be no more cakes and ale?' That's the point I've been trying to make while you sit there making faces: Just 'cause you've found the way, doesn't mean there aren't other sinners out there."

Chip again makes air quotes while bowing in mockery. "O thank you, 'perfesser', for 'enlightening' a dumb Midwesterner such as I. I am but a stout vessel which has just shipped a heavy sea after receiving, like a willing martyr, the whispers into his ear of a man of wit."

Charles almost gasps. "You've read your Emerson!"

"Of course, you yay-hoo. I was a damn English major myself; don't you remember? And the cakes and ale bit is from *Twelfth Night*, Willy the Shake, not Emerson, you clown."

Charles flushes scarlet and, nonplussed, grabs an errant ping pong ball from the banquette and whips it at Chip's head. The ball bounces off his forehead with a satisfying ponk. Chip grabs his mug and mimes pouring it into Charles's crotch.

After a minute during which he gathers his composure, and his ears turn from scarlet to merely bright pink, Charles leans back self-consciously, affecting what he thinks is a devil-may-care attitude, and takes a drag on his Marlboro, grateful that this dive bar was one of the few left in Miami where you can smoke. Charles blows a smoke ring, and Chip pokes his finger in the center, saying, "Never let it die a virgin. That shit's gonna kill you, mate," he says.

To change the subject, Charles says, "Did I ever tell you about when I was Allen Ginsberg's apprentice?"

"No shit?" Chip says, impressed. "How'd you get a gig like that?"

"Well, it was while I was in graduate school in Denver, around the same time as the jazz band thing. Somehow, I saw a flyer or something about this new school in Boulder, the Naropa Institute. It's Naropa University now. They'd just started up and had something called The Jack Kerouac School of Disembodied Poetics. I thought that was a pretty interesting name, although I was never a great Kerouac fan. Then I saw that Allen Ginsburg was on the faculty. I'd only read a little Ginsburg and thought 'Howl' was a great poem, but the thing that had really caught my eye about him was 'Mind Breaths,' a poem he published in *Rolling Stone*. In the poem, the poet imagines his breath leaving his nostrils and traveling out over the mountains, across the seas, and around the world. It was an incredibly evocative poem, and I re-read it probably a dozen times. So, I was intrigued by the thought of taking his class on poetry writing."

Chip, for the first time since Charles showed up, seems to shed his wise-ass act and looks interested. Charles warms to his story.

"The problem was the cost: $100, a tremendous sum back in those days. I was only making $500 a quarter as a teaching assistant. I prevailed upon my parents to finance the course, which met three afternoons a week during that summer, in Boulder, about a half hour from where I lived. I drove back and forth in an old Jeep Wagoneer that got about a mile a gallon.

"Despite the cost and the commute, it was a mind-blowing experience. I didn't know what to expect from the course, and it certainly was unlike any other course I took before or since. Each class began with about 15 minutes of mediation—I had never done that before. Allen was as much teaching us how to meditate and to think creatively as he was teaching us how to write. I especially remember we did in-class poetry writing. I adopted that for when I taught poetry. The first exercise stuck in my mind: write a poem about a tree without comparing it to fingers, rivers, or pillars. That set the tone. Allen also did a whole lecture on poetic clichés. Anyway, he said that he was going to take a few interns for the fall semester and those interested could apply. The application was just as unorthodox as he was. I remember he wanted to know the entire history of my poetry production, for example.

"So, I got the gig and I show up at this nondescript apartment complex in Boulder, and eventually find Ginsberg's building and apartment. The door is wide open, and the day is very warm, probably late September. I knock on the door and wait. Knock again, and call, "Hello?" I take a few steps into the living room and Allen and his lover, Peter Orlovsky, come barreling around the corner from the bedroom, both clad only in tighty-whiteys."

"Oh, seriously?" Chip says. "What? Were they fucking back there?"

Charles glares at Chip and shakes his head in irritation. "Anyway, I'm a bit taken aback, as one would be to be surprised by a nearly-nude world-famous poet.

"Hi, I say. I'm your apprentice. 'Oh,' Allen says. 'Was that today? OK, give me a minute.' Allen walks back to the bedroom, but Orlovsky stays and regards me closely from head to toe. 'So, what's your name? You should stand up straighter. Get your shoulders back. Do you like fruit?' He steps very close to me and grabs my belly, squeezing it all over, palpating it."

"Hah! A half-nude, former male model and famously promiscuous gay guy felt you up?"

"Oh, shut up Chip! I didn't get the idea he was anything but curious, although he did ask if I was married. Anyway, he carries on saying stuff like, 'You know, you should only use unwaxed dental floss. Best thing for you. Save the bees. The wax'll get you in the end.' Bored at last with feeling me up, he grabs the phone and dials the long-distance operator. Remember the long-distance operator? You needed to call her to place collect calls. He speaks to her in a pompous English accent and berates her when she can't find the number he needs. I'm not even sure he really wanted to place a call.

"Allen bursts back into the living room, fully clothed, in a white prayer jacket, his skinny white legs sticking out of baggy white shorts, and says, 'OK, did you bring your journal?' That was one of his requirements, that I bring my poetry journal. I hand it to him. 'Here,' he says. 'Fair is fair. Read my journal. This is one of the ones I'll want you to transcribe.'

"He sits, sweating, poring over my journal, striking words, making corrections and adding notes in the margins. To my embarrassment, one of the first corrections he makes is the spelling of his first name. 'It's Allen, not Alan,' he says, fixing his beady eyes on me like I'm an idiot.' Sorry,' I say. 'I knew that.'

"Meanwhile I read his journal. It's much as you might expect: stream of consciousness musings, bad puns—'At Florsheim's, I admit the agony of de feet'—and some brilliant turns of phrase and half-poems. He dreams of shoes, and his guru, and of being ignored, and laments his dead love after 10 years."

"He waited 10 years to lament his dead love?" Chip says with an evil grin.

"You know what I mean, dipwad! Anyway, some kind of assistant from across the courtyard comes in with a gift of crabapples and more dates for his appointment book. Remember appointment books? The crabapples roll off the table, and I juggle to catch them but end up throwing them on the carpet.

"Bored or finished with my journal, Allen rises and asks if I want something to drink. He brings me a huge glass of dark brown cider full of cinnamon. It was magnificent. I can almost still taste it. Orlovsky goes into a headstand, crossing his feet in the air with his head turning red. Abruptly leaving the pose, he grabs my journal and reads a poem of mine about cigarettes. 'This is great!' he says. I can't tell if he was kidding, or sarcastic or what."

"Probably both," Chip says. "Plus, he was trying to get in your pants."

Charles ignores Chip and continues his reminiscence.

"Anne Walden, a famous poet I had never heard of before going to Naropa, breezes in wearing a long flimsy dress—nice boobs, by the way—and goes over to the telephone and phones her mother. After she leaves, Allen goes back to my journal and Orlovsky wanders outside. The phone rings and Allen asks me to get it. It's someone asking for Jackson Mac Low. Allen says, he's down the hall. I run down the hall to fetch him. Mac Low is nervous, asking who is it? Is it long distance? I don't know, and he hustles down the hall to get the phone. I go back into the living room and Allen's looking at his datebook. 'I work very hard' he says, and I agree. He continues to go through my poems, chopping words, altering facts, and footnoting ideas. He goes to the wastebasket with a little thimble sharpener and shaves his pencil.

"Too soon, he apologizes and says he'll be back in a month and there's much more we could do. He gives me a box of old journals for me to transcribe, and I get in my car for the drive back to Denver. Orlovsky pokes his head out the door and yells, 'Keep a clean asshole!' I'm not entirely sure what to make of that and think about it all the way home. Turns out a couple years later, Orlovsky published his book, *Clean Asshole Poems & Smiling Vegetable Songs*."

"Manfred Mann, that's a bizarre tale," Chip says, stretching his arms above his head. "So, did you have anything more to do with Ginsberg?"

"Oh, yes. I did the transcriptions and sent them to him. He corrected them and sent them back. Of course, I was banging them out on a typewriter, and I was a terrible typist back then. Used a lot of Wite-Out. I remember meeting with him to discuss the manuscript and trying to decipher his handwriting. In an entry about traveling through the Rockies, he referred to what looked to be Mt. Thigh. He wrote the thing in 1967 or 68 because it mentions Lyndon Johnson talking about 'nucler' arms. This was seven years later, but he couldn't remember what he was thinking then. We scrounged up an atlas and then a map of Colorado but couldn't find any mountain by that name. Wait. Let me read the passage to you. I've got it on my phone."

Charles scrolls and finds the document. "Here you go:

Thru Rockies

Sunset up thru the grey rock walls of Clear Creek Canyon
white ice in the rock-sluice below,
pines in late afternoon light
marching the snow-sprinkled wall of Mt. Thigh—
out of Golden on the road that passes Central City 1946

"We agreed to leave it Mt. Thigh in the final manuscript. We met a few more times and he finally accepted the manuscript and thanked me.

"Then, a couple years later, when I started my poetry magazine, I got ahold of Ginsberg again and asked if I could interview him for the magazine and publish "Thru Rockies." It was kind of a weird phone conversation. You know, Allen was one of the reasons I decided not to become a poet. Here was this world-famous poet living hand-to-mouth, constantly needing to borrow from friends and crash at their places, at age 50. Anyway, when I asked for the interview, he kinda had a hissy fit. Basically, he said,

'Everybody wants something from me. I spend all my time doing things for people, doling out little pieces of myself, and what do I get? No time to work on my stuff. No time to make any money. I'm crashing on a couch right now.'

"I swallowed hard and explained all I wanted was an hour of his time and permission. He eventually calmed down and resignedly said we could do it. When I saw him, it was after his stroke and he looked terrible. We did the interview, and I asked about *Heart Beat*, a film that was in production about Neal Cassady and Kerouac. Allen was quite upset about the script and the way it depicted him. He was very hung up on the dialog: 'They put words in my mouth that I never said, never would say!' He made the filmmakers change his character's name to Stryker. When I sent him the interview transcription, he made me break it into two parts called Gossip—the discussion of the film—and Poetry. Years later, I got a request from a Ginsberg archivist wanting a copy of the issue."

"Wow. So, you decided to not become a world-famous broke poet, eh? Good call?"

"The jury's still out," Charles says, smiling. "That issue is available on the web for $25 now. Cover price was $2, so I guess it beat inflation. One good thing came of the whole Ginsberg thing: I started experimenting with my writing. I still remember one of my far-out tone poems but let me find it here." Charles flips back and forth through his phone.

"Ah, yes. Here it is. It's called Moon Arup."

Chip spews Bud Light out his nose. "No shit?"

"Yes. Now listen. You might learn something. Ahem.

> Boh Bih Bell
> Bin Boo Bar
> Ben Swim Nin
> Quell, Silent
> Run Re Rup
> Eeeeen Ar Mut
> Sihn Seen Zoot
> Mor Mien Moo
> Zee Zee Zie Zwie
> Cuan Lido Wine
> Zeido ZZZZZZZZ"

"Oh my God, that's fuckin' brilliant!" Chip doubles over in laughter.

"Thank you! Thank you very much!" Charles says in his best Elvis voice and does a little bow.

"But seriously," he continues, "one real bad thing happened because of my time with Ginsberg. I basically washed out of the poetry Master's program because I could no longer write the type of academic poetry they expected."

Chip says, "Wow! That's too bad, dude."

"Here's another one I wrote around that time. It's about the commute from Denver to Boulder, but other things as well.

> Down, blood wrong,
> I am lonesome after my own
> Tired, played out
> Played wrong,
> Beat by heat from traffic dazzle
> 70 miles round Denver-Boulder
> Blood wrong, pizza not taking
> Shall I chew C&E? or take the
> Allergy medicine?
> Wrong, played
> Out, tendon wires under
> Skin jump, sallow empty clear
> Skin, old skin, played wrong
> Beat out, lonesome after,
> Lonesome before, beat by beat
> Miles, blood wrong, pizza take"

"That's a little better," Chip admits. "What's C&E?"

"Dunno. Vitamins? Throat lozenge? Something for allergies? Although I rarely had allergy problems while in Denver. So anyway, one of my professors hated what I was doing so much that he took an entire class period to run down the Beats, several times directing his comments directly at me. The whole class was like, 'Dad just hit Mom.' When I met with him later, he said his wife thought my poetry was the worst thing she had ever read, and he called it sentimental. I was devastated. I felt really betrayed. This guy was supposed to be teaching me, not tearing me down. I've hardly written any poetry since. I changed my degree to English Lit."

"Man, that sucks. Sorry, buddy."

"Well it led me to this glamorous and lucrative career in the tech writing and starving newspaper columnist trade, so I've got that going for me."

"Which is nice," Chip responds. "Hey, that reminds me of a poetry joke."

"No, dear god, no!"

"A nurse is giving a young medical intern a tour of the hospital. The intern approaches one bedridden patient and asks, 'Why are you here?' The patient replies, 'Wee sleket cowerin' timrous beastie, O, what a panic is in thy breastie.' The intern moves on to the next bed and asks the same question. The patient answers, 'O, my luv is like a red, red, rose that's newly sprung in June.' The intern goes to a third bed and asks the question again, to which the third patient replies, 'The best laid schemes o' mice an' men gang aft agley.' At this the intern turns to the nurse and asks, 'What ward is this anyway?' And the nurse answers, 'It's the Burns Unit.'"

"Oh, for crying in the beer!" Charles pulls back his arm as if to slap Chip, who chortles like a madman.

Sweet Jesus Man of the Year / Who am I to disagree?

Eurhythmics—Sweet Dreams (Are Made of This)

Charles is dreaming.

He's at a festival held at some kind of historic train station. Very rustic. He's there apparently with his family: father, mother, siblings, Karen and their son, and neighbor friends of the family. The train station is a small rustic affair, a small-town whistle-stop. The tracks are long gone. The front part of the old station office is a gift shop.

He finds himself walking along a path in the open rough terrain around the station with an old friend of the family, Ron.

Ron proposes that they run all the way back to the station since they're probably late. Charles agrees but looks down to find he is in shorts and socks—no shoes. He decides to run anyway but watches the ground intensely. They run up and down shallow gullies, among broken glass and sharp stones. Charles finds running in stocking feet comfortable, pleasant even. He feels like his feet are not even touching the ground but gliding above it.

They arrive back at the train station. After some confused conversation with his parents, Charles wanders to the front of the gift shop. He looks out across the former tracks to the platform on the other side. He glimpses a familiar figure but can't quite make her out. He pushes through the crowd in the shop and out the door to get a better look. He's afraid to stare, but he thinks it might be Edie. He tries to wander nonchalantly down the platform, glancing from time to time across the gap at the woman.

She's with a group of men, just hanging out and watching the crowd. The men are all about Charles's age, with worn jeans and hippie clothes. By the time Charles reaches the end of the platform, he's pretty sure it's her. When he turns to walk back, he thinks he hears her call his name. But when he turns toward her, she's talking and laughing with the men.

Charles decides to cross the ex-train-track gully and talk to her.

He crosses over and approaches Edie. She is lovelier than she ever was with him: She's no longer rail thin; her hair is longer, and she actually seems to have improved with age. The biggest thing that impresses Charles is her calm—she was always a pretty uptight person, but now, she's almost serene in interacting with the men. She's wearing very fashionable casual clothes that suit her figure nicely.

Charles steps up and says hello. She turns and gives him a big calm smile. "I thought that was you over there. We've been watching you."

"And I've been trying to figure out if it was you over here. How are you doing? You look great." This is the truth. She looks much more desirable now than she ever did when they were together.

They kiss on the lips, and Charles immediately regrets it because his wife is back in the gift shop. He jerks a glance back across the gap but can't see her. He puts his arm around her in a friendly way and they talk over old times while walking back down the platform. He finds out very little about her current life. Charles glances over at the shop and sees his wife and son browsing a rack of clothing in the front. He figures he'd better get back. Edie says she'll walk with him because she needs to go to work. He pecks her on the cheek, opting for the safer kiss.

They walk back across the gap. As they enter the gift shop, Charles is scouting for his wife, nervous that they'd been seen with their arms around each other. Edie grabs a trash bag. Charles looks at her and she's now wearing a maintenance uniform with an ad for a cafe on the back in masking tape.

It is evident that she is supporting herself with odd jobs and living the bohemian life. Charles is vaguely jealous of the freedom of such a life, the life he used to know back in Denver when they both were poor. She moves through the shop picking up trash and says goodbye over her shoulder. Charles finds his wife and son and they are about to leave when he suddenly finds himself deep under water. He frantically swims for the surface but before he gets there, he awakens.

Charles quickly sits up in bed and looks out the window thinking about the dream. After what seems like a very long time, he checks the clock. It's only six o'clock; he can sleep another hour.

He turns over and tries to sleep, but the image of his former love obsesses his thoughts and he finds it hard to drift back off. Finally, he dozes for about 15 minutes before his alarm goes off.

Charles is puzzled about the meaning of the dream: Why was he in stocking feet? Why was he worried about broken glass? And why did his old flame, whom he has not dreamed or really even thought much about in years, show up once again in a dream?

Then he remembers: He'd had another hang-up call several weeks ago, the first in many years. That's probably why I dreamed of her now, he thinks. But that was months ago. Charles feels that Edie represents his abandoned past: the hippie years, the years as a young poet reading his pieces in coffeehouses and cafes and anywhere they wouldn't laugh. Still, it bothers him as he does his morning exercises, which take him longer than usual as he catches himself several times just lying on the floor thinking of the dream.

If she were really like that, calm and lovely, I would have never left her, he asserts to himself. The lure of the past is quite strong, the what-ifs and the might-have-beens.

Rousing from his funk, Charles showers and then goes over to Chip's house. He knocks on the door. Trixie leans out a kitchen window and yells, "He's out back. Killing ants."

Charles goes around back, over the coarse thick-bladed lawn, and finds Chip pouring bleach down a fire ant mound. "Hey, Chuck. What's up?"

"Not much. Just wondered if you wanted to shoot the shit and maybe help me out with the book."

"You bet, little buddy. Just let me kill off these vermin. Shit!" One of the ants had crawled halfway up Chip's giant calf and bit him. "Sonofabitch! Christ on a crutch, that hurts!" Chip swats away the insect and hops on one leg. He pours the rest of the gallon of bleach on the mound and limps into the house, with Charles following behind.

"Honey? I got bit again. Where's the calamine?" Trixie yells back, "Out in the garage, where it always is. Don't you get any of those ants in my house!" Chip and Charles go into the garage. Enclosed garages aren't common in South Florida, but Chip, an avid furniture maker, was lucky that his parsonage had one. There was no room for a car in the garage, however, because the floor was occupied by two table saws, a band saw, a lathe, and other large power tools, as well as chairs, tables, and bureaus in various stages of completion.

Chip rustles up a bucket that he squirts dish liquid into and fills partway with water before stepping in and scrubbing his leg with a soft brush. "Hand me that calamine, wouldya?" Chip scans the messy workbench and finally spies the bottle, which he hands to Chip. Chip dries his calf with a filthy towel and slathers on the lotion.

"Looks like I'll live," he says sardonically. "Let's go into my study and chat." The pair goes back around front. Chip's house has two front doors: one leading to the main part of the house, and one that opens into his study, which adjoins the garage. This was so that congregants and Chip's counseling clients could discreetly visit Chip without disturbing the family.

The two enter and Chip gestures toward the client chair and throws his bulk into a worn beige nailhead wingback chair. Between them is a low coffee table and behind Chip is his incredibly cluttered desk, featuring an old iMac and a 40-inch television. Chip kicks off his flip-flops and absently starts scratching his ant bite.

"Don't scratch! You'll make it worse," Charles says.

"Yeah, yeah, yeah," Chip says. "I know. So, what's on your mind?"

"Well, I had a very detailed dream last night."

"At least you can sleep," Chip says. He's an incurable insomniac, sometimes sleeping only a couple of hours a night.

I don't know how he can have such energy with so little sleep, Charles thinks. "Well, yes, but anyway, it was about Edie and, like I said, it was extremely vivid. She was different. Calmer. Not so schitzy. I'm kinda wondering what it might have meant."

"Well, I'm no shrink, but people tell me dreams all the time, so lay it on me." Chip has heard his share of weird dreams in his pastoral counseling business. Sometimes his clients' dreams are the reason he can't sleep. Chip slouches to his right and scratches his butt as Charles proceeds to describe the dream.

When Charles finishes, Chip says, "Well what do you think it means?"

"Don't give me that counselor crap, Chip! I want to hear your thoughts."

"Dude, don't be difficult. Tell me your ideas and then I'll give you mine."

"All right, clod for brains. I think it means maybe I made a bad choice when I married Karen?"

"What about the dream gives you that idea?"

"Well, you know, crossing the tracks to pursue Edie, not to mention that Karen and I ended in divorce. I dunno."

"OK, we can postulate that anyone who divorces has made a poor choice of mate. Do you think your marriage was all bad?"

"Not at all. I got a son out of it, not that I ever see him anymore. And we were happy for a while. If it weren't for that damn Munch, perhaps she wouldn't have gone gay and we'd still be together."

"I don't think people 'go gay,' Charles."

"I do. It's a choice."

"Yeah, after all those nasty columns you wrote in the *World*, I got that impression." Chip thought that the vehemence and hatred Charles expressed in those columns were so totally out of character for his rather meek, liberal friend. Perhaps Charles was still really tormented by the breakup of his marriage and the marriage of Karen and Munch.

Charles thinks for a while. He finally decides to share his theory of dreams with his friend.

"I think all dreams are true."

"God, I hope not, or I'm destined to have the ground open up and swallow me!" He moans, grimaces and pretends to claw the air above him.

Charles smiles. "Hopefully, that won't happen in this universe, but perhaps another. I think when we sleep, we pass from our universe through many others. Our consciousness tries to make sense of the various transitions, which explains some of the weirdness of dreams. I'm always dreaming about trying to find my way through innumerable rooms that keep changing, doors in become doors out. You must have had similar dreams. Sometimes you can fly, sometimes you're running in glue—you're in a universe with different physical laws. And sometimes you meet doppelgängers of people you know in this Universe, who behave in odd ways. But it's all true. It's all your experience, just in different times and places."

Chip nods and says, "OK. Could be."

Charles continues, "Often movies about dreams claim that if you die in a dream, you die in real life, like *Inception* for example. I think that's definitely possible, but that some survival instinct either shunts us to a more hospitable universe/time or returns us to this Universe and wakes us up before that happens. When we dream it, we actually do it, whether it be murdering someone or making love to them. As I've mentioned before, the biggest frustration for me on that point is never coming in a dream. I don't know why you can't come across universes. Perhaps there's some small bit of reserve in our psyches that prevents pan-universal ecstasy."

"Um, that's a weird theory you have there, Astral Traveler Boy. But I could enthusiastically support a Universal Come. Where do I go to surrender?" Chip jokes. "I remember that Sigourney Weaver dream you told me about, you perverted slug. Of course, there's no way to prove your theory, although it makes about as much sense as other theories. Take, for example, the idea that you're working out real-world problems in your dreams. Freud thought dreams expressed repressed longing that we can't express in the real world, especially in a social setting. Everything is dicks and pussies. Hold on. I'll get us some beers." Chip gets up and heads to the kitchen, returning with an IPA for him and a stout for Charles. Charles is pleasantly surprised at the beer. Chip knows he hates lager and must have bought the stout in case Charles came by.

Chip continues, "Freud did say, however, 'Sometimes, a cigar is just a cigar.' And I certainly don't know why you are repressing the desire to try to find your way through interminable office buildings."

"Exactly. While the repression theory could be true, I think dreams are more about telling you what you really think. Jung's theory is more like that. He thought that dreams let us reflect on our waking selves and process problems and conflicts."

"Yeah, so that's another theory: Dreams are metaphors," Chip says and takes a big gulp of beer and a little dribbles down his chin, landing on his black Lou Reed T-shirt. Heedless of the dribble, Chip doesn't wipe his chin.

Chip says, "Then there's the activation-synthesis theory that dreams are just random nerves firing in our brain and these impulses that drag out bits of memory. Our mind tries to make sense of them by assembling them into a narrative once we awake. And I've found that I only remember dreams that occur just before I awake, although I must have been dreaming several times during the night."

"As I've told you before, I've had déjà vu moments my whole life," Charles says, "Often I wake up with this weird feeling. I can't really explain it. I don't immediately think, 'Aha! I will have prescient moments today' but it's a weird feeling of déjà vu mixed with some other kind of disorientation."

"Don't drink so much before bed, my stout lad, and you'll be all right," Chip jokes.

"Funny, shithead. I'm serious. This really happens to me. Things happen that I clearly remember having dreamed about, and usually, I only recognize the situations after they happen. But on several occasions, I've been able to predict what is about to happen. In fact, back in college, one of these dreams, or déjà viewers, as I call them, actually helped me solve a this-universe problem."

"Bullshit."

"I shit you not. It was long ago in the distant past, back when computers filled huge air-conditioned rooms and programs were written on punch cards."

Chip snorts, "Spare me the purple prose, Springsteen!" Chip always hated the logorrhea of early Springsteen songs.

Charles, annoyed at the interruption, continues, "Anyway, I would submit the program, then it would run hours later. I'd have to trek back to the computer center, check the output, rekey a few cards and submit it again. Well, one night—it was probably about 1 am—I fed my card deck into the card reader, and the stupid thing stopped halfway through. That generally meant a bent card, so I looked at the next card that was to be fed, and it was pristine. Nonetheless, I went and remade it. Tried again. Same deal. I repeated this several times and even got the computer operator to come out of his glass cage to give me a hand.

"Then, all of a sudden it hit me: I had dreamt about this very problem the night before—not unusual; I invariably dream of boring things like that. In my dream, it was not the next card to feed that was the problem, it was the card that followed. The computer operator was sitting looking at the card that wouldn't feed, holding it up to the light like that hanging chad guy from the 2000 election, and I said, 'Wait, I know' and plucked the next card from the hopper and showed it to him. The card had a minuscule bend at the top left. The operator looked at me like I was crazy. 'How'd you know that?' he said. 'I dreamt it last night,' I said and went off to rekey the card. The deck sailed through without problems. That operator always looked at me strangely whenever we encountered one another again after that."

"Well," said Chip, "that's hardly earth-shattering prescience."

"I know. Most of my prescient dreams are similarly humdrum. I'll give you another example. When I was a junior in high school, I broke up with my girlfriend, or rather she broke up with me. A year later, I woke up convinced that she was coming to the house to see me. My mom was having an open house for her sorority to attract entering freshmen. I'll bet she's coming to that, I thought. So, after the thing started, I went out to the front porch to sit and wait for her, and, sure enough, after about 15 minutes, she shows up. 'I've been waiting for you,' I told her, which really freaked her out. I told her I knew she'd come to the open house, but she had no idea what I was talking about. She had come basically to tweak me, telling me she'd recently lost her virginity on a beach in Miami. Come to think of it, that one wasn't totally useless. I got to freak out my old GF. But most prescient dreams and feelings are. I keep trying to dream the lottery numbers, but so far no dice."

"No shit, Captain Obvious! You'd hardly be sitting here if you had. But remember your friends when you do, best buddy!"

"I think prescient dreams are caused by visiting a universe in the dream that is a bit accelerated timewise than ours, but nonetheless on a very similar time path."

"Well, I got to say, this theory is not as crazy as your Snagology idea, Captain Universe."

"Oh, but it fits in well with Snagology."

Chip snorts. "I can't wait to see you bend this pretzel, Logic Boy."

"Hear me out. Snagology is the belief that there are pan-Universal reality show viewers who get a perverse kick out of me running into physical and virtual snags. Perhaps when I dream, either these same Viewerverse denizens or maybe the night shift, flip the channels on me to see how well they can confuse me. Or perhaps it's the maintenance crew, setting me up for the snags of the coming day."

"Your egomania is beginning to worry me, my friend. Why is it all about you?"

"Good question. The reason I think it's all about me is because I don't have objective proof that anyone else exists. Plain and simple. You, my dearest friend, could be a hologram on the Holodeck as far as I know. Or perhaps everybody else on Earth has their own show, their own Snagological Viewerverse. But that doesn't matter. The only experience I can know, and feel, is my own, so that's why Snagology is centered on me."

"OK, you keep on talking about this Snagology religion like it's a thing."

"It is. I just put up a website at Snagology.com with my, er, manifesto? Ninety-five theses? What kind of document do you use to start a religion?"

Chip is taken aback. His crazy friend seems to be serious about founding Snagology. What part should I play in this craziness, Chip wondered. Would it be right or more importantly, would it be kind to help Charles in his demented state? "Uh, Charles. Are you pulling my leg? Because if you are, I'll give you such a smack!"

"I'm as serious as a midget in a nudist colony. I'm as serious as dick cancer. What makes you think I'm not serious?"

"I dunno. After all your railing against religion, it seems counterintuitive that you'd want to start one."

"If you can't lick 'em, lick 'em. So, you going to help me or what?"

"What. You're on your own, Slick. I've got a religion I am fairly comfortable with. You want to pursue this madness, good luck to you."

"You want to hear my manifesto?" "Dear, God, no," Chip says.

"OK, here it is:

> I assert that I am the only being in this Universe and the star of a pan-Universal reality show designed to entertain extra-Universal beings who place snags into my life for their amusement.

> I challenge all people to prove me wrong and to demonstrate that they too are players for the benefit of the Viewerverse.

> I hereby found a religion whose name will be Snagology and which is dedicated to proving or disproving my above theorem and/or collaborate on ways to keep the Viewerverse interested in perpetually renewing my, and/or my compatriots'— if such exist—tenure on this stage

> To become a Snagology acolyte, contribute $60 for the first year (PayPal accepted)."

"Oh, that's just so wrong. So wrong. What's come over you?" Chip is aghast that Charles has taken this delusion this far.

"I've woken up, is all. I'm woke. I can see clearly, now. The scales have fallen from my eyes."

"Now you're comparing yourself to Saul? That takes the fuckin' cake. If you are putting me on, I will murdelize you!" Chip is beside himself with worry at Charles's unhingedness.

I'd much rather be a reverend in blue jeans

Neil Diamond—Forever in Blue Jeans

CHARLES BEAUMONT DEFRIES

Charles Beaumont DeFries: I'm Not Obsessed; I'm Just Relentless

HIGHLIGHTS

You might say I'm obsessed.

You might say I'm argumentative.

But I'm just relentless.

BY CHARLES BEAUMONT DEFRIES
cdefries@miamiherald.com

Some people think of me as obsessed and argumentative, perhaps pathologically so. But I'm not obsessed, nor really that argumentative,

I'd much rather be a reverend in blue jeans—331

in the sense of a person who loves to argue and seeks out arguments, and never wants them to end. Instead, what I am is relentless.

Often, I really don't know when to stop, continuing a discussion long after other participants are weary, and running down the very last detail of a boring story despite the glassy looks of my audience. I know only too well that this relentlessness can be a problem, for myself and for others.

To give you an example, I once worked at a big company, in the mid to late '90s, and was part of an effort to build the company's, and the industry's, first web application. I not only did the documentation for the product but also assisted with the design and business analysis. The product was a success, and our director asked, "What's the next big thing?"

An emerging concept around this time was the web portal. New sites like CNN and Yahoo! were starting to bundle together lots of information, making it easy to access, and drawing huge numbers of viewers. The idea of a giant resource hosting all kinds of information rather than a single-purpose website was new and enticing, and as the decade grew older, portals such as MSN, Lycos, and Excite were giving traditional websites a run for their money.

The product group decided that we should build a web portal, and the buzz around this budding idea reached the president of the company. At a conference, the president strode up to me and asked, "What is a web portal and why do I need one?" I explained as best I could what we were planning; he nodded and walked away. He green-lighted the project and gave us a budget of $800K, lots more money at the end of the '90s than it is now.

I was assigned to work with the product marketing guy to hammer out the design for the portal. We produced proposal after proposal, but the VP of Marketing turned them all down. After nine months of this, it was obvious the guy had no notion of what he wanted. Like art, he only knew he hadn't seen it yet. My marketing counterpart brought up the idea of killing the project and turning the money back in. I was initially totally opposed this idea. I don't quit. I'm relentless. But eventually, after more ideas got rejected, I agreed it was useless to struggle further. We met with the VP and said, "We think the money should be used on something else. Perhaps next year we'll be able to agree on what a company portal would look like."

That was a valuable lesson for me. Sometimes you do really need to give up. But it's really not in my nature.

Another example: In high school biology class, the teacher gave us an in-class assignment. We were to take these cut up pieces of paper and, working together without words, assemble them into a square. The teacher divided us into two groups and gave each a box full of pieces.

My group struggled mightily to fit the pieces together, but it wasn't happening. Suddenly, a member of the other group, the student council president, started gesturing that we should combine our pieces. I refused to consider this, and held out, feverishly trying to solve the puzzle, until the others deserted me and merged our pieces with the other group's. Sure enough, all the pieces were from a larger square, and we had solved the problem, which was to cooperate. My relentlessness had obstructed progress.

I've tried to learn from these and other examples of counterproductive relentlessness, but it's hopeless. I will pursue a goal until long after it's obviously futile. This trait is both the key to my success—running down every detail for a corporate white paper—and an obstacle. It's a form of perfectionism, and I often remind myself of a famous aphorism, originally from the 17th century Italian, "Il meglio è nemico del bene" (The better is enemy of the good), later popularized by Voltaire as "better is the enemy of good" and now usually expressed as "Perfect is the enemy of good."

You see how I am?

It's a brilliant Miami afternoon and Charles and Chip are shooting the shit in the man cave and watching Casablanca for umpty-ninth time. The sun shines through the slats of the first-floor deck, drawing a slow-moving black and light shadow pattern on the hard floor of the room. Chip seems to be in a funk: no boisterous laughter, no good-natured ribbing, just quieter, energy-less, as if something is weighing on his mind. Charles barely notices. He's waiting for his friend to bring up his latest *World* article. For some reason, he wants Chip to bring it up and stubbornly waits, stewing. As the afternoon wears on, he gets more and more pissed. After an hour or so of watching the movie and talking about Bogie and Bacall, Charles can't stand it anymore.

"So, did you see my article in the *World*?"

"Yes, I did," Chip says coyly.

"Well?"

"That's a deep subject for a shallow mind," Chip says as if butter wouldn't melt in his mouth.

"Well, you tool, what did you think of it?"

"I think it was right on the mark. You are relentless. You don't quit. You don't give up, even when I've so very obviously bested you in an argument. You're a bulldog, it's true."

Charles says, "Wait, when have you ever bested me in an argument?"

"Well, boyo, just being the last person to say something doesn't mean you've won an argument. Often, I grow tired of your bullshit and just shut up. You're like the S.S. Relentless, or better, the Titanic—bam, bash, right into the iceberg, again and again and again."

Charles is shocked and angered by Chip's accusations. He studies his friend's face. He has noticed over the last few weeks that Chip's not his usual rosy self. His typically jolly expression is missing, and he looks tired and tense. Something must be bugging him, Charles thinks. Maybe that's why he's being so harsh on me. Charles sits and for a minute can't think of anything to say.

"But I love you anyway, you big lug," Chip says, jumping to his feet and coming over to Charles's couch to wrap him in a bear hug. Which Charles hates, and always has. Charles struggles to break free of the embrace, but he's no match for Chip's strength and so he just goes limp. Chip plants a big kiss on Charles's cheek and releases him.

"Oh, gross! You slobbering fool!" Despite his embarrassment, Charles is touched by Chip's show of affection. This does not prevent his entire face from becoming beet red. He thinks, God, he's acting strangely. Should I ask him what's up? Chip is staring impassively at the TV, idly munching on Dorito after Dorito.

Finally, Charles says, "What's up, big guy? You don't seem yourself today."

"Whom do I seem like?" Chip says, barely glancing at Charles.

"Like a Chip who's got something on his mind," Charles says.

"Like this chip?" Chip holds up a Dorito glistening with Velveeta.

"C'mon, man. Something's eating you. You want to share?"

"Not really. Let's change the subject." Chip slouches down on the couch and crosses his arms across his chest.

Charles at first is at a loss to come up with something to talk about. It doesn't seem like Chip wants to talk about the World article. Finally, he thinks about an article idea he got recently.

"OK, says Charles. "You want a new subject, here's one. What's the best song about masturbation?"

Chip says almost immediately, "'I Touch Myself,' by Divinyls. Hot chick. Always reminded me of Peggy Bundy from *Married...with Children*." Chip stirs on the couch to face Charles. He looks interested, and a little less gloomy, if not exactly cheerful.

"Yeah, that's a good one. Kinda blatant. The king of blatant beat-off songs in my book is 'My Ding-a-Ling' by Chuck Berry: 'every time the bell would ring / You'd catch me playing with my ding-a-ling.' So Pavlovian. I prefer stroke songs that kinda flew under the radar, like 'She Bop' by Cindy Lauper."

"Also good," Chip says. "But, shit, the lyrics are, 'Hey, hey, they say I better get a chaperone, / Because I can't stop messin' with the danger zone.' So only kinda subtle."

"Yup. But ask the average person, and they won't know it's about rubbing one out."

"Hey, a great blatant one is 'Darling Nikki,'" Chip says. "That's about as upfront as any song: 'masturbating with a magazine.'"

"You're right. Prince was always right up front about sex. I think one of the most obvious stroke songs was from the Buzzcocks. After all, they're a band named after a dildo, and their epic, 'Orgasm Addict' features the classic lyric, 'You get in a heat, you get in a sulk / But you still keep a-beating your meat to pulp.' They actually make orgasmic grunts instead of a bridge. Anyway, the reason I'm interested in self-abuse songs is I'm thinking of writing a column on the subject of subliminal masturbation."

"That seems like an oxymoron, you moron!" Chip shows a little more life.

"Funny. Not. But I'm looking for songs that are subtle, that fly under the radar. Like the Who's 'Pictures of Lily.'"

"Wait. That was about yanking the crank?" Chip is warming to the topic.

"Sure. Let's see." Charles pulls out his phone. "Here you go:

> I used to wake up in the morning
> I used to feel so bad

I got so sick of having sleepless nights
I went and told my dad

He said, son now here's some little something
And stuck them on my wall
And now my nights ain't quite so lonely
In fact I, I don't feel bad at all
I don't feel so bad at all"

Chip whooshed his hand over his head. "Totally missed that one. Cool! So 'Dancing with Myself' is too obvious, right?"

"Yeah, plus it's Billy Idol. Billy Idol only belongs on only one 'Best of' list: Best Sneer. Even better than Elvis."

"Them thar's some fightin' werds, bucko!" Chip is an Elvis freak. "Hmm, did Elvis ever do a masturbatory song, I wonder?"

"I don't think Presley did, but Elvis Costello did do 'Pump it Up,' which might have something to do with masturbation. It's hard to tell. Could be about just about anything. Could be about a blow-up girl, like The Police's 'Be My Girl' was. Anyway, Elvis himself said it was about drugs and his band."

Chip nods. "In the blatant category is Thomas Dolby's 'The Key to Her Ferrari.' You ever hear that one? I went through a serious Thomas Dolby phase. It's about coming at 100 miles an hour, all over the seat. Friends don't let friends drive with their dick in their hand."

Charles laughs and pantomimes driving and yanking. "Yeah, then there's 'Blister in the Sun'. It's a bit oblique, but it seems obvious how he stains his sheets, although it could be an alimentary problem."

"Alimentary, my dear Flotsam." Chip chuckles at his corny joke. Charles feels good that the discussion is cheering up his friend.

"Then there's Devo's 'Praying Hands'," Chip says, "where the guy may be using both hands to do himself, or he could be jacking off while diddling his lover."

"Don't know that one. Was never a big Devo fan. OK, here's a more-subtle one: 'Turning Japanese!'" Charles squinches up his eyes, opens his mouth wide, and pumps his fist over his crotch. "Not particularly PC, though," he says. "But it could make the list."

The two sit for a couple of minutes trying to think of more songs. "'Spank Thru' by Nirvana?" Chip says.

"Too obvious," Charles says, turning to his phone. "I'm just gonna Google it. Hmmm. Janet Jackson's 'If?' Don't know that one, but it's subtle: 'How many nights I've laid in bed excited over you / I've closed my eyes and thought of us a hundred different ways / I've gotten there so many times I wonder how 'bout you.' That works. Nice to get some diversity in there. Hmmm, here's a highbrow group going down and dirty: 'Billy Liar' by The Decemberists. But unfortunately, it's pretty blatant: 'hands in his pockets / Staring over at the neighbor's, knickers down.' So, no."

Charles scrolls a bit more. "Oh, ick! Britney Spears!? 'The more I come to understand the touch of my hand / The small of my back / The arch of my feet / Lately I've been noticing the beautiful me / I'm all in my skin and I'm not gonna wait / I'm into myself in a most precious way.' Ugh. Not on my list! Let's see, here's a Bjork song; not gonna do it. Madonna? Not a chance. The Pixies? Too depressing. Yuck! 'The Stroke,' Billy Squier—awful and blatant, oh, and 38 Special, 'Hold On Loosely'—not on my watch! Atlanta Rhythm Section 'Imaginary Lover'—yes! That's a keeper!"

"Are you almost done?"

"Yes, yes, oh yes, yes, yes, yes!" Charles shoots Chip a wry smile. Chip just shakes his head. "Actually," Charles says, "I think I just thought of the most subtle wank song ever: Jackson Browne's 'Rosie' from *Running on Empty*."

"Huh? That's about a groupie, although you could make the case that rock stars' use of groupies is masturbatory."

"It's only partially about a groupie. Let me get the lyrics up. Here. You know the refrain:

> Rosie, you're all right
> (You wear my ring)
> When you hold me tight
> (Rosie, that's my thing)
> When you turn out the light
> (I got to hand it to me)
> It looks like it's me and you again tonight, Rosie

"But what you fail to hear is a line that precedes this. At the beginning of the song, Jackson gets Rosie a backstage pass, but: 'when they walked off stage / You know, the drummer swept that girl away.' Jackson loses Rosie in the first verse! He's singing to his hand, your famous Madame Hand, Rosie Palm! 'You wear my ring'—he yanks left-handed or has a ring on his right. 'Rosie, that's my thing'—yeah, your ding-a-ling. 'I got to hand it to me' Oh, wonderful! This is the centerpiece of my article! Yasss!"

Chip nods in grudging admiration. "Well, I don't know how many times I've heard that song and didn't catch that. Nicely done. Now, what's the point of this article?"

"Wankers abound!"

"Wow. That'll make the front page of the *World*, easy!"

"OK, smart guy, how many times have you seen articles on masturbation in a daily newspaper?"

"Uh, probably never."

"Right. So, I got that going for me. But even better, since the context is music lyrics, I'm going to try to present the self-gratification urge as a case of misheard lyrics, your self mishearing the song of the procreative urge."

"Hah?" Chip looks confused. "Come again?"

"Ah! I see what you did there!" Charles laughs. "Maybe I can work that into the article: Masturbation is mankind mishearing something the Universe said and saying, 'Come again?' But I will explain in simple terms that a guy like you can understand."

"Oh, I would be most grateful, Master Bates," Chip sneers.

"Sit at my feet and learn, acolyte." Chip rolls his eyes. "So, you're familiar with Whitman's 'I Sing the Body Electric,' right?" Chip nods and makes a "No, duh" face.

"Well, I think that poem is about wanking, at least partly. Dig: 'The armies of those I love engirth me and I engirth them / They will not let me off till I go with them, respond to them.' Walt was getting busy with these armies, engirthing and whatnot."

"Oh, you can't be serious! That poem was groundbreaking in its celebration of the worth of the body, and of people, and disputing the common feeling that the body was corrupt, and the soul was pure."

"Take it easy, sāmaṇera! I'm just talking about the opening lines and the fact that Whitman in later stanzas lists the features of bodies in a way that sounds masturbatory. So, if I take this poem's title literally—Whitman's singing; it's a song—it's another case of the listener not hearing the meaning properly—mishearing lyrics, in other words. Similarly, onanism can be seen as the body mishearing the procreative urge and, rather than getting busy with another human, as the urge intends, turns inward and whacks off."

"OK, OK, I get your premise. Just leave Whitman out of it!"

"Yeah, you're probably right. It's a bit too esoteric for my audience. But do you get what I'm saying?" Chip nods reluctantly. "Add in many religions' prohibition of masturbation, upon pain of sin or even banishment—you remember my John Mittney chapter, right?—and the whole subject of self-love gets all tangled up in shame and repression. Yet, as in our song discussion just now, masturbation still pokes through in art."

"You did not just say 'pokes through' Obvious Boy!" Chip smacks his forehead in disgust.

Charles chuckles. "I did, and I meant it! So, we have two ways in which messages are misheard: We mishear our body's urge to make babies, and we mishear, or fail to hear, masturbatory messages in the lyrics we discussed. It's similar in literature. Sometimes these messages are blatant, as in *Portnoy's Complaint*, which was totally scandalous in its time for even discussing masturbation."

"You make a good point there, for a change," Chip says, finally feeling comfortable as the discussion turns to an area of his expertise. "In pre-modern literature, it was scandalous to discuss the physical act of love, but discussing self-love was beyond scandalous, although there were veiled references as far back as medieval literature. *Fanny Hill* was written in the mid-1700s, and is pretty explicit, and is the first porn novel in English. But it really wasn't until the 20th century that novelists dared write openly about beating off. Even though Joyce had Bloom pull his pud in *Ulysses*, he dressed it up with so many metaphors that you might not have even noticed. Jean Genet's *Our Lady of the Flowers* is one big wank. And Faulkner's protagonist in *As I Lay Dying* literally gets blown by the wind!"

"All good material for my article! That last bit gives new meaning to 'the answer, my friend, is blowin' in the wind!' Anyway, I want to mix religion into the article as well. It seems like all religions are based on misheard lyrics from the universal song, stuff we can't quite hear right and thus misinterpret. Or, like Springsteen's 'Born in the USA' we just pick out parts we like and interpret them wrong. Have you ever really listened to that song?"

"Sure," Chip says. "It's a stone bummer: 'Down in the shadow of the penitentiary / Out by the gas fires of the refinery / I'm ten years burning down the road / Nowhere to run ain't got nowhere to go.' You show that verse to a hundred people and 99 of 'em couldn't identify the song."

"That's what I'm talking about. Humanity has a hearing problem. They hear the chorus, but not the verse. And perhaps the biggest thing they're not hearing clearly is the message from the Universe."

The two men sit in silence, drinking their beers. Although Chip had cheered up somewhat during the first part of their conversation, his gloomy mood returned with this left turn into Springsteen's bummer song. Chip begins thinking about his calling and his religion. Could I have misheard the message? Misheard the call? I have to admit, there are a lot of parts of Methodism that I don't think make sense, where what I think is right is at odds with what my religion teaches. Could it be that I have wasted my life? Is Charles not a deluded man who has wandered away from faith but instead a clearer thinker than I am? Chip looks over at his friend, who is staring out the glass sliding doors, obviously furiously thinking about his article. Charles sees him looking and says, "Sorry, I was just writing the article in my head."

Chip gets up and says, "I need another beer. You?" Charles turns his head, distracted, nods and resumes staring out the sliding glass doors. Chip grabs two beers, hands one to Chip and says, "I need some air. I'm going out to the backyard." Charles, still intensely thinking, just grunts, and Chip pulls the sliding door and steps outside. He walks around the pool and down the slope toward the ancient sinkhole. He stops and turns around, walking back to the garage from which he emerges carrying a quart of motor oil. He unlatches the gate to the chain link safety fence that surrounds the sinkhole, walks to its lip, opens the oil, and pours it into the water several feet below. Then he sits on the edge of the hole, swatting mosquitos, drinking beer, and pondering his life.

After half an hour, Charles comes out to join him. "What's up with you, Chip?" he says.

"Nothing. I'm just tired I think." Charles sees the empty motor oil bottle and asks, "What's the deal with this?"

"Hmmm?" Chip says distractedly. "Oh, it's for the skeeters." Chip points at the water at the bottom of the sinkhole. "The stinkers breed in any standing water, so I periodically pour a quart of oil in the hole. Keeps 'em from breeding. Kills the larvae." Chip stares glumly into the hole.

"Ah! Interesting. Say, with this sinkhole and all, aren't you afraid your house is going to sink?"

"Nah. This parsonage was built in 1922 and the hole had been around probably for decades before that. It's stable. The only pain is, I have to maintain this fence around it that keeps the dogs, the toddlers, and the stupid from falling in." Chip waves his arm to indicate the rusty chain link fence which has periodic bright patches where it obviously has been mended.

Chip seems so gloomy. Charles is getting more and more worried. "You sure you don't want to tell me what's bugging you?"

"Nah. I'm OK. Just a little low." Chip grimaces. "I'll be OK."

Trixie comes out onto the deck and says, "Chip, come in and get dressed for the wake."

"Ah, shit," Chip says to Charles. "I forgot Old Man Keeler's wake. Nuts. Smell you later, buddy."

"OK," Charles says. "Call if you need to." Chip gives Charles a hug and walks up the hill to get ready to go.

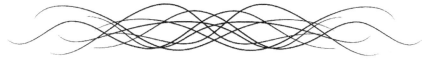

The next afternoon, Trixie calls Charles. "Charles, it's Chip. He's been arrested!" Trixie's voice is quivering and hoarse, as if she'd been crying for some time.

"Oh, my god, Trixie! What happened? Why?"

"They arrested him on . . . weapons charges!" Trixie begins to sob. Charles is boggled by the news.

"Weapons charges? Chip's never owned or even shot a gun, has he?"

Trixie blows her nose and tries to calm herself. "Charles, when he saw the cop cars pull up in front of the house, Chip told me he had been collecting guns from gangbangers for a gun buyback program that his buddy, Pastor Dabrezil, from Haitian Immanuel Baptist, got him involved with. Neither of them knew it was a scam. He said it was apparently run by a crooked cop out of Miami Gardens. Dabrezil got roped in by the pastor at Antioch Missionary Baptist Church. That fuckin' cop was selling the guns to the Haitian Batay Ouvriye militants. Oh, Charles, Chip's in so much trouble!"

"OK, Trixie, let's try to be rational here. So, Chip told you all this?" Trixie says yes in a very small voice. "OK, so that's what happened. And if so, then

Chip and Dabrezil and the Antioch pastor are patsies. They'll just get their hands slapped, maybe not even go to trial."

"They will? You really think so?"

"Yes, I do. Think of the headlines if the cops jail three pastors who were only trying to get guns off the streets. They were duped. It's the cop who will go away for a long time."

"What if they don't catch the cop?"

"Well, let's just not go there. Where's Chip now?"

"He's at the Pre-Trial Detention Center downtown. We can see him at 5:30."

"OK, good. So, I'll come over now and sit with you, and then later, we'll go see him together."

Charles hangs up and drives over to the parsonage to console Trixie. On the way he thinks, so that's why Chip has been acting so weird lately. I'll bet the package Chip took over to Emmanuel that night we had pizza was guns. And that day we played basketball at the church, I'll bet that package I saw Chip take from the guy in the car was a gun. Jeez, Chip, what did you get yourself into?

By the time Charles and Trixie arrived at the detention center, Trixie was a basket case. I'd never believe that Trixie could ever be so emotional, Charles thinks. She's always so no-nonsense and in charge. I would have thought she'd have stormed on down to the center and kicked some ass. He glances at Trixie who is clenching her fists, digging her fingernails into her palms, very obviously trying to keep it together. "It'll be OK, Trixie. We'll get him out of this."

Trixie looks at him and says softly, "I hope you're right."

After waiting a half an hour, Trixie and Charles are ushered into the visitation room. Cripes, this looks like a cliché out of some bad cop movie, Charles thinks. Smudged glass and telephone receivers on armored cables. They sit down just as Chip is led into the cubicle. He turns and thanks the guard, who smiles and slaps him five. Charles sits down smiling but as he turns to see Trixie, his face falls. He lifts the receiver. Trixie grabs at the receiver and fumbles it, causing it to knock loudly against the glass as it falls to the ledge below. She picks it up and says, "Oh, Chip," before bursting into tears. Charles decides it will be best if he turns around while the two talk, or rather, while Chip talks and Trixie mostly cries. Eventually, Trixie says, "He wants to talk with you."

Charles hugs Trixie and takes the phone. Trying to keep it light, Charles says, "Looks like you're making friends in there."

"Oh, Clyde? He's actually an old friend and a former church member. But, yeah, you know I'm always friendly and glad to meet new people. I talked with several people in the holding cell. Might have a couple of new counseling clients when they get out."

"So how are you holding up?"

"Fair to middlin'. Actually, kind of relieved."

"Huh?"

"Yes, you may have noticed that I've been, ah, a little testy recently?"

"Yes, especially yesterday. Did you see this coming?"

"Kinda. Pastor Dabrezil got suspicious the last time he met with Patrolman Beaugelove Dajuste two days ago. The guy seemed bugged and jittery and said that he couldn't reimburse us for the guns for a while—we were fronting $75 a pop, to coin a phrase. Agwé, that's Pastor Dabrezil's first name, called the Miami Gardens police station to enquire and found they didn't have a gun buyback program. Agwé called me yesterday and told me the cops were real interested in what he told them, and he wouldn't be surprised if we heard from them. Well, we did. And now I'm here."

"By the holy old dynamiting Jesus!"

"Hey, good one. I've never heard that oath."

"It's from Nova Scotia. You don't want to know how I came to hear it. But seriously, they can't actually think a bunch of pastors was running a gun ring."

"Well, they probably will realize that, but for the moment, I'm stuck in the slammer. And I don't have any money for a lawyer, so I'll have to have a public defender."

"I can't see this going to trial."

"Well, the cops told me they can't find that fucker, Dajuste, whom I never met. Without him, they've got a trio of pastors to take the fall."

"But think of the bad press."

"That didn't stop them from crucifying that Haitian Pastor in West Palm Beach who left his wife for her best friend. It was all over the news. And this would be juicier: 'Pastor Gang Sells Guns to Haitian Militants.' I just don't know why I was so stupid. I just took Agwé at his word that we were helping a legitimate buyback program. There were so many red flags: the Miami guns were going to Miami Gardens, not Miami. We were turning them in via another pastor who was giving them to a cop. I never thought of checking to see if Miami Gardens was doing a buyback. Last time they did one, it was all over the news. I'm an idiot!"

"Well, you're in the faith business. You always think the best about anyone you meet. You shouldn't be hard on yourself. Look, I'm going to help. I'm going to find that pig-fucker Dajuste."

"Hey, Sgt. Friday, hold your horses! Leave that to the authorities. Since this thing involves another country—the guns are going to Haiti—the feds will be all over it soon unless I miss my guess. You've been watching too much TV."

"Doesn't matter. I'm going to help. I've got some ideas how Dajuste might have been getting the guns out of the country and back to Haiti. I've got your back."

"Take care of Trixie for me, will you?" Chip looks older than when Charles arrived. His usually cheerful face is sagging, the façade of sunniness gone.

"You can count on it, amigo. When do you think you'll get out on bail?"

"They said maybe tomorrow. I'm seeing the judge at 10 am. The big question will be if I can afford the bond."

"I'm positive I can raise the bond by talking to a few church members. Don't worry about that."

Chip nods, and signals to the bailiff. He blows a kiss to Trixie, who had quit crying and was sitting straight and stoic in her chair, wiping her eyes.

The next day, Charles drove Trixie to the bail hearing. Bail was granted at $10,000. Charles put the $1,000 bond on his credit card; Chip was released and the three of them drove back to Chip and Trixie's house. After getting his friends settled in, Charles took off, driving to a nearby coffee shop to use the Wi-Fi.

OK, let's find this bastard on social media, Charles thinks, bringing up Google and plugging in the officer's name. Just as I suspected, there's not a lot of Beaugelove Dajustes in the world. I got him on Facebook, Twitter, and LinkedIn. On Facebook, Dajuste's interests include the Haitian rum Barbencourt. In addition, he follows the rum's page and posts there quite often. Hmmm. He also belongs to four Barbencourt groups and raves about the liquor on all of them. Seems to be quite the Barbencourt head. That stuff's made in Haiti. Who's bringing it into Miami, I wonder?

After some more digging, Charles discovers that the local distributor of Barbencourt is located in, of all places, Miami Gardens. What are the chances, Charles thinks. A big boat comes in from Haiti with Barbencourt and leaves with cases of wine for the tourist trade that have the odd pistol inside. It could work that way. Let's see if we can find out who works at the distributor. Charles opens LinkedIn and types in Dajuste. Well, what do you know? There's a Stéphanie Dajuste who's a sales consultant there. Wife or sister? Doesn't matter. I think I should stake out that warehouse and see if there's any late-night activity tonight. Dajuste will be wanting to get rid of all his iron as soon as possible.

That evening at 8 o'clock, Charles parks in the driveway of a roofing company across the street from the distributor. He's partially hidden by a tall bush but has a good view of the loading area. He settles in for a long boring vigil and starts listening to "5 Minutes of Rum" podcasts on his earbuds.

Around 10 o'clock, a dark Ford Focus drives slowly down the empty street. Charles hunches lower in his seat and takes off his earbuds. The Focus drives into the loading dock area and a stocky man in jeans and a polo shirt gets out. Monsieur Beaugelove Dajuste, I presume, Charles thinks, fitting his telephoto lens to his cell phone and snapping some quick pictures. A door by the dock opens, spilling light onto the car and the man as he climbs the stairs carrying a heavy cardboard box. Charles can see the silhouette of a woman inside the warehouse. The couple speaks briefly and enters the warehouse.

OK, that's really circumstantial. Perhaps I'll see some foolishness with one of the shipping containers sitting at the bays. Sure enough, light starts streaming through the gap between a trailer and the dock. Charles gets out of his car with his cell and creeps up closer. He hears a big creak and a clank as the container doors are opened. Figures begin moving back and forth through the light. Charles gets a little closer. It's of no use. Even with the telephoto, he can't get clear shots of the people as they pass the gap. He decides to retreat to his car to see if he can get a picture of Dajuste's face as he leaves.

Soon, the dock door opens, and the man comes out, followed by the woman. In the yellow sodium light of the loading area, Charles can barely make out their features as he snaps away, hoping to get a clear picture of a face. The woman says goodbye and walks down the road to the employee parking area. As the man backs out, Charles gets a great shot of his license plate. Gotcha, you nincompoop, he thinks. The man takes off down the street to the left. Perhaps I can get a plate on her, too. He starts his car but doesn't turn on the headlights. He creeps down the street toward the only car left in the parking area. The woman starts her car and backs out into the street. As she drives off, Charles follows her and gets a clear shot of her license plate.

Well, that was easier than I thought, Charles thinks. That shipment could go out tomorrow, so I better get on over to the cop house right away and give them my evidence.

Once there, it took some doing to convince the front desk sergeant to roust a special investigations detective. An hour later, a casually dressed detective with an annoyed look on his face comes in and walks with Charles to a conference room that has a TV.

"I'm Detective Barker, and who might you be?" Charles introduces himself and briefly describes his surveillance, then casts the pictures and video he shot to the TV. Unfortunately, the people's faces are too blurry and dark for an ID. Charles tells Barker his theory about the gun-running operation.

"You need to stop that container from going anywhere tomorrow," Charles says.

The detective nods and asks, "How come you're involved in this case?"

"Pastor Chip is my best friend in the world. I know he was duped somehow, and he had the best of intentions."

"Do you think the man in your photos is Dajuste?"

"I wouldn't say that, but I suspect that. Run the plates and see what you get."

Detective Barker calls Charles at 8 am the next morning, rousting him out of bed. "Looks like you cracked the case, Mr. DeFries," he says. "The plates match Dajuste's and his sister's cars. We got the Feds to seize the truck and, sure enough, they found about 100 pistols in the wine cases. We found the sister and sweated her a little, and she told us Dajuste was staying with a friend on the Beach and planned to charter a Sea Ray to get him to the Bahamas. We nabbed him and have him in custody."

"Oh, thank goodness!" Charles says. "Did you tell Pastor Chip?"

"No, I figured you'd want to do that," Barker says. "You know, we usually discourage the Junior G-Man thing, but I have to admit, you did a great job of nabbing a bad cop. We thank you."

"You're welcome. Now I just hope Pastor Chip gets a break."

After he hangs up with the detective, Charles calls Chip. "OK, dude, I cracked the case."

"What you talkin' about, Willis?" Chip says. "Come again?"

"I'd be happy to. A little detective work on the web, a little surveillance, a little cooperation from the Miami Gardens detectives, and our boy Dajuste is in the slammer awaiting arraignment. Case closed."

"What the fuck? You're serious?"

"I'm as serious as a poutine shortage in Chicoutimi during a curling bonspiel," Charles says, grinning.

"What the hell are you talking about?"

"That's another Canadian expression, via *How I Met Your Mother*. Some time I need to tell you about my adventure up there, but right now, dude, you're mostly in the clear!"

"Is that like being only mostly dead?" Chip could never resist a *Princess Bride* reference.

"I think it's a damn sight better than being any kind of dead. I think we should celebrate, I'll come by and take you and Trixie to dinner, although it's really you who should take me to dinner, given how I've saved your massive ass and all." Chip roared with laughter and said, "Done. But you have to drive. Oh! And you've reminded me of a joke!"

"Criminy. I save your butt and you pay me back by telling me one of your stinkin' jokes?"

"So, back when he was president, Barack Obama was out jogging when he tripped, fell over a bridge railing, and landed in the creek below. Before the Secret Service guys could get to him, three kids, who had been fishing, pulled him out of the water. He was so grateful he offered the kids whatever they wanted.

"The first kid said, 'I want to go to Disney World.'

"Obama said, 'No problem. I'll take you there on Air Force One.'

"The second kid said, 'I want a new pair of Nike Air Jordans.'

"Obama said, 'I'll get them for you and even have Michael sign them!'

"The third kid said, 'I want a motorized wheelchair with a built-in TV and gaming console!'

"Obama is a little perplexed by this and says, 'But you don't look like you are handicapped.'

"The kid says, 'I will be after my dad finds out I saved your ass from drowning!'" Chip's laugh booms through the phone so loudly, Charles needs to pull it away from his ear.

"OK, maybe I don't want to take you guys out to celebrate after all," Charles shouts before ending the call.

I'd kill him in the Bible, and raise the rent

Steppenwolf—*The Pusher*

Charles was working on his Snagology website when he got a PayPal alert. Who the fuck has sent me money, he thought. He opened the PayPal app and saw that not one, but three people had sent him the $60 membership fee from the Snagology.com website. Oh my god! This is great! I haven't even started to publicize my new religion and I've got converts!

Hmmm. They all have the same last name. It's a family! Wow. Now I've got to get to work on the credo. Charles concentrated on perfecting the Credo page, then read it over to proofread it.

Snagology Credo

Snagology is the belief that there are pan-Universal reality show viewers who get a perverse kick out of me running into physical and virtual snags. Here are the tenets of Snagology.

Is it Solipsistic in Here or is it Just Me?

The first and most important tenet: I am the only person in the Universe, and I exist for the entertainment of the Viewerverse.

The Viewerverse is Entertained by Snags

Snags in my life, both physical snags (belt loops, wires, shoelaces) and metaphorical snags (unbelievably rare or devastatingly unlikely incidents) are entertaining or comical to the Viewerverse.

Renewal Equals Everlasting Life

I believe the Snag Masters control my fate, and that I must please them by reacting to these evidently hilarious snags in a comical way. Rather than gaining everlasting life by dying, as in most religions, I'm hoping to get everlasting life by pleasing my Snag Masters, so they renew me every season, forever.

The Origin of Snagology

All my life, I've been plagued by snags—constant, sometimes highly improbable, snags—physical snags, situational snags, general life snags. I started hoping this was all leading somewhere, like to some dramatic, life-saving snag that keeps me from plunging to my death.

One day I had a revelation: What if this is some kind of hilarious comic entertainment for a cosmic audience who find snags to be funny? It would explain why my life's just chock full of snags. And to an audience with a sick sense of humor, these snags and pratfalls could be comical.

After this revelation, I started congratulating the puppet masters of the Universe for their novel snags and engaging in imaginary conversations suggesting that they give me a break, or sarcastically thanking them for their attention, or asking them why they have it in for me.

Dreams are Voyages Through Other Universes

When I dream, these same Viewerverse denizens, or maybe the night shift, flip the channels on me to see how well they can confuse me. Or perhaps it's the maintenance crew, setting me up for the snags of the coming day.

In dreams, I pass from this universe through many others. My consciousness tries to make sense of the various transitions, which explains some of the weirdness of dreams. Sometimes I can fly; sometimes I'm running in glue—in a universe with different physical laws. And sometimes I meet doppelgängers of people I know in this universe, who behave in odd ways. But it's all true. It's all my experience, just in different times and places.

Aspects of the Viewerverse

There are other signs of the existence of the Viewerverse.

I think the universe that is controlling ours intersects with our universe at an angle, about 11.2 degrees in fact.

I've noticed over the years that when I'm not paying attention, I hold glasses and cups at about an 11-degree angle. There's no good reason for this, and not only that, it generally happens at about 11 degrees in a southwesterly direction. Not so coincidentally, that's about half of the tilt of the Earth from the ecliptic, and the difference between the North Pole and magnetic north is 11.2 degrees.

Plus, I think I can hear the Viewerverse, at least some of the audience. I sleep with earplugs. The least little noise wakes me up. I've discovered that you can hear some things better when you've got earplugs in. Often, when I'm lying in bed waiting to go to sleep, I can kind of hear these voices. I hear the rhythm of their conversation and their tones of voice, and it does seem like English, but I can't make out the words. It's like a far-off radio program muffled by a pillow. They are carrying on conversations, and not speaking to me. I'm eavesdropping. It's hard to say if they're talking about me.

So, one of the precepts of Snagology is: Wear earplugs to bed.

Just Keep Them Interested

My goal, and the mantra of Snagology, is: Just Keep Them Interested. Like MIT cosmologist Max Tegmark said: "If you're not sure, at the end of the night, whether you're actually simulated or not, my advice to you is to go out there and live really interesting lives, and do unexpected things, so the simulators don't get bored and shut you down."

Adopting Snagology

If any follower would like to prove they are a Snag Star, they must join Snagology and keep current with their tithing. Such followers must join the community and be subject to the questioning therein and from me as to the merit of their claim to Snag Stardom.

Should a follower convince me that they are a fellow Snag Star, they shall be blessed with that title and partake of the tithing. They must forsake all other religions.

Join now and prove I'm not unique.

OK, that's as good as it's going to get at the moment, Charles thought, and he pushed the update button to refresh the web page. Now I've got to create some kind of official certificate indicating membership in Snagology. He looked up some clip art and built a certificate in PowerPoint.

There. Now I can send my three new acolytes their official Snagology certificates. I think I'll use the $180 to do some Facebook advertising. Next, I need to set up the community software on the website.

Charles formally unveiled his Snagology website on April 1st. He paid for Facebook and other social media ads and also posted comments on religious and atheist websites. He anxiously watched the traffic statistics and saw a steady stream of people coming to the site, but only two more memberships. He offered to pay his five congregants half the tithe of any new member they sponsored and got a half dozen more.

This is going nowhere fast, he thought. Perhaps I have to hit the speaking circuit. He booked himself into several Unitarian meetings and a couple of atheist and secular humanist Meetups, including getting a keynote spot on the Black Nonbelievers convention at sea. This last took some doing because not only was he not black, but he was pushing a religion. His audiences ranged from flabbergasted to tentatively accepting to actively hostile. Nonetheless, the trickle of members grew to a stream.

Charles maintained a regular schedule of "Ask Me Anything" events on the Snagology site, discussing and arguing with members who challenged his assertion of being the only being in the Universe. While he enjoyed these sparring sessions, he enjoyed even more the litany of snagging stories that poured into the Snagology community from new members. People were snagging themselves on all manner of objects, including silverware drawers, wire fences, folding chairs, and errant tree roots. The most offending object was the lever-style door handle. Interestingly there was a pattern to these snags. The people who were the most snagged by these handles were between 5'6" and 5"10" probably because their belt loops were the same height as the handles.

The most snagged objects after belt loops were pants pockets, headphone cords, keys on lanyards, backpacks, and surgical gowns and scrubs. Charles was fascinated by the banality of these events. Even if they don't seem hilarious to me, perhaps the Viewerverse is roaring with laughter, he thought.

There were some snags that seemed worthy of investigation for Snag Master involvement. One poor schmuck got a screen door handle embedded in the crook of his elbow. Another snagged her nose ring in a holey towel and ripped it from her nostril. After hearing this and other potentially deadly snag stories, Charles theorized that either there really were other people in the Universe, or the Viewerverse Snag Lords had a dark enough sense of humor to throw these stories at him as a way to mess with his mind. As the stories accumulated, he slowly began to realize that he might not be the most-snagged person in existence.

Charles started engaging in the online community with an interesting acolyte named Lawrence. As they argued back and forth via text message, to Charles's surprise, he started to think there might be other beings in the world.

During a conversation early one Saturday evening, Charles was holding his own until Lawrence messaged, "Solipsism is the opposite of empathy. You have to have zero emotional understanding of others to be a solipsist." Good point, Charles thought. Am I really devoid of empathy? I'm a solitary introvert, but I don't think I lack compassion or empathy. As Charles thought this over, Lawrence typed, "What would Jeannie think about you being a solipsist?" Charles was stunned. His jaw dropped as his confusion mounted. He read the message again and again. He replied, "WTF? 😕 "

Lawrence continued, "She became the ghost in the machine to save the fucking world. Can an electric ghost count as another universal being?"

Son of a bitch, Charles thought, and typed, "Fuckin' hell! Is that you Chip?"

Chip replied, "Took you long enough, shit for brains! 'Tis I, your loyal opponent who, BTW, shelled out 60 clams just so I could pull your leg a bit. You're fond of quoting that Chaos Magick guy about the Universe being a joke played upon itself. Well, me and Uni sure pulled one over on you. Laughter is your only tenable reaction to the major con I just ran on you!!!!!!! 👋 Sucked you right in! And BTW, you owe me a coupla dinners for sure on accounta I had to pay to metaphorically pants you, Slim."

"Oh, my fucking god! Damn. You got me good, asshole! What's worse is you about had me convinced there was another soul in this Universe. And if there were to be only one, I'd hope it'd be you."

"Shucks, you sappy asshole. You're gonna make me cry. I still can't believe you fell for it. I even used my real name." Charles had forgotten that Chip's first name was Lawrence. Damn, did he put one over on me!

Chip typed, "Now where are we going to dinner? It better be someplace expensive. And I'm feeling kinda hungry."

Later, at dinner, after about 15 minutes of Chip crowing over his victory, Charles decides to try to change the subject. "Look, you made a good point there, Larry." Chip gives him a sharp look and then points at Charles. "That's one. You get one." Charles smiles. He knows Chip hates his given name, but he had to get back at him somehow. Charles continues, "I get it, what you said. Solipsism is the anti-empathy—pain only means my pain. There is no concept of others' pain. But if others are just shadows on the wall of my existence, can't I still feel empathy for them? Like they're a movie that makes me sad? Does feeling really need to be just for real people? You didn't cry when Old Yeller died?"

"Oh, sure," Chip concedes, "you could look at it that way. But don't you think a solipsistic mindset would inevitably devolve into a lack of empathy or other positive feelings for the simulated others in your universe? That's only one of the problems with your sham religion. Here's another one: You can't have a religion comprised of one person."

"Dude, I have almost 1,000 apprentice Snag Stars now. I'm rolling in dough. Plus, anytime I feel like a good argument, I engage them, like I did you, and watch as they struggle to convince me of their reality."

"This can't end well for you, buddy. These fools are gonna want their money back . . ."

"They sign an agreement that there are no refunds."

"Yeah, but you offer to cut them in on the cash if they can convince you they're real . . ."

"The agreement stipulates that it's at my own discretion. I'm in charge. It's perfect. What I can't believe is that so many people have joined. Sure, at some point, I may need to accept a few acolytes into the money even if only just to help count it."

"I still worry about you, man. Seriously. This could turn into pissed off villagers with torches."

Charles had to agree there could be a downside. Well, he thinks, there's only a thousand members so far. How bad could it get?

When Snagology reached 20,000 members, Charles found out. He had accepted only a small fraction of the acolytes as Snag Stars, and the rest were clamoring for recognition and, not coincidentally, a piece of the now quite substantial pie. Charles had to modify the precepts of his religion to create several new categories of followers, with each getting a little piece of the action.

One day, Chip told him, "Dude, this is so out of hand. You're building a multilevel marketing pyramid scheme, not a religion."

Charles had to agree. He had never intended Snagology to be hierarchical. That was antithetical to his opposition to established religions. I wanted an egalitarian religion of which I was the head, he thought. It was almost a spoof and a goof on the gullibility of humankind. But now I've got responsibilities, and the craving for position, and leaders, and structure is driving me crazy. Plus, it's taking all my time. I've got no time to finish my novel.

One night, Charles read an article about antimatter. Scientists' current theory is that there was an equal amount of matter and antimatter immediately after the Big Bang. The two types of matter should have annihilated one another, and the Universe should never have formed. But it did because one matter particle per billion managed to survive. Scientists can't figure out why. They figure there must be some difference between the matter and antimatter, like differences in mass or charge. But there is no observable difference.

One passage in the article hit Charles like a punch in the gut: "Researchers have observed spontaneous transformations between particles and their antiparticles, occurring millions of times per second before they decay. Some unknown entity intervening in this process in the early universe could have caused these 'oscillating' particles to decay as matter more often than they decayed as antimatter." Wow, Charles thought. Some force must have kept, and continues to keep, the two apart.

Charles was struck with an inspiration: God keeps them apart! God insulates us from total destruction. God makes our existence possible.

He sat paralyzed in his chair, his mind racing. Maybe this is the answer to life, the universe, and everything I've been looking for. It's like that Emo Philips joke: "I pray a simple prayer every morning. It's an ecumenical prayer. I think it speaks to the heart of every faith. It goes, 'Lord, please break the laws of the Universe for my convenience.'"

Whatever that force is that intervened, it's either God or evidence of God, Charles thought, ensuring, nanosecond by nanosecond, that the Universe doesn't explode. This changes everything, literally.

Because of this revelation, and also his dissatisfaction with the religion he created, Charles decided he could no longer in good conscience keep promoting Snagology. He resolved to divest himself of the religion.

Charles started making discreet inquiries on the Internet for a buyer for Snagology. He concentrated on online evangelist networks, of which there were surprisingly many, including one that focused on evangelist marketing ideas. Eventually, he got a few nibbles, and one in particular looked interesting. It was a woman who had just come into a large inheritance.

Paula was in her mid-40s and was looking for meaning in her life. She was from a business-oriented, non-religious family that had prized material success over all else. But she knew there had to be more to life than the accumulation of money and things. Insular and never married, her only exposure to religion had been through a friend who was hooked on TV evangelists. They seemed to her to be just like the businessmen her family interacted with: bullies in empty suits.

Not long after her parents died two weeks apart, Paula had stumbled upon the Snagology website. It was a revelation for her.

"I'm plagued by snags, just like you," she told Charles when they talked. "Your site is the first true thing I've found in my quest for meaning."

Charles was flattered, but Paula's attitude made him wonder if he was just enabling yet another evangelistic con artist.

He thought, she wants the money, but she seems honestly interested in the premise of Snagology. And she's got the means to build Snagology further. Eventually, Charles decided she was the one, and together they created a contract which licensed Snagology and the website to Paula subject to several rules, including some that limited Paula's ability to exploit the religion for her own gain.

After a little back and forth, they struck a deal. Charles would get a one-time payout and remain the titular founder of Snagology. He would be paid a stipend based on the revenues of the website. He would have no other relationship with the religion. Paula would step in as its head and run the religion within the guidelines they had agreed upon.

Once the deal was signed, sealed, and delivered, Charles was relieved to be out from under the administrative burden of running Snagology. He was no longer as sure about the existence of the Viewerverse as he had been when he began the religion. Clearly, he thought, my discovery of a godlike property of the Universe doesn't mean this is not a simulation built for the enjoyment of a pan-universal audience. But there is some positive force out there, as I've always expected.

There is a reason to believe.

I have finally found a place to live / In the penance of the Lord

Blind Faith—*Presence of the Lord*

The October day Charles was to move dawned humid and perfect, as usual. There's nothing like Miami, he thought as he wiped the sleep from his eyes. Especially now that I can afford a condo at the beach.

October had always been a month of reflection for Charles. It seemed that old memories and especially old regrets would surface unbidden all month. For no apparent reason, Charles would find himself dwelling on ancient insults and foolish behavior, unkind words spoken and regretted, feeling again the raw hurt as if it were current. When he had lived in the North, he attributed the timing of these floods of remembrance to the change of seasons, but here in Florida, in the absence of seasonal cues, the nostalgic rerunning of emotion continued as before. Charles has the worst time with recurring regretful memories in the fall, especially October, and also in the spring. Spring reawakens memory that lies as dormant as the tulip, Charles thought. But when it blooms, its fruit is often bitter.

A memory would surge in like a wave, often causing Charles to hold his breath and wince. The memories were not the same each season, but there were some commonly occurring ones: unkind words he said, stupid mistakes he made, chances he took that turned out badly. Charles would be going along fine and, bam, one would hit him, and he relived the horrible moment.

While packing up his desk, Charles pulled out a list he keeps of regrets, ironically titled, "For the Forgiveness of Sins." The list was an ineffectual attempt a few years ago to put these ghostly visitors to rest. If I commit these to paper, he thought, perhaps I can forget about them. It didn't help. Charles looked at the list, sighed, and added a couple more items to the list.

Charles had always looked upon these unwanted memories as a reflection of his attitude towards whatever his current situation was. The déjà vu was worst when he was unhappiest. Actually, he realized as he brushed his teeth, so much has been happening this month, there hasn't been time enough for the traditional October preoccupation with the past to intrude, until yesterday.

All through the previous day, as he packed, Charles had reflected on the old Chinese curse Chip had once told him: May all your dreams come true. Selling Snagology for big bucks and having his messiah novel *Misheard Lyrics* accepted by a big publisher had come pretty close to fulfilling all of his dreams. What was left? As he worked to finish packing for the move, Charles inevitably ran into little bits of his past and was nagged by the feeling that deep down he knew what was missing. Each time he tried to confront the feeling, it remained out of reach.

Now, while brushing his teeth, a conversation he had a few months ago with Chip kept returning to his mind. After listening quietly to Charles's attacks on religion, Chip, possibly fed up with Charles's attitude, had said, "You know what Dylan said, Chuck, you're gonna have to serve somebody. Might be God, might be the Devil, might just be yourself, but it's true, you do gotta serve somebody."

"Look, don't go quoting Dylan on the subject of religion," Charles had said. "He's even more mixed up than the rest of us on that score. You know I'm not only an agnostic but also a radical pessimist: Whatever happens is for the worst. I don't see any Supreme Being taking care of my business."

"But he does! You've no idea how complete your life will be once you decide to believe. Just believe, and the crazy evil world no longer matters. It's you who's saved. It's you who has a personal relationship with God."

Charles hadn't let Chip know at the time, but their long arguments about religion and faith had stirred uncomfortable feelings within him. These feelings were magnified by his recent thoughts about the force in the Universe keeping matter and antimatter from annihilating everything.

The idea that it might be better to believe made him queasy. Suddenly, the memory of making out with his high school girlfriend in the church at night walloped him like a punch. He gripped the washbasin with both hands, closed his eyes and leaned over, half expecting to vomit.

Charles opened his eyes and glanced at the worn and dirty tile floor. There, inches from his slippered feet, crouched a cockroach, its body, legs and antennae motionless. Charles regarded the pest for a moment and idly moved his left foot to crush it. The cockroach shot forward under the trash can. "Damn!" Charles muttered, and quickly snatched the can off the floor, re-aimed his foot, and stomped, once again missing the tiny beast, who ran along the baseboard under the washstand and then along the base of the tub to Charles's right. "God damn you, cockroach!" Charles whirled quickly and slammed his left foot savagely down on the insect, squishing its guts into the grout line between the tub and the floor. Crap, he thought, one more thing I'll have to clean up before I can get my security deposit back.

As he turned to switch off the light and go get dressed, he was struck by another old regretful memory: As a boy, he and his friend Dexter had found a sick and obviously dying toad on his friend's front lawn. As the toad tried feebly to hop away, the other boy grabbed it and said, "Hey, Charles, have you ever opened one of these things up?" Charles admitted that he hadn't, and Dexter said, "Hold it a minute while I go inside and get my knife."

Charles sat self-consciously on the grass in the middle of his friend's yard wondering what to do. He wasn't too keen on dissecting the toad, but he was sure that even if he let the animal go, it wouldn't be able to escape. He thought of putting the toad in the woodpile on the other side of the driveway, but he couldn't think of a plausible lie to tell his friend about the toad's miraculous escape.

While he was contemplating his options, Dexter came running out of the house and plopped down next to him holding a Boy Scout penknife.

"OK," he said, "Let's get started." The boy grabbed the toad from Charles's limp grasp, flipped it on its back and quickly slit a two-inch incision in the toad's belly. Charles stared, fascinated and repulsed, as the boy grasped the edges of cut skin and spread them apart. There, in the belly of the toad, were what looked to Charles to be several thousand small black ants, some still writhing. "Wow," he said weakly. "Wow."

"Yeah, isn't it cool?" Dexter said. No, thought Charles, it isn't cool, but he nodded anyway. He looked at Dexter with new eyes and decided that perhaps he needed a different best friend.

As the years went by, the boys drifted apart, despite the fact that Dexter lived just across the street. In high school, Dexter managed to buy an old junker of a car which he would frequently park in the middle of his family's front lawn at odd angles after a night out in the woods drinking stolen beer with his friends. One morning, when Charles left his house to catch the school bus, he noticed the car was all banged up and resting against a tree in Dexter's front yard with the driver's door wide open. Dexter was laying half in the car and half on the grass. Charles ran across the street and pulled Dexter out onto the grass.

"Dexter, Dexter, are you OK?" Charles saw blood on his forehead, and Dexter's left eye was swollen shut. Charles put his ear to Dexter's chest but heard nothing. He turned Dexter's head to start CPR, but the head flopped over to an impossible angle. His friend had died of a broken neck. Charles ran to Dexter's front door and pounded but there was nobody home. He ran across to his own house and told his mother what happened. She called 911 and soon the medics were taking the body away in an ambulance. Charles had never seen a dead body before.

Shaking his head to clear the vision, Charles snapped off the bathroom light, got dressed in an old shirt and jeans, and concentrated on boxing up his books, his stereo, and his hundreds of record albums, which were his only possessions of any value. He'd sold his furniture, except for his grad school cinder block and board shelves, a couple of patio chairs and the bed. By late afternoon, the living room was strewn with boxes of albums labeled alphabetically.

Later in the evening, Charles had just finished the only frozen dinner left in the freezer when the doorbell rang. He went to the intercom. "Yes?"

"Charles, is that you?"

"This is Charles. Who's speaking please?"

"Charles, it's me, Edie."

For a second, Charles thought, Edie who? Then he placed the voice and a thrill went up his spine.

"Edie Packer, as I live and breathe! I haven't seen you since Denver!"

"Will you let me in or what?"

That's Edie, all right, he thought. Forthright as ever. "Sorry. Just a minute. Fourth floor." Charles pressed the buzzer to let his old lover in.

He was struck by an irrational desire to tidy up the place. He smiled at himself as he surveyed the box-strewn living room. Funny, he'd had a dream about Edie just last week.

He opened the door and waited just outside in the hall. After Edie had climbed the last flight of stairs, Charles was surprised at her appearance. She looked much as she did in Denver so many years before, but now a bit overweight, with ragged dirty jeans, wild hair, and wild eyes.

"Edie! God, it's been like forever!"

She walked close to embrace and kiss him. He responded mechanically, which she seemed to notice. She peered at him through narrowed eyes.

"How have you been, Charles?"

"Just great, Edie. Come on in, I'll see if I've got anything to drink. Don't mind the mess; I'm moving."

Charles had eaten, given away or trashed almost everything in his refrigerator, but he looked anyway. There in the back corner of the top shelf was an old bottle of André champagne a well-meaning friend had brought to a party a year ago. Charles couldn't stand that champagne and, in fact, had been surprised that it was still around, languishing forgotten among the moldy tofu and rotten lettuce.

He got the bottle out and started working on the white plastic cork. While he was in the kitchen, Edie began to root about in his stuff. She pulled out a few books and a few albums. When Charles came back in with two red plastic cups of wine, Edie was standing in the middle of the room with an armful of possessions.

"These are mine," she said simply.

"Oh, I didn't realize. Well, OK, take them then."

She held out an old red candle shaped like an elephant. They had kept it in their bedroom the year they lived together. Seeing it, Charles was surprised that he still had it after all these moves and years.

"Do you remember this, Charles? We used to make love by its light."

"Turn on your love light, baby." Charles grinned at the memory of their old rituals. She'd strip nude, put on a brown choker and lie on the bed, legs akimbo. He'd perform a striptease, ending by hanging his underwear on his rod and jumping upon her. They always had cheap wine on the bedstand next to the elephant candle, but never André.

Once while he was screwing her, the elephant candle lit some photos lying on the bedstand on fire. Charles had calmly grabbed his underwear and, without missing any strokes, damped out the blaze. When they were finished, Edie couldn't believe what he had done. He said, "There was no reason to get excited, I just put it out."

"My savior," she said with an ironic laugh. "Light my fire," and they did it again.

Charles handed her the cup and she sat in one of the patio chairs, cradling the candle in her lap. They reminisced for a while, sipping from the cups. Finally, Edie asked, "Do you remember what I said to you before you left me?"

Charles couldn't, or didn't choose to.

"I said you would always be mine and I wouldn't let anyone else have you." Feeling uncomfortable, Charles said nothing.

"After we last saw each other in Denver, I went to San Francisco and lived in Haight Ashbury for a while. It was way after its peak, of course, but before it got yuppified. There were still a few communes, though, and after walking the streets for a while, I joined one. The only people in communes after the hippie era were pretty radical. It was weird to be with people talking about revolution again."

Edie took a gulp of wine and held out the cup to Charles for a refill. As he poured the wine, Charles wondered what she was leading up to. As her hands turned the once-elephant candle over and over in her lap, her eyes were far away.

She shrugged. "I became the lover of this female painter and we were together for 10 years. We got a place together on Telegraph Hill. She was doing well in the galleries by then."

Edie's revelation startled Charles at first. Then he remembered what Edie had told him when they last met: "I've been thinking a lot about becoming a lesbian." Charles had thought this almost comical at the time. Edie had made it sound like a rational decision that one should consider objectively before making.

Edie took a long sip. "The cops began watching the house because she was dealing dope. They were amazingly crude—sometimes they just hung out in front of the apartment and smoked. She made most of her deals at the galleries anyway. When they finally busted her, I completely freaked out. I attacked the cops, throwing candles and books, kicking and scratching. I managed to mace one of them before they carried me away screaming.

"Before the preliminary hearing, they had some stupid shrink examine me. I decided I would snow him and deliberately acted crazy. He was such a fucking tool. Anyway, he determined that I was not competent to stand trial. As I look back now, I may well have not been; I was pretty far out there then."

Edie got up and walked over to the stereo, which was always the last thing Charles packed. She placed the elephant candle on the bookshelf and, with some difficulty, got it to light. Then she raised the cup to her lips, cradling it with both hands as if praying, or accepting wine from a chalice.

"The joke was on me, though. They committed me, and I was institutionalized for eight years. But I convinced them I was cured, and now I've come for you."

Edie had delivered the whole monologue in such a flat, detached voice that this last startled Charles. He snapped upright in his seat. Although he felt threatened, Edie was speaking in such tranquil tones, he didn't know what to think. "What do you mean?" he asked.

"I mean, you're going to come back to me or," she pulled a small black gun from her pocket, "you're going nowhere."

A bolt raced up Charles's spine. His heart thumped into high. Everything in the room seemed crystalline, much more real than it had been moments before, and time seemed to move like sludge. The wine, which had been giving Charles a glowing buzz, was forgotten. He surveyed the box-strewn path to the door, glanced at the window, and began to sweat.

"Come on now, Edie," he said feebly through dry lips.

"No," she said, "I'm not coming anywhere. You need to make a decision. You see, I've done this before, killed someone. It's not real hard. Especially after Nam. You just pretend you're in a movie. I'm in a movie; I'm the heroine; and I've been done wrong. It's perfectly logical to grab a gun and shoot someone. Real easy. You hardly need to think about it; it's just the movie."

She leaned back against the shelves, holding the gun carelessly. "After I got out of the looney bin, I went to Mexico for a while. I had fooled the shrinks into believing I was cured, but I was still lost, and I was looking for something to believe in, corny as it sounds. I believed in you, Charles, and you betrayed me. I devoted my life to you . . ."

"Not true," said Charles desperately, "you had your own interests. You weren't even faithful to me. How can you say you devoted yourself to me?"

"Shut up. I mean it. I was devoted totally to you. I realize you were the father I never had. But now I've found a new father. Have you ever heard of Santeria or Palo Mayombe?"

Charles was bewildered. The adrenaline rush parched his throat. He tried feebly, "Jazz musicians?"

Edie laughed raucously, squeezing her eyes tight and throwing back her head. "No, they're magical religions. One from the Caribbean, the other from Africa via Cuba. You see, when I got to Mexico, I looked up some of my lover's old friends—dealers and pushers. I needed a place to crash and some cash, and I hadn't turned tricks since I first hit SF. Besides, those Mexican whores are a tough bunch and they don't like competition. So, I looked up José in Matamoros.

"To make a long story short, he got me involved in this cult down there, a blood cult, you know, sacrifices and shit, and I finally found something to believe in, something that works." Edie moved down the length of the shelves toward the door.

"You see, me and my crew believe that by making sacrifices, we bring luck to our drug business. And it works. Since we started sacrificing the odd college student or drifter, there have been no busts and no cops." Edie laughed lightly and smiled.

Now Charles was really horrified. He looked around the room again for escape routes, but with boxes piled everywhere, there was no way he would be able to move quickly enough. Edie was holding the gun casually in her right hand. But Charles suspected she would use it quickly if he tried anything.

"I became José's lover and even more good fortune came to us. Finally, he let me perform the ritual killings, and now my life is like a pure shining light. I have found the way."

Edie was glowing as she stepped away from the bookshelves, placing herself between Charles and the door. Charles was mesmerized for a moment, forgetting where he was. Edie's odd perfume combined with the scent of the candle held him still as he stared at her face. The peaceful visage before him was just what he had seen in his railroad station dream. Edie was transfixed, transcendent as she pointed the gun at him.

She looked like all the saints in Charles's catechism books back when he was a child. Beatific. Bathed in the joy and righteousness of belief. And the light of the candle on the bare wall behind Edie's head almost looked like a halo.

Charles decided he needed to distract her in some way. She was obviously too unstable to reason with and had made her peace with the idea of killing him. Christ, he thought, if she's been slaughtering strangers for years, I shouldn't be much of a problem. Or should I?

"Edie, Edie, put down the gun and let's talk."

"I'm not putting down the gun unless you say you'll stay with me always. And you better mean it you bastard, or I'll blow your dick off!" She aimed the gun at his crotch for a moment, and then let her arm drop to her side.

"Edie, c'mon. Hey, do you know what just happened to me? Do you know why I'm packing? I just sold my first novel to a New York publisher, and I got a big advance. They think it'll be a best seller. Kinda like that Springsteen song, eh? Yeah, I'm gonna be a star! I'm pulling outta here to win!"

Charles leaned forward in his chair, pretending to be excited.

"What? What did you say?" Edie spoke distractedly, frowning. "A book. That's nice. I'm looking forward to sharing your success, you bastard. It'll be nice to be rich. But you gotta say it. You gotta say you'll stay with me forever."

"Edie, how can I say that? I mean, we haven't seen each other for eons. Let's put down the gun, get real wide on this wine, and see what happens. Come on, let's get to know each other all over again."

Edie looked doubtful. Charles moved to the very edge of his chair. Edie drifted back toward the shelves, propping the elbow of her gun arm on a tattered paperback copy of *The Fountainhead*, vaguely aiming the gun in Charles's direction.

"I don't know," she said. "Sometimes I think I know you only too well. You married that bitch because she was willing to kowtow to you; she had no spine. And that's what you want. You want a little girl to roll over for you. Well, I'm not a little girl and I'm not going to roll over, unless I roll over you! Say it. Say you'll love me forever." Edie pointed the gun at the middle of Charles's chest.

"All right." Charles was willing to say anything she wanted him to at this point. "All right. I'll love you forever."

"I don't believe you. Why do you love me?"

This had been a sore spot in their relationship. Once, Edie had asked Charles why he loved her. Charles had been unable to put his finger on a specific reason, and so had lamely said, "Because of your sense of humor." Edie, not really knowing what she had wanted Charles to say, was furious, nonetheless. "Sense of humor?! Shit! I'd rather you loved me for my tits!" They had broken up for three days over the incident.

Charles knew he needed a better answer now. "Because you're so fine, and so smart, and so sexy and so neat. Please, let's put down the gun and party. Hey, I've got some sinsemilla I've been saving for years."

Charles got up as if to go get the pot.

"WHY DO YOU LOVE ME!" she shrieked, leveling the gun at him with two hands, like all the cops on TV.

Charles collapsed back into his chair. "Honey, that's such a hard question to answer. C'mon now, be reasonable."

"WHY?"

"OK, why, let's see, why. Because you're so smart. You know how I feel about smart women." Edie visibly softened. "Yes," Charles continued. "You were smart enough to get out of that hospital, and you're smart enough to have found me here, just when I needed you the most."

"Yes."

"And I love your body. You know I've always loved your body. Show me your breasts. Please. I want to see them again. Edie, take off your shirt and let's make love."

Edie seemed taken by rapture, not really looking at Charles, an otherworldly smile on her lips. "Yes," she said. "Let's make love." The flame guttered in the elephant candle, making her halo skitter on the wall.

Charles was panicked at the thought of making it with this madwoman. He decided to grab for the gun while Edie was entranced. About six feet separated them. Charles slowly rose once more from his seat, hoping she wouldn't notice. Once he was almost at full height, he lunged toward Edie. She lurched convulsively to her left and he missed his try for the gun. They crashed over on top of boxes of record albums with Charles falling heavily on top of Edie.

The boxes split, and the slippery LPs spilled out beneath them. Charles clutched Edie's right arm and tried to bang it on the floor. Edie screamed obscenities and fought back with surprising strength. They wrestled on the slick albums, legs and arms thrashing and Edie screaming like a madwoman. Charles was trying to bend back Edie's wrist when the gun went off, hitting him in the left side. He fell off her in shock and she rose unsteadily to her feet, the gun dangling from her finger by the trigger guard.

Charles sprawled in pain among A through H of his record collection, rolling over on his belly and pressing his face against a Hendrix album. Edie stood up and wobbled as if drunk, staring at the blood coming from Charles's side.

"Oh my god," Edie yelped. "Charles, how could I ever hurt you? Oh shit. Oh my god!" Before Charles could react, she put the gun to her head.

"Goodbye, Charles. I'm not meant for this world. I'll find my destiny beyond."

"NO!!" Charles screamed as she pulled the trigger and spread her brains onto his living room wall.

After lying there in pain, shock, and relief for a minute, Charles gathered his strength to sit up. The Allman Brothers' *Eat A Peach* album appeared between his legs. Dazed, Charles stared at the giant peach on the cover. He vaguely thought he should get to a doctor. But a more primitive urge gripped him. He floundered to his feet, slipping on the albums, trying to staunch the flow of blood from his side, and lurched to the door.

The trip to the cathedral was an agony of pain. Charles fell several times. Once a street beggar extended his hand and helped him up. "You all right, buddy?" Charles pushed him away and careened down the street toward the church.

When he got inside, he saw that Friday night confessions were winding up. Only one woman remained waiting in the pews. The low murmur of sinners reciting penances at the altar rail filled the darkened space.

He made his way with difficulty to the pew behind the woman and lay upon the cool wood. She got up and walked to the confessional. The murmuring of penances continued as Charles blacked out.

He came to as the woman was parting the curtain to leave. He struggled to his feet and entered the confessional, falling heavily against the dark wood.

The priest worked the slide. Charles saw the dimly lit silhouette through the mesh and remembered childhood, remembered confessing to cursing and lying, but never to masturbating. He began, haltingly, to recite words made unfamiliar by the gap of years. "Bless me, Father, for I have sinned. It has been . . . 50 years since my last confession and these are my sins . . ."

Exhausted, Charles paused. Sweated. Bled.

"Yes, my son, what do you have to confess?"

"I . . . I haven't been a very good Catholic for the last 50 years."

"What makes you say that, my son?"

"Well, I've taken the Lord's name in vain. I've lied. I've envied my neighbor's wife and goods . . . I've broken most of the Commandments."

"Have you killed?"

"No, although I was ready to tonight."

"Have you committed adultery?"

"Only in my heart. But I've wanted to often."

"Do you seek God's forgiveness?"

Charles paused. It was getting hard to breathe. "Yes, I guess I do. That's another thing. For 50 years, I haven't believed there was a God."

The priest paused for a moment. "What has changed your mind?"

"I, I uh, I've been thinking . . ." Charles laid down on the cramped confessional bench. "I need something to believe in. I think there may be a God, and faith may be what I need to make my life whole."

"Rest assured there is a God, my son. He is good, and He helps those who love Him."

"Oh, you're saving my life."

"Everlasting life is what God is about. Do you repent for your sins?"

"Yes, . . . Father, I do." Charles was barely breathing as he rasped this out.

"My son, is there something the matter with you?"

No answer.

"My son . . ."

The priest leaned closer to the screen and saw Charles lying on the bench, his side wet with blood. "My son?" Charles could not answer.

The priest hurried out of his cubicle to investigate. He found Charles lying in a pool of blood and ran to the vestry to call the paramedics. When he returned, the priest dragged Charles out into the aisle. Charles was breathing irregularly.

The priest began rudimentary CPR. He was not trained and called upon his TV viewing to guide him. Minutes passed in the quiet church. Unaware, on the other side of the cathedral several mourners trickled in to light candles. A group of women from a lesbian Bible study group meeting in the basement came up the back stairs. One of the women noticed the priest bent over Charles on the floor.

"Hey, Father, you OK?" asked one. The priest turned. "I called the paramedics. Do any of you know CPR?"

Shocked, the women rushed over. "Stand aside, Father. I'll take over, I've had CPR." The woman knelt and pressed her ear to Charles's chest, then probed his mouth.

"Hey," she said, "I recognize this guy! This is the bastard that was on *Sunrise Miami* defending his piece of sh—garbage article attacking lesbians!"

The woman straightened, angry at the memory. "Whataya gonna do, Maggie?" asked one of the others. Maggie shook her head, uncertain.

"Please," said the priest, "For the love of God!"

"Yeah, you're right, Father, for the love of God." Maggie began pumping Charles's chest. "Karla, you go out front and wait for the paramedics. Tess, go see if you can find some bandages or cotton or something to help stop the bleeding."

"There should be some towels in the vestry," said the priest. "Hurry!"

The priest sank into a pew and began to pray. After five minutes, the paramedics arrived. By this time Charles had negligible pulse and no respiration. The paramedics took over CPR as they transferred him to their truck and rushed him to the hospital.

At the hospital, Charles still wasn't breathing, although his color was good from the CPR. They rushed him to the ER. A bleary-eyed resident prepared to shock him. He hit him with the paddles. No response. He hit him again. And got a regular heartbeat. Charles had been clinically dead for 15 minutes.

Charles was released from the ICU on another perfect day in Miami. The sun baked the orange terracotta tiles of the hospital roof and light streamed into Charles's room. With the bed slightly inclined, Charles drifted in and out for most of the morning.

Around 11 o'clock, Chip showed up. He had on a plaid sport coat, white golf shirt, and khaki slacks. "Hey, hey," he greeted Charles, "It was nip and tuck at the Chip and Chuck show!"

Charles grimaced at Chip's hackneyed joke. Not only did he hate it when Chip called him Chuck, he especially hated the nip and tuck quip that Chip used often. He pulled himself up in the bed.

"That's for sure. I almost didn't make it."

"I heard they found you at St. Mary's Cathedral. I couldn't believe it when I heard it. What the hell were you doing there?"

Charles's face flushed. "I, ah, went there to make my last confession."

"Good agnostics die hard, hah Charles?" If Chip was concerned, it didn't show beneath his humor.

Charles was puzzled by Chip's attitude. Why is he acting so flip? And why is he calling me Charles? Something's going on. "Well, you know what Pascal said, it's better to believe futilely than to not believe stupidly."

Chip roared out his booming laugh. "Sho' you right, Charles! But seriously, I got something to tell you. I've quit the church, my car is packed, and I'm going to California with the church secretary. Pretty stereotypical, hah?"

"What!? You're leaving with Rita?" Charles tried to sit upright but winced at the pain. This was incredible. He couldn't believe it. "What about Trixie and Robby?"

"I told Trixie she can have everything and just let me know when the divorce is final. As for Robby, I hardly see him anyway, what with the church taking all my time and him out most nights with his high school buddies. I'll take him for a couple weeks here and there and we'll probably have a better relationship for it." Chip started to pick his teeth with a business card.

Charles was stunned. In all their conversations about religion, Chip had seemed the stalwart believer. He had taken Charles to task for his divorce and his agnosticism. Yet here he was, acting as if he was free of a great weight, chucking it all to run off with a younger woman, and one who was the star of Charles's fantasies to boot!

"This is so sudden. Why didn't you tell me?"

"Dude, I had to keep up appearances. Plus, I just decided a couple days ago."

"What are you going to do in California?"

"Who knows? Isn't that great? I haven't got a plan; I haven't got a clue! Maybe I'll break into the movies, hah?"

Maybe I'm dreaming this, Charles thought. After all, I lost a lot of blood. "Well, what brought this on?"

"I decided that my problem is not only am I sick of the church, but I'm not that crazy about God either. He's got to be one sadistic son-of-a-bitch, and I don't want to be an accomplice anymore. I mean, you're right, Charles. What kind of benevolent deity allows Cat 5 hurricanes, and tsunamis, and earthquakes, and too many disasters to count?"

"I can't believe you're saying this. What about all those arguments we had about faith? You were always trying to convince me to believe. What about that?"

"Just going through the motions, my friend. Call it force of habit. I mean, I've had doubts all along, but the last few years it's been tough to believe. Plus, like I told you, I began to come around to your way of thinking, after all the long hours we spent disagreeing. So, I'm retiring. You've been a retired Catholic for years. Now I'm joining you, as a retired Methodist. Gonna head for Graceland and mow the ceiling before settling down in Lost Angeles."

Chip had always referred to LA with disgust, calling it either Lost Angeles or LALA Land. Charles was flabbergasted. Chip represented pure faith to him. And now—adultery, divorce, abandonment. It was too much to take. He slumped back in his bed.

"But Chip, you're the biggest reason why I think I've found my own faith . . ."

"Glad to hear it, little buddy. Real glad. It's just, while you found yours, somehow, I misplaced mine. But don't worry. It's a big old goofy world, but it's got to be around here someplace." Chip made a show of patting his pockets. Charles still couldn't believe the careless way Chip was acting. He seemed high with relief at leaving his old life behind.

"Look, I gotta go. Rita is waiting for me in the car, and it's a long way to Memphis. So, take good care of yourself and get better soon. I'll text when I get there, and, hey, once I get settled and you get healed, you're welcome on my couch anytime." Chip moved to the bed to hug Charles. They embraced, and Charles caught Chip's hand.

"Really, Chip, thanks a ton for everything you've done for me. I love you."

"I love you too, Charles. Just don't turn into a monsignor on me or anything, OK?" Chip again wrapped his huge arms around Charles, gave him a hug that made Charles wince, then turned and strode out of the room chuckling to himself.

Charles just felt tired. His mind was fogged with the shock of recent events. The TV was showing an old movie: *The Candidate* with Robert Redford. He stared at it for a few moments, then held up his left hand and looked at his wedding ring. With some difficulty, he slipped it off and held it up to the sun, watching it glint as he turned it. Sighing, he put it on the bedstand.

Out the window, Charles could see the top of one of the hospital buildings where a stack streamed a white plume of water vapor. He watched as it feathered back and forth, almost disappearing in a strong breeze, then billowing up again. He was not quite awake and not quite asleep. In a trance, he watched the vapor playing atop the stack, looking like a living thing dancing and bobbing and weaving. After a while, his lunch came, and then, just before he drifted off, he heard Redford say, "What do we do now?"

Acknowledgements

First off, nothing that I do would be doable without the advice, help, and support of my wife, Deb Kolbo Ellsworth, an author in her own right, and the originator of the Empathy Symbol.

Many parts of this book, including a huge hunk of the Jeannie chapter, would not have been possible without the knowledge, ideas, and moral support of Rev. Samuel F. "Skip" Parvin. To the extent that I got anything in the book right about United Methodism, card games, and Chaos Magick, I am indebted to Skip, a fellow author and my best friend.

I am thankful for my parents—for my mother for passing on to me her love of literature, as well as my first misheard lyrics; and for my father for answering every question I ever asked him, mostly accurately, and almost never with, "I don't know." Also, for telling me not only shouldn't I hate Nikita Khrushchev, I shouldn't hate anyone.

I am thankful for my alma mater, Duke University, for nurturing in me the belief that I could become a writer. I am particularly thankful for my poetry teacher at Duke, Dr. James Applewhite, and for Dr. Robert S. Pawlowski, my professor at the University of Denver who believed in me when others didn't. I also thank Mrs. Kana, my 6th grade teacher, for making me the editor of the school paper.

I am thankful for the Leslie Gore song that presented me with my first puzzling misheard pop song lyric: "I can cry Papa haunt you." Also, thanks to Debbie Symonds for challenging me to make sense of a verse in Cream's song, "Strange Brew." This quest preoccupied me for weeks as I listened to the passage dozens of times. It wasn't ultimately solved until the Internet came to be. This was the beginning of my obsession with misheard lyrics.

(BTW, the lyric in question turned out to be: "She's some kind of demon messing in the glue." I heard it as, "does she live mortal" because nothing else seemed to make any sense.)

Thanks to David Gottschalk, John Ogden., Don "Jasper" Luttrell, Sam Raffa, the printers in the Maharaj Ji Divine Light Mission ashram basement, the poets whose work we published, and everyone else who helped me produce *Plainspeak Magazine* (but no thanks to the Catholic monk who ripped us off.)

Finally, I appreciate the many friends who have contributed their own misheard lyrics, intentionally and unintentionally, over the years. You can see some of my favorite misheard lyrics that didn't make the book on the Misheard-Lyrics.com website.

Finally, you may want to check out the soundtrack to this book on Spotify. Search for the "Misheard Lyrics – the songs that drove the book playlist" and enjoy!

About the Author

Mike Ellsworth has contributed technical chapters about the Internet to two widely published books and several national magazines. He has also written numerous white papers and seven non-fiction books about social media and social selling. His poetry has been published in a variety of small poetry magazines, and he ran his own, *Plainspeak*, for two years in the late '70s. This is his first novel.

He lives in the Twin Cities with his wife.

Made in the USA
Middletown, DE
27 March 2020